RULES OF THE HUNT

VICTOR O'REILLY

G. P. Putnam's Sons
New York

G. P. Putnam's Sons
Publishers Since 1838
200 Madison Avenue
New York, NY 10016

Library of Congress Cataloging-in-Publication Data

O'Reilly, Victor.
Rules of the hunt / by Victor O'Reilly.
p.   cm.
ISBN 0-399-13869-2
I. Title.
PR6065.R65R85   1995   94-32242   CIP
823'.914—dc20

Printed in the United States of America

1 2 3 4 5 6 7 8 9 10

Book design by Chris Welch

This book is printed on acid-free paper.

For my two research assistants, my eldest son, Christian O'Reilly, and Sheenagh Goggin. It is a pleasant thing indeed for a father to work with his son.

For Budge and Helmut Clissmann, for support in the learning curve, and for Alma, Evie, and Bruff—and Kira and Shane—and Liz O'Reilly.

For my distinguished editor, Neil Nyren. He requires a pickax and a miner's lamp to get to know—and I am still digging—but the effort is worth it.

For Phyllis Grann and David Shanks (who knows how to run a dinner even if the temperatures in New York are subzero—just melt the snow with grappa) and Lou Aronica and the entire Putnam Berkley team.

For my agent, Sterling Lord, whom I value greatly, and for Pat Bradshaw, a lady of significant beauty and grace.

For Jane and Chris Carrdus, the best of friends.

For the remarkable people I met in the course of researching and writing this book and who could not be better represented than by Robert Edison Fulton, world traveler and inventor extraordinary—as the world of Special Operations well knows. And for his wife, Anne, one of the most charming and attractive women I have met in a very long time.

For my friends in Japan who, generally speaking, have a somewhat quieter time than Hugo Fitzduane experiences in this book—and particularly for Chifune Murase (who has all the good qualities of the fictional Chifune in this book—though I have to say I cannot vouch for her firearms expertise).

And so to action . . .

PROLOGUE

The killing team needed a cover story for their presence.

As Japanese in a Western environment, they were more likely to be noticed and remembered.

They decided to come in as a film crew. Gold had been discovered in the region amid some of the most scenic terrain of the West of Ireland, and there was controversy as to whether it should be mined. It was a classic environmental issue and attracted international media attention. Film crews came and went, and most hired some kind of aerial transport. Ireland looks glorious from the air.

The team carried out their initial reconnaissance in a four-seater Piper Aztec. Discretion minimized their amount of flight time over the island itself, but it was sufficient for them to become comfortable with the lay of the land. On the second day, to allay suspicion, they telephoned Fitzduane's castle, explained the story they were working on, and requested permission to film from the ground to add some local color. They were politely refused.

The island itself was like a finger, ten kilometers long and four kilometers across at its widest, pointing west into the Atlantic toward America some three thousand miles away. It was joined to the mainland by a bridge set into the cliffs over a treacherous-looking divide; land access elsewhere looked impossible. The jagged coastline consisted of high, overhanging cliffs or, in the few places where the fall of land was more gentle, was guarded by concealed rocks and changing currents.

From the air they could see shadows of darkness in the sea and in two locations the remains of ancient wrecks. The sea seemed beautiful, moody, and dangerous. It was not a hospitable-looking spot.

There were two castles on the island.

The westward castle, Draker, was a sprawling Victorian Gothic structure which they knew had once been an exclusive school but which was now boarded up.

The castle nearer the landward side was Fitzduane's castle, Duncleeve.

It was this that interested them. It stood on a rocky bluff at one end of a bay. Inland was a freshwater lake overlooked by a small, white, thatched cottage.

Their reconnaissance covered many things: access, terrain, population, security, cover, threat assessment, and weather conditions. But their main concern was with confirming the killing ground.

They booked the helicopter and a faster, longer-range aircraft for the last two days. They explained that they were on a deadline and had to fly some exposed film to make a connection in London. Their credentials were double-checked by a cautious reservations clerk but were verified as satisfactory.

They would contour-fly in at fifty feet or less by helicopter, and land on the north side of the island in a clearing to seaward of one of the hills. They would be neither heard nor seen. They would then proceed on foot to the spot they had chosen. Fitzduane tended to vary the route he took on his daily ride, but there was one spot he normally visited either coming or going.

The child and his desires were the man's weakness. A watcher had monitored his movements for several weeks before the killing team had moved in.

The team members were experienced, well-trained, and totally motivated. After the hit, they would escape on foot to the waiting helicopter, fly to the aircraft, and enplane immediately for France. There, they would vanish.

It was now down to implementation and that intangible—luck.

TOKYO, JAPAN

The bodyguard tensed as he saw the gates in the outer perimeter wall swing open and the gleaming black limousine enter the drive.

The gates should not have opened without his checking the visitor on the TV monitor and, even more to the point, without his activating the release of the electronic lock. The master received a constant stream of visitors and petitioners at certain specified times of the day, so black limousines were more the rule than the exception. But this was seven in the morning, and the master's insistence on privacy while he bathed and prepared himself for the day was well-known.

It was a running joke in the circles of power that more careers were made and broken by the decisions made by Hodama-*san* while he soaked in his traditional copper bath than by the rest of the government put together. The joke had more punch when you realized that Hodama held no official position.

The drive through the formal gardens to the single-story traditional Japanese house was short. Even though Kazuo Hodama was one of the wealthiest men in Japan, custom dictated a certain modesty in lifestyle. Overt displays of power and wealth were frowned upon. Further, Hodama's simple house and grounds were in the exclusive Akasaka district of Tokyo. The ownership of a property at such a location was a message in itself. Tokyo property prices are the highest in the world. Hodama's dwelling and grounds, not much more extensive than a typical American ranch-style bungalow and yard, were valued conservatively at tens of millions of dollars.

The bodyguard, a grizzled veteran in his sixties, was kept on less for his physical skills than for his memory and his sense of protocol. Threats were not seriously feared. Those days were long over. Hodama's power and influence were too great. Instead, the bodyguard was primarily concerned with the procedural niceties of controlling the flow of visitors. Appearances and appropriate behavior were of enormous importance. The wrong greeting or an inadequate bow by one of Hodama's retainers could be misinterpreted, and damage the harmony of the relationship between visitor and Hodama himself. And Hodama attached great importance to his relationships. The people he knew and influenced, the people he flattered and pampered and manipulated and betrayed, were the basis of his power.

With these thoughts in his mind, and concerned not to upset some dignitary, the bodyguard took no action for the few seconds it took for the long black vehicle with its shining chrome and tinted windows to sweep around in front of the house and purr gently to a halt. The sight of the license plate and the discreet symbol it bore was instantly reassuring. The bodyguard relaxed, immensely relieved that he had not initiated any precipitative action and caused embarrassment and loss of face. The opening of the perimeter gates was now explained. The limousine belonged to one of Hodama's intimates.

The driver's door opened almost as soon as the vehicle came to a halt, and the chauffeur, immaculate in navy uniform and white gloves, jumped out and opened the rear passenger door.

The bodyguard had also been hastening down to open the passenger door, as one of the gestures of respect he would employ for the distinguished visitor. Now, his first actions rendered unnecessary by the speed of the chauffeur, he stumbled to a halt and bowed deeply, his eyes cast down in respect, as the limousine door was opened.

A pair of expensively trousered legs emerged.

Something was wrong. Decades of bowing had made the bodyguard expert at making quick assessments with his head at waist height. Something just did not look right with the trousers. His master's visitor was very particular and consistent. His suits were exclusively English-tailored, and these trousers were definitely of Italian material and cut.

There was the sound of spitting—three distinct short spitting sounds—and the bodyguard's uncertainties were abruptly terminated, as three 9mm hollow-point bullets entered the top of his skull, expanded as designed as they smashed through the bone, and then wreaked fatal havoc as they ricocheted around inside.

The bow became abruptly even more respectful until gravity exerted itself to the full and the bodyguard's corpse collapsed in an undignified heap. Blood from his head wound trickled its way into the carefully raked gravel of a Zen stone garden.

The chauffeur spoke one word into a miniature two-way radio, and seconds later another black limousine sped into the grounds of the Hodama residence and the gates were closed. A total of ten attackers had now emerged from the two cars. Their sureness of movement re-

vealing much training and rehearsal, the attackers swiftly surrounded
the house and then entered simultaneously at one command.

Inside the house, Hodama was looking forward to the simple pleasure of a good long soak in a hot bath. Although U.S. bombers had destroyed the original property which had been on the site and the house
was merely a meticulous reconstruction, the bath itself was an original
and had been specially built into the new house, which was otherwise
equipped with the most modern of plumbing.

Special construction had been required because the bath, a heavy,
open-topped copper cylinder with a curved base that made it look
more like a deep cauldron than a Western bath, was heated by a small
fire located directly underneath it. For convenience to the external
woodpile, the firebox was placed in an outside wall and was accessible
only from the outside. Inside the bathroom, the copper bath was built
in flush to the tiled floor. Operation was a matter of filling the bath with
water, lighting the fire until the water reached the required temperature, putting out the fire, and then—having carefully tested the water
again—stepping gingerly into the steaming water and sitting on the
built-in wooden seat to luxuriate in the soothing heat.

Hodama was deeply attached to his copper bath. He liked to say that
it had been in his family for more generations than he could count. He
could sit in it with the water up to his chin and his legs dangling and
think in a way that did not seem to be possible in a chilly, drafty, low-
slung Western bath.

That morning, his manservant, Amika, who had the responsibility for
lighting the fire and making the other preparations, had just told
Hodama that the bath was ready.

Slowly, Hodama shuffled into the tiled bathroom. He was feeling
mentally alert but physically every one of his eighty-four years. He no
longer slept much and had already been working for several hours. The
soothing water beckoned.

Hodama was wearing a light cotton *yukata,* a form of kimono, with
the left side over the right side. Right over left was used only for
corpses. The *yukata* was held together by a simple *obi.* Over this he
wore a *haori,* a half coat like a cardigan. At his age he was susceptible to
the cold, particularly in the chill hours of early morning. On his feet he
wore sandals.

The bathroom was a good-sized room with a place to change his clothes and a massage table, in addition to the washing and changing areas. When he was younger he had enjoyed many women on that couch. Now it was used merely for its formal purpose.

Amika helped Hodama to undress, hung up his clothes, then followed him across to the bathing area. Wooden boards placed across the tiles allowed drainage. There Hodama sat on a small wooden stool and soaped himself down. When he was ready, Amika ladled water from a wooden bucket over him until the last trace of soap was removed. He would enter the bath clean and thoroughly rinsed, in the Japanese fashion. The idea of soaking in his own effluvia, as Westerners did, was repellent.

The water temperature was perfect. Hodama smiled in anticipation and nodded approvingly at Amika. The manservant acknowledged the look with the deferential smile and slight bow that was appropriate for his status as a long-serving retainer, and then the front of his face dissolved and he leaped headfirst into the steaming copper bath.

Crimson leached into the water.

Hodama gave a cry and staggered back in shock. He felt himself being seized and then flung facedown on the massage table. His hands and feet were held and then bound with something hard and thin that cut into his flesh. He was then hauled to his feet.

Men in dark business suits, three or four that he could see, their faces covered in hoods of black cloth, faced him. Two, at least, held silenced weapons.

There was a sound of a heavy metal object dropping onto the wooden laths and someone started tying something to his feet. He looked down and saw a cast-iron weight.

Blood drained from his face. Suddenly he realized what was about to happen, and his fear was total.

"Who are you?" he managed to croak. "What is it you want? Don't you know who I am?"

One of the figures nodded grimly. "Oh yes, Hodama-*san,* we know exactly who you are." He gave an exaggerated bow. "That is precisely the point."

Two of the figures went to the edge of the bath, crouched down, then hauled Amika's dead body out of the bath and flung it into a corner of the room.

Hodama stood there bound, naked, slight, and wizened—smaller by several inches than the men around him—and tried to preserve what dignity he could. The heat increased in the room. The water in the bath began to bubble gently. As the bubbles increased, his composure collapsed.

"*I have power,*" he screamed. "*You cannot do this and hope to escape. It is madness. . . .*"

The figure who had bowed made a gesture and one of the other figures hit Hodama very hard in the stomach. He doubled up and fell to his knees and retched. Through a haze of pain, he looked up. There was something familiar about the figure. Both the laugh and the voice had struck a chord. "Who are you?" he said quietly. "I have to know."

The figure shook his head. "You have to die," he said grimly. "That is all you still have to do." He made another gesture.

Two of the hooded figures lifted Hodama, suspended him over the copper bath, and slowly lowered him into the bloody, boiling water.

1

H ugo Fitzduane placed his Swiss-made Sig automatic pistol on a high shelf in the bathroom and reflected that firearms and small children did not mix well. On further consideration, he decided that much the same could be said about more than a few adults.

For his own part he had adjusted to being under terrorist threat as well as one reasonably could—security precautions were time-consuming and tedious—but then Peter had arrived on the scene, a small, pink, rather creased-looking little package with a dusting of blond fuzz at the noisier end, and Fitzduane had started looking at the world very differently.

He tested the water with his hand. He had read in one of the baby books that the right tool for this was an elbow, but that seemed a ridiculous way to go about such a straightforward activity, and Peter normally seemed quite satisfied with the result. If he wasn't, he yelled. Children, Fitzduane had found, were believers in direct and immediate communication.

"Boots," called Fitzduane, trying to sound stern and in command of the situation, "bath time." He added a threat. "Come here or I'll tickle your toes." Peter's nickname had evolved from the consequences of the weather in the West of Ireland. Given his fondness for running around outside and splashing into puddles and playing with mud, Peter had learned to ask for his red Wellington boots on one of his first deter-mined forays into speech.

There was no response. Fitzduane checked the bathroom closet and behind the laundry basket, half expecting to see a small, blond-headed three-year-old crouched down and shaking with barely suppressed gig-gles.

Nothing.

He felt mildly concerned. The castle in which they lived, Fitz-duane's ancestral home on a remote island off the West of Ireland, was not large as such places go, but it had stone stairs and battlements and a high wall around the courtyard, and there were many locations where a child could come to harm. From the point of view of a nervous parent, Duncleeve was not the ideal place to bring up a child.

Frankly, Fitzduane was surprised that any of his ancestors had made it to maturity. An accidental long drop onto the rocks below or into the freezing waters of the Atlantic seemed much more likely. But the Fitzduanes had tended to be a resolute and hardy lot, and they had survived.

He opened the bathroom door and looked around the dressing room. Still nothing.

The dressing room door-handle began to turn very slowly.

"Boots!" called Fitzduane. "Come here, you little monster."

There was silence. A sudden chill swept over Fitzduane, as disbelief battled intuition. He had feared the threat for so long, but never seri-ously believed in it. Now, perhaps, it had become reality.

He stepped back into the bathroom, picked up the Sig, slid it out of its holster, and removed the safety catch. A round was already in the chamber.

His mind ran through the available options. The windows of both the bathroom and dressing room had twentieth-century double glazing but had been designed as firing slits by the original Norman architect. No way in and certainly no way out for Fitzduane's six-foot-two frame.

The dressing room door-handle began to turn slowly. Then it slid back noisily, as if suddenly released.

Fitzduane didn't think; he reacted at the potential threat to the per-son he loved most in the world. He flung the door open, his weapon traversing an arc of fire that took in the whole corridor. There was nothing. He looked down. The muddiest little person he had ever seen stood there, dripping. It didn't look much like anyone he knew, though the boots and body language seemed familiar.

"Daddy!" said the mud boy indignantly.

Fitzduane felt weak with relief. He slipped the safety catch back on the Sig and looked at the mud boy. "Who are you?" he said sternly.

"DADDY!" shouted the mud boy. "I'm Peter Fizz . . ." He paused, a look of concentration on his face, to assess the situation. He had a problem with the Fitzduane part of his name. He brightened. "I'm BOOTS," he shouted.

Fitzduane swept him up and kissed him. Small muddy arms encircled his neck. A small muddy face was pressed to his. Fitzduane had never associated Irish mud with absolute happiness, but at that moment he was as happy and content as a human being can ever be.

He hosed down Boots in the shower, and when a recognizable three-year-old had emerged, they both went for a soak in the big Victorian bath. As Fitzduane lay back in the soothing water, eyes closed, Boots lay in his arms for the first few minutes. Then the normal mischievous nature of Peter Fitzduane took over. He slid from his father's body and went to play in the water.

Minutes passed. Fitzduane, eyes closed, was practically asleep. Playing with taps was forbidden, and the hot faucet had been made too stiff to turn, but small hands wrestled with the large brass cold outlet and very quietly half filled a jug. The boy stood up, protected from falling by an unconscious reflex action of his father's legs. He held the jug over Fitzduane and started to giggle.

Fitzduane opened his eyes just as the icy water hit him. His shout of indignation could be heard through the double doors and echoed through the stone passageways beyond. It was immediately followed by the sound of Boots in an advanced fit of the giggles and then Fitzduane's laughter.

COLONEL—TO BE General in two days' time, despite the opposition of more conservative military figures and countless politicians and civil servants he had crossed over the years—Shane Kilmara flipped back the cover of his watch and began to check the time.

Just as he focused, the plane lurched again and his stomach surged toward the top of his skull. He still felt nauseated, despite the motion-sickness pills, but had been saved the indignity of actually throwing up. Low-level combat flying was an effective way to penetrate airspace undetected, but in a special-forces-modified Lockheed C130 Combat Talon—where functionality was awarded a decidedly higher priority than comfort—you tended to have a hard ride this close to the ground, or the sea, or whatever terrain you happened to be over.

The Irish Rangers had initially been set up as an antiterrorist unit in the mid-seventies, following the assassination of the British Ambassador by a culvert bomb. The political establishment felt they could also end up in the firing line unless they took some precautions, and that gave the founder of the new organization some extra leverage. Kilmara, who had served in a special-forces capacity with other national forces for many years after a falling-out with the Irish authorities, had emerged as the most suitable candidate to head up the new unit.

The entire Irish army, cooks and mascots included, was tiny—at around 13,000 personnel smaller than one U.S. Army division—and was chronically underequipped and underfunded. Accordingly, Kilmara, whose own special-forces unit was actually quite well-equipped, thanks to special supplementary funding, had become a world-class expert in the art of scrounging. It helped that he was something of a legend in the Western special forces community, and that said community was a small, highly personal world which tended to transcend national boundaries under the banner of a motto aptly propounded by David Stirling, founder of the SAS: "If you need something, do not be put off by bureaucracy—find a way to take it."

Kilmara hadn't taken the Lockheed Combat Talon—it actually belonged to the U.S. Air Force—he had merely borrowed it and its highly skilled crew in a complex arrangement with Delta. He had a tendency toward elegantly complex barter deals, because then, in his experience, no bureaucrat could ever possibly unravel them. A much-simplified interpretation of this particular arrangement was that the Irish were given access to the Combat Talon and certain other goodies in exchange for Delta being allowed to train in Ireland, and in particular with the new high-speed, heavily armed FAV—Fast Attack Vehicle—known as the Guntrack.

None of this, needless to say, had been arranged through official channels. However, all of it was supported by appropriate paperwork. Kilmara had operated in this outrageous manner for years. He got away with it because he was very good at what he did. And he was consummate at working the system.

The Guntrack was a Rangers innovation and had been inspired by Fitzduane. The primary purpose of the exercise was to test the dramatic-looking, black, tracked vehicle under simulated combat conditions. The C130 would infiltrate the "enemy" airspace of Fitzduane's island, flying little higher than the roof of a suburban house, and then drop down to the approximate level of the top of the front door. The rear doors of the Lockheed would be open. At a precise point, a cargo parachute attached to the palleted Guntrack would activate and the vehicle would be pulled sharply out of the rear doors and fall only a few feet onto the ground—hopefully in one piece.

The technique was known as LAPES—low-altitude parachute extraction system—and provided the pilot didn't sneeze while flying a bulky cargo plane at 120 miles an hour five feet above the ground at night in new terrain, LAPES was considered a safer way to put cargo on the ground than by actually dropping things from a height. It was regularly used by airborne troops, even for substantial items like armored vehicles.

The whole procedure tended to scare the shit out of Kilmara. He could just see the pilot absentmindedly spill his coffee at the wrong moment. Fortunately, LAPES was not recommended for people. The drill was to drop the equipment first, then climb to five hundred feet and start throwing out the human element. Five hundred feet just about allowed a parachute to open, but the enemy didn't have much time to shoot you as you dangled silhouetted against the sky. And, with luck, they would be asleep.

The pioneers of airborne had tried dropping people first and then the heavy equipment on top of them. The survivors had suggested that this had not been a good idea.

The trouble with Europe was that it was too congested. There just weren't enough places where you could drop things and shoot things without damaging the locals. The nice thing about Fitzduane's island was that all you were likely to flatten, if you picked the right spot, was the heather.

The warning light came on. Hydraulics began to whine. Outside, the night was dark and cold and looked bloody miserable. The Combat Talon was now so low that Kilmara found he could look *up* at some of the terrain. He just hoped that all the microchips that made this kind of lunatic flying possible were getting on well with their electrons. He wanted to live to be a general in two days.

FITZDUANE HAD REACHED the stage of an evening where, although he knew common sense dictated getting some sleep, he just hadn't the energy to make a move.

He was thinking about what he was going to do with his life. Apart from the part-time occupation of acting as something of a "think tank" for the Irish Rangers as they expanded their operations, for the last few years he had tended to take the easier way out, to let his accountant take care of his affairs and to concentrate on bringing up Boots. It was not good enough. He now had a feeling that this course would change, and it brought with it a sense of foreboding.

He checked the security system and then went to pot Boots. His small son lay there, long eyelashes over closed eyes, cheeks pink and tanned from the wind, lithe young body sprawled in over and around the duvet. He looked very beautiful. His bed was very wet.

Fitzduane stripped the bed, meditated briefly on bladder control and a three-year-old's potty training, then carried his son to his own big bed. He hadn't the energy to remake the cot—or that is what he told himself.

Father and son slept side by side in the big bed throughout the night. Fitzduane's sleep was somewhat disturbed, since Boots tended to wriggle. In the early hours he thought he heard the sound of a familiar aircraft, but before the thought had fully registered he was asleep again.

2

January 2

Boots was giving Oona, the housekeeper, a hard time in the kitchen.

It was staggering, thought Fitzduane affectionately, how much time, effort, and emotional energy such a very small person could soak up. He imagined having twins or—he went pale at the thought—triplets. In fact, right now, he couldn't really contemplate looking after more than one child at a time.

How did women do it, and, as often as not these days, combine raising a family with a career? In truth, he had considerable sympathy for Etan, Boots's mother. It was partly her strength of character that he had initially found so attractive. It was scarcely surprising now that she wanted to make her mark on the world.

That was where the age difference came in. Fitzduane had personal wealth, and, after the army, had reached the top of his chosen profession of combat photographer, strange occupation though it was. He had been ready to settle down.

Etan still had to achieve some personal goal before she would be content. They hadn't fallen out of love. It was more a case of being out of sync. How many relationships foundered on career conflicts and bad timing? But Etan had gone her own way, and that was the way of it.

Fitzduane tried to convince himself that someday soon she would return and they would at last get married and be a family unit, but deep down he no longer believed it. He suddenly felt a terrible loneliness, and tears came to his eyes.

He was lost in thought, staring out the glass wall at a choppy green black sea, when Boots came tearing in, hood up, garbed for the outdoors, bright red Wellington boots flashing. "Daddy! Daddy! Let's go! Let's go!" He skidded to a halt. "Daddy, why are you crying?"

Fitzduane smiled. Children were disconcertingly observant at times. "I've got a cold," he said, sniffing ostentatiously and wiping his eyes.

Boots reached into his anorak and explored a pocket. A small hand emerged, clutching a tissue that looked like it was beyond recycling. A half-eaten hard candy was stuck to it. He proffered the combination to Fitzduane. "Sharing is caring," he said, repeating Oona's carefully drummed-in propaganda. "Can I have a sweetie?"

Fitzduane laughed. "Three years old and working the angles," he said. He had read all the books about the importance of feeding children properly and not encouraging bad habits, but he was fighting a losing battle where Boots and candy were concerned. He tossed Boots an apple taken from the fruit bowl on the sideboard.

Boots made a face, then grabbed the apple with one hand and Fitzduane's arm with the other: "Daddy! Let's go! Let's go! Let's go!"

THE SNIPER REFLECTED that the vast majority of his fellow citizens had never even held a weapon, let alone fired one.

Japan had abjured war. An army, as such, was specifically forbidden by the constitution. There was no conscription. The self-defense forces were manned exclusively by volunteers. The police carried guns but almost never drew them, let alone used them. The streets were safe. Criminals threatened only each other, and even then mostly used swords.

The sniper spat. His country was degenerating, suborned by materialism and false values. The politicians were corrupt. The rulers of his country had lost direction. The warrior class had been contaminated by commerce and were effete. The true wishes of the Emperor—views he never communicated or expressed but which they knew he must, at heart, profess—were being ignored.

A new direction was required. As always in history, a few people of strong will and clear vision could change destiny.

The sniper emptied the magazine of his rifle and reloaded it with hand-loaded match-grade ammunition. He checked every round. Beside him, the spotter had placed his automatic weapon to hand and was sweeping the killing ground in front of them with binoculars.

The watcher was in position fifty meters above and to the left of them.

All three saw the portcullis of the castle rise, and horse, rider, and passenger emerge.

The killing team settled in to wait. It would be about an hour.

They could hear the sounds of the small waterfall flowing into the stream below them. The stream widened and became shallower at this point. It was a location where people had traditionally established a crossing point or ford. The name wasn't marked on any map, but it was known, by the Fitzduanes, as Battleford.

At that spot, centuries earlier, Hugo's ancestors had fought, held, and died.

IT WAS A TRUISM of special forces that nothing ever went entirely to plan.

In this case the objective was to test the air deployment of three Guntracks and nine personnel onto the ground at night via LAPES, then mount a simulated assault on the abandoned Draker Castle, which was at the opposite end of the island to Duncleeve. Kilmara didn't want Fitzduane complaining about having his beauty sleep disturbed. He had longer-term plans for the island which depended on his retaining his friend's goodwill. Good training areas were in short supply.

The first two Guntracks had made an uneventful landing by the standards of this truly terrifying technique. The third Guntrack, mounted on its special shock-absorbing pallet, had its landing even further cushioned by a flock of panic-stricken sheep. Seven seemed unlikely to wake up again. Kilmara winced. He knew Fitzduane, and was having nightmares of an outsize trophy board being delivered to Ranger headquarters. He was never going to live this down.

The second hitch was that they had misplaced three Rangers—actually Delta troopers on secondment from Fort Bragg. The Irish were well-practiced in jumping in the unusually windy and gusty conditions of the West of Ireland. The Delta team were at the start of the learning curve and were going to have to leg it, cross-country and at night, to catch up.

Still, they hadn't vanished into the Atlantic, as Kilmara had at first feared. He thanked the Great God of Special Forces they weren't keeping full radio silence, as would have been the case on a real operation. After more than thirty years of the military, he had never gotten used to losing men. The Texas drawl in his earpiece had reassured him. He had acknowledged briefly and caustically and was then able to meditate, with rather more equanimity, on the matter of the dead sheep.

The sun was well up when Kilmara suspended the exercise and they laid up and prepared food. It was only then that one of the Delta team mentioned the civilian helicopter he had seen land on the north side of the island. He had assumed it was connected with some local inhabitant, and, since it was away from the official exercise area, he brought the subject up only in passing.

Kilmara knew the topography and the context. "A forced landing?" he said hopefully, a mug of tea in his hand.

"Maybe," said Lonsdale, the Texan, who as a reflex had examined the helicopter briefly with his night-vision binoculars.

He sounded unconvinced. There had been no smoke or erratic maneuvering. The flying had been purposeful, skilled.

"It came in low and fast." He thought again. "It was a civilian bird, but it was more like he was heading for a hot landing. Probably an army hotshot reliving his past."

Kilmara sipped his tea without tasting it. "What then?" he said.

"Three guys got out. They were dressed in vacation gear, you know, hats with flies and those sleeveless jackets with lots of pockets. They had fishing poles with them. They seemed to know where they were going. They headed towards Duncleeve, your friend's place. I guess they fucked up on their navigation and landed a little short. They wouldn't have been able to see the castle from that height with the hills in the way."

"Fishing poles?" said Kilmara.

"I guess they call them rods over here," said Lonsdale. "They had them in those long bags you use when you're traveling. You know, kind of like a gun c—" It hit him. "Oh, shit!"

Kilmara's unfinished tea cut a glistening swath through the air as he flung the mug to one side. "It's *not* the fishing season," he snarled. His command echoed through the clearing. "RANGERS: MOUNT UP! THIS IS NO DRILL!"

They were at the wrong end of the island.

IT HAD BEEN Fitzduane's practice to ride the length of the island along the cliffs of the southern coastline and past Draker Castle to the headland.

This pleasant routine had lost something of its attraction one morning when he had found young Rudi Von Graffenlaub with a rope around his neck hanging from a tree. And it was that hanging that had brought him into the world of counterterrorism. It was a world that had no exit. That particular incident had ended with the destruction of the terrorist known as the Hangman, but the dead terrorist had been the linchpin of a worldwide network, and revenge by one of the surviving terrorist groups was no small possibility.

The memories of that incident and its consequences lingered on all too well without the added stimulus of a sight of the hanging tree. Also, Boots had a three-year-old's attention span. He liked shorter rides, more variety, and to finish up at the waterfall.

The cascading water at Battleford entertained him and distracted him sufficiently for Fitzduane to be able to enjoy his surroundings without having to answer a question every thirty seconds. Boots liked to splash and float sticks and throw stones into the water. The stream was shallow there and relatively safe.

That day, with Boots secure between his arms on a special seat on the saddle in front of him, Fitzduane first headed west toward Draker, as had been his old routine, but then turned inland, past a section of particularly treacherous bog, and veered north across the track that ended with Draker Castle and on toward the hills that guarded the northern coastline.

Fitzduane loved the feeling of the young body next to his. Boots's curiosity and sense of fun were contagious. His excitement and enthusiasm were total. From time to time, unconsciously, Fitzduane would pull Boots to him and caress the top of his head with his lips or stroke his cheek. He knew that this was a special age and a special closeness, and that this time would pass all too soon.

The center of the island was relatively flat by the standards of the terrain, and here, just north of the track, Fitzduane and Boots found a neat row of dead sheep. A note written on milspec paper was wired to a stick and fluttering in the wind.

It read: "Hugo—if you find these sheep before I have had a chance to hide them, I can explain everything! See you for dinner this evening." It was signed, "Shane (Colonel, soon to be General) Kilmara."

Fitzduane smiled. Kilmara tended toward the incorrigible. It was a miracle he was making general, given the number of enemies he had made, but occasionally talent will out.

He was curious about how Kilmara's exercise would work out. He had high hopes for the Guntrack concept, small light fast vehicles festooned with weaponry and capable of outrunning and destroying a tank, and costing a fraction of the amount.

There was evidence of several of the tracked vehicles around. The tracks seemed to have sprung out of nowhere and then headed north. He followed them, and behind a clump of rocks found the drop pallets and Kevlar restraining straps under a camouflage net. The tracks then headed in different directions. Well, he would find out the details that evening.

Boots was enjoying himself playing with the camouflage net and jumping from pallet to pallet. Fitzduane dismounted and let Pooka, their horse, nibble. Boots soon worked out a game whereby he would throw himself off a pallet and Fitzduane would have to catch him. Boots jumped fearlessly, utterly confident that his father would keep him from harm.

Boots suddenly screwed up his face, so Fitzduane pulled down the little boy's pants and let him pee away from the wind. The exercise was a success. They mounted up and headed due east, parallel more or less with the hills, and toward Battleford.

THE WATCHER SAW them first. He took no action. His main concern was guarding their rear and their escape route. It was all clear.

Below him, the spotter picked them up as they emerged around the base of a foothill and headed toward the waterfall. He spoke to the sniper.

The rifleman adjusted his point of aim in response to this information.

Seconds later, rider and son on horseback entered the limited field of vision of his telescopic sight.

KILMARA HAD OFTEN NOTICED there was a natural temptation to consider movement in itself a positive result. In his opinion, this tendency had bedeviled maneuver warfare since Cain initiated the process by terminating Abel.

But Kilmara was an old hand. He went for the high ground—a protruding foothill—and there positioned himself on a reverse slope. He then spoke into his headset microphone, and a telescopic mast began to extend from the back of the Guntrack. It stopped when it was just over the brow of the hill. A higher slope behind them meant nothing was silhouetted against the skyline.

Kilmara could now view most of the low-lying terrain as far as Duncleeve and beyond. There was some dead ground due to natural variations in the fall of the land and there were the hills on the north side of the island—to his left from where he was positioned—but it was the best he could do in the time available, and Kilmara rarely worried about the theoretical optimum. He wasn't an idealist; he was a pragmatist. He had learned over more than three decades that the profession of arms was a practical business.

Mounted on the extended mast was a FLIR—forward looking infrared observation unit. This operated like a variable, very-high-magnification telescope, but with the added advantage of a wider angle of vision linked with the ability to see through mist and rain and smoke and darkness. The image was transmitted to a high-resolution television screen which was built into the console in front of him.

Methodically, he began an area search, operating the FLIR head with a small joystick. Concurrently, he had ordered the other two Guntracks forward. One was following the line of the foothills. The other was advancing toward Duncleeve at high speed on the track that ran the length of the island.

Behind Kilmara, in the heavy-weapons gun position, a Ranger tried to link up with Duncleeve by radio. His satellite communications module was capable of bouncing a signal off a satellite orbiting in space and reaching around the world through a network of relay stations, but it could not get through to Duncleeve about three miles away. The satcom was connected to Ranger headquarters in Dublin, who had then patched the call into the Irish telephone system.

This was one link too far. Fitzduane's local telephone exchange was old and tired and low on the priority list for modernization. Some days it just seemed to need to rest up. And this was one of those days.

Master Sergeant Lonsdale sat in the driver's seat, irritated at himself for not reporting the helicopter sooner, despite the fact that the Colonel, when he had cooled down, had said there was no reason he could have known its significance. The Colonel was right, but that didn't make him feel any better. He had a strong sense of unit pride, and the U.S. Army's elite Delta Force was his world. He felt he had been shown up in front of the Irish, and he was determined to redeem himself.

The Irish were good—damn good, in fact—but nobody could touch the best of the best, and in Lonsdale's opinion that designation went to Delta. Beside him was a heavy piece of milspec green metal topped by a telescopic sight. The awesome-looking weapon looked oversize and brutal when placed beside a conventional sniper's piece. It was the newly developed Barrett .50 semiautomatic rifle. Each round was the size of a large cigar and could throw a 650-grain bullet over three and a half miles. That was the theoretical range. On a practical basis, given the limitations of the ten-power telescopic sight and human eyesight, the maximum in the hands of an absolute master was about one third of this, or 2,000 yards. The longest combat shot that Lonsdale had ever heard of was around 1,800 yards.

Hits in excess of 1,000 yards from even the best of sniper rifles were the stuff of myth and legend until the Barrett came on the scene. They still required extraordinary skill.

"I've got Fitzduane," said Kilmara, and tightened the focus on the FLIR. He passed the location to the two other Guntracks. One continued toward the castle. The other was in a side valley and out of sight of Fitzduane's location.

Kilmara put himself in the position of a killing team with unfriendly intentions toward Fitzduane and searched accordingly. The team would want to oversee their target and have good cover. They would have an escape route back to the helicopter. They would not wish to fire into the sun—not much of a risk in this part of Ireland.

With binoculars alone he would have seen nothing—the killing team was excellently positioned and concealed. The FLIR changed the ground rules. It could pick up body heat.

"Two hostiles," said Kilmara, and indicated the TV screen. He had activated the laser system. The target was now illuminated by a laser beam which was visible only if special goggles were worn. The range was also determined. On the screen it read 1,853 meters, well over a mile.

"It's yours," he said to Lonsdale. Supposedly they were on a training exercise. The Guntracks were not carrying longer-range standoff weapons.

Lonsdale had already moved when Kilmara spoke. He positioned himself on the brow of the hill, the Barrett extended on its bipod in front of him. In his heart he knew it was a near-impossible shot—and anyway they were almost certainly too late.

But he also knew, the way you do sometimes, when everything comes together, that this was a special time—and on this day he would shoot better than he ever had before in his life.

Through his goggles he could see the laser beam pinpoint the target. The 16× telescopic sight was calibrated to the ballistics of the .50 ammunition. He acquired the target. The sniper's body was totally concealed in a fold of ground. He could just see a burlap-wrapped line that was the rifle barrel and an indistinct blob that was the head.

Behind him, Kilmara fired off two red flares in a desperate attempt to distract the assassins and alert Fitzduane. The flares in this color sequence had been the abort signal twenty years earlier when they had fought together in the Congo. It was an inadequate gesture, but it was all he could think of.

As they approached the ford, Boots grew animated. The place he particularly liked to play in required crossing the stream, and he loved the sensation of traversing the water on high, perched safely on Pooka's back.

From this vantage point he could sometimes see minnows or even bigger fish darting through the water, and there were interesting-looking stones and dark, strange shapes. The hint of hidden danger that provided part of the excitement was nicely offset by the reassuring presence of his father.

They crossed at walking pace, the peat-brown water gurgling around Pooka's hooves. Halfway across, Boots shouted, "Stop! Stop!" He had pieces of stick he wanted to drop into the stream so that he could follow them as they bobbed in the rushing water.

Red blossomed in the sky. Fitzduane looked up at the flare, then leaned back slightly to see more easily, as the second flare exploded. A sense of imminent danger coursed through his body, and Pooka shifted uneasily.

The sniper fired.

His rifle had an integral silencer, and he was using subsonic ammunition.

Fitzduane heard nothing.

He just saw the back of Boots's head open up in a crimson line and felt his son grow limp. Stunned at first, he screamed in anguish and desperation as the horror of what he was seeing hit home.

Pooka reared up.

Distracted, the sniper fired again before fully reestablishing his aim. Blood spewed from Pooka's head as he collapsed, throwing Boots several feet away into the shallow water.

The sniper's third shot hit Fitzduane in the thigh, smashing the femur. Fitzduane was now partially caught under his dead horse. With a desperate effort he tried to roll free, but then his strength gave out.

"BOOTS!" Fitzduane cried, oblivious of his pain, his arms outstretched toward the boy, who lay faceup in the water just out of arm's reach.

The horse was shielding his target, so the sniper had to rise for the killing shot. He had the luxury of a little time now. His victim was down and defenseless.

The spotter decided to help finish the business.

He fired a burst from his silenced submachine gun at the boy as he lay in the water. The rounds impacted in a ragged group around the boy's head, causing Fitzduane to make a superhuman effort to release himself and go to the assistance of his son. He pulled free and tried to rise, and as he did so, he exposed his upper body.

Two more shots for a certain kill, thought the sniper: one to the heart and one through the head. He didn't believe in relying on a one-shot kill. Subsonic ammunition might not inflict the massive trauma of a fully loaded round, but it did make for a silent kill and the corollary of extra time to make sure the job was properly done.

He and Master Sergeant Al Lonsdale fired at the same time.

The sniper's round created a small entry wound as it entered Fitzduane's body one inch above his right nipple and two inches to its left at the fourth rib space.

Continuing its path of destruction, it pierced the chest wall, smashed

the front of the fourth rib, and then—now combined with bone fragments—divided the fourth intercostal artery, vein, and neurovascular
bundle. Fragments of rib became embedded in the right lung and the
bullet plowed through it, damaging minor pulmonary arteries and
veins.

The round missed the trachea, went slightly lateral to the esophagus,
missed the vagus nerve and thoracic duct, grazed the skin of the heart,
went to the right of the aorta, and entered the posterior chest wall.
Traveling slightly downward, it then smashed the back of the fifth rib,
went to the right of the vertebrae and exited out of the upper left side
of the back, producing a large exit wound.

Fitzduane made a slight noise as the shock of the bullet drove the air
from his body, and folded slowly, his arms stretched out toward Boots.

Lonsdale's bullet had longer to travel. It was approximately five
times the mass of a modern automatic-rifle projectile and had a muzzle
velocity of 2,800 feet per second. Part of the mass consisted of explosives.

The spotter saw the center of the sniper's body explode as the corpse
was flung back against the hillside. He could see no sign of threat ahead
of them.

He was turning when Lonsdale's second round arrived and drilled
through his right arm from the side before exploding inside his torso.

KILMARA WATCHED his friend and his young son through the FLIR.

The image of Boots and then Fitzduane getting hit and tumbling
into the rushing water was replaced by the sight of Fitzduane's desperate attempts to help his child. And then he lay still.

The Ranger Colonel continued to monitor developments and to
issue orders, his face immobile. The Guntrack originally tasked for the
castle was the first unit that could make it to the scene, and at full cross-
country speed it arrived in less than two minutes.

Three Rangers—Newman, Hannigan, and Andrews—jumped out.
All Rangers were BATLS, Battlefield Advanced Trauma Life Support,
trained. BATLS was a combat version of the ATLS techniques pio-
neered in the U.S. The reasonable assumption, given the Rangers' line
of work, was that they would be under fire. The emphasis was on
speed.

Newman and Hannigan ran to Fitzduane. Of the two, he was clearly the more seriously wounded. Drenched in blood, he was dying before their eyes. He was bluish, very agitated, in severe respiratory distress, and in deep shock. His wounded leg looked bent and visibly shorter. It was clear the femur was shattered.

"Chest and leg," said Newman into his helmet-mounted microphone. "Lung penetrated; leg looks bad; looks like the femoral."

Andrews went to Peter. The boy's wound looked like a graze. He was mildly concussed and the back of his head was bleeding, but he was very much alive. Within a few moments, he regained consciousness. "Boy grazed but OK," said Andrews.

Fitzduane was critical, however. "Hugo," Newman said, "can you hear me?" A reply would have meant that Fitzduane was conscious and his airway clear.

There was no reply. "Shit," said Newman. Their patient was dying. Newman gave him five minutes at best. He moved to check Fitzduane's airway. Satisfied, he inserted a hollow tube, a Guidel airway, which would act to maintain access.

The whole procedure took about twenty seconds. "Airways OK," said Newman.

Hannigan had been cutting open Fitzduane's clothing and assessing the two wounds. Blood was everywhere but was cascading from the thigh wound in a positive torrent. He estimated that the man had lost up to a liter of blood in the first minute, and though the pressure had now eased off slightly as the blood supply diminished, the flow was still major. The femoral artery was like a power shower.

Fitzduane's clothes were saturated and the ground was sticky with blood. Immediately, Hannigan wrapped a bandage above the area of the thigh wound and applied pressure on it. The flow diminished, though it did not stop.

Newman suspected a tension pneumothorax. The man's lung was punctured. The likelihood was that air was leaking into the chest cavity and could not escape. Pressure was building and blocking blood flow to and from the heart. In addition, the pressure in his chest kept his ribs and diaphragm expanded, so he could not breathe in and out properly. Fitzduane was gasping. He was running out of oxygen.

Working very fast, Hannigan checked Fitzduane's trachea, then percussed his chest. The first dull sound confirmed the leakage of blood into the pleural space. The second sound, a booming resonance, confirmed the excess of air.

"Fuck it," he said. "We've got a tension."

Without hesitation, he thrust a wide-bore cannula into the front of the chest. The cannula looked like a slim ballpoint-pen refill and consisted of a hollow needle protruding slightly inside a hollow plastic tube.

As the needle penetrated, he heard a massive blow-off of trapped air. Immediately, Fitzduane's breathing improved. There was still blood and air in the space, but it was no longer under tension.

The procedure had taken one minute.

Fitzduane regained partial consciousness. "C-ca . . . brea . . . ," he gasped faintly. "My son, look after . . ."

"Be my guest," said Hannigan, and put a Ventimask over Fitzduane's mouth and connected it to a cylinder of compressed oxygen. At a rate of ten to twelve liters per minute, the oxygen would last only fifteen minutes or less. Time was still critical. As Hannigan slipped on cervical and neck collars, Newman secured the Ventimask tapes. Another minute had passed.

"I'll plug," said Newman. He would try to stop the bleeding while Hannigan worked at establishing intravenous access. There was no point to inserting drips if the liquid was immediately going to leak out, and yet Fitzduane needed extra liquid fast. He was in a state of shock. His normal blood volume was five and a half to six liters, and he looked close to losing half of that.

His brain was not getting enough oxygen. He was confused, extremely weak, his heart rate was fast, his eyes glazed.

His system was closing down. He was losing the physical strength to live.

The chest wound will just have to wait, thought Newman. The thigh wound still represented the main bleeding problem. He applied direct pressure against the leg, above the area of the wound. He knew he would have to maintain the pressure for at least five minutes, probably longer.

But there was now a plug in the bath.

"You can fill him up," said Newman.

Hannigan inserted a cannula into a vein of each arm, then connected the fluid bag. The solution would make it easier for the remaining blood to circulate and keep the vital organs supplied with adequate amounts of blood, and hence oxygenated. Lack of oxygen to the brain for more than three minutes meant that parts of it would start to die: permanent brain damage.

Establishing intravenous drip access to each side had taken less than four minutes.

Fitzduane's blood pressure began to improve from sixty to seventy systolic. It was critical. Normal was around one-twenty.

Newman was still maintaining pressure on the thigh wound.

Keeping a close eye on Fitzduane's airway to make sure that the Guidel tube was not spit out, Hannigan applied a dressing to the entry and exit wounds, taking care to stick each dressing down on three sides only, while leaving the fourth open so that air could escape. Sealing the wound totally could once again cause a buildup of internal pressure.

Newman glanced at his watch. They had been working on Fitzduane for just over eleven minutes. He was now stabilized to the best of their ability, but he remained close to death.

As Hannigan began to administer small incremental doses of morphine intravenously to Fitzduane, Newman bandaged Fitzduane's legs together to form a splint, and together they slid him onto a "scoop" stretcher and strapped him into place.

Master Sergeant Lonsdale, Barrett at the ready like a modern-day incarnation of an avenging angel, watched over the Rangers at the ford.

When it was over and the helicopter had departed, he rose and walked back the few paces to the command Guntrack. The Colonel looked up from the console, his expression unfathomable. He looked as if he was going to speak but said nothing.

The radio operator in the back of the Guntrack had the miniature folding satellite dish extended. There was a break in his arcane work and he looked up and shook his head. "It doesn't look good."

Lonsdale stood there, knowing he had shot better that day than ever before in his life, but that it still had not been good enough. Could he have been just a few seconds faster?

THE WATCHER, higher up the hill, had a better overview of the terrain and was also less tightly focused.

He had first been alerted by the sight of a vehicle traveling at high speed toward the castle. He hadn't warned his people below, both because they were so close to achieving their goal and also because the vehicle did not seem to represent any threat. At first it did not appear to be heading toward them. Apart from its speed, there was nothing unusual about it that he could see from a distance. Then it turned toward them.

They had been warned to expect a Land-Rover and maybe a car or two. Nearer, this thing was unlike anything he had ever seen before. At first he thought it must be some piece of tracked farm machinery.

He watched it through his binoculars. As it got closer, his heart started to hammer as something close to panic gripped him. He could see a machine gun on a mounting by the front passenger, and he realized that he was looking at something designed solely for the purpose of killing.

The two flares went off in the sky.

He looked up, then at the killing team below, and felt a sudden terrible fear.

He began to run. He had chosen his escape route well. He had found a slight dip in the ground between two hills, which was so angled that it could not be seen from the land below. In addition, there was cover from rocky outcrops and heather. He ran and ran, his very being telling him that whatever mysterious force had slaughtered his companions was now searching for him as well.

From time to time as he fled, the watcher waited for a few moments to see if he was being followed. As he grew more confident, he waited longer and it became clear that he had gotten away without being spotted. He started to relax. Soon he made it to the bowl in the hills where the helicopter lay.

He was halfway across the open ground to the helicopter when he heard a voice behind him. His automatic rifle was in his hand and it was cocked and loaded. He had practiced many times for this contingency and could turn and hit a target at fifty paces in a fraction of a second.

His practice nearly paid off. He might have been a shade faster than the Ranger behind him, though whether he would have got a shot off in time was entirely another matter. It was a moot point much debated thereafter.

As he turned, the remaining two crew of the Ranger Guntrack that had been tasked for the hills and redeployed to ambush the helicopter site double-tapped him twice each through the upper body, then through the head, with armor-piercing ammunition. Body armor was getting better and better and was turning up on the most undesirable people. It was best to be sure.

A REGULAR ARMY unit was ordered in to search the island, together with armed detectives.

The nearest mainland hospital, Connemara Regional, was alerted and an army trauma team experienced in gunshot wounds helicoptered to the hospital.

Other precautions and contingency plans were implemented. Nationwide, the Rangers and the various security organizations were put on full alert. Passengers and vehicles entering and leaving the country were suddenly subject to intense scrutiny. Such precautions were usually a massive waste of time, but not always. There were certain security advantages to Ireland's being an island with limited access and exit points.

3

TOKYO, JAPAN

January 2

etective Superintendent Aki Adachi was lying on the couch in his private office in Keishicho, the Tokyo Metropolitan Police Department's headquarters, with his shoes off, his shirt open, and his tie hanging from a desk lamp.

He rarely used his office, preferring to sit in the general office with his team when he was officially working, but for serious relaxation such as that required after a particularly energetic *kendo* bout at the police *dojo,* a horizontal position and a couch were more appropriate.

The only trouble was that the couch was not long enough. In Adachi's opinion, the bureaucrats who supplied such things were like civil servants the world over and running a couple of decades behind the times. They had not yet wised up to the fact that today's Japanese were several inches taller than their parents—and their children, brought up on McDonald's hamburgers and milk shakes in addition to sensible things like rice, raw fish, seaweed, raw egg, and miso soup, looked like they were heading skyward still further.

Adachi looked at his feet, which rested on the armrest of what was supposed to be a three-man sofa. At forty-two, and five foot ten inches, he was a little long in the tooth for the Big Mac generation, but had grown to above average height anyway. This was useful if you were staring down a suspect, but a bit of a pain if you were trying to tail somebody. Still, those days of pounding the streets and hiding in doorways were mostly over. Rank was a wonderful thing.

He wriggled his toes and practiced his foot-stretching and ankle exercises. He had been a paratrooper for ten years before transferring on fast-track promotion to the Tokyo Metropolitan Police Department, and jumping out of airplanes meant that sometimes you landed in the wrong way and in the wrong place. Which at times was not healthy. His tendons complained. His ligaments were appalled. Still, what the hell; it had been a lot of fun. And he still jumped occasionally. It was a thoroughly ridiculous activity for a sane adult in his middle years, and that appealed to him.

Adachi swung his legs off the sofa and poured himself a generous slug of *sake,* then another. The alcohol on top of the pleasant lethargy imparted by his recent violent exercise gave him a pleasant buzz. He swung his legs back on the sofa and idly picked up a report. It showed comparative crime statistics. The twenty-three wards of Tokyo, with a population of eight million, had seen ninety-seven murders last year. New York, with a slightly smaller population, came in at just under two thousand. Robbery came in at three hundred and forty-three for Tokyo and ninety-three thousand for New York. The rape figures were a hundred and sixty-one compared to over three thousand two hundred.

He smiled in satisfaction. It appeared as if the Tokyo cops were doing something right. On the other hand, paradoxically, he liked New York and wouldn't mind at all living there. Man does not live by crime-free streets alone. Still, for making his outstanding contribution to Tokyo's law-enforcement efforts, he felt entitled to a rest. And he did not grudge his forty-one thousand fellow metropolitan cops their share of the glory. He closed his eyes, thought of Chifune looming over him naked and beautiful and sexy, and slept.

Outside in the general office, the seven members of the special task force investigating the links between organized crime and politics nodded approvingly to one another. They had wagered useful money on Adachi winning the detectives' *kendo* championships, and they wanted their man to keep his strength up. Besides, things were quiet.

And then the phone rang.

SENIOR PUBLIC PROSECUTOR Toshio Sekine, a gray-haired man in his early sixties and actually rather slight, had the kind of physical presence and gravitas that would have dominated the big screen if his orientation had been that way. Instead, he had settled for the law and a life of public service and a career of distinction even by the high standards of the Tokyo Public Prosecutor's office.

Sekine-*san* specialized in putting bent politicians behind bars. In most countries that was a career with unlimited lifetime potential. In Japan, there was the additional complication of major links with the Boryokudan, the organized crime syndicates. Further, the whole corrupt mess was so institutionalized that it was becoming hard to know what was actually illegal anymore. If the norm in politics was corruption, was it corruption anymore or merely the way the system worked?

The prosecutor sipped his green tea. He came from a *samurai* background with a tradition of service to the state. He regarded the Japanese political system with distaste. It seemed to him that most elected politicians were small-minded and venal. Fortunately, they were largely irrelevant to the orderly governance of Japan. The country had an excellent and largely incorrupt civil service and a law-abiding population driven by the Confucian work ethic. In Sekine's opinion, elected politicians were more akin to a branch of the entertainment business. They provided distraction but had little to do with the serious business of running a country.

Superintendent Adachi was shown in. He bowed respectfully. He had enormous respect and affection for the senior prosecutor. They were both of the same social class, their families knew each other, and both the prosecutor and the superintendent were graduates of Todai— Tokyo University. Even more to the point, they had both taken law degrees. That made them the cream of the crop. Tokyo University graduates constituted an elite, and the inner circle came from the law faculty. Todai alumni practically ran the country. Senior Prosecutor Sekine had not selected Superintendent Adachi by accident. The investigation of political corruption linked to organized crime was a tricky and dangerous business. It was essential to have people on your team you could trust and who were predictable. Sekine trusted Adachi to serve him well.

The prosecutor gave Adachi time to relax, collect his thoughts, and sip his tea. The policeman had just come from the crime scene and had supervised the removal of Hodama's body. He had had a long day, and his fatigue was showing.

"Hodama?" the prosecutor said, after Adachi had sipped at his tea.

Adachi grimaced. "An extremely unpleasant business, *sensei,*" he said, "a massacre. Everyone in the house was killed. The bodyguard in the front was shot where he stood. Two others died inside the house. The manservant was shot in the bathroom. Hodama himself was boiled alive in his own bathtub."

The prosecutor made a sound of disapproval. "Guns," he said disdainfully. "Guns. This is very bad. This is not the Japanese way."

Adachi nodded in agreement but silently speculated whether or not the victim would have been any better off chopped to death with a sword in the more usual Japanese style. On the issue of being boiled alive, he thought a couple of 9mm hollow-points were preferable any day of the week. Anyway, execution by boiling had not been much in vogue since the Middle Ages. The last person he had heard of being killed that way was Ishikawa Joemon, a notorious robber. He had been a Robin Hood figure, supposedly robbing the rich and giving to the poor—less deductions for expenses. Hodama had not quite been in the same tradition.

"The method of Hodama's death," he said. "I wonder if that is indicative in its own right."

The prosecutor shrugged. "Let's not speculate just yet. First the facts."

"We think the killings took place around seven in the morning," said Adachi. "Hodama was a man of regular habits, and the physical evidence would tend to support this. The police doctor cannot be quite so precise. He puts the time at somewhere between six and eight.

"The bodies were not actually found until 3:18 P.M. Hodama normally received from 2:45 P.M. onwards. Today, the outer gate was not open and there was no reply to either the bell at the gate or the phone, so eventually a local uniform was called. He nipped over the wall to check out if anything was wrong and left his lunch all over the first body he found. They are not used to blood and guts in that part of the world."

"So the Hodama residence was unguarded from about seven in the morning until after lunch," said the prosecutor. "Plenty of time to remove what needed to be removed."

Adachi nodded. He knew exactly what the *sensei* was getting at. Hodama was one of the most powerful men in Japan, and a constant stream of visitors brought money in exchange for favors. The operation was extensive. There should have been some written records and considerable sums of money on the premises. The first question the prosecutor had asked when they had spoken by phone earlier in the afternoon was whether any records had been found.

"We went over the place again," Adachi said. "We used the special search team, optical probes, and all the gizmos. We turned up nothing written at all—nothing—but we found thirty million yen in a concealed safe." He grinned. "It was in a series of Mitsukoshi shopping bags."

The prosecutor snorted. Thirty million yen—roughly three million dollars—was chicken feed for Hodama. As for the shopping bags, Japan was a gift-giving country and Mitsukoshi department stores were favorite places to buy gifts. Their elegant wrapping and ornate shopping bags were part of the symbolism. Shopping bags were also the containers of choice for carrying the large bundles of yen notes that were the preferred currency of Japanese politicians. He had heard that American politicians preferred briefcases.

"Do you have any leads so far?" he said.

Adachi took his time answering. He felt extremely tired, but the thought of a nice long soak in a hot tub was not as appealing as usual.

"The scene-of-crime people are still rushing round with vacuum cleaners and the like," he said, "but it does not look encouraging. We found a couple of empty shell casings and a neighbor reported seeing two black limousines arrive around seven in the morning. And that is mostly it."

"Mostly?" said the prosecutor.

Adachi removed an evidence bag and placed it on the table. The prosecutor picked it up and examined it carefully. Then he took a file out of his desk and opened it. He removed a photograph from the file and compared it to the object. There was no doubt. The symbol was the same. The object was a *shasho*—a lapel pin—of the kind worn by tens of millions of Japanese to identify their particular corporate or social affiliation.

The symbol on that particular pin was that of the Namaka Corporation.

"Namaka?" he said, puzzled. "Where did you find it?"

"In the copper bath, jammed down by the wooden seat under Hodama's body," said Adachi. "Very convenient."

The prosecutor nodded and sat back in his chair and closed his eyes. His arms were folded in front of him. He said nothing for several minutes. Adachi was used to this, and quite relaxed about waiting.

The telephone rang. The prosecutor took the call facing half away from Adachi, so the policeman could not hear much of what was being said. It did not seem to be a deliberate gesture, and after he put the phone down the prosecutor went back to his eyes-closed position. Eventually he opened them and spoke.

"This investigation will be difficult, Adachi-*san*," he said. "Difficult, complex, and quite probably dangerous. There is scarcely a politician or an organized-crime leader who has not had something to do with Hodama over the years. Whatever we find, powerful interests and forces will be displeased."

He smiled with some affection, and then his expression turned serious. "You will always have my support. But you must be careful who you trust. You must take the fullest security precautions. At all times, you—and your team—will be armed."

Adachi's eyes widened. Although the uniforms were armed, he rarely carried a gun. It just was not necessary except in certain specific circumstances, and it was difficult to get his suit jacket to hang right with a lump of metal strapped to his belt. He said the Japanese equivalent of "Holy shit!"

"One extra thing," said the prosecutor. He pressed a button on his desk twice, and a buzzer rang in his assistant's office. "Koancho will be involved."

Adachi heard the door open, and he could smell her perfume before he saw her. Koancho's brief was internal security and counterterrorism. It was a mysterious and sometimes feared organization and officially reported directly to the Prime Minister's office, though there were links with Justice. It was generally considered that it was something of a law unto itself. It did what was necessary to preserve the constitution. Whatever that meant. It was not an organization that pissed around. It was small. It was effective.

"Involved how?" said Adachi.

"A watching brief," said Chifune.

"Quite so," said the prosecutor.

Chifune Tanabu bowed formally at Adachi, who had risen from his chair. He returned her bow.

"I think you two know each other," said the prosecutor, "and, I hope, trust each other. I asked specially for Tanabu-*san*."

I know your lips and your tongue and your loins and every inch of your exquisite body, thought Adachi, but trust? Here we are in uncharted waters. "I am honored, *sensei*," he said to the prosecutor, but including Chifune in the remark. He bowed again toward her. "It will be a pleasure," he added, somewhat stiffly. He felt decidedly disconcerted.

Chifune said nothing. She did not really have to. She just looked at him in that particular way of hers and smiled faintly.

ADACHI'S APARTMENT was not a ninety-minute commute away in some godforsaken suburb. It was a comfortable two-bedroom, one-living-room affair of reasonable size on the top floor of a building in the Jinbocho district conveniently close to police headquarters. The area specialized in bookshops and, for some obscure reason, cutlery shops selling an intimidating array of very sharp instruments.

Just up the road was Akihabara, where anything and everything electronic could be purchased. Turn in the other direction and there were the moat and grounds of the Imperial Palace and, nearby, the Yasukuni Shrine, the memorial to the war dead.

The area had character and amenities, and it was on a subway route. It was a nice place to live. Occasionally, Adachi jogged up the road and rented a rowing boat and paddled around the moat of the Imperial Palace. Other times, he took his ladder and went up through the roof-light onto the flat roof with a bottle of *sake* and sunbathed. There was a low parapet around the edge of the roof, so he had a modicum of privacy.

He also used to make love on the roof from time to time, but the advent of the police airship rather took the fun out of that. It tended to hang around central Tokyo quite a lot, and he had been up in it and knew what you could see from a thousand feet with good surveillance equipment.

Like most Japanese homes, Adachi's was decorated in a mixture of Japanese and Western styles but all blended in a distinctively Japanese way. Western furniture, where used, was modified for the shorter and slighter average Japanese physique. In Adachi's case, since he was tall, it was a modification he could have done without.

Adachi had been reared to sit upright on the floor when required like any civilized human being, and could maintain that position for hours without any discomfort. But his present posture was less traditional. He was sprawled out on the *tatami* mat floor of his living room with his head on a pillow. The room was in semidarkness, lit only by two candles.

Facing him, slightly to one side, was Chifune, also on the floor but sitting in a manner considered more appropriate for her sex. Her legs were tucked under her and she was resting back on them, her hands in her lap. She looked submissive and demure, every Japanese man's dream, which only goes to show, thought Adachi, that what you see is rarely what you get.

She was wearing a short Western skirt of some soft beige material, and in that position it was well above her knees. She had removed the matching jacket. Her blouse was cream-colored and sleeveless.

She was truly delectable. The Beretta automatic pistol she carried in a holster tucked inside the waistband of her skirt in the small of her back had been removed and placed in her purse. She also carried a silencer, Adachi knew, and two spare magazines of hollow-points. The weapon was more than a precaution. It was meant to be used. Still, she did not look in a shooting mood at the moment.

Adachi tried to remember where he had left his revolver and when he had last trained with it, but neither answer came quickly to mind. Those were tomorrow's problems. He looked through the skylight at the glow that was the Tokyo night sky when it was cloudy, and missed the stars.

He looked back at Chifune and then raised himself on one elbow. He drained his glass and she refilled it. As she came closer to him, he was acutely conscious of her body and the softness and texture of her skin. She returned to her original position.

"What is Koancho's interest?" he said.

She shook her head. "I can't tell you. You know that."

He smiled. "I know very little about you," he said. "I don't know what you may or may not do. I only know what you do where I am concerned, and you do that extremely well."

Chifune returned his smile. "You're a male chauvinist," she said sweetly, "but perhaps a little less extreme than most Japanese men. Make the most of it. Times are changing."

Adachi had to admit that she was correct on all three points. He did like—and had been brought up to expect—subservience in a woman. But he also had learned to enjoy and respect independence in the opposite sex. Truth to tell, Adachi liked women.

"Tell me about Hodama," he said.

"You know about Hodama," she said.

"Tell me anyway," he said. "Then what *I* know will join with what *you* know and that will add up to what *we* know, which quite probably will be more than *I* know right now. I think it's called synergy."

"Gestalt psychology," she said. "The whole of anything is greater than its parts."

"Tell me about the whole Hodama," he said. "Who would want to boil a nice little old man like that—to death? Actually, it looks like he died of a massive heart attack almost immediately, but you know what I mean."

"I think our problem is going to be too many candidates," said Chifune. "Hodama led a long, active, and mostly evil life."

" 'Our problem,' " said Adachi. "That's encouraging. I thought observer status meant just that. Koancho is not really into the sharing business." He grinned. "Like most security services, more into paranoia."

" 'Our' problem," Chifune repeated quietly.

"Ah!" said Adachi, savoring this new insight. He decided not to pursue it for the moment, at least verbally. Instead he stretched out a bare foot and slipped it between Chifune's knees and then a little further. She did not resist. There was a faint flush in her cheeks.

"Hodama," he said, "but perhaps the shorter version for now."

Chifune was an expert in various martial arts and related disciplines. They all put a heavy emphasis on mind over matter. She drew on this training as she spoke.

"Kazuo Hodama was born in Tokyo early in this century, the son of a civil servant. He actually spent much of his early life in Korea. His father was part of the Japanese occupation forces. Hodama therefore grew up with both military and other government connections—which he was to put to good use later on in life."

The occupation of Korea was not one of the high points in Japanese history. Japan had annexed the country in 1910, and for the next thirty-six years Korea had been subject to an arbitrary and frequently brutal Japanese military-dominated regime.

"In Korea, Hodama worked extensively for the authorities and specialized in putting down resistance. Mostly, he worked behind the scenes. He organized gangs of thugs to beat up or kill Koreans who wanted independence, thus enabling the administration to pretend they were not involved in the more extreme acts of repression.

"Hodama returned to Japan in the 1920s. The world was in recession. That was a period when there was major conflict in Japan between democratic government and the ultraright headed by the military. Since the moderates could not seem to do anything about fundamental issues like feeding the people, it is scarcely surprising that the rightists won out. The same thing happened elsewhere—in Germany, Italy, Spain, and Portugal. Empty rice bowls are not good for democracy."

"That was a period of secret societies and assassinations," said Adachi. "Various moderate government ministers were assassinated. Wasn't Hodama involved in all that?"

"So it is rumored," said Chifune. "Whether he did any of the actual killing, we don't know. Anyway, for plotting to assassinate Prime Minister Admiral Saito, Hodama was actually sent to prison by the moderate regime in 1934, and served over three years, but then he was let out when the extremists took over. And, of course, having been in prison for the cause put him right in there with the new regime. His rightist and nationalist credentials were impeccable. He had endless contacts in government and in the military and through the various secret societies he was involved with. From then on, he was into everything—but always operating behind the scenes. He was already a *kuromaku*."

Kuromaku, thought Adachi. The word had a sinister ring. There was a long tradition of such figures in Japanese life. *Kuromaku* literally meant "black curtain," a reference to classic Kabuki theatre, where a concealed wire-puller controlled the action on the stage from behind a black curtain. The English equivalent would perhaps be godfather or string-puller or kingmaker, but a *kuromaku* was more than all these. The word implied a person of very special caliber, and more recently it suggested links to both organized crime and politics at the highest level. Above all, the very sound represented power.

"Into everything?" said Adachi. His eyes were closed. He was rubbing Chifune's soft wet center with his toe. The sensations were incredibly exotic. Her voice in itself was an aphrodisiac.

"Everything," said Chifune. There was a slight quaver in her voice. Aikido, a martial art which taught self-control, could take a woman just so far. "He wheeled, he dealed, he traveled, he traded, he spied, he made and broke people. He had vast commercial interests. He finished World War Two with the rank of Admiral, though there is little evidence that he knew much about the navy except how to make money out of it. He both supported and used the Tojo militarists."

"And," said Adachi. This was an area where Koancho files would be more complete than his own. The police were not invulnerable to political pressure. The war was a sensitive issue. Detailed records of behavior during that period were not encouraged by those in power.

"Prior to Pearl Harbor," said Chifune, "he had connections with U.S. Army intelligence. He supplied them with information about China. He was there a great deal. Prior to the actual outbreak of war, there were certain mutual areas of interest between the U.S. and this country."

Adachi whistled. "Energetic little fellow, wasn't he? Was he actually an American spy?"

"We don't know," said Chifune. "They may have thought so, but I doubt that he was in the sense you mean. Certainly he balanced things out by actually funding part of the Kempei Tai—the secret police—operations in China."

"And then came the bombs," said Adachi. "Distracting even for a *kuromaku.*"

"Very distracting," said Chifune. "Japan surrendered, the Americans landed, MacArthur arrived, and within a short space of time Hodama was arrested and slung into Sugamo Prison to await trial. He was classified as a Class A war criminal."

"I imagine he was," said Adachi. "But nobody hanged him."

"He had a great deal of money hidden away," said Chifune, "on the order of hundreds of millions of yen—and he was a good talker. And he knew people and things, and he could make connections. And he had people outside who worked for him. Part of his money went to found a new political party—democracy now being in fashion again."

"The Liberal Party," said Adachi, "which merged with the Democratic Party in 1955, which as the Liberal Democratic Party has ruled this country ever since. Ouch! Why couldn't somebody less controversial have got himself killed?"

"You're leaping ahead," said Chifune. She looked straight at him as she slowly unbuttoned her blouse and then removed it. Underneath it, her skin was golden. She removed her bra. She had small but full breasts and prominent nipples. "Don't," she said.

Adachi raised an eyebrow. He was glad he had changed into a

yukata when he had returned to his apartment. Its light cotton could accommodate his growing excitement. Western trousers would have strangled the thing. Heavens, in some ways the West had a brutal culture.

"The war crimes trials took place. They lasted for two and a half years right here in Tokyo, and on December 23, 1948, seven of the defendants—six generals and one premier—were executed. Shortly afterwards, Hodama was released. He was never formally charged, let alone tried."

"The guilty are punished; the innocent go free," said Adachi. "That's modern justice for you."

"Ha!" said Chifune. She unzipped her skirt, raised herself slightly off her knees and then slid the garment over her head with a technique that would have done credit to a striptease artist. Adachi wondered how many times she had performed that movement before, and for whom. The thought hurt a little.

She moved forward and untied his *yukata* and gently slid him inside her. Adachi groaned with pleasure. Sex with Chifune was decidedly not like that with other women he had known. Chifune was an artist. Sight, touch, sound, taste, smell: she played on all his physical senses, but most of all she played games with his mind. He was obsessed with her, but he feared her. He loved her, but did not trust her. There was no certainty or predictability to their relationship. He knew little about her, and her file, as an employee of the security service, was sealed.

"Until 1952 when a formal treaty was signed with the U.S." said Chifune, "we were an occupied country. And as always, Hodama gravitated to where power lay. His release came neatly in time to avail of a major opportunity—suppressing the rise of communism."

As the full scale of the threat to the West of Stalinist communism became clear, anti-communist opinion in Washington hardened. The Central Intelligence Agency was founded. The West began to fight back. The threat was worldwide. The scale of the menace demanded drastic solutions. Some were legal. Some were not.

In what the Japanese called the *gyakkosu,* or political about-face, SCAP—the predominantly military administration of Douglas MacArthur, Supreme Commander for the Allied Powers—and the conservative Japanese government in power at the time carried out an official purge of communism. It was decided that a strong Japan was needed to stand against Soviet communism, and if that meant leaving some of the militarists and their prewar industrial support structure in power, then so be it.

But just so much could be done through official channels. Where more drastic methods were required—to break up a communist union or intimidate a left-wing newspaper, for example—SCAP and the new organization, the CIA, used gangs of local thugs. Fairly soon, it became clear that these ad hoc arrangements required organization, and into this opportunity stepped Hodama. Heavily funded by the CIA, he used the *yakuza* to do the strong-arm work and bribery to ensure that the appropriate anti-communist politicians got elected.

Japanese politics, as the prewar assassinations and other excesses showed, were never exactly squeaky clean, but the contamination of Japan's new and fragile postwar democratic system by institutionalized bribery could be traced directly to the CIA. The same thing was happening in France and Italy and in many other countries.

Communism was checked, but at a high price. Organized crime received a major cash injection and direct links with the political establishment. And links with the politicians meant protection.

In such an environment, Hodama, the *kuromaku,* thrived.

Adachi opened his eyes. Chifune had stopped speaking and was reaching behind her head, her breasts uplifted by the gesture. Her hair, glowing richly in the candlelight, came tumbling down. Then she leaned forward to kiss him, and he put his arms around her and held her and caressed her while they kissed.

Connemara Regional Hospital

January 2

There was no time to bring in a rescue helicopter, so Kilmara had decided to use the aircraft in which the terrorists had arrived.

There was no margin for any other decision. The Rangers had done the best they could, but it was not enough. Fitzduane had been too seriously wounded. He was losing ground.

Kilmara made the reasonable deduction that a machine meant to be used in such a covert mission would be fully fueled, and the tank would probably have been topped up when they had landed on the island.

So it proved. One of the Delta men was Unit 160 trained. He could fly low and fast and land on a dime. Unfortunately, he had no idea of the local geography or Irish radio procedures. Anyway, thought Kilmara privately, his Georgia drawl would be practically unintelligible to the locals. Sergeant Hannigan went with him to monitor the injured, navigate, and act as an interpreter.

Flying low was vital. Fitzduane had a punctured lung. The higher he flew, the thinner the air, the greater the pressure put on his lung as he struggled to breathe—and the greater the risk of his lung collapsing.

To the Delta warrant officer, trained in contour flying, low meant low. It was the most hair-raising and exhilarating flight of his Ranger comrade's life. Unfortunately, Hannigan was able to enjoy little of it. Seatless, he had to work from a kneeling position. The noise and vibration of the helicopter meant vigilant observation of the injured passenger's essential signs. He took blood pressure and pulse repeatedly, monitored airways obsessively, fought to keep the drips in place in the exposed interior.

By the time the helicopter arrived at Connemara Regional Hospital, Hannigan was of the opinion that on the balance of probability, Fitzduane was going to die.

THE HELICOPTER TRIP took thirty minutes. It was now forty-five minutes since the shooting.

Mike Gilmartin, the casualty consultant, had been briefed ahead by radio, and made his own diagnosis now while his team went to work.

The consultant anesthetist, Linda Foley, checked the airway for obstructions. Clearly, he could not breathe adequately for himself. "Bag him," she said. An oxygen venting mask was attached and connected to an Ambu-bag, and an anesthetic nurse began manually compressing the bag, forcing oxygen into the patient.

The patient was waxy white and his skin was clammy and cold to the touch. He was struggling and bewildered, straw-colored serous fluid leaking from his wounds, his clothing saturated in clotting blood. Closer examination showed his breathing to be thirty-five gasping breaths per minute and his blood pressure to be over eighty and unrecordable. His pulse showed one-forty beats per minute.

Fitzduane was showing a basic animal response to severe injury. Unbidden by his conscious mind, he was cutting off the blood supply to the less important areas and preserving the blood supply to his brain so that his body could fight back.

Gilmartin percussed Fitzduane's chest, and hearing the dull sound, immediately ordered a chest drain. Quickly, he injected a local anesthetic, and without waiting for the three to five minutes it took for the drug to be fully effective, made an incision in the muscles over the lower end of the fifth rib space and opened up the muscle with a forceps.

It was not enough. He inserted his surgical-gloved finger to open the wound up more, then replaced it with a forty-centimeter-long plastic tube.

Blood, a mixture of bright-red arterial and bluish venous, rushed out in a bubbly, dirty-red stream through an underwater seal and into a container on the floor. A second tube protruded from the container and released the air that was escaping from Fitzduane's lung. Half a liter of blood came out in the first two minutes.

Oblivious to his surroundings, semiconscious, confused, and terrified, Fitzduane was struggling. The anesthetist and her staff watched with concern and quickly moved to tape down the cannulas. It was all too easy for them to dislodge from the veins and go into tissue.

Gilmartin exposed the wounded leg and applied a fresh pressure dressing, while a nurse applied a direct manual pressure. The leg was unnaturally white, a sign that the femoral artery and vein were damaged. Further, the patient had clearly sustained a multiple fracture.

"What a bloody mess," he said. "Let's prep him for theater."

The preparations continued. Fitzduane's blood pressure slowly improved to ninety to one hundred systolic and his heart rate had slowed to a hundred beats per minute.

He was now adequately resuscitated for surgery.

Thirty minutes had passed since his arrival at the hospital. It had been one hour and fifteen minutes since the shooting.

He was wheeled into the operating theater.

4

Chifune left sometime around dawn.

Adachi had opened one eye as she touched her lips to his but had not protested. She had never yet stayed a full night with him and refused to explain why, and that was just the way of it. In time things might change. Meanwhile, murder and *kendo* and lengthy lovemaking were exhausting. He drifted back to sleep.

He awoke officially when the alarm clock shrieked. The Japanese electronics industry was a great believer in innovation, and this ridiculous thing, which was a clock in the form of a parrot, had been bought for him one Sunday when they had been browsing around Akihabara. It looked horrible, the digital clock face that peered out of its stomach was obscene and sounded revolting, but it did wake him up and it had some sentimental value. Nonetheless, he was determined to shoot it one of these days. Which reminded him. Where was his gun?

He went hunting and found it under his socks. It was a .38 Nambu Model 60 with a five-chamber cylinder. It was not exactly state of the art compared to American personal firepower, but in peaceful Japan it looked like overkill. He buckled on the damn thing, and two speedloaders to balance out the weight, with regret. Orders were orders.

The thought came to him that the vast majority of Japanese had never handled a gun. Neither would Adachi if he had had any choice in the matter, but weapons were not an option, even in the Japanese Defense Forces.

Adachi had had a good time in the paratroops but had never seriously associated his military life with the need to kill anyone. He just enjoyed the camaraderie and jumping out of airplanes. He regarded with both puzzlement and awe the U.S. Airborne soldiers with combat infantry badges and Purple Hearts that he had met at Atsugi during training. He just could not imagine deliberately killing another human being.

Adachi slurped a bowl of herb tea and ate some rice, a few pickles, and a little grilled fish. He bowed toward the ancestral shrine he kept in a niche of the living room and headed for the subway. He had looked a little hollow-eyed when he checked himself in the mirror earlier, but apart from a certain understandable fatigue—he had slept only about three hours—he felt great.

It was not yet seven in the morning, but the train was jammed with work-bound *sararimen*—male salaried employees in their uniforms of blue or gray business suits, white shirts, and conservative ties. Squeezed in between them were OLs—office ladies—the catchall title given to women office workers. Some OLs might have university degrees and other excellent qualifications, but even so, the serious work belonged to the men. An OL's job was to make the tea and do the chores and bow prettily and get married. An OL was a second-class citizen.

Adachi thought of himself as moderately progressive, but he admitted to himself that he had more or less accepted the status quo until he had met Chifune. Now he found himself looking at OLs and other Japanese women with renewed interest. If Chifune was representative of the true nature of Japanese womanhood, Japan was in for some interesting times.

He slipped his folded copy of the *Asahi Shibumi* out of his pocket and scanned the news. There was another bribery scandal in the Diet, the Japanese Parliament, and the Americans were getting upset about the trade balance.

Nothing ever changed. He refolded his paper with some skill—it was an art form like origami to do such a thing in a subway car during rush hour, but you got good with practice—and checked the stock market. Nothing had changed there, either. The Nikkei was still going up. Day after day, that was all it did. Half of Japan seemed to be buying shares. Property values were going insane. Adachi was glad he had been a paratrooper. There was nothing like jumping out of a perfectly good aircraft to remind you that what goes up must come down. He invested, but cautiously.

The train swayed and Adachi looked up. Several feet away, a young and rather pretty OL was looking his way, an expression of subdued distress on her face. Then she looked directly at him, a silent cry for help in her eyes. The carriage was jammed. Pressed up directly behind her was a round-faced middle-aged *sarariman,* his face expressionless.

The practice was all too common. A man would press up against a woman in a crowded subway and grope her or otherwise excite himself sexually, confident that the woman would not complain. A Western woman would tear herself away from her assailant or otherwise protest. Japanese women were taught to be submissive. Other travelers, packed together but isolated in their own worlds, would not interfere.

Adachi sighed. Chifune would be the death of him. He squeezed toward the beleaguered OL until he stood beside her, then smiled at the *sarariman.* The man smiled back uncertainly. Adachi reached out and put his hand in a friendly manner on his shoulder and squeezed. He thought he had the place about right. The *sarariman*'s face glazed over with pain and he went very white, and at the next station shot from the train as if rocket-propelled.

The girl looked at Adachi uncertainly. He had helped her, but this was not usual behavior. She was not sure what was coming next. Adachi winked at her and she blushed. He could not think what else to do, and then he remembered that he had a bunch of those idiotic MPD public relation cards in his pocket. The cards featured the MPD mascot, a mouse called "Peopo," and promoted the emergency service 110 number and the name, rank, and telephone number of the officer concerned. It was the kind of thing you gave to a citizen and not to a *yakuza,* if you did not want to be laughed at. The girl looked reassured and gave a little bow of thanks. Adachi's station came up and he smiled briefly and left.

ADACHI'S TEAM WORKED in a large open office on the sixth floor.

The layout was designed so that everybody could see what everybody else was doing. It was not ideal for concentrated individual work, but it was excellent for supervising and integrating the group.

There were thirty detectives, including the superintendent himself, in Adachi's department. The layout in this case consisted of three islands of eight detectives headed by a sergeant—with the remaining three desks by the windows occupied by two inspectors and Adachi himself, when he was not using his private office. Down the corridor were individual interview rooms, and anybody who needed privacy or to concentrate went there for the period necessary.

However, being apart from the group for long was frowned on. The group system, the basis of Japanese social culture, had served them well. The most frequently heard saying in Japan was "The nail that protrudes gets hammered down." The system did encourage individual initiative, but only in the sense that it contributed to the progress of the group.

Personally, Adachi was surprised how many nails were protruding these days, but thought it had probably always been so in reality. The trick was to avoid the hammer, and the best way to do that was not to be perceived as a nail. Alternatively, the nails could come together as a group. One way or another in Japan, it was hard to avoid the group.

Most of the desks were occupied when Adachi walked in. His detectives were handpicked, and selection for the elite unit was regarded as a privilege, but the level of commitment demanded was high. Typically his detectives worked seventy to eighty hours a week, on top of commuting up to three hours a day and attending the near-obligatory group drinking sessions after work.

Quite a number of his men were unshaven and bleary-eyed from having been up all night. The killing of the *kuromaku* was a serious business, and its resolution demanded every effort. Also, it was well understood that the twenty-four hours after a murder were a particularly crucial time. Physical evidence quickly got lost. Human memory had a short shelf life. You had to search and interview as quickly as possible. That was the well-understood routine.

Adachi felt a pang of guilt for not having been up all night with his men as well, but then reflected that in his own way he had been making a contribution to the inquiry. Anyway, his right-hand man, Detective Inspector Jim Fujiwara, was about as reliable as another human being could be. They had worked together for the last three years and knew each other well. Fujiwara, a stocky powerful man in his late forties, had worked his way up through the ranks. He had more street experience than Adachi and an encyclopedic knowledge of the *yakuza*. Their respective skills were complementary and they worked together well. Adachi felt fortunate.

Adachi sat down at his desk and Fujiwara sat down facing him. A detective brought tea. He was wearing house slippers. Most of the detectives were. In Japan, workers spent so much time in their offices that it was customary to make yourself comfortable and as much at home as you could. And, of course, no one wore shoes inside the home. They were removed as you entered and placed by the door. It was a barbaric idea to bring dirt from the street into the home, and, anyway, outside shoes were not comfortable to relax in.

There was a pile of reports on Adachi's desk. It stretched several inches high. He might have sneaked in a little relaxation last night, but such interludes would be scarce until Hodama's killers were found. There would be work, work, and more work. It was the Japanese way.

Adachi gestured at the reports. "Fujiwara-*san*, I see you have been busy."

Fujiwara acknowledged the implied compliment. Specific praise was uncommon. You were expected to do your work as well as you could and you did it. Nothing else would be appropriate. There was nothing exceptional about doing your duty.

"We have completed the house-to-house questioning and we have in all the reports from the *kobans* and mobiles in the area. In addition, we have the preliminary pathology reports and those of the Criminal Investigation Laboratory. There have been some developments."

"The case is solved?" said Adachi with a smile.

"Not exactly, boss," said Fujiwara with a grin. "I think on this one we are going to earn our pay."

Adachi became serious. Fujiwara continued. "We now have several reports of two black limousines in the area at around seven in the morning—within the time window, anyway. The models were current-year Toyota Crown Royal Saloons. They were noticed because the two cars were in convoy and there was some speculation as to what dignitary was inside. Otherwise there was nothing suspicious. The windows were tinted, so the witnesses have no idea how many people were inside or who they were. Still, we now have sufficient evidence to indicate that the killers came and went in those cars."

Tokyo was wall to wall with shiny black executive limousines, thought Adachi, and tens of thousands of them would be current-model Toyotas. It did not seem a promising line of inquiry. It was a pity the killers had not favored Cadillacs or Mercedeses. Both makes were comparatively uncommon and were favored by the *yakuza*. At least he would have a pointer as to where to look. Also, the good thing about leaning on the *yakuza* was that you normally got a result. To get rid of police harassment, the *yakuza* had the useful custom of giving up a suspect. The suspect might well not be the guilty party, but he would plead guilty and confess and the police could mark the case closed. In return, the nominated perpetrator would receive a light sentence and when he came out would be greeted by the gang and feted. It was a common way for a gang member to establish himself with his gang. It was, so to speak, part of the apprenticeship system.

Adachi had once described the custom to a visiting police group from the West, and they had been horrified. Personally, Adachi thought the custom had a lot to recommend it. No *yakuza* operated on his own initiative anyway; actions were always dictated from the top, so the idea of specific guilt or innocence was somewhat academic. Second, the custom incorporated a built-in check on the crime rate. A *yakuza* gang did not mind giving up a member now and then for a few years, but it did not help practical operations or morale if half the gang was behind bars. Finally, it made the job of both the police and courts a lot easier, which was good not just for them but for the taxpayer. Everyone gained.

"Nothing helpful like a license plate?" said Adachi helpfully.

"And a signed confession," replied Fujiwara. "Nothing so convenient at the scene. However, a policeman in a *koban* several blocks away saw a Toyota Crown Royal Saloon of the right year and color parked, and took its number as a matter of routine. The driver was fiddling in the trunk. When questioned, he said he had had a puncture and had just finished changing the tire. The beat cop expressed his sympathy and let the man go, and apart from making a record in his log, thought no more of it. But when he was questioned again, he said one thing struck him afterward—the driver's hands were clean and his uniform was immaculate. Of course, he could have been wearing gloves when he was changing the wheel."

"Did he look at the driver's ID?" asked Adachi. The thought occurred to him that the driver would certainly have had gloves. Even the cabdrivers wore white gloves in Japan, and a conscientious chauffeur would certainly come prepared for such an eventuality as a puncture.

"No," said the inspector. "There was no apparent cause. It did not seem polite to question someone who had just had a puncture who was obviously in a hurry."

Adachi grunted. Treating the citizenry politely was all very well, but like most policemen he believed that an extra question or two seldom went amiss. The innocent should have nothing to hide. Of course, everybody really had something they would rather not be known. He thought of Chifune and her secrets and the discretion with which they conducted their sporadic affair.

"One car, not two?" he said.

"One car," said Fujiwara. "Though it could have linked up with a companion nearer its destination. But the make, model, description, and timing fit."

"Was there anyone else in the car?" said Adachi.

"The *koban* cop did not know," said Fujiwara. "The windows were tinted. He said he thought he saw someone else in the passenger seat, but hadn't a clue about the rear."

"Put that cop on my shitlist," said Adachi sourly. "He seems to think he's a social worker, not a policeman. What's the point of having *kobans* all over the place if the cops stationed there don't keep their eyes open?"

"He got the number," said Fujiwara, in defense of the beat cop. Actually, he thought that Adachi's criticism was justified, but he had sympathy for the cops in the field. And the inspector had spent considerably more time working out of a *koban* than Adachi. "And we have traced it."

"This is not a TV quiz show," said Adachi.

Fujiwara laughed. "You'll like this, boss," he said. "It's registered to the Namaka brothers. It is one of their personal vehicles."

Adachi just stared at him. "Well, I'm buggered," he said. "First a lapel pin, and now this."

The phone on Adachi's desk rang. He picked it up. "*Moshi, moshi,*" he said—the Japanese equivalent of "Hello." The caller was brief. Adachi put the phone down and stood up. He checked his appearance.

Fujiwara spoke. He knew the signs, and it was not unexpected. "The top floor?" he said.

Adachi nodded. He had a thought floating around he could not seem to be able to grab hold of. He headed out the door.

THE TOKYO METROPOLITAN Police Department was headed up by the Superintendent-General. Like Adachi, he was a graduate of Tokyo University law school and a highflyer. This high flying kept him busy mixing with the movers and shakers of the Tokyo power structure and much too busy with his social obligations to spend a great deal of time on actual police work.

The man who really ran the MPD was the Deputy Superintendent-General, the DSG. And everyone knew it.

Adachi headed for the elevator. A group of policemen heading up to a training session were also waiting, and it was clear there would not be room for all of them and Adachi. He was bowed into the elevator and no one followed. The group would travel as a group.

The Deputy Superintendent-General, Saburo Enoke, was not a graduate of Todai. He had gone to a quite respectable provincial university, but owed his advancement to considerable ability and enormous political cunning. The apparently mild-mannered Enoke-*san* was a force to be feared.

Adachi bowed with deep respect. The Deputy Superintendent-General had always treated him politely, but he could not warm to the man. He had a gray personality that revealed nothing. The eyes behind the designer glasses were intelligent but enigmatic. Enoke-*san* was an extremely hard man to read.

The chain of command, as far as Adachi was concerned, was clearcut enough but potentially politically fraught. He was a policeman and a member of the Tokyo MPD and reported ultimately to the Deputy Superintendent-General. However, the direction of specific investigations came from the prosecutor's office. Additionally, both the prosecutor's office and the Tokyo MPD were, in the final analysis, responsible to the Ministry of Justice. And the ministry was headed up by the Minister of Justice, who was a politician and a member of the Diet; and Adachi's little department specialized in investigating corruption of Diet members.

Effectively, Adachi was reporting to some of the very people he was investigating. It was, he thought, an interesting relationship.

The DSG, in addition to the offices of his secretariat, had a conference room of some size at his disposal, and an even larger private office with windows on two sides and an excellent view of central Tokyo. It was generally considered a good sign if he used his private office for an interview. Such was the case on this occasion.

Black coffee was brought after the initial pleasantries. If you spent all day meeting people of a certain social class in Tokyo, you spent all day drinking something or other. Even the *yakuza* bosses followed the social customs. One of the first things Adachi had learned in his anti-corruption job was to pee as and when opportunity presented itself. Sitting cross-legged with a full bladder on a *tatami* mat or on one of those damn low-slung sofas was agony.

"Superintendent-*san*," said the DSG, "how is your father? He is well, I trust?"

Adachi thanked the DSG for his consideration. People were always asking after his father. That tended to happen when your father was a senior adviser to the Emperor. The Emperor was no longer considered divine. He exercised no direct power. But his symbolic influence was considerable. A senior adviser to the Emperor was someone with friends in the highest places. It was a key reason why Adachi had been selected for his job. He had enough connections at the highest level to be considered reasonably invulnerable to political influence. And he had a temperament to match.

"The death of Hodama-*sensei* is extremely unfortunate," said the DSG.

Adachi nodded his agreement. He imagined Hodama, himself, had not been overly enthusiastic either. He noted that Hodama's staff, who had also died rather abruptly, did not get a mention. The DSG, who was an exceedingly small man, sat in a very large and well-padded black leather swivel chair. He swiveled his chair around so he could look out of the window after he spoke, and was silent. Adachi fought an impulse to peer over the DSG's desk. It was rumored that his legs dangled.

"Unfortunate," repeated the DSG quietly, almost as if talking to himself. He did not seem to expect a reply.

It was a characteristic of Japanese discussions that what was said was significantly less important than what was communicated in other ways. The ranking of the participants, the context of the discussions, body language, shades of tone—all these elements were as important as the spoken word, and together added up to the dominant aspect of a meeting. Adachi understood all this as well as the next man, but considered that the DSG carried the whole process to excess. The man never seemed to say anything specific. He never committed himself. There was no feedback on recent developments. He just sat like a spider spinning some invisible web; and around him, senior street-hardened career policemen jumped if he called. He was not a popular man, nor even respected as a leader, and yet the consensus in the force was that the Tokyo MPD had never been in better shape. Whatever it was, the Spider had something. And, so it was rumored, part of that something was political clout.

"Hodama-*sensei*." The DSG's use of the term *sensei* was interesting and possibly disturbing. *Sensei* literally meant "teacher" and was used as a term of respect. That Deputy Superintendent-General Enoke should talk about Hodama, a man who had been under active investigation by Adachi's own department, in such a way had implications. It implied connections which implied potential embarrassment for these connections; embarrassment which must be avoided. The DSG was warning Adachi to proceed carefully, to be cognizant of the political ramifications. Where the DSG stood on the matter was far from clear. He might be supportive. He might be warning Adachi off. The superintendent had not the faintest idea where the DSG stood, and he had not the slightest intention of asking. It would be pointless and it would offend protocol. The DSG was his superior, and Adachi was well-schooled in what was appropriate in such situations. This was Japan. Respect for one's seniors was fundamental.

The small man in the big chair turned to face Adachi. "Superintendent," he said, "do you have all the resources you need?"

"Yes, I do, Deputy Superintendent-General-*san*," said Adachi. "I have my own department, additional manpower seconded to me as it may be required, and the work of the technical support services has been exemplary." Internally, he was taken aback. It seemed he was being both warned off and offered help. It was typical of the Spider, extremely confusing.

The DSG made an approving gesture. "It is important that this matter be resolved satisfactorily."

Adachi agreed respectfully. He had the feeling that the operative word was "satisfactorily."

The Spider changed the subject, or appeared to do so. "I was examining the latest crime statistics," he said. "I am concerned about the foreign element. Our own Japanese criminals behave predictably and they know how far they can go. Foreigners have no respect for authority. Their motives are often obscure. Their behavior is frequently impermissible."

Adachi agreed again. "Foreigners can indeed be difficult, and yet some are required for the economy."

"Korean criminals are a particular problem, I have noticed," said the Spider. "They have a tendency towards violence." He looked at Adachi. "Sometimes random violence. They can be a cruel people. They lack adequate respect for office and position." He rose to indicate that the interview was over.

Adachi bowed deeply and left. The DSG might be suggesting he clean up the whole Hodama business by framing some obliging Koreans; he might have remembered Hodama's early years in Korea and be suggesting a line of inquiry; he might merely have been making polite conversation. Adachi was not about to ask exactly what he meant. If the DSG had wanted to be specific he would have been. And more to the point, it was not appropriate to question a superior. Japan was a disciplined and hierarchical society, and the Tokyo MPD was a disciplined and hierarchical organization. Where would anyone be if sufficient respect for one's superiors was not shown?

Still, thought Adachi, there are times . . . He felt vaguely frustrated. He went down to the *dojo*, found a *kendo* partner, and worked out energetically for an hour. Bashing somebody over the head with a split bamboo cane meant loosely to simulate a *katana*, the long sword, while being hit as little as possible yourself was an excellent way to restore equanimity.

After the session, he bathed and went back to work refreshed. The Spider's observations he stored in the back of his mind. The pile on his desk had become even higher. There was work to be done.

5

CONNEMARA REGIONAL HOSPITAL:
INTENSIVE CARE UNIT

January 4

A terrible feeling suffused him.

He could not identify the feeling, nor did he understand where he was or what had happened. Tears coursed down his cheeks. He opened his eyes. He had no sense of place or time or reason.

Brightness. Noises. Electronic noises. Strange breathing sounds. He was not breathing! Terror; absolute terror. Darkness. Sadness. Blackness. Nothing.

A little peace.

A time for nightmares. He awoke again, choking, and knew only despair. He fainted.

DR. LINDA FOLEY was working with the senior intensive care nurse, Kathleen Burke. Fitzduane would have one-to-one attention until he left ICU. If he left ICU.

Linda Foley had a sense of unease when she looked at her patient. Something was definitely wrong, not just the physical things but something else. Dr. Foley tended to feel this kind of thing. It was a gift and it was a burden.

Working together, they checked his BP and blood gases through the arterial line; checked his CVP; checked his oxygen levels; checked his air entry with a stethoscope; watched the monitors.

Linda Foley noticed that Fitzduane had high blood pressure and a fast pulse rate. "He's in serious pain," she said, "poor sod." She prescribed morphine in the form of Cyclimorph.

Kathleen, concerned about his body temperature, added some blankets. She checked his wounds for oozing through the dressings, and changed them where necessary.

Foley looked around the futuristic-looking room as if for inspiration, and moved her neck to try to release some of the tension. Her muscles ached. She was bloody tired and too much black coffee was fraying her nerves, but she was not going to quit on this one until it felt right. And so far, it did not. No, something was decidedly wrong.

He had been drifting in and out of consciousness. He was gradually regaining some—albeit drug-laden—awareness. It was going to be a frightening awakening. In her opinion, the intensive care unit was about as un-people-friendly as could be. It was a monument to hygiene and advanced technology, but it did nothing for the human psyche. It was overlit and cold and sterile and full of cables and bleeping monitors, and it was a truly terrifying place to wake up in, even if you knew you were being treated.

In Fitzduane's case, he would have no sense of continuity. He had been ripped from his normal life, massively traumatized and then cast ashore in this alien environment. He would be paranoid and disoriented. All his systems—cardiovascular, respiratory, renal, immune—had mounted an immense physiological response to his injuries, and the effect would be total mental and physical exhaustion. To make matters worse, the first people he'd see would be masked and gowned.

He would see only eyes.

His main reassurance would come from the ICU staff's voices. Voices in ICU were vital. They provided the human element, the link to the human spirit. In Linda Foley's experience, recovery was only partly physical; it was predominantly a matter of the mind . . . shit, that was it. This patient's spirit was damaged in some way. How she knew it, she could not say, but that was it. He lacked the will to recover.

In consideration of his high blood loss and low body temperature, Foley had kept him on the ventilator, the life-support machine, for a further six hours after surgery and then had gradually weaned him off. He was now breathing for himself with an oxygen mask over his face. He had been wearing it for two hours. It would soon be time to remove it.

Fitzduane opened his eyes again. Kathleen leaned over him and spoke: "Hello, Hugo. I'm Kathleen. You've had an operation, and all went well."

Fitzduane's eyes filled with tears. His vision was blurred and his throat was dry and sore. He tried to speak. No sound came out. Kathleen moistened his lips with a small sponge.

A gasping sound came out. Kathleen bent closer. He spoke again, and then consciousness faded.

"What did he say?" said Linda Foley.

Kathleen looked puzzled. "Boots or roots," she said. "He said he—they—were dead, I think. He's still drugged to the eyeballs. He's just rambling."

Linda Foley looked down at Fitzduane. Desecrated though his body was, he was a striking-looking man. He did not look like someone who would surrender life easily, and yet the fighting spirit was missing. "Fuck it," she said. "We're missing something here. I'm going to find out more about this guy."

She turned on her heel, walked out of ICU, and pulled her mask down. She wanted a cigarette but had quit while an intern. A good stiff drink would do fine. In the corridor outside were two men in combat uniform carrying automatic weapons. "I want to talk to someone," she said. "Someone who knows my patient—and quickly."

A pair of legs also wearing combat fatigues swung off a couch, and a figure emerged. He was in his early fifties, bearded, hollow-eyed from fatigue, but a commanding presence.

"Talk to me," he said. "My name is Shane Kilmara."

FITZDUANE WAS BEGINNING to remember.

He could hear the sound of flowing water and feel Boots against him. Then came flares in the sky and a sense of unease and a line of blood across the back of his son's head.

He sobbed. Bullets splashed around the unconscious boy. He could not move. He wanted to help—was desperate to help, to do something—but he could not move.

He felt weak and confused, and his throat hurt. He opened his eyes, but the light was too bright.

"Daddy!" said a voice. "Daddy! Daddy!"

Fitzduane started and cried out, "I'm coming . . ." and fell silent.

Linda Foley looked at the monitors with concern. This might not be the best idea. She and Kathleen exchanged worried glances.

Fitzduane could feel a small hand in his.

He felt small lips against his cheek and he smelled chocolate. He opened his eyes.

A small, rather grubby face looked down at him. "Want some, Daddy?" said Boots's voice. He thrust the remains of his bar into his father's mouth. Fitzduane could taste it—*really* taste it.

"Boots is fine," said a familiar voice. "He was grazed by one round, but he's fine. Now it's your turn to get better. He's wearing me out."

The monitors went crazy—and then stabilized strongly.

Fitzduane smiled and, using all his strength, put his left arm around Boots. The little boy lay beside his father in the narrow bed for a short while and hugged him, then was removed by Kilmara.

Fitzduane was already asleep. He was still smiling.

Kilmara looked at Foley and then at Kathleen. "You're a hell of a pair," he said. "You don't know when to quit. Good people." He smiled. "You can join the Rangers anytime."

Linda Foley and Kathleen Burke smiled back tiredly. They had now done just about as much as they could for the time being, they considered. Linda's beeper went off and she shrugged in resignation and went to answer the call. As she was leaving, she turned around and made a gesture of success.

Kathleen was played out. She looked at Fitzduane and not at the monitors. It was unscientific rubbish, she knew, but she could just see the difference. The man now had an aura. He was fighting back.

"How long is it going to take to get him fully back into action?" said Kilmara.

"That's an impossible question," said Kathleen, taken aback. "And premature. He's still critical."

"Only his body," said Kilmara.

Kathleen looked at him. "Four months, six months, a year," she said. "He's been badly hurt. It depends a great deal on the individual. Who is he, anyway? Apart from the odd farmer who trips over his shotgun, gunshot victims are an uncommon occurrence in this part of the world. And then there are you people." She gestured at Kilmara and the armed Rangers on security duty. "Men with weapons in my hospital. I don't like it. I would like to believe it is necessary. I would like to know why."

Kilmara gave a slight smile. "I'll tell you over a cup of tea," he said, "or maybe something stronger. You've earned it."

They found a small office beside the nurses' station. A nurse brought in two mugs of tea and Kilmara produced his hip flask. Kathleen would have killed for a shot, but she was still on call. Kilmara topped up his tea, and the aroma of Irish whiskey filled the air. He really did not know why anyone drank Scotch.

"Your patient, Hugo Fitzduane, is an anachronism," he said. "The first Fitzduane to come to Ireland was a Norman knight seven hundred years ago. I sometimes think that Hugo has more in common with him than with the twentieth century. Hugo still lives in the family castle and retains values like honor and duty and putting his life on the line for causes he believes in and people he cares about."

Kathleen leaned across and read Kilmara's name tag. "And what's your connection with him, Colonel Kilmara?"

"He served under me in the Congo," said Kilmara. "You fight beside somebody and you get to know what they are like. We became friends. Hugo left the army and became a combat photographer and went from one hot spot to another, but we stayed in touch. A few years ago, he decided he had had enough, but then he ran into something pretty nasty on his own island. It was a terrorist thing and he put an end to it with a little help from my people. There was a lot of killing. After it, he just wanted to settle down in his castle and raise a family. He is quite a gentle man at heart."

Kathleen nodded, her mind going back to Fitzduane's desperation, then his transformation when he realized his son was alive. She knew she was callused by the day-to-day realities of her job, but she had been touched by what she had seen.

"So he has a wife?" she said.

Kilmara shook his head. "That didn't work out," he said. "Hugo looks after Boots."

"And now we come to the matter of why this gentle knight living in isolation off the west coast of Ireland should be struck down by assassin's bullets," said Kathleen. "This was no training accident."

"It was no accident," agreed Kilmara. "And I suspect it is no deep mystery, either. The counterterrorist world is characterized by action and reaction. If you get involved, you are always at risk. I think this is a simple revenge shooting for what happened three years ago. These people thrive on vengeance."

Kathleen shuddered. "Warped minds. It's sick. But it's been three years. Why wait so long?"

Kilmara shrugged. "That we don't know as yet. But delayed revenge is more common than not. The target starts off taking extensive precautions and being alert to every nuance. And then time passes and he starts thinking the threat is less likely and he lets his guard down a bit. And so it goes. And there is also the saying . . ."

" 'Revenge is a dish best eaten cold,' " completed Kathleen.

"Just so," said Kilmara.

Kathleen studied Kilmara. Here was a man who had seen and tasted much of what life had to offer, she thought, and had come to terms with it. Here was a man whose daily currency was lethal force and who hunted other men. And who was a target himself. What a terrible existence.

"How do you live with all this," she asked, "the fear and the violence and the knowledge that any day some stranger might strike you down?" She regretted her words as soon as they were uttered. It was a remarkably tactless question and a clear manifestation of her fatigue.

Kilmara laughed. "I don't accept sweets from strangers," he said, "and I play the percentages. And I'm very good at what I do."

"But so was Mr. Fitzduane, you have implied," said Kathleen.

"Kathleen," said Kilmara, "when you have got his attention, Hugo is the most dangerous man you are ever likely to encounter. But he can be a little slow to start. His values get in the way of some of the more direct requirements of this business. But when he is motivated, he makes me look like a wimp."

Kathleen found it hard to reconcile the horribly wounded man in ICU with any element of menace at all, but Kilmara spoke with quiet certainty. Then a disconcerting thought occurred to her.

"The armed guards you've placed here," she said. "Do you expect more trouble? Would these terrorists try again in such a public place?"

Kilmara took his time replying. He did not want to create a panic in the hospital. On the other hand, Kathleen did not look like the panicking kind and he owed her more than a little for what she was doing for Fitzduane.

"The kind of people we are dealing with will do anything anywhere," said Kilmara. "That is one of the rules of their game. There are no limits. Zero. Zip. Nada. None. That's what keeps me young," he added cheerfully, "trying to outguess the fuckers."

"So you think they will try again?" said Kathleen.

"Possibly," said Kilmara slowly.

"So we're all at risk," said Kathleen, "as long as your friend remains in this hospital."

Kilmara nodded. "There is an element of risk," he added, "but let's not go overboard on it. There will be heavy security."

"Jesus Christ!" said Kathleen, quite shaken. "Who are those people? Why can't you find them and stop them?"

Kilmara emptied his hip flask into his mug. "Terrorism is like cancer," he said. "We have our successes, but the enemy mutates and we're still looking for a cure. It is a long, open-ended war."

"I guess the sooner we get your friend recovered and out of here, the better," said Kathleen.

Kilmara lifted his mug in a mock salute. "Way to go, Kathleen," he said. "Now you're getting it."

Kathleen gave a thin smile.

6

Fitzduane opened his eyes.

What had awakened him? Who was out there? He must react. He had dropped his guard before and look at what had happened.

The imperative to move coursed through his body and was counteracted by his painkillers and sedation.

Still the warning screamed at him.

Sweat broke out on his forehead. He tried to rise to a sitting position, some body posture from which he could react more forcibly than when lying down helpless and defenseless.

The effort was terrible. His body did not want to respond.

He drove it into submission and slowly he could raise his head and bandaged torso, but he was too weak. He screwed up his eyes as the pain hit, and a low cry of agony and frustration escaped from his body.

He heard a voice, and it was the voice of a friend. There was no threat. He was safe. Boots was safe. Suddenly, he knew where he was.

And then he saw her and felt her hand soothe his forehead and heard her voice again. "Hugo," she said. "You're safe. Relax. Lie back. There is nothing to worry about. You must rest and get well."

The digital wall clock read 2:23.

Kathleen, a warm, dark-haired woman in her early thirties, was changing his drip. On Linda Foley's initiative, she had been seconded from Intensive Care. Kathleen Burke's patients tended to do better than most. She had the touch.

She finished her task and checked his pulse. She had an upside-down watch pinned to her uniform and she was looking at it as she counted silently. He liked the touch of her fingers and the clean, warm smell of her body. There was the mark of a recently removed ring on the third finger of her left hand.

"Can I get you something, Hugo?" she said very softly.

Fitzduane smiled. It was strange. The pain was still there but somehow remote. He felt rested and at peace. He lifted his hand and took hers. There was nothing sexual in the gesture. It was the kind of thing you might not do in broad daylight but which is somehow appropriate when it is two in the morning and the rest of the world seems asleep.

"Tell me about it," he said sleepily. His fingers stroked the spot where the ring had been.

Kathleen laughed quietly. She was a very pretty woman, all the better for the signs of the passing of the years etched on her face. "It doesn't work that way," she said. "You're supposed to do the talking. It doesn't do for a nurse to give away her secrets to a patient."

"It takes away the mystique," said Fitzduane quietly, with a smile, quoting what a nurse in Dublin had once told him. "Patients want support and strength—solutions, not problems. It doesn't do to get emotionally involved with a patient." He grinned. "One way or another, we move on."

He started to laugh, but the pain hit him. He gasped, but almost immediately recovered. "Basically, we're a fickle lot."

This time, Kathleen laughed out loud. Outside in the corridor, the Ranger on duty heard the sound and felt mildly jealous. It would be nice to recline in bed with a pretty nurse as company. Then he contemplated what he had seen and heard about Fitzduane's injuries and decided that he had the better part of the bargain, after all.

The nurse came out of the room some ten minutes later and there was a smile on her face. She looked more relaxed, happier somehow. Earlier on, when he had checked her on screen before letting her through the double security barrier, the Ranger could have sworn she had been crying.

A message sounded in his earpiece, and he responded by pressing the transmit button in the day's coded sequence. Then he concentrated on the routines that the General had laid down to keep Fitzduane safe from another attack. The Ranger hadn't needed any reminders that lightning can strike as often as it takes. He had been one of the force that had relieved the siege of Fitzduane's castle three years earlier. As far as he was concerned, if you were a player in the war against terrorism, you were in a state of permanent danger.

Simply put, either you killed them or—sooner or later—they would inflict lethal force on you.

January 24

General Shane Kilmara—it was really rather nice being a general at last—thought that Fitzduane looked terrible.

On the other hand, he looked less terrible than three weeks earlier. The sense that you were looking only at a receptacle for tubes, electronics, and the drug industry was gone. Now Fitzduane looked mostly like a messed-up human who was still being stuck together. Shades of Frankenstein when he needed more work, only Fitzduane was better-looking.

He was pale, he'd lost weight, and he was strapped, plastered, and plugged into a drip and a mess of other hardware, but he was sitting up and his green-gray eyes had life in them again. And that was good. Also, he was talking. That, perhaps, wasn't so good. Hugo was a particularly bright human being, and his questions meant work. And tended to have consequences.

"Who and why?" said Fitzduane.

"How about 'Good morning,'" said Kilmara. "I haven't even sat down." He pulled up an armchair to demonstrate his lack and began to nibble at Fitzduane's grapes.

It was curious how hard it was to talk to the sick. You tended to meet and deal with most people in full, or at least reasonable, health. A person laid low was like a stranger. You no longer possessed a common frame of reference. The same applied to a soldier on the battlefield. When he was mobile, he was fire support and valued. After injury he was a statistic, a casualty—and a liability. It wasn't very nice, but it was true. And like many things in life, there wasn't much you could do about it.

Fitzduane, it appeared, wasn't going to accept the convention. He might look like something the cat had chucked up behind the sofa, but his brain was working.

Kilmara formed the view that his friend—actually his closest friend, now he thought of it, except maybe for Adeline, who was his wife and therefore didn't actually count in that particular census—was on the mend; maybe. The medics were still hedging their bets.

But it was going to be a long haul. Being shot with a high-powered rifle tended to have that effect. As they used to say in Vietnam, "A sucking chest wound is nature's way of telling you you've been hit." Hugo had been hit twice, and it showed.

"Shane," said Fitzduane. There was something about the tone.

Kilmara was caught in mid-munch. He swallowed the pits.

"No speeches," he said. "I embarrass easily."

Fitzduane was silent. "In case I forgot to mention it," he said, after a very long pause, "thank you."

"Is that it?" said Kilmara, sounding incredulous. "Is that all?" He grinned. "Truth to tell, we were lucky. Well, relatively lucky."

Fitzduane raised an eyebrow. "That's a matter of perspective," he said. "Now let's get to work. The white suits have cut back on the pills and needles, so I'm beginning to be able to string together a thought or two, and these first thoughts are not kindly. I want whoever is behind this. You've got some of the puppets and that's nice, but that's not what counts. What really matters is nailing the puppetmaster."

Two nurses came in and started to do things to Fitzduane before Kilmara could respond. They asked Kilmara to wait outside. When he came back in Fitzduane was paler, but his pillows were puffed up and his bed looked neater.

Kilmara had been shot earlier in his life and had had malaria and other reasons for being hospitalized. He had formed the view that the medical professionals sometimes had their priorities mixed up. They liked their patients to look sharp so that they could show them off to the doctors. The patient's rest didn't seem to come into it. Nonetheless, he had a weakness for nurses. He could forgive most nurses most things.

He switched his mind back to Fitzduane. He had been told in words of one syllable that the patient was not to be worried and that stress was to be avoided at all costs. And now Fitzduane, his medication at last down to manageable proportions so he could think reasonably clearly, wanted to dive straight into the investigation. Tricky. Hard to know what to do.

"Hugo," he said, "are you sure you're ready for this? You're still a very sick fellow."

Fitzduane looked at him long and hard, eyes blazing.

"Shane," he said deliberately, the words punched out, "they nearly killed Boots. I saw the back of my son's head open up and his lifeblood pour out. I thought he was dead. Next time they could succeed. Don't fuck with me. You're my friend. Help me. These"—he paused now, shaking with emotion and weakness, searching for the right word— "these vermin have to be found, fixed, and destroyed. And I will do it, with or without your help."

"Found, fixed, and destroyed."

The military phrase brought back a flood of memories to Kilmara. Fitzduane as a young lieutenant in the Congo. His first recon mission. The brutal firefight that had followed. Other missions. Other demonstrations of his effectiveness at the skills of deadly force. The man had a natural talent for combat. But then, that was his heritage.

Kilmara picked his words to ease the tension.

"There were three men in the team that attacked you," he said. "Unfortunately, all were killed. Their identification papers were all false. Their clothing had been recently purchased and revealed nothing. There were no distinguishing marks."

Fitzduane still looked at him. It has been three weeks, the look implied.

"The one characteristic they all had in common was that they were Asian, or at least looked Asian. More specifically, they looked Japanese," continued Kilmara. "We put in an inquiry worldwide through Interpol and specifically to Japan through the Tokyo Metropolitan police. We trawled through other sources as we normally do when a terrorist profile is involved. And we phoned our friends and called in a few favors and otherwise did a little rousting along the Information Highway."

"And?" said Fitzduane.

"The replies have been a little slow in coming. Of course, Interpol is not renowned for its reflexes and the Japanese like to chew things over before they swallow. Finally, it emerged that the three were members of a right-wing extremist group that had supposedly been broken up nearly three years back. Our three had been locked up on some techni-cality but were released about eight months ago."

"The timing is about right," said Fitzduane. The motive would have stemmed from his encounter with Kadar, the Hangman. If this was a revenge mission, he would have expected it to happen earlier. The des-ignated hitters' being out of circulation at the Japanese government's pleasure could explain the timing. "But why Japanese?"

"The only thing," said Kilmara, "is that according to Tokyo our three violent friends shouldn't have turned up on your island."

"And why not?" said Fitzduane.

"They are supposed to be in the Middle East," said Kilmara cheer-fully. "That's what the computer said. But what do computers know? More to the point, there is a slightly strange rhythm to the way some of the other sources have been responding. Silence, then the absolute minimum, and then a veritable feast. It's as if some people have figured out that we might be able to make a contribution to their particular game. As to who these people are . . ."

He looked at Fitzduane with some concern. The man was looking decidedly strange. "Hugo," he inquired tactfully, "are you sure you want to get into this?"

"Aahh!" said Fitzduane, in what sounded like a long sigh of under-standing or acknowledgment.

"Adeline says that sometimes," said Kilmara cheerfully, "and I'm never quite sure if it's good or bad. It's a contextual noise."

"Aahh!" said Fitzduane again. He was propped up by pillows in an uncomfortable-looking hospital bed. He had turned frighteningly pale. Now he leaned forward, as if propelled from the back, and was vio-lently sick.

Kilmara hit the emergency button, conscious that even medical help would be delayed for precious seconds by the security he had put in position. To die because of your own security, what an irony. Hugo would certainly appreciate that.

He looked at his friend. Fitzduane had sunk back against his pillows. He was now more green than pale. "Apologies," he muttered. His eyes closed and he slid to one side, unconscious. Some color came back into his cheeks.

The door burst open and white-clad bodies filled the room. Fortu-nately, they seemed to know what they were doing.

It's not nice being shot, thought Kilmara; it's not nice at all. And it's about basic things we don't like to think about—like the spilling of blood and the discharge of mucus, and splintered bone and traumatized flesh and time and pain.

The room smelled of vomit and things medical. But there wasn't the faintest trace of the smell that accompanies the passing of a life, the reminder of each and every human's mortality. The air was clean of the smell of fear.

Kilmara, sitting in the visitor's armchair, temporarily ignored by the focused emergency team, felt immensely relieved. He knew at that moment that Fitzduane was *really* going to make it. Hope became certainty. He felt curiously weak, as the reaction to endless days of tension set in. He wanted to laugh or cry or shout out loud, or just lie down and sleep. His face showed no change of expression.

An intern turned around to get something from a nurse and noticed Kilmara. The intern had been on duty for some ridiculous length of time and was tired, unshaven, irritable, and short on words. "Out," he ordered. "You there—get out of here."

"Get out of here, *General*," said Kilmara agreeably.

He exited. Fitzduane was clearly back in the ballgame, but it was going to take a little time before he became a serious player. But, knowing his friend, not too long.

TOKYO, JAPAN

January 24

Wearing fatigues to avoid the distinctive smell of propellant clinging to her street clothes, Chifune shot for forty-five minutes on the Koancho Number Three internal range, working mostly under low-light conditions.

She fired at least a hundred rounds a day five days a week to keep her edge.

The work demanded total concentration. The scenarios she had selected to be projected on the target screen covered hostage-taking and similar complex situations where, apart from shooting accurately, only brief seconds—and sometimes even less—were allowed in which to determine who were the targets and who were the victims. The poor light made the work even harder, but she was practicing this way because it was the nearest thing to the environment where she was going next.

She practiced both with and without an optical sight. The EPC subminiature optical sight, of British design—the U.K. had considerable expertise in the manufacture of counterterrorist equipment—allowed her to keep both eyes open, and replaced the conventional sight with a prismatically induced red dot which automatically adjusted to the infrared level of ambient light. The sight was passive—it did not project a line of red light like a laser sight—so it was ideal for covert operations. It was proving to be particularly effective under low-light conditions. The optics gathered the light like a pair of high-quality binoculars, and where the large red dot was placed, so went the rounds.

Using the EPC optical sight on her Beretta, Chifune found she could aim and fire accurately—hitting a nine-inch plate at twenty meters—in one third of a second. The qualifying standard was double that time.

Chifune Tanabu was an exceptional shooter.

ADACHI WAS GOING through the standard checklists that were used for a murder investigation and then updating his personal operational plan on his word processor.

The investigation of the last few weeks seemed to indicate that Hodama had met everyone and been everywhere. And he had lived too damn long. The classic routines of interviewing all friends and acquaintances and cross-checking their stories was taking forever. And as for trying to work out who had a motive to kill him, well, who didn't? Hodama had schemed and manipulated and bribed and double-crossed all his life. His list of enemies must be endless.

Somewhere, Hodama must have records. The house was clean and, more important, there was no indication that any volume of papers had been removed. There were no empty shelves or open filing cabinets or safes with doors open. No, Adachi was of the opinion that he had kept his goodies elsewhere. He was a devious, cautious son of a bitch, and that would be in character. Alternatively, the place had been sanitized by a true professional; and that in itself was food for thought.

They had discovered the security video—the recorder that taped all the comings and goings at Hodama's house—but could not read it. Evidently, Hodama liked to keep a permanent record of his visitors, but in such a way that it was secure. The video recording was scrambled and needed a decoder to work. Right now, the technical boys were trying to decode the thing. It was bloody frustrating; they might have a complete recording of the killers, but they could not view it. But why had the killers not removed the tapes? Elsewhere, their preparation had been so meticulous. Would they slip up on a visual record? For some reasons of their own, did they deliberately want to leave a record?

"Boss!" shouted Fujiwara.

Adachi looked up.

Inspector Fujiwara was waving his telephone handset around and grinning. "Progress. We've turned over the homes of all of Hodama's people, and we've hit pay dirt at Morinaga's."

"Who the fuck is Morinaga?" said Adachi. He was tired and felt drowned in paper. Reports written on the heat-sensitive paper used by the built-in printers of the little word processors used throughout Japanese officialdom seemed to be curled up everywhere, interspersed with even curlier faxes. Adachi longed for good, old-fashioned plain paper. Apart from being horrible to handle, heat-sensitive paper had an annoying habit of fading when exposed to direct sunlight. He could just see the crucial report, "And the murderer is . . ." fading as he looked.

"Harumi Morinaga was one of the Hodama bodyguards shot inside the house," said Fujiwara. "He took a burst in the torso and a couple in the neck. Kind of a slight physique for his line of work. Aged mid-twenties."

Adachi flipped through the file. He knew most victims through the photos taken as they lay dead. They were the ones that left the most vivid impressions. Somehow, the pictures collected afterward of a victim while still alive seemed to have an air of unreality. The real thing, the most memorable image—the most recent picture—was that of the corpse. He nodded at Fujiwara as he found the bloody mess that had been Morinaga.

"Morinaga's father," said Fujiwara, "was with Hodama for many years. Father and son, it appears, were estranged for a while. Father wanted son to work for Hodama and carry on the family tradition, and son wanted to go his own way. He went to work for one of the big corporations. Then, unexpectedly, he left the corporation, acceded to his father's wishes, and went to work for Hodama."

Adachi nodded. They had expected an inside man. It was common in such killings, and there was the detail that the front gate had not been forced. Someone had given the intruders the combination—or they already knew the code.

"We found young Morinaga's financial records," said Fujiwara. "He's been buying more on the stock market than he could ever afford from a bodyguard's salary—and there was over a million yen in cash in his apartment."

Fujiwara was still grinning.

"There's more?" said Adachi.

"We found a nightclub receipt and a couple of cards in one of his suits. We went to the places concerned and had them identify Morinaga and the company he was with. Young Morinaga was out with some people from the Namaka Corporation."

"Eenie, meenie, miney, mo!" said Adachi.

"What does that mean?" said Inspector Fujiwara.

"Damned if I know," said Adachi. "Let's grab a few of the boys and go have a beer."

CHIFUNE LAY CONCEALED behind a pile of packing cases on the third floor of a warehouse near the Fish Market at the back of the Ginza, and reflected upon the psychology of informers.

One of the packing cases held the pungent Vietnamese fermented fish sauce Nuoc Mam, and clearly a bottle or two had broken. The stuff stank. What the hell was wrong with good old-fashioned soy sauce? she wondered. The Japanese had the longest life span of any nationality, living proof that the traditional diet was superior.

Strictly speaking—if you wanted to evaluate the pure functionality of the issue—it was scarcely ever necessary to actually meet an informant. Information could be communicated by phone, by radio phone, by fax, or even posted—and that was without the more exotic methods of communication beloved of spies: dead-letter boxes, loose bricks, hollow trunks of trees, and the like. If you were computer literate, you could even use CompuServe, for heaven's sake.

No, the communication of information in itself did not require a meeting. It was the human element that dictated such an impractical, functionally unnecessary, and dangerous activity as a face-to-face encounter between informant and controller.

In accordance with standard Koancho operating procedure, Chifune had been trained not only by Koancho themselves, but also by a designated foreign intelligence agency. Traditionally, the foreign agency of choice had been the CIA, but Japan's ever-growing economic success had fostered a desire to exert some degree of independence, and in the late sixties, America's—and the CIA's—prestige being at somewhat of a low point thanks to the Vietnam War, Koancho had started trolling the field. There was plenty of precedent for Japanese traveling abroad to pick up foreign expertise. The initial impetus for the success of the Japanese economy had come from exactly this approach.

In the case of intelligence, Koancho hit pay dirt with Israel. Chifune's foreign training stint had been spent with Mossad, "the Institute"—in Hebrew, Ha Mossad, le Modiyn ve le Tafkidim Mayuhadim, the Institute for Intelligence and Special Operations.

She had undertaken the arduous course at Mossad's training center north of Tel Aviv that produces the elite of highly effective *katsas*—case officers—which are the backbone of Israeli intelligence. Chifune's grandmother was Jewish, a fact known to Mossad, which played no small part in the care they put into her training.

It was the Japanese side of her character that had Chifune waiting for a meeting with her informant. The Israelis had emphasized the inherent dangers and threats to security of such meetings, and had stressed that sheer logic dictated the importance of keeping such arrangements to a minimum. In contrast, her Japanese upbringing and even her Koancho training stressed the importance of *ninjo*, human feelings.

Ninjo were fundamental in all human relationships, even between police and *yakuza* or in the grubby world of case officer and informer. Even in the deadly business of counterterrorism, in Japan there was a need to respect one's *giri*, or obligations. For her part, Chifune felt a strong sense of obligation toward her informants. This was sensed and normally returned, and the resulting bond helped greatly toward her operational effectiveness.

The price she paid was that her life was not infrequently in danger. Her solution was her own personal version of "Walk softly and carry a big stick." She put a great deal of care into the preparations for every meeting and carried not a big stick, but her silenced Beretta.

Unless there was a foolproof cover story, Chifune varied the location of each meeting with an informant and tried to make each meeting place a plausible scenario.

In this case, her informant—code-named Iron Box—had a brother who was the accountant for the food importers who owned the warehouse and had his office in a partitioned-off area of the floor below. Accordingly, Iron Box had a solid reason for visiting the place, and right now, though the regular warehouse staff had gone home, her brother was working away downstairs on his abacus trying to reconcile stock. This was never an easy task where food was involved. The damn stuff was too portable and too easy to dispose of. The brother was convinced that packing cases of food had legs.

Iron Box was a code name randomly selected by the Koancho computer, and by design it was singularly inappropriate for the slight, demure, and rather pretty twenty-seven-year-old medical receptionist, one Yuko Doi, that Chifune was waiting to meet.

Miss Doi was also a terrorist, a member of a group known as The Cutting Edge of the Sword of the Right Hand of the Emperor—a name which did not roll easily off the lips, even in Japanese, and which was known as Yaibo—Japanese for "the cutting edge"—for short. But Yaibo, despite their ridiculous name and rightist propaganda, was no laughing matter. It was the most effective Japanese terrorist group since the Red Army, and its specialty was assassination.

Yaibo also operated a five-person cell structure and was exceedingly difficult to penetrate. Iron Box was something of a coup. She was a by-product of Yaibo's habit of conducting regular purges, of killing its own people who were suspected of being informers.

Iron Box's lover had been just such a victim. He had been beaten to death over several days by her cell—including Iron Box herself—and the experience had dented her idealism. She had made a rather shaky call to the *kidotai*, the riot police who were in the front line of the battle against terrorism as far as the media were concerned, and then the connection had been quietly handed over to Koancho.

Slowly and carefully, Chifune shifted her location from the cover of the fish sauce to a pallet of bags of rice. Whatever the smell, the thought had occurred to her that if shit started to fly, then undoubtedly rice had better ballistic stopping properties than glass bottles of fish sauce. Better still, it was Japanese rice. Thanks to subsidies, it might be many times the world market price for rice, but every good Japanese knew it was superior.

The elevator started to creak and groan. The warehouse floor was rectangular in shape, with the elevator and stairs located side by side to one end. Directly facing the elevator door, but to one side, Chifune was concealed. Her position gave her quick access to either the fire escape or the stairs if she had to make a run for it. Locating the fastest way to get the hell out was one of the first lessons you learned in training. Heroics were not encouraged.

There was a rattle, a further series of groans, and a crash, and the doors of the goods elevator were open.

Chifune's gaze was fixed on the opening. She was expecting Iron Box, dressed in her normal smart suit, too-high heels and crisp blouse, but it could be the night watchman up to check the stock and decide what to steal that night. Chifune had noticed in her reconnaissances that with typical Japanese modesty he limited himself to one case per night.

The minimal warehouse lighting, presumably a gesture toward security, was provided by a series of low-power naked lightbulbs dangling above the intersections of pallets. The filthy ceiling of the room and the matte colors of the packing cases absorbed the light, and clear visibility was difficult.

It was dawning on Chifune that she should have brought an image intensifier. Still, perfection was an aspiration, not a human characteristic. Instead she focused the EPC optical sight of her silenced Beretta on the elevator entrance, just as a small figure wearing either slacks or trousers stepped out and looked uncertainly from side to side.

It was Iron Box. Chifune registered that fact just as the significance of the flared sighting dot in the sight hit home. The sighting dot reacted to infrared light. Someone was scanning the gloom with an invisible infrared beam—invisible except to someone with an infrared viewer or the EPC sight. Someone else, who wanted to be covert, was in the warehouse.

Chifune tracked the source of the beam. Through the sight, it was like tracking a beam of light. Her gaze terminated at the crude wooden structure on top of the elevator shaft that housed the motor. She had considered that very hiding place herself, and she went cold at the thought. Her next question was, How did someone get up there without being seen by me?

There were two alternatives: either the watcher had arrived before Chifune and knew the Koancho agent was there, or else the watcher, or watchers, had entered the small motor room directly from a roof trapdoor in the elevator. Chifune tried to remember if she had seen such a trapdoor and decided she had not. It was an old, crude installation dating back to the postwar building rush, by the looks of it, and constructed with scant regard for building regulations.

Iron Box walked out hesitantly onto the warehouse floor, just as Chifune came to her disturbing conclusions. A split second later, flame flashed from the motor room, there was a hollow explosion, and almost immediately afterward, the Vietnamese fish sauce behind which she had been hiding exploded in a lethal mist of shrapnel and glass shards.

The destruction was near total. Two seconds later, there was another flash and double explosion from the grenade launcher, and what was left of the warehouse's trial shipment of Vietnamese Nuoc Mam sauce was vaporized. Chifune flinched behind her rice as hot metal thudded into the rice sacks, and gagged at the smell. She was spotted from head to toe with the awful stuff.

Iron Box was crouched on the floor, trying to take cover behind a pallet-load of drums of cooking oil. She was screaming, and oil was spewing from several of the drums where grenade fragments had penetrated.

The access door of the elevator motor room flew open and three figures in black ski masks jumped down onto the main warehouse floor.

Two figures with slung automatic weapons grabbed Iron Box. The third stood guard, a U.S.-made M16 automatic rifle fitted with an underbarrel grenade launcher in his hands.

Chifune realized that she was supposed to be dead, and certainly it was not for lack of trying. Two M79 grenades against one slight Koancho case officer and a few cases of fish sauce was overkill. The explosions had blown out the lightbulbs in her section. She crouched down behind the rice bags, thankfully shielded by the darkness. One handgun against three automatic weapons was not good odds. It did not make sense to die for an informant.

For a split second, Japanese *giri* and Israeli pragmatism fought a battle, and in the end sheer irritation at being fucked around by three goons won out. She heard a cry of fear and, looking over the top of her barrier, caught a glint of metal. Iron Box was struggling in one terrorist's hands, and he was pushing her onto her knees as the other raised a sword above his head. The third terrorist still kept a lookout, his weapon traversing the gloom of the warehouse as he scanned from side to side.

Chifune placed the red dot on the third terrorist and fired four shots when the combination was pointed well away from her. In case he was wearing body armor, she aimed for his head, and all four rounds impacted. The grenade launcher exploded with its characteristic double blast, and a pallet of the local version of Scotch whisky at the other end of the warehouse went up in flames.

Distracted by Chifune's attack, the terrorist with the sword looked away from his victim toward this new assailant, and Iron Box kicked him very hard in the balls.

He doubled up in pain just in time to be missed by Chifune's next burst of fire. She swore and ducked down, as the remaining standing terrorist got his automatic weapon into play. Rice showered in the air. It was like a wedding.

She sprinted a dozen paces to fresh cover, changing magazines as she ran, then rolled into the aisle and fired again in a long burst of aimed shots, just as Metsada, the action arm of Mossad responsible for the more direct approach, had trained her.

The standing terrorist was ducking down to change magazines as Chifune surfaced. Her rounds hit his torso, neck, nose, and the top of his skull, blowing his brains back over Iron Box.

Chifune ran forward at a crouch and then crashed to the ground, as she skidded on the cooking oil, invisible in the gloom. Her weapon slid under a pallet.

The surviving terrorist had raised himself to his knees and now brought his *katana* down in a sweeping blow. Chifune just managed to roll to one side, but her left arm was gashed and she felt suddenly weak with shock.

Iron Box cried out a long "Noooooo!" and then there was a dense dull sound as the terrorist's next blow cut down through the side of Iron Box's neck and on through her torso to terminate close to her pelvic bone. Nearly split in two, the informant, a look of horror on her face, slumped forward.

The terrorist looked fascinated at her as she collapsed.

Chifune picked up the fallen M16, switched the fire-selector switch to automatic, and with two bursts forming a rough Y, which she thought was appropriate, terminated the killer's short career as a swordsman.

Flames were licking up the warehouse, the floor was slick with blood, and the smell of the slaughterhouse and burning whisky mixed with Vietnamese fermented fish sauce was indescribable.

Iron Box had been due to tell Chifune about the involvement of

Yaibo in a hit on an Irishman called Fitzduane. The terrorist group was indeed "The Cutting Edge," but the real issue had been who was wielding the blade. Chifune had her suspicions, but proof was in short supply.

It did not look as if Iron Box was going to be of much assistance.

1

CONNEMARA REGIONAL HOSPITAL

January 31

Fitzduane had worked out a routine which—as he thought of it—allowed the hospital ghouls to do their thing, and him to do his.

In the morning he seemed to be an object for the medics to play with. He was woken at an ungodly hour, washed, fed, and otherwise got combat-ready, and then inspected.

The inspection tended to be detailed. He now knew what a packaged chicken must feel like as it waited on a supermarket shelf. He was getting used to being poked, prodded, and otherwise examined in the most intimate ways. He felt like hanging a sign around his neck saying: "Despite a little wear and tear, I am a human being; I am not a dead chicken."

Trying to persuade the medical profession to treat patients as real, thinking, sentient people seemed an unwinnable battle. Perhaps a doctor had to have a certain distance to survive mentally in the midst of a constant stream of damaged humanity. By thinking of yourself as separate—a different and superior life-form—you could fool yourself into thinking the same kind of things you were witnessing daily couldn't happen to you.

Well, that was his benevolent theory. It was suspect because the nursing staff—who worked in exactly the same environment—didn't conform. Almost without exception, they tended to be warm and caring, even when emptying bedpans.

Lunch was early. After it he would sleep for a couple of hours. Then, refreshed, he would work or receive visitors until his evening meal. Again he would sleep for a few hours and then awake in the early hours, for what he was beginning to think of as the best part of the day. It was quiet. There were no distractions. He could think and plan. And there was Kathleen. He was growing very fond of Kathleen.

The wall clock read 1:00 A.M. The curtains, at his request, were only partially drawn, and the room was bathed in moonlight. The room was on the third floor and could not be looked into from the ground, but nonetheless this was a breach of security. Fitzduane knew it wasn't wise, but he found the confines of the hospital claustrophobic at times and he loved moonlight.

Boots was asleep on a camp bed beside him. He lay sprawled on his back, one arm behind his head, his eyelashes long, his cheeks plump and full. His breathing was deep and regular. In Fitzduane's opinion, there was nothing more beautiful than a sleeping child—except his very own child.

Boots's sleeping over in the hospital was not a nightly routine, but it did happen two or three times a week. He had been told by Oona that it was "camping," so there was an added spice to the adventure. A small plastic sword lay on the floor beside him. He was now quite unfazed by either the hospital surroundings or Fitzduane's injuries, but he was determined that no bad men were going to harm his daddy again.

For his part, Fitzduane had much the same idea but a different taste in weapons. Kilmara had left him with a Calico submachine gun. This U.S.-made high-technology weapon held a hundred rounds of 10mm in a tubelike helical magazine which lay flat on top of the receiver, and which were fed in a spring-loaded rotary arrangement rather like an Archimedes screw. It had a folding stock. The end result, without the traditional magazine jutting out of the bottom of the weapon, was unsurpassed firepower in relation to its size. It was so small and light, it looked like a toy. It rested discreetly in something like a saddle holster clipped to the right side of the bed.

He could hear Kathleen's footsteps outside.

He had become adept at identifying individual cadences. Her walk was quiet but firm. This was not the rapid squeaky walk of an overworked student or the consciously measured stride of a consultant. This was the walk of a person of serious caliber.

Kathleen closed the curtains and put on the monitor light. Then she went to Boots and potted him. He was wearing a long T-shirt covered in small bears. There was a satisfying noise as he peed to order. He was still fast asleep and warm and pink-cheeked and floppy. Kathleen gave him to Fitzduane for a kiss and a quick cuddle and put him back under the duvet. She emptied and rinsed out the pot in the bathroom that adjoined the private room. Then she sat down on the bed beside him. Their conversation continued virtually where it had left off. It had become that way with them. Neither questioned the reasons or where it was all heading. Both valued the warmth and the closeness.

Last night they had been talking about her failed marriage. It had been a classic case of sexual incompatibility. This night, Kathleen was asking the questions.

Fitzduane interested her. She had spent all her life comparatively sheltered in Ireland in a caring profession. Here was a man who had traveled the world and was an intimate of danger. Here was a gentle man who had killed.

She looked at him as he lay back against the pillows. He had a strong yet sensitive face curiously unlined for his years. His eyes were an unusual green-gray and twinkled with humor. The steel-gray hair was cut *en brosse*. Wounded and weakened as he was, he still looked formidable. He was a big man, lean and well-muscled. There was gray in the hair on his chest. He had clearly seen much of life, the good and the bad.

Kathleen wanted to ask about Etan but started on another subject. Despite their growing intimacy, Kathleen sensed that Boots's mother might be off-limits—or then again, he might want to talk about her. She would take her time.

"How did you meet General Kilmara?" she said.

Fitzduane looked at her a little amused, as if he knew that was not the question she had intended to ask, but he answered nonetheless. "He was my commanding officer," he said, "back in the early sixties. He was something of a maverick—a fighting soldier rather than a politician in uniform—but there are times when fighting soldiers are needed."

"The Congo?" questioned Kathleen.

Fitzduane nodded. "You know, it's funny. When most people hear that you have fought in the Congo they automatically assume that you were a mercenary. They don't seem to know that a United Nations force was there and that the Irish Army provided part of the U.N. man-power."

"The Congo is forgotten history," said Kathleen, and smiled. "I don't know very much about it."

"It's not something I'll forget," said Fitzduane quietly. "My wife was killed there."

Kathleen took his hand but did not speak. After a minute or so, Fitzduane continued. He seemed to want to talk.

"Anne-Marie was a nurse," said Fitzduane. "She wanted to get some experience of life and do some good. Those were idealistic days. I met her at a bush hospital near Konina. She was tall, red-haired, and beautiful. We were married within weeks. A couple of months later, less actually, a group of rebels known as the Simbas started rampaging. They took hostages and assembled them in Konina and threatened to kill them if they were attacked. Some they tortured and killed anyway.

"Well, we mounted a rescue mission and infiltrated a small advance unit into Konina where they were being kept. There were only twelve of us and thousands of rebels, so we were under strict instructions not to fire until the main force arrived. We were in the upper floor of a house overlooking a square where the hostages were being kept. For eight hours we had to watch people being tortured and killed below—and we could do nothing. Finally, some Simba kid—he can't have been more than thirteen or fourteen—hauled Anne-Marie out and, just like that, hacked her head off. It was very quick, mercifully quick."

Fitzduane continued. "I can't really describe how I felt. I was only fifty meters away, and through binoculars she looked close enough to touch. I remember getting sick and then just a feeling of numbness. Soon afterwards, the main attack began. I couldn't stop killing. Machine gun, automatic rifle, grenades, garotte, fighting knife—I used them all that day. It didn't make me feel any better."

"There was nothing you could do," said Kathleen.

"I have been told that again and again," said Fitzduane, "but I have never been quite sure. Another irony: her tour of duty was over. If she hadn't married me and signed on again to be near me, she would have gone home before the Simbas attacked."

He looked across at Boots, who was now sleeping on his right side, his right cheek resting on his hands. "Now here I am putting someone I love in harm's way again."

"Guilt is not a very constructive feeling," said Kathleen.

Fitzduane smiled. "I don't feel guilty anymore," he said. "I've learned enough about the random nature of violence not to feel personally responsible for Anne-Marie. I've come to terms with her death. However, I cannot accept a threat against my family. There, whether I'm directly responsible or not, I'm still responsible."

"Do you think you're directly responsible in this case?" said Kathleen, indicating both Fitzduane and Boots.

" 'Directly responsible,' " replied Fitzduane, quoting her words back, "probably not. Responsible, in that all of this happened as a consequence of my actions, probably yes."

"I don't quite understand," said Kathleen.

"About three years ago," said Fitzduane, "I found a dead body on my island. I could have reported the matter to the police and left it at that. Instead, I started trying to find out what had really happened. One thing led to another and I found that there was a terrorist involved. His plans were foiled and he was killed."

"You killed him?" said Kathleen.

Fitzduane hesitated before he replied; then he nodded. "I killed him," he agreed.

"He was a terrorist," said Kathleen, but there was uncertainty in her voice. This was an alien world. "How can you be blamed for that?"

"The issue isn't really blame; it's responsibility," said Fitzduane. "What I did was necessary—indeed, unavoidable. However, the man I killed almost certainly had friends. This is about cause and effect and consequences. I may have done the right thing, but in so doing I put myself and those dear to me on the firing line."

"So you think you were shot by friends of this dead terrorist?" said Kathleen.

"Well, I'd like to think that it wasn't some complete nut," said Fitzduane. "I would prefer to be shot for a reason."

"It makes a difference?" said Kathleen.

"It makes a difference if you want to stop it happening a second time," said Fitzduane. "And this isn't the kind of thing I fancy happening twice."

It was slowly dawning on Kathleen that merely by being in Fitzduane's company she was putting herself in danger. For a moment she tried to imagine what it must be like to be under permanent threat. It was a horrendous notion.

She reached out and stroked his face and then leaned over and kissed him. She pulled away before Fitzduane could react and ran the tips of her fingers over his lips.

"Daddy! Daddy!" cried a sleepy voice. "Where are you?"

Fitzduane laughed and squeezed her hand. "Bring him here," he said.

Kathleen picked Boots up and slid him in beside his father. There wasn't much room in the narrow hospital bed, but Fitzduane cradled Boots's head in the crook of his left arm, and within seconds Boots was asleep again.

DUBLIN, IRELAND

January 31

Jiro Sasada, whose visiting card stated that he was a vice president of the Yamaoka Trading Corporation, sat in his room in Dublin's Berkley Court Hotel and sipped a Scotch from the mini-bar.

His initial shock at the disappearance of the killing team four weeks earlier had worn off after a good night's sleep, and he had immediately applied himself to learning what had happened to the missing men and the current status of the designated target. Sasada-*san* was typically Japanese in his belief in the work ethic, and setbacks in his value system were merely temporary inconveniences which could be solved by even more dedication.

His backup plan involved using a splinter group of the IRA—the Irish Revolutionary Action Party, or IRAP—that owed his group, Yaibo, a favor. Since unfortunately a Japanese involvement in the attack on Fitzduane had almost certainly been established by now, it made sense to use a local team which could more easily blend into the indigenous population.

Fitzduane's location had been determined through a sustained operation using radio scanners. Though technically illegal in Ireland, these devices were readily available and could pick up Garda—Irish police—communications which, for budget reasons, were in clear.

The Rangers had their own budget and operated with secure encrypted radio and telephone networks, but they were short of manpower. Accordingly, they worked extensively with the police, and therein lay their weakness. Kilmara was, of course, perfectly aware of this security flaw in his operational procedures, but there was nothing he could do about it in the short term. He needed the extra manpower the police provided, and he needed to communicate with them.

The IRA had been socially respectable when Ireland was fighting for independence from the British. However, for twenty-six counties out of a total of thirty-two, that goal had been achieved in 1922. Thereafter, the vast majority of Irish people wanted to live normal peaceful lives, unhindered by men with guns. The IRA became illegal. Operating undercover, it split into various groups with different objectives and ideologies. As with the Mafia, different gangs fought over territory. In some cases, fighting between different IRA factions was at least as vicious as that against the British.

The IRAP were under sentence of death by the Provisional IRA for excesses even by terrorist standards, and the three leading members of the IRAP—Paddy McGonigal, Jim Daid, and Eamon Dooley—had headed south out of the British North of Ireland into the safer territory of the independent Republic of Ireland, so, for an appropriate financial reward, they were ready and willing to help Sasada-*san* with his task.

Sasada-*san,* who despite his papers was actually a senior member of Yaibo, had met the IRAP in Libya. He had helped to train them at Camp Carlos Marighella. It had been a matter of an obligation to the Libyans. The Libyans backed a wide array of international terrorist groups, but, in turn, called in favors. It was like any other business.

IRAP was a lethal group. So far in its bloody career, it had killed more than sixty people in a series of bomb and gun attacks in the North of Ireland, Britain, and continental Europe. It would certainly be able to take care of finishing off Fitzduane.

Sasada-*san* poured himself another Scotch and went back to studying the plans of the hospital where Fitzduane lay. You could, he thought to himself, get most things with a strong yen.

It was just as well. As far as the world was aware, Yaibo was a completely independent terrorist group. In actual fact, they were obligated to the Namaka brothers, and the brothers were exceedingly dangerous when their wishes were not fulfilled.

TOKYO, JAPAN

January 31

Kei Namaka, cofounder and president of the vast Namaka Corporation, stood staring out through the windows of the top floor of the Namaka Tower.

Below him, as far as the eye could see, was the neon-bedecked ferroconcrete, glass, and steel sprawl that was modern Tokyo. In the middle distance, the police airship, the favorite toy of the Superintendent-General of the Tokyo Metropolitan Police Department, floated serenely, monitoring the congested arteries that struggled inadequately to cope with the city's traffic. Through the tinted bullet-resistant plate glass, the repetitive rotor-thump and high-pitched engine buzz of a passing helicopter could scarcely be heard.

Namaka, his eyes open, saw nothing and heard nothing. He was awake but he was having the dream.

It was near midnight on December 22, 1948.

The night was cold. They stood outside the gates of Sugamo Prison, waiting for the execution to happen. The gates were guarded by armed, white-helmeted U.S. Army military police. The weather-stained gray stone walls of the prison were floodlit by security lights.

Plentiful electricity meant the occupation forces. For the defeated Japanese, everything—power, water, food, cooking fuel, clothing, housing—was in short supply. Tokyo still lay devastated by the firebombing from the B29s of the U.S. Air Force. Most of the population were barely subsisting.

Recovery had begun, but it was a slow and painful process. Governing authority was in the hands of General Douglas MacArthur and the two hundred thousand mainly U.S. troops under his command. The Emperor had renounced his divine status. The old Japan was dead. The new Japan was having a difficult and painful birth, and there was much suffering.

Kei, a tall scrawny teenager, stood on one side of his mother. On the other side was his brother, Fumio. Fumio was small for his age and his right leg was crippled. A year earlier, he had been hit a glancing blow by a U.S. Army jeep as it careered out of control down one of Tokyo's labyrinth of alleyways, and the compound fracture had healed badly. Medication, bandages, good food—all the requirements for a full recovery—were virtually unavailable. Fumio's growth would be stunted and he would remain severely crippled for the rest of his life.

The Tokyo War Crimes trial had taken two and a half years. Eleven judges representing three-quarters of the world's population had presided. Witness after witness spoke of massacres, genocide, the slaughter and starvation of prisoners, death marches, the destruction of cities, wholesale rape, torture, executions without trial, germ warfare, forced medical experiments, a catalogue of crimes against humanity.

Six generals and one prime minister had been sentenced to death by hanging.

The executions were to take place at 00.01 hours on December 23, 1948, at Sugamo Prison.

One of the condemned men was General Shin Namaka, Kei and Fumio's natural father. Their mother, Atsuko Sudai, had been his mistress for many years. The General's legal marriage had been arranged, unsuccessful, and childless. Atsuko, their mother, had been his true love, and he had cared for her and his children with the greatest diligence and affection.

The evidence against him at his trial had clearly established that he was directly responsible for the death of over a hundred thousand slave laborers in China, and there were other crimes to do with medical experiments on prisoners.

But he had been a loving father. With his arrest, Kei's world had collapsed. The eldest son, he had been closest to his father.

The condemned men were kept in Block 5C of the prison, one to a cell. Each centrally heated cell, eight feet by five and a half feet, contained a desk, a washbasin, and a toilet. A futon mattress was placed on the floor and blankets were provided. To avoid suicide, cell lights remained on and prisoners were kept under twenty-four-hour surveillance.

The executions were carried out according to the U.S. Army's regulations for such procedures.

Each prisoner was weighed in advance to determine the appropriate drop. A table of effectiveness had been determined by trial and error in the nineteenth century. General Namaka weighed a hundred and thirty pounds and would fall seven feet seven inches when the trap was sprung. Too long a fall, and his head could be torn off. Too short a drop, and he would slowly strangle to death: The objective was to snap his spinal cord and kill him almost instantly. It was not a precise science.

The condemned men's last meal was rice, chopped pickles, miso soup, and broiled fish. They drank *sake*. They spent their last day writing letters and praying.

Half an hour before the official time of execution, the condemned men were brought to the death house. Each man was handcuffed to two guards.

In the center of the execution chamber was a platform reached by thirteen steps. Four ropes made from one-inch manila hemp hung from the gallows above. The hangman's knot had been greased with wax. Before each prisoner ascended the steps, his handcuffs were removed and his arms pinioned to his sides with two-inch-wide body straps.

The final climb was slow. At the top, on the platform, the ankles of each prisoner were secured with a one-inch strap. The noose was then placed around the neck with the knot directly behind the left ear.

The traps were sprung, the sharp crack echoing throughout the death house and across the prison yard.

The executions took place in two groups.

General Shin Namaka was in the second group. He entered the death house at 12:19 A.M. At 12:38, he was pronounced officially dead by the senior medical officer.

Each corpse was transported to Yokohama Municipal Crematorium, placed in an iron firebox, and incinerated. Afterward, the ashes were scattered to the winds.

The dream faded.

In its place was emptiness and despair and then a grim determination to survive and never to forget, whatever the cost.

Kei Namaka, tall, well-built, muscular from his daily workouts at the *dojo*, and looking a decade younger than his age, uttered a terrible, anguished cry. He fell to his knees, his eyes wet with tears, and sobbed.

He had had the dream countless times over the years.

The Namaka Tower stood on the site of what had once been Sugamo Prison. The whole development, which included a hotel, aquarium, offices, and a large shopping center, was no longer called Sugamo. After an open competition, the name Sunshine City had been chosen.

Just a simple inscription on a boulder placed in a small outdoor sitting area at the foot of the Namaka Tower recalled the executed.

WHEN KEI AND FUMIO Namaka had first started their entrepreneurial activities, administration was comparatively simple.

Fumio would scout for a victim and then Kei, bigger, stronger, faster, and decidedly dumber—though far from stupid—would do the actual deed. It was a simple system and administratively undemanding. No paperwork was required. Counting the proceeds of armed robbery and related activities could scarcely be called financial planning, and personnel management was nothing more than the two brothers agreeing between themselves.

That was no problem. The two were devoted to each other and painfully aware that they had no one else to turn to. Further, their roles were clearly defined by age and natural attributes. Kei was the official leader, man of action, and decision-maker. Fumio was the loyal second in command, the thinker, and, quickly and discreetly and in absolute privacy, and in such a manner that Kei was not really aware of the process, told Kei what decisions to make.

The Namaka brothers were a pair of ragged, street-smart hoods in the late 1940s. As he grew older, Fumio found that more and more he recalled those early postwar days.

They were the benchmark of the scale of their achievement. So much from so little; so much from virtually nothing. They were driven by desperation, for the immediate postwar period was indeed a desperate time.

Their initial capital, Fumio Namaka remembered vividly, had come from a major in the Imperial Army. It had been late January 1949, a month after the executions. The little family was shunned by many who were fearful of the imagined wrath of the occupation forces. Mother was seriously ill. The brothers were near-starving and desperate. They were living in a bomb site, really little more than a hole in the ground with a roof made of flattened U.S. Army ration cans.

Priorities were elemental. Whereas before and during the war, people had been occupied with such issues as strategy, patriotism, social standing, and career prospects, by 1949 the issue was survival.

You did whatever you had to to make it through the day. You dressed in rags and castoffs, you slept in ruins or worse, and you ate anything you could. Pride was irrelevant. Social status was a joke. Moral standards and ethics were an abstraction.

You did what was necessary and you lived. You stood on principle and you died. You killed if you had to. After a while you got used to it and you killed because lethal force worked. It got results. It was effective.

There was a thriving trade in Japanese Imperial Army militaria. Two hundred thousand occupation troops wanted war souvenirs and several million Imperial Army veterans wanted to eat. The action came together in street markets around Tokyo, and particularly in the Ginza.

The major was of the *samurai* class and had been a member of the Imperial General Staff after distinguished service—initially in Manchuria and subsequently in the invasion of Burma. The latter exercise had cost him his left arm above the elbow after a British .303 bullet had shattered the bone into multiple fractures, but it had added to his chestful of medals and gained him promotion to the staff, where he was highly regarded. More medals soon followed. Promotion was a certainty, until Hiroshima and Nagasaki and the reedy voice of the Emperor, never before heard on the radio, called for surrender.

Selling his medals one by one had kept the major alive. Now, on that freezing cold day in January 1949, his medals were gone and he was down to his last item of value, the long sword, or *katana,* that had been in his family since the eighteenth century. It was a blade signed by Tamaki Kiyomaro. It was bought for a fraction of its true worth by one of MacArthur's bodyguards.

Inwardly, the major died a little as he sold it, but there was no choice. He and his family had to eat. Everything else of value had been sold. His wife had earned some food and a little military scrip from sleeping with members of the occupation forces, but her looks had gone and there was too much competition. They were starving. There was no other choice. He had to sell the last item of value they owned.

The purchaser of the major's *katana* was not short of compassion and, by the standards of the time, paid generously for the blade. The exchange and the amount paid caught the attention of Fumio Namaka. Undersized and limping, he tended to be either ignored or dismissed as insignificant, and, as such, he was an ideal scout.

The brothers had been searching for a worthy target for several days. The soldier's generosity toward the destitute major clinched their choice of victim. He had paid not in restricted military scrip, which could only be used in designated locations, but in *U.S. dollars,* green-backs—in 1949 the hardest, strongest, most desirable currency in the world.

Kei Namaka, skinny but tall for his age, and still, despite the hunger, reasonably fit and strong, followed the major home through the back streets and when he stopped to relieve himself in a deserted section, hit him with a rock.

The major fell to the ground as Fumio limped up. The two brothers looked at each other, and then Fumio cut the unconscious man's throat with some broken glass. They had agreed in advance that there would be no witnesses. They had owned a knife but had to sell it to buy food. The broken glass did the job adequately but was slow. It was also messy. The brothers did not mind. They now had more money than they had ever seen before in their lives.

Suddenly, the Namaka brothers did not just have enough money to buy food; they had capital. It was not much, but it was a beginning. They were no longer looking at bare survival. They could plan. And Fumio, crippled and physically less gifted than his brother, was a natural planner. He was gifted with a strategic sense, a decided cunning, and a talent for manipulating his fellows. In short, he had brains.

When they returned to their shelter with a little boiled rice and some *sake* to celebrate, they found that their mother was dead.

OVER THE DECADES they had evolved into the Namaka Corporation, a vast corporate network of interlocking companies whose interests had spanned the length and breadth of Japan, most of the developed world, and much of the third world.

The core operational group of the Namaka Corporation was not the Torishimariyakukai—Board of Directors—which was really about public image and strategic alliances and was kept well away from detail. The real planning and decisions were made by the more conveniently named General Affairs Department, or Somu Bu.

The Somu Bu had served the Namaka brothers well. Nearly three decades after its creation, it now consisted of Kei and Fumio and six handpicked, seasoned *buchos*—department heads—of unquestioned loyalty.

In the typical corporate world, a *bucho* would not have vice-presidential status, but in the case of the Namaka Corporation there were obvious security implications, which dictated a tighter vertical structure.

THE GUARDED, soundproofed, and electronically swept meeting room of the Somu Bu of the Namaka Corporation was decidedly luxurious.

Eight overstuffed handmade tan leather executive armchairs were placed around a boardroom table made from a single piece of hand-worked wood. Each chair was embossed with the Namaka crest in gold. The chairs at either end of the table were even larger and more luxurious, with deeper padding and higher headrests. The walls were covered in silk. Some of Kei Namaka's vast collection of antique Japanese swords and Western weapons from the same periods were in illuminated glass cases on the walls. Underfoot, the carpet was thick and soft.

The six *buchos* rose to their feet and bowed deeply as the Namaka brothers entered. Bows in Japan come in three grades: the informal, the formal, and the slow, deep, right-down-to-the-waist kind known as *saikeirei,* used for the Emperor and the less democratic *yakuza* bosses.

The bows delivered to the Namaka brothers were of the *saikeirei* class. Japan's entire society was based on ranking, and the brothers were not known for their democratic approach to discipline.

Kei entered the room first through the special padded double doors which led directly to the luxurious office the brothers shared.

Fumio followed, at a respectful distance, limping and supported by a stick. He had not aged as well as his brother. His hair had gone completely silver and he looked as if he could easily have been in his mid-sixties. But his age gave him a dignity and gravitas that was not unhelpful.

Kei sat down first, and Fumio followed some seconds later. All the *buchos* now took their seats. Kei called the meeting to order formally and then looked at Fumio. The younger brother ran it, but always gave the appearance of deferring to the chairman. This was the first formal meeting since the murder of the *kuromaku.* Kei had been attending secret talks in North Korea when the event had occurred, and had only recently returned.

"The first item," said Fumio, "concerns the death of Hodama-

sensei. His passing means that we have lost our most influential friend. The manner of his passing gives some cause for concern." He stood up and bowed his head in silence, and all the others followed suit.

After several minutes, he sat down. The mention of Hodama was enough to get everyone's full attention. The *sensei* had been the behind-the-scenes fixer for the Namaka brothers and had helped to give them a charmed life with the authorities and the competition over the last three decades.

His untimely death was proving a disaster.

The *kuromaku* had been an unparalleled protector but had been jealous of his power and influence, and now there was no obvious candidate to replace him. Despite his age, he had not nominated a successor. Because of his age and his sensitivity on that matter, the Namakas had not pushed the subject.

The Namaka brothers' position had been that of two men in a sturdy boat in a shark-infested sea, with Hodama representing the security of the boat. Now that boat had been arbitrarily removed and they had been dumped unceremoniously into unfriendly waters to swim with the sharks. It was going to take a period of adjustment.

There was also the matter of the Hodama's killers' methodology. After the *sensei,* who was next for the cooking pot? The assassins were efficient, brutal, and did not seem to be deterred by the status of the victim. These were disconcerting thoughts.

"It would be helpful," said Kei to the gathering, "for the corporation if your thoughts on the current implication of the passing of Hodama-*sensei* could be prepared."

The assembled *buchos* bowed their heads respectfully in acknowledgment. They knew exactly what the chairman wanted. He was asking for a detailed paper and proposals on the full consequences of the Hodama affair. The procedure was known as *ringi seido.* It referred to a circulated written proposal which would be signed by the assembled team but only after a great deal of informal and behind-the-scenes discussion, known as *nemawashi*—literally, "binding the roots."

The *ringi seido* system could be slow and bureaucratic. At the Namaka Corporation, particularly in the General Affairs department, the system had been refined to an art.

"Next item," said Kei. He was wearing a Savile Row–tailored dark-blue pinstripe suit and a handmade silk shirt. His tie was regimental. His hair, though streaked with gray, was still full and he wore it brushed straight back, the wings meeting behind his head. He had a high forehead, a strong nose, and firm, regular features. He looked every inch the chairman of the board. Fumio was very proud of him.

"Our obligation in Ireland, Kaicho-*san*," said Fumio, with the appropriate honorifics. Privately, his brother was called by his first name. In public, the formalities were always followed. There were no fewer than seven different ways to address different social ranks. It was an area where foreigners—even if they spoke Japanese, a rare occurrence—normally fell down. Well, what could you expect? No *gaijin* could ever really understand Japan.

One of the *buchos*, Toshiro Kitano, Vice President for General Affairs, cleared his throat. He was a slight, studious-looking man with thinning hair in his late fifties; he reminded some people of a priest or monk. There was an ascetic, spiritual quality about him. It was not entirely misleading, since he was a martial arts master—a field in which the spiritual was regarded as at least as important as the physical.

Kitano's role in the group was security. Within the ethos of the Namaka culture, that had less to do with conventional industrial security than with the direct application of force against those who opposed the wishes of the brothers. Kitano was an enforcer and assassin, and had been with Kei and Fumio since the early years. These days, he rarely carried out assignments himself. He was now an executive, and in Fumio's view had made the transition rather well. He was an invaluable man, with the advantage of hands-on practical experience and organizational talent.

Skilled killers with the administrative talents required by the corporate environment were not easy to find.

"Kitano-*sensei*?" said Kei respectfully. Although Kitano was an employee and his junior in the Namaka Corporation, the master was his mentor and trainer in the martial arts field and as such was treated with an appropriate deference.

"Several years ago, we had dealings with a terrorist, a *gaijin*, known as the Hangman," said Kitano. "He had many names and we never did find out his real background. But we cooperated on several assignments. It was a successful partnership."

"He approached us, as I recall," said Kei. He did not add that it had been a major breach of security. It was not appropriate to embarrass Kitano in front of his peers. Anyway, the *sensei*, once he had recovered from the shock, had handled the situation extremely well.

"He had extensive connections," said Kitano. "A number of apparently separate groups in different countries reported to him. Some of his people trained with some of ours in the Middle East. This led to his attempting to penetrate our organization to find out more about us. Fortunately, we were able to block this infiltration, but not until he had learned rather more than he should. The situation was difficult. The solution was cooperation. His people were not known in some areas; our people were not known in others. By exploiting this we were able to carry out a number of assignments successfully."

There were approving noises from around the table. The *buchos* were all aware that the subject was difficult for Kitano, and they were anxious to show support. The harmony of the group—*wa*—was very important.

"I remember," said Kei. "It was an excellent solution, *sensei.*"

Kitano bowed slightly in acknowledgment. Actually the whole business had been extremely serious. He had never been able to identify that damned *gaijin,* whereas the foreigner had penetrated the entire Namaka organization and their direct-action arm. The operations they had carried out together had been successful, but they had all been planned by the Hangman and carried out on his own terms. Then the fates had intervened. Just when the security chief had been at his wit's end, the Hangman had vanished. Subsequently, they had learned that he had been killed. It had been the best news of the decade, as far as Kitano had been concerned.

Unfortunately, the Hangman's death was not the end of it. He was a player of games and a man with a warped sense of humor. He had left behind a request in the form of a video sent only to Kitano. If he was captured, he was to be freed. If he was killed, he was to be revenged. If his request was ignored, there would be one warning, then the detailed information he had on the Namaka Corporation would be given to the authorities and there would be other unpleasant consequences. Above all, the security chief would be disgraced in front of his colleagues and the brothers themselves. The brothers knew about the request; Kitano had not told them about the threat. They might consider it his fault, since the *gaijin*'s infiltration was his responsibility—and Kitano shuddered to think of the punishment. No, he had to take care of this himself.

"This *gaijin* was killed three years ago," said Fumio. He had more serious matters on his mind, and as a result was more direct than was customary in a formal discussion. "I am a little puzzled as to why the matter of this obligation has come up now."

"It was a small matter," said the security chief, "not worthy of the meeting's attention. As to the passing of time, it was difficult to ascertain who had been responsible for the Hangman's death. Then there was the matter of finding an appropriate team to do the job. And there was no urgency. It was a matter of little operational consequence. It was delegated to Yaibo. The team they allocated was then held by the security forces for some time. All of these matters contributed to the delay. If it had been a priority, we would of course have acted sooner."

Kei wanted to move on to other things. The security chief was an experienced enough man. A routine action six thousand miles away should not be occupying the time of the meeting. Delegation was about someone else getting on with it while you did what was really important. But still he hesitated. The security chief himself had put the item on the agenda.

Kei looked at the security chief. "There is something you want to say, Kitano-*sensei?*"

"The assassination attempt took place as planned," said the security chief, "but it was not entirely successful. Our team, it appears, was killed. The target was merely seriously wounded. Our lack of complete success is regrettable."

There was a palpable feeling of relief around the table. The loss of a killing team was something they had to be made aware of, but it was not something to be concerned about. There was a steady supply of young men who wanted to prove themselves in action. Casualties in the field were almost inevitable these days, given the ever-increasing expertise of counterterrorist units, but were just an overhead of doing business. And it was infinitely better that the team were dead rather than captured. Dead men were poor material for interrogation.

"We thank you for reporting this matter, Kitano-*sensei,*" said Kei, "but we have confidence that you will resolve it satisfactorily."

Kitano acknowledged the confidence.

"What is the name of the target, *sensei?*" said Fumio. "Is he of any significance to us?"

"The target is an Irishman called Hugo Fitzduane, Namaka-*san,*" said the security chief. "He is of no significance. It is merely a matter of *giri.* Further action is being implemented."

"Next item," said the chairman.

8

Kilmara surveyed Fitzduane's hospital room.

Fitzduane, propped up into a sitting position by his bed, was wearing a T-shirt over his bandaged torso and actually did not look medical for a change. He was pale and had lost weight, but there was some color in his cheeks and his eyes were sharp and alert. The T-shirt had a picture of a group of skunks on the front and was printed with the word "SKUNKWORKS!"

Fitzduane noticed his glance. "The Bear sent it over," he said.

Kilmara grinned. "And while we're on that substantial subject, how is the Bear?"

Police sergeant Heini Raufman, the Bear, was a large, overweight Bernese policeman with a heavy walrus moustache, a gruff manner, and a taste for large guns, which, like many Swiss, he shot exceedingly well. He and Fitzduane had become very close during the hunt for the Hangman in Bern, and they had fought together during the siege of Fitzduane's castle. Subsequently, the Bear, a widower, had remarried. Fitzduane had been the best man.

Fitzduane smiled. "He's still officially with the Bernese Kriminal-polizei, but he's got some kind of liaison sweetheart deal with the Swiss federal authorities. He's not doing normal cop work anymore. He's not getting normal pay, either. He is into counterterrorist work and similar exotic territory."

Kilmara was not surprised. The Bear was the kind of man that you might easily pigeonhole as no more than a solid street cop who had reached his level. But appearances were deceptive, though useful in his line of work. The Bear had a subtle brain. It wasn't surprising that it was being used at last.

Mind you, he could be a little short on patience. When Fitzduane had first met the Bear, the detective had been in disgrace for thumping some German diplomat who had got out of line at a reception. Bern, being the Swiss capital, was full of diplomats with nothing to do except fornicate and drink and look at the bears. All the diplomatic action took place in Geneva and the financial in Zurich.

Kilmara remembered Fitzduane's smile. He was still smiling—expectantly. "Am I missing something?" Kilmara inquired politely.

"I need a gun permit," said Fitzduane.

"You've got a gun permit," said Kilmara, "not that the lack of one has ever seemed to worry you." Fitzduane's extensive gun collection in his castle was not quite in conformity with the Irish legal system.

"A rather large gun permit," continued Fitzduane. "Or perhaps I should say I need a permit for a rather large gun."

Kilmara raised his eyebrows as the lightbulb blinked on. "For a rather large man," he said.

"You're razor-sharp today," said Fitzduane agreeably. "The Swiss seem to think I may need some protection, so they are lending me the Bear."

"More likely they smell blood and would prefer the bodies to pile up in this jurisdiction than theirs," said Kilmara. "Can't say I blame them." He stood up and started looking in a cabinet that Fitzduane had had brought in for the wandering thirsty. A modest selection of bottles greeted him. There was a small fridge and ice-maker built into the lower half.

"I thought this thing looked familiar," he said. "Want one?"

"Not yet," said Fitzduane. He waited until Kilmara had mixed himself a large Irish whiskey. The General sipped it appreciatively and resumed his seat.

"They tell me alcohol and getting shot don't mix," said Fitzduane. "I'm drinking fizzy water, though I'm not sure how long my resolution will last."

Kilmara looked shocked at this statement of sobriety. He took another drink. There was nothing to beat good Irish whiskey, even if the major Irish distillers were now owned by the French.

He looked back at Fitzduane, then gestured toward a three-inch pile of folders on the bedside table. "You've read the files, Hugo?"

Fitzduane nodded. "At last," he said, with a grimace of impatience. "The medics have not allowed anything more stressful than Bugs Bunny until recently."

"I'd like your perspective," said Kilmara—he smiled—"seeing as how you are intimately involved. There is nothing like being shot to encourage tight focus."

Fitzduane gave a very slight smile in response. "Very droll," he said. Then he looked down at a yellow legal pad. "Let me start with a summary. There is a lot of stuff here."

"Summarize away," said Kilmara.

"The actual hit," said Fitzduane, "was carried out by three members of a Japanese terrorist group called Yaibo, the Cutting Edge. They would be a run-of-the-mill bunch of extremist nuts except for their track record of viciousness and effectiveness. Whereas most terrorist groups are ninety-five percent talk, Yaibo focuses on action. The secret of their success seems to be their leader, a very smart lady in her mid-thirties called Reiko Oshima.

"Yaibo's motive," continued Fitzduane, "seemed clear enough at first. A direct connection has been traced between Yaibo and the Hangman's group. And to make it more personal, it looks like Reiko Oshima and the Hangman were lovers for a while—though scarcely on an exclusive basis."

"So far so good," said Kilmara. "And though a bunch of us were involved in the Hangman's demise, Yaibo picked on you because you did the actual deed. Hell, you killed their leader's lover with your very own hands. This isn't just business. She really does not like you."

Fitzduane sipped some water. "Well, it all looked fairly straightforward," he said, "until I read on. Suddenly, a nice clean-cut terrorist revenge hit gets complicated. It turns out that maybe Yaibo is not the freewheeling bunch of bloodthirsty fanatics they would like us to believe. Instead we find that Yaibo has been involved with a series of killings that seems to have benefited a fast-rising Japanese group known as the Namaka Corporation. Your American friends in Tokyo have linked the Hangman to the Namakas. So what we have here is an outwardly respectable Japanese *keiretsu* which uses a bunch of terrorists for its dirty work. And a further implication is that the hit was ordered by the

Namakas and is not Yaibo's little notion. It was, you might say, a corporate decision."

"That's supposition," said Kilmara.

Fitzduane shrugged. "The connection between Yaibo and the Namakas might not stand up in a court of law, but it will do for me. But I agree on the issue of who ordered the hit. It could have been the Namakas, but it could equally have been a lower-level initiative by Yaibo."

"Do you have an opinion?" said Kilmara.

"Not yet," said Fitzduane. "There is absolutely no hard evidence one way or another. But what does puzzle me is the orientation of much of this stuff against the Namakas. On the face of it Yaibo is the logical candidate, and yet the main thrust of these reports is that the Namakas should be taken out. Hell, the Namakas are nearly as big as Sony. This is heavy."

Kilmara swirled his ice. "The main accusations against the Namakas," he said, "come from Langley's operation in Tokyo. You may care to know that it is currently headed by the unlovable Schwanberg."

Fitzduane looked puzzled.

"Let's flash back nearly twenty years," said Kilmara, "when you were rushing around South Vietnam with a camera trying to get yourself killed and on the front cover of *Time*."

"And Schwanberg was racking up the body count under the Phoenix program, only the VC cadres he was having killed weren't VC," said Fitzduane. "I thought the CIA threw him out. Hell, he was an unpleasant piece of work."

"He was connected," said Kilmara, "and ruthless fucks like Schwanberg can have their uses. He worked in Greece under the colonels and did a spell in Chile, then was posted to Japan as an old Asia hand. And the rest is history. The CIA have many good people, but scum floats to the top and does not always get skimmed off."

Fitzduane rubbed his chin. He was suddenly looking very tired. His friend was definitely making progress, observed Kilmara, but there was a long way to go. "So Schwanberg has it in for the Namakas for some reason," said Fitzduane. "So where does that leave us?"

"With you getting some rest," said Kilmara, "and me and my boys doing some more digging. Remember, Schwanberg may have his own agenda regarding the Namakas, but that does not mean he is wrong."

"Watch Schwanberg," said Fitzduane. "I remember him cutting the tongue out of someone he claimed was a VC suspect. She was thirteen years of age. This is not a nice man."

Kilmara stood up and drained his whiskey. "Get some sleep, Hugo," he said. "Don't overdo. We need you fit and well."

Fitzduane smiled weakly. It was maddening how little stamina he had. But it was returning.

He closed his eyes and within seconds was asleep.

THE WEST OF IRELAND

February 1

Except for certain special detective units, the Republic of Ireland's national police force, the Garda Siochana—literally, Guardians of the Peace—are unarmed. They strike many people, who do not know better, as being likable but somewhat traditional and, not to put too fine a point on it, *slow.*

On the other hand, the *gardai,* many of whom come from rural backgrounds, have their own ways of doing things, and on the top of the list is knowing exactly who is who and what is what on their own patches.

This is not always so easy in the cities. In rural Ireland, especially outside the tourist season, every stranger is noted and observed by someone. And sooner or later—if the sergeant is doing his job right and knows how to work with rather than against the local population—that information finds its way back to the local police station.

In the case of a Northern Irish accent, which is quite distinctive to an inhabitant of the Republic, that information tends to find its way to the *gardai* very fast indeed. There are, of course, a few pockets of sympathizers—less than one percent of the population, if the voting rolls are to be believed—but there were no such pockets in the area around Connemara Regional.

Routine radio communications were in the clear. Intelligence reports were treated more carefully and were communicated by secure fax to Garda Headquarters in Dublin and from there to the desk of

General Shane Kilmara, commander of Ireland's antiterrorist force, the Rangers.

As it happens, Kilmara was not there when the intelligence report arrived. He was in the West of Ireland.

KATHLEEN'S FATHER, Noel Fleming, had been a successful builder in Dublin for many years before retiring early to the West of Ireland during one of Ireland's all-too-frequent economic downturns.

In his spare time he had liked to paint, and the light and scenery of the West presented a never-ending challenge. His wife, Mary, was from the area and loved horses, so their way of life was convivial and pleasant. They built a large bungalow some miles from the town, and when Kathleen's marriage broke up it seemed only natural that she would live at home for a while. She was an only child. Connemara Regional was nearby, and she applied for a job and was accepted.

Kathleen had married a solicitor in Dublin. He was young and ambitious and did not want children. She had continued working, so when it became clear the marriage was not going to work it had been relatively easy to make a break.

She had left Dublin without regret. The city had its merits, but it seemed to her that it was losing the human values that had made Ireland special without gaining proportionately material advantage. She had found her husband's friends—mostly lawyers, accountants, and bankers—to be narrowly focused yuppies. They lacked dimension and breadth of vision.

She was no fan of the direction of modern Ireland. The country was the least socially mobile in Europe. She witnessed the injustice of the structures every day in her work. If you were born underprivileged, the chances were you would die that way. A rich and powerful element guarded the status quo. The majority lived on the margin. One-fifth of the population was without work. Emigration was the norm for most of the young. And this is the fruit of our independence, she thought. For this we fought; for this so many died.

Ireland's redeeming feature, in Kathleen's opinion, was its land. It had a beauty and a quality that was duplicated nowhere else in the world. And the most beautiful part of Ireland was the West. In the West there was magic. It wasn't just a matter of how the land looked.

It was how it felt. It was a place of the spirit, of romance, of sadness. It was a land of mystery and past heroes and great deeds and tragedy. It was a land that touched your soul.

Night shift over, she drove her little Ford Fiesta along the narrow country road toward her parents' bungalow and thought about Fitzduane. Though security kept most of the staff from ever actually seeing him, he was something of a conversation piece in the hospital. Occasionally they had a criminal or a mental patient kept under guard while getting medical treatment, but this was the first time anyone could recall that an assault victim was being guarded for his own protection. Also, the security did not consist, as normal, of one rather bored unarmed *garda* whiling away the time with endless cups of tea.

In this case, there were *gardai* on the perimeter all right, but there were also armed Rangers carrying weapons of a type she had never seen before.

It was rather scary, but it was also exciting. It would also have seemed unreal, except for the grim evidence of Fitzduane's wounds. It was truly horrifying, the damage two little pieces of metal could inflict.

She braked as she rounded a bend and saw a herd of cows up ahead blocking the road, then brought the car to a complete halt. Behind them, a farmer and his dog followed. They were taking their cows from a stone-walled field to be milked in the yard half a mile up the road. While this was going on, the road was blocked. It was possible to pass from behind, but it tended to alarm the cattle and they were heavy with milk.

The air was heavy with moisture, but the sun had broken through and droplets sparkled on the spiders' webs in the hedgerow. To the left there was a lake and in the distance the purple silhouettes of mountains. To her right, the hills were closer. Small rocky fields bordered with dry stone walls gave way to bog and heather and lichen-covered rock. Sheep grazed the higher land. Overhead, a kestrel soared.

The tragedy of Ireland, she thought, is that with all this beauty in our laps we can't seem to find a way to make a living here. The Irish did well enough abroad. There were supposed to be over forty million of Irish descent in America. There were more first- and second-generation Irish in Britain than in Ireland. Meanwhile at home, lack of vision, corruption, begrudgery, an inadequate education system, horrendous taxation, poor communications, and straightforward bad government played havoc with the prospects of generation after generation of Irish men and women.

She remembered the James Joyce quotation: "Ireland is an old sow that eats her own farrow." In her experience and observation, it was all too applicable.

Her thoughts switched back to Fitzduane.

He attracted her more than any man she had ever met. Unlike many Irish of their generation, her parents were tolerant and enlightened; she was not inexperienced sexually and had slept with several men before her marriage. She had met other men who had attracted her strongly and aroused her physically.

What was different about Fitzduane was that he combined a strong physical presence and sex appeal with a keen intellect and an approach to life she found deliciously refreshing. The man was not constrained by the dead hand of custom and practice which seemed to stultify so much of Irish society. He had an open and inquiring mind, and he did not seem to care a damn for convention.

Despite its reputation for great conversation and friendliness, Ireland was an indirect culture in which it was the custom to say what people wanted to hear rather than the truth. Accordingly, much of the friendliness was a surface patina rather than the manifestation of a relationship based on mutual understanding. In contrast, though his timing and manner belied any offense, Fitzduane tended to be direct and to cut to the heart of the matter. He was not glib or witty in the surface manner that tended to be a success in Irish pubs. He was kind and amusing, and he was so damn interesting.

She wanted him, but she was not at all sure she was going to get him. Still, she had a window of opportunity, and that in itself was rather fun. Night shift didn't use to be like this.

Ahead of her, the last cow raised its tail and deposited one of the less attractive aspects of rural life on the road before plodding into the yard. Washing a car in the country was something of a pointless exercise.

Kathleen accelerated slowly and skidded through a succession of cow pats as the farmer closed the gate and raised a hand in salute. She took a hand off the steering wheel in a casual wave of reply. Everybody saluted everybody in this part of the world, which was pleasant enough, though not entirely conducive to road safety.

A car, a white Vauxhall Cavalier, had come up behind her when she had stopped for the cattle. She noticed idly that there were two—no, three—men in it and it did not look local. It drove behind her for the next two miles until she came to her parents' isolated bungalow, and as she turned into the tree-shaded drive it followed her.

She parked and got out. She could smell wood smoke. Inside, her mother would be preparing breakfast. She felt tired, but it was very pleasant to chat with her parents over a cup of tea before heading off to get some sleep.

She walked toward the Cavalier. The roads were not well sign-posted, so this was probably people lost again. The network of minor roads was quite confusing.

As she approached the car, the two front doors opened and two men got out. The driver had crinkly reddish hair and pleasant open features. He was smiling. He put a hand inside his coat. When it reappeared, it was holding an automatic pistol.

Kathleen looked at the gun in shock and a terrible, all-encompassing fear gripped her. She was about to scream when the smiling man kicked her very hard in the stomach. Roughly, he pulled her up and hit her again hard in the face. "Let's go inside, Kathleen," he said. "We'd like a wee word with your parents."

KILMARA DID NOT take kindly to using such scarce and expensive re-sources as his elite Rangers on something as mundane as static guard duty.

He liked to take the initiative. Guard duty, he believed, wasted the expertise of his men. A Ranger on guard duty was just one more target with scant opportunity to utilize his unique skills. Waiting for some-thing to happen left the terrorist with the freedom to strike when and where he wished, and to have local firepower superiority even when outgunned on a national basis.

He had to look no farther than Northern Ireland across the border to have this truth demonstrated. There, a few hundred IRA activists kept thirty thousand British troops and armed police fully stretched—and still the killing went on.

In the case of providing security for Fitzduane, Kilmara was pre-pared to make an exception. The official justification was that Fitz-duane held a reserve commission in the Rangers—he had the rank of colonel—and therefore they were merely looking after one of their own. Actually, it had more to do with friendship and a long history together. Kilmara did not like to see his friends getting shot. Over a long and turbulent military career, it had happened more than a few times, and now he valued those close to him who were left.

Six Rangers had been assigned to guard Fitzduane. Allowing for shifts, this meant that two were on duty and two on standby at any one time, and the remaining two were off station. Perimeter security consisted of an armed plainclothes detective in the grounds below Fitzduane's window, and another detective in the hospital reception area monitoring the front stairs and elevator.

Primary internal security consisted of a control zone on the private ward where Fitzduane was located. Two sets of specially installed doors sealed off the corridor. The rule was that only one set of doors could be opened at once. Visitors were checked through one door, which was closed behind them, then checked again in the control zone before being allowed through the second set of doors. There was a metal detector in the control zone. All staff who had right of access had been issued special passes and a daily code word. Their photographs were pinned up by the internal guard, but by this time all the regulars were known by sight.

There were six private rooms off the central corridor once you got through the two sets of doors. Initially, four of these had been occupied, but after an epic battle with the hospital authorities, Kilmara had managed to get them cleared after the first week. Now one room was occupied by Fitzduane, a second was used for sleeping by off-duty Rangers, and a third functioned as a makeshift canteen. The other three were empty.

It seemed a reasonably secure arrangement and the police were quite happy, but the whole setup made Kilmara nervous. It might be good enough to keep a conventional killer at bay, but a terrorist threat was of a different order of magnitude. Terrorists had access to military-grade weapons. They used grenades, explosives, and rocket launchers. They had been known to use helicopters and microlights and other esoteric gadgetry. They were often trained in assault tactics.

In the face of a sudden commando raid and terrorist firepower, the defenders—security zone or no—would not have an easy time. Just one rocket fired through Fitzduane's window would not do him much good either. Sure, they had bolted in place some bulletproof glass, but an RPG projectile would cut through that like butter. The things had been designed to take on tanks. Unfortunately, there were a number of such weapons on the loose in Ireland. Quadafi had supplied several shiploads of rifles, explosives, heavy machine guns, and rocket launchers to the IRA. He had even thrown in some handheld anti-aircraft missiles. There were arms caches all over the country. Many had been found. Many others had not.

Kilmara tried to console himself with the thought that most of the time nothing ever happens. Many threats are made; very few are implemented. Most potential targets die in their beds of old age and good living. Such thoughts seemed logical until he applied them to Fitzduane. Then his instincts screamed. The man was a magnet for trouble.

In the second week of Fitzduane's stay in the hospital, when the basic precautions had been in place and the man himself out of intensive care, Kilmara had sent the problem to Ranger headquarters in Dublin. There the scenario had been evaluated by two teams. One team had worked out how to defeat the security and kill Fitzduane. The second had looked at current and past terrorist methodology and current and past counterterrorist protection techniques.

The findings had been pooled and the exercise repeated several times. The final conclusions had led Kilmara to implement several more security measures. Above all, he wished he could move Fitzduane, but that would have to wait a few weeks longer. He was recovering, but needed—absolutely had to have—the specialized care of the hospital. Set against that certainty, the possibility of another assassination attempt was a minor risk. Or so said the computer.

Kilmara looked at the screen when the finding came up. He remembered a game he used to play with his girlfriends as a teenager. You'd pluck the petals from a daisy one by one. "She loves me; she loves me not; she loves me; she loves me not." The last petal would decide the issue.

"I don't trust computers any more than I trusted daisies," he said to the screen. The cursor winked back at him. "Nothing personal," he added.

The first finding of the Ranger attack-scenario exercise had been that the maximum point of vulnerability at the hospital was not the security deployment as such, but the people.

"Between you, me, and these four walls," said Kilmara to the screen, "I really didn't need a computer to tell me that." He rubbed the gray hairs in his beard. "Life has a habit of instilling that lesson."

The computer continued to wink at him. He quite liked the beasts and they were damn useful, but sometimes they got on his nerves.

He pressed the off switch and, with some satisfaction, watched the monitor die a little death.

THEY HAD OPENED the door with Kathleen's key and then pushed her down the hall in front of them.

Her parents were in the large kitchen at the back, her mother at the Aga stove stirring porridge, her father sitting at the table reading yesterday's *Irish Times*. "The Pat Kenny Show" was on the radio in the background.

The kitchen had picture windows on two sides and there were no blinds. One of the gunmen went instantly to close the curtains, but the leader, the man with the smile, shook his head.

"Doesn't look natural," he said. "Bring them into the front room." He pushed Kathleen and grabbed her mother. She was still stirring the porridge, as yet unable to take in what was happening. The pot crashed to the floor. A third man came into the room and pulled the chair out from under Kathleen's father and half-pushed, half-kicked the gray-haired man out through the door.

Social life in the home in rural Ireland tends to revolve around the kitchen. The front room is kept for visitors and special occasions and tends to have the heating turned off and to feel somewhat unlived-in. The Flemings' sitting room was fairly typical in this respect. The room was chilly and the venetian blinds half closed. There were family photographs on the mantelpiece and a fire was laid but not lit. There were drinks on a low cabinet for visitors. The main seating consisted of a sofa and two armchairs, with several upright chairs set against the wall to deal with any overflow. An oil painting of Kathleen in nurse's uniform with her parents, Noel and Mary, hung over the fireplace.

Kathleen's parents were pushed onto the sofa, where they tried to regain some composure. Noel put his arm around his wife's shoulders. Kathleen was thrust into one of the armchairs, and the man who appeared to be the leader took the other. Sitting back in the chair, he reached into an inside pocket and removed a cylindrical object, which he attached to the barrel of his automatic.

"Fuck, it's bloody freezing," he said. "Jim, will you turn on the heating or something."

Jim, a heavyset man in his late twenties with black hair and facial stubble to match, turned on the radiator controls and then lit the fire. The firelighters caught and the kindling crackled. It was a sound that Kathleen associated with home and safety and comfort.

The sight of the silencer being screwed into place made her feel sick. None of the men wore masks. They did not seem to be worried about being identified later. The conclusion was all too obvious.

"My name's Paddy," said the leader. He pointed at the others. "That's Jim." Jim was now leaning against the radiator, soaking up the spreading warmth. He didn't react. "And the baldy fellow behind me"—he gestured with his left thumb over his shoulder—"is Eamon."

Eamon nodded. He looked to be only in his early twenties, but his bald head shone with a patina of sweat. He had an automatic rifle cradled in his arms. Kathleen recognized it as an AK-47 assault rifle. There had been a great deal about them on the news when a ship bringing in weapons for the terrorists had been arrested off France. Apparently, the armaments aboard had originated in Libya.

Paddy leaned forward and rested his elbows on his knees. The pistol was now clasped loosely in both hands between his legs. He looked straight at Kathleen and spoke softly, almost intimately. If the occasion had been different, he might have been addressing a lover. "Kathleen, my darling," he said, "I need your help."

Kathleen's mouth had gone dry. She was nauseous, her stomach ached from where she had been kicked, and her terror was so great that she felt paralyzed. At the same time, her brain was in overdrive.

This must have to do with Fitzduane. So this was the reality of his world. It was worse than anything she could have imagined. What could she do? How could she help? What did these frightening men want? Silently, she determined to resist when and how she could. If everybody fought these kind of people as best they could, they would be defeated.

Paddy McGonigal looked into her eyes. He could read the pain and the defiance. How little these people know, he thought. How fragile their lives are. How irrelevant in the scheme of things.

I bend my finger and she dies. An effortless physical act. That is all there is to it. And they think they matter, that somehow they can resist. The dreams of fools. He felt anger. Why do they not understand how fucking unimportant they are, these little people, these pawns of fortune?

"I need to know about the hospital," he said. "There is a fellow called Hugo Fitzduane I want to visit. I want to know where he is. I want to know about the security. I want the routines and the passwords and all the little details."

Kathleen had removed her nurse's headgear on going off duty but was still wearing her uniform under her cloak. The cloak was navy, but the lining was of some scarlet material. The effect over the crisp white of her one-piece garment was striking.

For the first time, McGonigal looked at her as a woman. She was, he realized, a very beautiful woman. Her eyes were particularly striking, her breasts were full, her legs were long and slender. He noticed that her dress buttoned up the front. The skirt had risen above her knees.

"I'm sorry," she said, shaking her head. "I'm afraid you've got the wrong person. I don't know who you're talking about."

McGonigal reached out with his automatic and placed the silencer and barrel under her skirt and lifted it. He undid the bottom button of her skirt with his left hand and then started on another button. There was the hint of lace.

Noel Fleming leaped to his feet at the same time that Kathleen's hand cracked full force against McGonigal's face. He could taste blood. Jim, the terrorist leaning against the radiator, jumped forward and smashed her father back onto the sofa with the butt of his gun.

Mary Fleming screamed and clasped her husband. A long gash had opened in his skull, and crimson leached into his silver hair and soaked his wife's blouse. He lay against her, dazed and in pain and bewildered by what was happening.

McGonigal put a hand to his lip. There was blood on his finger when he took it away. He licked his lips and swallowed, but the metallic taste remained in his mouth. The left side of his face hurt. This was a strong woman. But vulnerable.

"Kathleen," he said, "you're brave and you're beautiful, but you're foolish. How does it help you if you make me angry? Now answer me that."

Kathleen shook her head. The feeling of paralysis had left her since she had struck this man in front of her. She no longer felt quite so help-less, so afraid. She remembered that she hadn't called in. She had to buy time.

McGonigal stood up. He transferred the automatic to his left hand and removed from his pocket what looked, at first, like a large penknife. There was a click and a longer thin blade glittered dully in a shaft of light coming through the blinds. He looked at the portrait.

"You've a nice family," he said, looking down at Kathleen. "Close-knit is the phrase, I think." He transferred his gaze back to the portrait and slowly cut a large X through her image. The sound of the canvas parting under the pressure of the blade was unsettling. To Kathleen it was an obscene, wanton gesture.

"I could hurt you, Kathleen," he said, "but where would that get me? It's you I need to hear from." He turned back to the portrait. "Life is about choices," he said. "It just isn't possible to have everything."

He brought the blade up again and seemed to hesitate. He turned and looked carefully at her parents, then nodded to himself. His gaze reverted to the portrait.

He raised the blade again. "It wouldn't surprise me at all," he said, "if you weren't just a little bit keen on Hugo. He's a wounded hero and all that. Romance has blossomed at many a bedside—and has died in many a bed." He laughed. "But the thing is, darling, you can't have it all." The blade sliced through the image of her father.

Kathleen cried out. The terrible fear had returned.

Her mother screamed. "No! No!" she said. "This is—this is wrong. It's all wrong. You must go. You can't do this."

Anger flared in McGonigal. He turned and thrust the automatic pistol in his hand at the bald-headed terrorist, then grabbed Kathleen's father by his bloodied white hair and hauled the elderly man to his feet.

"Fuck you," he said. "Fuck all you little people. You know nothing." He placed the edge of his knife under Kathleen's father's ear and cut and pulled, severing his throat from ear to ear.

There was a dreadful, rattling, gagging sound that was mercifully brief, and blood fountained from the severed arteries and cascaded over McGonigal and Kathleen.

When the blood had stopped pumping, McGonigal released his grip on the dead man's hair and the body sagged to the ground. Mary Fleming had fainted. Kathleen looked at him, deep in shock. He slapped her face.

"I have little time," he said. "Your mother is next. It's your choice."

It was several minutes before Kathleen could speak. McGonigal used the time to wash himself off and lay the hospital plans out on a table in the living room. Then Kathleen told him almost everything she knew.

Her fingers still smeared with her father's blood, she outlined the security procedures and marked out the layout of Fitzduane's floor and the location of the control zone and other security procedures. She was questioned again and again, and finally McGonigal was satisfied. It all tied together with what he already knew. Kathleen was completely broken. They always broke.

When it was all over, he placed his pistol against Mary Fleming's head, but at the last second took his hand off the trigger. Hostages were handy in this kind of situation. They could be disposed of after the operation had gone down.

Kathleen had stripped off her cloak and uniform and was now huddled in a terry-cloth bathrobe in a state of shock. Her skin was cold and clammy. Her gaze was unfocused.

McGonigal was looking at her and mentally undressing her when the telephone rang for the first time since they had arrived.

9

February 1

Fitzduane looked at his visitor with affection.

He was very, very fond of the Bernese detective.

The Bear had slimmed a little after he had met Katia—his first wife had died in a traffic accident—but had now reverted to his normal shape. Fitzduane was relieved. Katia was a lovely woman and meant well, but the Bear was not really destined by nature to be lean and mean and to dine off bean sprouts. He was kind of big—well, closer to massive in truth—and round and gruff and had a heart of gold. And he was a good friend. Fitzduane valued his friends.

The Bear gave him a hug—a gentle hug. Fitzduane was not wearing his Skunkworks T-shirt that day, so the visible bandages inspired caution. Even so, a "gentle" hug from the Bear caused him to wince slightly. The main hazard was the Bear's shoulder holster. It contained a very large lump of metal.

"Men don't hug in Ireland," said Fitzduane, who enjoyed the cultural contrasts between the Swiss and the Irish. "We're not really a very touchy-feely nation. It's something to do with the church and sex and guilt, I think. What's the hardware?"

The Bear removed the largest automatic pistol Fitzduane had ever seen. "Everybody in Europe tends to use 9mm because that is what everybody uses. The manufacturers are tooled up for it. The ammunition is relatively cheap because of economies of scale. The round is easy to shoot because it has a good range and a nice, flat trajectory and doesn't kick like your mother-in-law. And you can fit fifteen rounds or more in a magazine, so you can generate some serious firepower. Everybody's happy.

"But the problem with 9mm," he continued, "is that it lacks stopping power. Analysis of actual gunfights in the States shows that a hit on a vital spot puts the victim out of action only about fifty percent of the time where 9mm is used, as opposed to over ninety percent when a .45 is involved."

Fitzduane was beginning to think that this conversation was somewhat lacking in tact. He remembered that he had only recently been shot. Still, the subject seemed to be doing the Bear some good. "So use a .45," he said helpfully.

"Aha!" said the Bear triumphantly, "so one might think. But . . ." He paused.

"But?" said Fitzduane.

"But . . ." said the Bear. He paused again.

Fitzduane felt as if he was in a slow tennis match and should be flicking his head from side to side to watch the shots. "But?" he said again. He couldn't resist it.

"What's that English expression about the importance of detail?" said the Bear.

It occurred to Fitzduane that if any nation should know about detail, it was the Swiss. "The devil is in the detail," he said.

"Exactly," said the Bear. He raised his huge automatic in demonstration.

A nurse came in carrying a kidney basin containing something unpleasant. Fitzduane had developed a profound dislike of kidney basins. Either he was being sick into one or a syringe was being transported in the damn thing, with some part of his anatomy as its destination. He was generally off needles. And kidney basins were what they used, he had been told, to carry away bits of him that had been cut out. These were not nice thoughts.

The nurse screamed and dropped the tray.

The Bear ignored her. "The problem with the .45," he said, "is that it hasn't got the range or the penetrating power. It is a big bullet with loads of shock value, but it doesn't have the velocity."

The door smashed open. A Ranger stood there with an Aug Steyr automatic rifle in his hands. The Bear ignored him, too.

Fitzduane suddenly noticed that he was in the line of fire. It would

be ridiculous to be killed by some gung-ho idiot in the higher purpose
of saving his life. Also, he had been shot up enough for one year.

"DON'T FUCKING WELL SHOOT!" he shouted.

"WHY THE FUCK NOT?" shouted the Ranger. Fitzduane looked
at him in shock. He couldn't instantly think of a good reply. This was a
ridiculous thing to have to debate. He just glared at the Ranger and
then relaxed. The man was grinning. It was Grady, who knew the Bear.

"So," said the Bear triumphantly, "I looked for a cartridge which
would combine the strengths of the 9mm and the .45 without the
disadvantages. I wanted stopping power, flat trajectory, good penetra-
tion, range, and sheer shootability. I wanted a nice big magazine."

He released the magazine from his weapon. "It's a 10mm Desert
Eagle. Trust the Israelis to know their weapons."

It was then he noticed the Calico in its holster clipped to Fitzduane's
bed. "What's that?" he said. Fitzduane showed him.

"And the caliber?" said the Bear.

"I don't want to steal your thunder," said Fitzduane, who couldn't
help grinning. "10mm."

"Oh," said the Bear, a little sadly.

KATHLEEN, exhausted from the night shift and the shock of her or-
deal, was dozing when the front doorbell rang.

She awoke feeling sick and disoriented, but associating the familiar
sound with help, with good news, with some positive development.
Visitors were a regular feature of the Fleming household. Neighbors
dropping in for a cup of tea were always welcome. Traditional Irish
hospitality had not been eroded by television. In fact, they had no television. This was not from some deeply felt conviction. It was merely
that the nearby mountains made adequate TV reception impossible.

The chair she sat on and the carpet were saturated and sticky with
drying blood. The body on the floor, half covered with a newspaper,
was her father. Shock hit her again, and she started to retch.

"Shut up, you cow, if you know what's good for you," said the terrorist by the window.

There was the sound of animated conversation from the hall, which
continued for several minutes. Then the door opened and the leader,
Paddy, came in. He moved to one side and gestured to others behind
him to enter.

Two other men entered the room, and then a figure who looked singularly out of place. Unlike the others, who looked Irish and were dressed in casual clothes, the man standing in the doorway was smartly dressed in a dark suit and white shirt with a club tie. His shoes were highly polished. And he was Asian, Chinese or Japanese.

"This is the nurse?" he said.

"The very same," said McGonigal.

"And you are satisfied with her information?" said the Japanese. His accent was pronounced, but he spoke clearly.

McGonigal smiled. "Oh yes," he said. "The wee girl saw reason"— he reached out and grabbed Kathleen's mother and again the knife was in his hand—"and there's still one blood relation to go." Kathleen swallowed a scream. "You told us everything, didn't you?"

Kathleen nodded weakly.

"And the phone call?" said the Japanese.

"She answered it," said McGonigal, "with me listening in. It was the matron inquiring could she do day shift next week."

Kathleen swallowed the bile in her throat and then spoke hesitantly. "We work a rota system. Sometimes someone is sick or needs time off and the matron makes the arrangements."

The Japanese looked at her for a little time before speaking again. Something about the phone call bothered him. "What time was the call?" he said to McGonigal.

"Twenty past nine, something like that," answered McGonigal. "Why? I heard the whole conversation. There was nothing to it. It was just as the girl said."

The Japanese was still staring intently at Kathleen. He was about to decide whether the operation went ahead or not, and this time he was going with the assault team. He didn't want to put his life on the line if the operation was blown. At the same time, the assignment must be completed. It was a matter of duty.

"It's a small hospital, the woman had just come off night shift," said the Japanese. "The matron would know that and would expect her to be asleep at the time she called." He slapped Kathleen hard across the face. "Is that not so? So why did she call?"

Kathleen spat blood. It was clear the bastard had never worked in a hospital, did not understand the pressures, the need to perform a task *now*. It was clear he did not know her matron. Inside herself, she smiled. He was a clever little sod, but he was on the wrong track.

"Losing sleep is pretty normal in our business," she said. "People don't get ill on just a nine-to-five basis."

"The caller—the matron—apologized when she called," said McGonigal. "She said that she had actually rung up to leave a message with the woman's mother. Our lady friend here"—he indicated Kathleen—"actually said very little. Just 'it doesn't matter' and 'yes' and a couple of phrases like that. Of course, she sounded tired, but then she would, wouldn't she? She was just off duty and games with her boyfriend." He grinned lasciviously at Kathleen.

Sasada was torn between the logic of what had been said and his instincts. In truth, nothing could be more normal than a brief phone call about a rota change, yet he would have felt much happier if this woman had never been allowed near the phone at all. Despite her rough handling and the killing of her father in front of her and the manifest shock that this had induced, there was still the faintest spark of defiance in her eyes. This was a strong, resourceful woman. Could she somehow have managed to warn the hospital?

"Why did you allow this person"—he pointed at Kathleen—"near the phone at all?" he said to McGonigal. He needed time to think.

McGonigal shrugged. "I've been through this hostage business before," he said. "The thing is to keep things as normal as possible from an outsider's perspective. Anybody who knows these people would have expected the phone to be answered. Secondly, I didn't want some neighbor calling round because she couldn't get through."

He looked squarely at the Japanese. "Anyway, man, my hide is on the line, too, and I'm telling you—she didn't say anything. There was no keyword, no password, no unusual phrase. I'm sure of it." His northern accent became more pronounced as he emphasized his words. There was a noticeable increase in tension in the room.

"Why didn't you use the mother?" said Sasada, indicating Mary Fleming, who sat motionless on the sofa, her face a blank, her eyes unfocused.

"Jaysus, Sasada, just look at her," said McGonigal. "She would have sounded like shit on the phone. There was no way she could have come across normal."

Sasada was convinced by McGonigal's denial. The reality of the situation was that the IRAP were vastly more experienced at this kind of thing than he was. The latest wave of IRA violence had been operating without a break for the best part of a generation. The younger members had grown up in a culture of violence. They had never known anything else. They learned about the techniques of terrorism in much the same way as the young in a normal society learned to drive.

He drew a knife from under his coat. Its blade was very slightly curved and the tip was angled. The shape, though much smaller, was very like that of a Japanese sword.

He is going to kill me, thought Kathleen. Sasada: I now know his name; I know what he looks like; I can identify them all. There is no way that they will let us live. A terrible sadness and feeling of regret swept over her, so strong that it dominated even her fear.

She thought of all the things in life she had not done and wanted to do. She thought of Fitzduane and his smile and his injured body that she so wanted to love and be loved by. She thought of her mother, who would now need her more than ever. She thought of the pain of dying at the hands of these terrible people, and suddenly felt weak with terror. She closed her eyes to try to mask her fear. If she was going to die, it would be with some dignity.

She felt the knife at her throat and then the warm trickle of her own blood.

STUDYING A MAP in one of the empty private rooms on Fitzduane's floor, Kilmara silently cursed the British and their road-building sins of the past centuries—most of their bloody little roads were narrow, winding things, but there were too many of them to block—and reviewed his options.

He was in an isolated hospital in an isolated part of the country with a target that was undesirable to move, and no safer location to move him to anyway. His defensive manpower was decidedly limited, particularly if unarmed police were factored out. There were too many roads and back lanes to block. He did not know how and when the opposition would strike.

He did not actually *know* anything. He suspected a great deal. Still, in the counterterrorism business you mostly worked with bits and pieces. You rarely had the luxury of complete intelligence. If you fucked up, well, you fucked up. People might die, but the world went on. One had to be philosophical. People killing each other was not globally threatening, like destroying the ozone layer. It was actually quite normal. But it was inconvenient for those involved.

Kilmara did not like to involve Fitzduane, who was supposed to be recovering from serious wounds and resting, but it was hard to deny that he had a vested interest in the outcome of what was happening. Also, Hugo had an excellent tactical sense. He had fought his own wars and covered others for twenty years. He had seen it done right and he had seen it done wrong, and he had learned from this experience in a way few people did.

As he reentered Fitzduane's room, Kilmara looked at his watch. It was a few minutes after ten in the morning. Fitzduane was being examined by a doctor and two nurses, and the Ranger general was peremptorily asked to wait outside. Ten minutes later, the doctor emerged.

Kilmara tried to enter but was again shooed away by the nurses. Eventually, they emerged. One held a partially covered kidney basin containing something bloodstained. The other held a similar basin in which there was a syringe.

It crossed his mind that Fitzduane, though now lucid and apparently recovering, was still a very sick man. He hesitated by the door. It then occurred to him that his friend could be a very dead man if they didn't come up with something pretty soon.

Fitzduane was propped up in his amazing new bed, eyes closed, looking disconcertingly pale. He had looked much better before his recent visit by the medical team. His bed, on the other hand, was beautifully made. The corners were a joy to contemplate. The sheets were crisp and smelled of starch. The blankets—taut, tucked, and without blemish—would have made a marine drill instructor's lip tremble.

Fitzduane opened his eyes. He no longer looked dead, which was reassuring. "Anything new?"

"We've had more intel in," said Kilmara. He hesitated.

"Want to tell me about it?" said Fitzduane.

"I'm not overburdened with good news," said Kilmara. "You stand a good chance of being cut off in your bullet-ridden prime."

"As in killed?" said Fitzduane with a faint smile. "These people are obsessive."

"I would guess that to be the intention," said Kilmara. "I'd like to move you, but where?"

"Tell all," said Fitzduane, and there was no humor in his voice.

"We heard a rumor a day or so ago that the IRAP were in the area. No big deal, though these are nasty people. Early this morning the guards picked up two of their local sympathizers with a scanner. They haven't talked yet, but a list of keywords was found on them—and you feature. Add to that, there is Kathleen. It's a standard ploy to suborn someone from the inside—the IRA have been doing it for years—so I arranged for all staff who entered this zone to ring in with a keyword when they went home and before they came back on duty. And Kathleen didn't ring this morning."

"You didn't tell me about this," said Fitzduane.

"You were supposed to be kept free of hassle," said Kilmara. "It was a procedure, nothing more. I didn't want you worrying about things you could do fuck-all about."

"Kathleen could have forgotten," said Fitzduane.

"People don't forget these things," said Kilmara. "This is life-and-death stuff, and I know how to get their attention. And they are reminded every time they go off duty. Anyway, we made a check call. She was very subdued—and no keyword."

"So that's how you knew," said Fitzduane.

Kilmara nodded. "Well, we still don't *know*. Strong suspicion is the phrase."

"Shit," said Fitzduane.

"The IRAP don't have anything against you?" said Kilmara.

"Not that I know," said Fitzduane. "I have never run across them before in any shape or form, and I steer well clear of the North."

Kilmara slid a piece of fax paper across to Fitzduane. "I faxed Dublin an hour ago and this came back." The paper showed a Japanese getting into a taxi outside a familiar-looking Dublin hotel.

"You're losing me," said Fitzduane.

"This is a small country and an island," said Kilmara, "with a small homogeneous population and a terrorist problem right on our doorstep. Accordingly, the security services can—and do—watch the comings and goings of our visitors fairly closely, and we keep a particularly keen eye on the big hotels."

Fitzduane nodded. Terrorism was normally associated with ideology, but it was surprising how often money entered the picture. Many terrorists liked to live well, arguing that since they put their lives on the line they deserved a good standard of living. A further justification for frequenting large expensive hotels was their supposed anonymity. In point of fact, these patterns of behavior allowed the security forces to focus closely on such well-frequented habitats.

Luxury hotels were particularly easy to monitor. They wanted to keep on the right side of the authorities. Rooms could be bugged, the telephone system could be tapped, and television cameras could be emplaced with relative ease. Finally, the reception staff were easy to reach an accommodation with. And hotel staff notice things. They are trained to. That is how they respond immediately to a guest's needs and it is how they ensure that they are well-tipped. And the security services tipped even better for the right information.

"A man with a Northern accent inquired at the Burlington reception for one of their guests, a Japanese. The accent rang bells and the combination was sufficiently unusual to get security to photograph the Asian. The Northerner was subsequently tentatively identified as Paddy McGonigal, the leader of the IRAP. The Japanese is a guy calling himself Sasada. He is actually a member of—guess who? Our old friends, Yaibo."

Fitzduane was silent, trying to absorb these latest developments. The thought of Kathleen's plight made him feel helpless and guilty. Physically, he felt weaker than normal. The doctor had lectured him on taking it easier and had not been happy with his self-imposed work routine. He spoke again to Kilmara. "Any news of the Bear?" he said.

"Nothing," said Kilmara. "And he's out of radio contact, thanks to these hills. He's got one armed detective with him and two unarmed uniformed cops. He'll do a reconnaissance. If it's a hostage situation, he won't be able to do much more except contain the situation until reinforcements arrive. Unfortunately, that's not going to be for some time."

"How long?" said Fitzduane.

"Two to three hours at least," said Kilmara, "possibly longer. And then only after we're sure they are needed. The problem is, the serious crime boys have a major operation on and the nearest army unit is tied up with a search on the border. There was a shooting there last night. We're not high on the list of priorities. We've got suspicion. They are dealing with ongoing operations."

Resources were a constant problem for the Irish security services. The mainly unarmed police and army together totaled not much more than twenty thousand, and only a small percentage of these were equipped to deal with heavily armed terrorists. Not unnaturally, they were concentrated in centers of population and likely trouble spots, like the border. The poor quality of the road system hindered fast vehicle deployment. Helicopters, the obvious solution, were in chronically short supply. And to further exacerbate the helicopter shortage, they were often monopolized by politicians visiting their constituencies. In the real world, chasing votes normally got a higher priority than hunting down terrorists.

"If they've got Kathleen," said Fitzduane, "they are going to make her talk. That means they'll know where to hit, location and number of guards, weaponry—basically everything they need."

"They'll know everything Kathleen has *seen*," said Kilmara, "which is not quite the same thing. There are quite a few other precautions in place a layperson wouldn't notice."

"They'll know the essentials," said Fitzduane, who was thinking furiously, "and they'll do it quickly. And my guess is that they will blast their way in. This isn't a job for a rocket through the window. They will want to make sure, and heavy firepower is the IRAP style."

Kilmara was somewhat taken aback. The normal style in the North was to seize a hostage half a day or so ahead of the operation, and he had been thinking in terms of this pattern.

He now realized that Fitzduane could well be right. Allowing for time to make Kathleen talk and to put together a plan based on her information, travel, and reconnaissance, the hit could happen any minute. But they would almost certainly wait until doctors' rounds were over. On the other hand, if this was going to be an assault—a quick in-and-out—they wouldn't want a clutter of visitors getting in the way, so it would happen before visiting hours.

They probably had an hour to prepare—at the most.

Kilmara picked Fitzduane's brain for a few more minutes and then briefed his small force. Certain changes were made. Fitzduane himself was moved from Room Number 2 on the left-hand side of the corridor to Room Number 4, the corner room on the right.

Kilmara did not fancy a firefight inside the hospital, but he had nowhere else to put Fitzduane that was secure, and at least the private wing had no other patients in it. He would have preferred to take any attackers in the parking lot, or otherwise away from the hospital, but he did not have enough manpower for that option and there was always enough activity directly outside the hospital to make civilian casualties likely.

The attackers could pick the time, the strength of their force, and the weapons, but Kilmara had picked the ground. It crossed his mind that a famous Irishman, the Duke of Wellington, had specialized in this tactic. He never fought a battle on terrain that he had not scouted in advance, and he never lost. However, sometimes he took truly terrible casualties.

Kilmara was confident his unit could survive an assault, but he was far from sanguine about the price.

FOR FORTY-FIVE MINUTES, Sasada, knife in hand, interrogated Kathleen.

Over and over again, he asked the same questions, until the spark of defiance faded from her eyes and he was satisfied that she had told as much as she knew.

By the time he had finished, Kathleen's upper body was slippery with blood and she was deep in shock. Sasada had punctuated his questions with small, threatening cuts of his knife. The blade was so sharp, each cut in itself did not hurt at first, but the streaming blood and the terror he induced drove practically all hope from her mind.

McGonigal had watched the questioning with mounting irritation. He was operating away from his home turf, and he felt uneasy in strange surroundings. He was from the North of Ireland and knew the habits and methods of the British Army and the RUC—the Royal Ulster Constabulary. The *gardai,* the police of the Republic of Ireland, and the Irish Army were less of a known quantity.

When Sasada was finished, he ordered the two women tied and gagged, and they were dumped unceremoniously on the floor of the front room. An extending table was pulled out from the wall, chairs put in place around it, and the detailed assault plan rehearsed.

McGonigal carried out the briefing. That he had survived on the run as long as he had was a tribute to his professionalism. Every attack was rehearsed meticulously, but he had trained all his men to improvise if things went wrong. He emphasized the importance of timing and of discipline. He restated the rules of fire and movement so that no one man advanced without cover from another. Ironically, he had served in the British Army as a young man. Subsequently, he had received further training in Libya and was an expert with Soviet-bloc weapons.

"It's a small hospital," he said, indicating the plans Sasada had brought, "rectangular in shape. The entrance is in the middle, with the reception desk on the left. Straight ahead, there is a staircase that runs up the center of the building. On each floor, the wards are to the left and to the right. The ward we want—what they call the private wing—

is on the third floor on the left. The third floor is the top floor, although the stairs run up to a half-landing above it, where there are toilets and storerooms."

McGonigal used a knitting needle as a pointer. He had been reminded of his mother when he had found the knitting basket. She had loved to knit. She had been knitting when she had been killed by a stray bullet fired by British paratroops.

"The nurse says that since our target arrived, there is normally a uniformed *garda* or sometimes an armed detective at the foot of the stairs. He screens everybody going up and alerts another man on the third floor if anyone is heading up there. The uniformed cop isn't armed, but he does have a radio."

Jim, the black-haired terrorist, interrupted. "The fellow on the third floor?"

"The third floor—the private wing on the left—is guarded entirely by Rangers. They have installed what they call a control zone. There is a Ranger outside, then two sets of specially installed armored doors. The outside man checks you through one door. In the middle is a metal detector. If you are clear, then you go through the second set of doors, where there is the second Ranger. The doors are never opened together. Indeed, I gather they can't be. They have some kind of integrated electronic locks."

"Is there video surveillance?" said another terrorist.

McGonigal nodded. "There is a camera on the wall overlooking the outside of the two doors. It can see the length of the corridor to the top of the stairs. There were fire doors there, but they were removed by the Rangers. Anyone coming up the stairs or leaving the elevator, which is beside the stairs, is on camera from the moment he hits the third floor."

There was silence in the room, as each man evaluated what he had heard so far. Taking care of the policeman at reception would be no problem, but getting up three flights of stairs without alerting the armed Ranger at the top would not be so easy. Still, McGonigal normally had an idea. He was good at this kind of thing.

"Fire escapes?" said Jim. He found building plans hard to read and would have preferred a recent photograph and a hand-drawn sketch. He also had a suspicion of old plans. It was not the Irish way to be meticulous in record-keeping. Whatever the regulations, buildings were modified and amended without up-to-date plans necessarily being filed. He looked at the date on the drawing. These were not the originals, but they were still forty years old. He wondered just how reliable they were.

McGonigal nodded. "There is one at either end of the corridor, and they both go right up to the flat roof. However, I think it is safe to assume that the Rangers will have done something with the one at their end."

The planning continued. Lying bound and temporarily ignored in the corner, Kathleen listened to an assault scenario being outlined which seemed impossible to stop. She despaired when weapons were pulled out of canvas bags and she saw what the terrorists had assembled. There were not just automatic rifles. These people had rocket launchers and grenades—overwhelming firepower.

She clung to one thought. She had told the terrorists everything except the correct number of Fitzduane's room. It was one lie she had stuck to despite everything, one lie that she had now convinced herself was the truth, so these bastards would not see through her. Fitzduane was in Room Number 2. She had persuaded them that he was really in Room Number 4. It was all she could do. It was pathetically little.

Shortly afterward, the terrorists, five in number including Sasada, departed, leaving behind just one man to guard them in case hostages were needed. If the attack went off as planned, there would be a phone call and, lying there helpless, Kathleen and her mother would be killed. They would no longer be needed and they could identify their attackers. Sasada had wanted to kill them earlier, but McGonigal had persuaded him to wait an extra hour or so.

It was not much time to live. Silently, Kathleen sobbed. Their guard, Eamon, he of the bald head, listened to the radio and occasionally glanced in their direction. An AK-47 rested on his knees, but he was planning to kill them with his knife. He had killed before, but never in that particular way.

He had thought of fucking the nurse, but, banged about and drenched in blood as she was, she was not an attractive sight. Still, this waiting was boring. He was supposed to remain in the front room with the blinds down, but that was ridiculous. What difference would it make if someone saw him—just a shape—from outside? And who would, in this remote bloody spot?

He stood up, stretched, and went into the kitchen to make himself some tea.

THEY USED the Bear's car. It would be less likely to attract attention than the unmarked, but still well-known, police vehicles. The Bear's car had an Avis sticker, the badge of a tourist in that part of the world.

The series of little roads were narrow and winding, and the Bear was still adjusting to driving on the left-hand side of the road. The stone bridges were narrower still. He thought it quite likely that he would be leaving some paintwork on the local stonework before the day was out.

As they drove around one bend, about a mile from Kathleen's home, two cars came toward them from the opposite direction. The Bear saw the lead car only at the last minute and swerved desperately to avoid a collision.

His tires locked, and he skidded off the road and slid inexorably into a patch of boggy ground. When the car came to a rest, using the clutch and gears with care, he tried to drive out but in vain. Next he tried to get out, but his door was stuck.

The Bear felt very foolish and not a little angry with himself. He should have let one of the policemen drive. He was a good driver in Switzerland, but Ireland always took him a few days to get used to and the roads in the West were worse than most. His front passenger had slid out, and he followed by sliding across with some difficulty. The Bear was not built for confined spaces.

The four men tried for fifteen minutes to push the car back on the road, but their efforts were fruitless. The Bear fell in the mud several times as he pushed. None of their personal radios could pick up anything in the valley.

Finally, the four men set off for the Fleming house on foot. The Bear was not overly fond of walking, but could manage a brisk enough pace if it was absolutely essential. The armed detective brought up the rear of the little party. He had taken his Uzi out of the briefcase it was normally carried in and slung it over his shoulder.

After the men had walked for five minutes, the sky became black and menacing and suddenly it began to rain in sheets. Lightning flashed and thunder rumbled in the distance.

The Bear's moustache began to droop. He was soaked from the thinning hair on his head to the well-designed tips of his expensive Bally shoes—a gift from Katia and not typical Bear apparel. Not for the first time, he thought the Irish climate was ridiculous.

He wondered why he was prepared to behave in a decidedly un-cautious and un-Bernese way when in Fitzduane's ambit. Somehow, this damned Irishman brought out the adventurer in him.

The Bear straightened and began to whistle a Bernese marching song. Behind him, the two uniformed guards, who had had the sense, being local, to wear uniform caps, long raincoats, and Wellington boots, looked at each other and, when they had got the hang of it, joined in. Behind them, the detective checked the condom on the muzzle of his Uzi for effectiveness in conditions which might be deemed somewhat harsher than its normal design parameters—and beat time with his hand slapping against the receiver.

Soon, they were all marching in step. Ahead of them as they rounded a bend lay the Fleming bungalow.

There was a light on at the back of the house.

10

CONNEMARA REGIONAL HOSPITAL

February 1

There is a rule of thumb in the traditional military world that the attacker needs more manpower—three to five times is recommended—than the defender to ensure success.

Paradoxically, in terrorist and counterterrorist operations, the reverse has often turned out to be true. A small attacking force armed with high-firepower weapons has time and again inflicted damage out of all proportion to its size. That does not invalidate traditional military lore. It merely means that in the world of terrorism, the attacker rarely needs to seize and hold territory. Instead he is primarily interested in the logistically simpler task of inflicting maximum destruction in a strictly limited period of time. In his favor, he has tactical surprise on his side. He can choose when and where and how to strike. He can ensure that, though outnumbered and outgunned on an overall basis, *at the point of contact he has superiority.*

Kilmara, whose entire military career had been spent in the world of special forces and counterterrorism, knew the rules of the game as well as anyone. It was why he disliked being on the defensive. To Kilmara, the initiative was everything. Temperamentally, he was not a believer in the big battalions. He had more faith in planning, timing, audacity, and firepower.

But he was also a pragmatist. On an operation, he rarely allowed himself to be distracted by aspirational thinking. He worked within the context of the situation, and if it was not to his liking he merely swore more than usual and worked even harder. He was a believer in the work ethic in his arcane special forces world. He could not understand why all military men did not follow this creed, since the alternative was, not infrequently and quite predictably, death.

The hard core of the IRAP unit was only three men, Kilmara knew, but that was often fleshed out with manpower drafted in for a specific operation. Reviewing past IRAP operations on his computer linked to Ranger headquarters in Dublin, he noted that as many as twenty terrorists had been involved in some attacks, and that in some instances, armed with heavy firepower, they had stood their ground and gone head to head with regular army troops.

It was generally thought that the terrorists bombed and sniped and immediately ran away, but that was not always the case. And IRAP, in particular, liked to play hardball. McGonigal was a murderer and arguably a psychopath, but he did not lack either bravery or daring. On the side of the angels, he would be considered a hero.

He was sitting in a swivel chair in Room Number 4 of the private wing, looking at a bank of television screens linked to microminiaturized cameras that had been installed to cover all key points both inside and outside the hospital. Apart from light from the television monitors, the room was in total darkness. A dense black fabric had been pulled down over the windows and stapled in place. The same had been done to every room on the private ward.

In the corner of the room, Fitzduane, tired from talking to Kilmara earlier, was asleep.

MARY FLEMING was evidently fond of home baking.

Eamon had found freshly baked soda bread in the kitchen, together with a pound of creamery butter and some homemade raspberry jam. He put his AK-47 on top of the dishwasher, rooted in the drawers for a bread knife, and went to work with a will. He was in seventh heaven. You could take your French cuisine and stuff it. The high point of Eamon's culinary life had been bread and jam at his mother's table, and this little feast evoked strong and pleasant memories.

The weather outside was atrocious. It was so dark that without the light on in the kitchen he would have been scarcely able to see, and sheets of rain lashed at the windows and made looking outside a matter of squinting and peering. It was like looking through Vaseline. But in these conditions nobody would be out walking and he would hear any car that drove in. Even with the noise of the rain, the wind, and distant thunder, there was a loose cattle grid at the entrance that clanged noisily when driven over.

He had the radio on quietly in the corner. It was really very pleasant, this cocoon of warmth, light, and comfort in the midst of the worst the elements could do.

As his hunger was being satisfied, his other needs surfaced. Out of sight, the attractions of the nurse increased. He conveniently forgot the bloodstained upper body, the knife nicks on her throat and breasts. Instead he remembered slim thighs and long legs. She was wearing only a bathrobe and panties. He felt pressure against the front of his pants. He would have a couple more slices of bread and jam and then service this woman. He might as well. She would be dead meat soon enough. He did not fancy fucking a corpse. It was obscene.

He had left the bread board on the counter by the window. As he picked up the bread knife, there was a sudden flash of lightning and a loud crack and the kitchen light went out.

He looked up at the lifeless tube, then noticed the radio had gone dead. Either the lines were down or a couple of fuses had blown. Ah, well, it was of little matter. What he planned to do next was as often as not done in the dark. And with Kathleen in her present condition, it might be better that way.

He turned around to finish cutting his bread, and screamed. Through rain-smeared glass he could see a face looking down at him. The face was like something out of a nightmare. It was large and hairy and grim, and the man himself was a giant. He wore some kind of matted mud-smeared garment.

The window in front of him exploded into shards of glass and a massive hand reached out for him, grabbed him by the collar, and hauled him off his feet.

Desperately, he lashed out with the bread knife, felt the blade make contact, and pulled free.

There was a crash at the front of the house, and he could feel the wind whistle down the corridor. Someone had broken in, but that was the least of his worries. His AK-47 was on top of the dishwasher only feet away. He dived for it and knocked it onto the floor as he grabbed.

He rolled, found the weapon, and turned. A massive fist holding the largest handgun he had ever seen was pointing right at him. There was a stab of flame, and he felt a terrible blow on his right shoulder. The weapon slid from his arms and he slumped back, half lying on the floor but partially propped up against the kitchen unit.

He could see blood seeping from his body, but he could not move and he felt nothing. He heard more smashing of glass and then a huge figure came through the kitchen door, kicked away his automatic rifle, and stood looking down at him.

Eamon found he could not raise his head. He noticed that the mud-stained figure was wearing wet, muddy, but expensive shoes. They were Swiss, he recalled, but he could not remember the name.

The plainclothes detective came into the kitchen. His grandfather had been in the old IRA in the fight for freedom against the British and he had served on the border in Dundalk for several years. What today's terrorists did made him sick. And time and again, they seemed to evade the security forces through legal technicalities and playing one side against the other.

How could you fight a completely ruthless terrorist organization within the context of a legal framework designed for peacetime civilian application?

One of the uniformed *gardai* had broken down the door, but the detective, being armed and experienced in such things, was the first man to enter the house. The front room was on his right. With one of the uniforms keeping an eye on his back, he kicked open the door, but kept to one side, half expecting an answering burst of fire. There was nothing—which was just as well. The protection of the thin partition wall was an illusion.

He entered the room in a sudden movement and rolled to find cover. He could see very little. There was no light and the blinds were drawn. Outside, the rain had stopped as abruptly as it had started, but the sky was still overcast with black clouds. There was a disturbing sweetish metallic smell in the air. It set his nerves on edge. It was the smell of blood and body matter and fear, the odor of the slaughter-house.

His eyes adjusted to the gloom. Tentatively, he stood up, glanced around, and opened the blinds. The floor and furniture and part of the walls were drenched in blood. There was something on the floor half covered in a newspaper. He pulled the paper aside and gagged. The man's throat gaped at him and the expression on his face was that of utter horror.

One of the uniforms came in. "Jesus, mother of God," he said, and crossed himself. He then went across to the two bound figures in the corner and, removing a clasp knife, cut their bonds.

One of the figures, the younger woman, was trying to say something. Her face and upper body were sticky with blood, and she smelled of vomit. The policeman suppressed his nausea and put his head close to hers. "I had to," she said. "I had to."

The policeman did not understand. He tried to say something reassuring, but the bloody figure reached out a hand and gripped his arm with such intensity that it hurt. "They made me talk," she said. "They killed my father."

She started sobbing. "They killed my father. They killed my daddy."

The policeman was a kindhearted man, used to dealing with farmers who had not licensed their cars and poachers who were overly fond of other people's salmon. He felt tears come to his eyes, and he put his arms around the woman.

Her grip tightened. "Now they are going for Hugo," she said, "in the hospital." Then she was silent, and the policeman could see her gathering her strength. Her next words came out almost in a shout.

"They know everything," she said. "They know everything, the guards, the layout, the routines." She made a final effort. "But I told them the wrong room. I told them Room Number 4."

The policeman gently disentangled himself and wrote down what he had heard in his notebook.

The second policeman had telephoned for an ambulance and other assistance and then ministered to Kathleen's mother. The ambulance would come from Connemara Regional, but where it could safely go would require some thought.

The detective, a father of four and an experienced graying sergeant in his forties, a man noted if not for brilliance, then for reliability, went into the kitchen and saw Eamon sprawled on the floor.

"One of them?" he said to the Bear.

The Bear indicated the AK-47 and nodded. Blood dripped from a long cut on the back of his hand, but he seemed oblivious to it.

"Have a look next door," said the detective heavily. His Uzi was now pointed at Eamon.

The Bear lowered his pistol and headed toward the front room.

The detective walked closer to Eamon. The terrorist smiled at him nervously. The man looking down at him was more of a known quantity. A policeman always looked like a policeman. There would be an ambulance and medical assistance and a cop by his bedside while he recovered. There would be questioning and a trial and a sentence to some high-security prison. He would either escape or be with his own kind. It wouldn't be too bad. It went with the job.

The detective took up pressure on the trigger and looked into Eamon's eyes, and for an instant Eamon knew he was about to die.

He was screaming as the detective fired and continued firing until the magazine was empty.

The Bear carried Kathleen out of the charnel house that was the front room and laid her on the big bed in the master bedroom. She had fainted briefly, but her eyes opened again as he covered her. He sat beside her and held her hand.

There was a glimmer of recognition in Kathleen's eyes. She had never seen this man before, but she *knew*. "You're . . ." She paused. He nodded encouragingly. "You're the Bear," she said. "Hugo told me about you."

The Bear knew his nickname well enough, but he was never so called to his face. There were conventions in these matters. Anyway, he rather liked his given name of Heinrich—Heini, for short—and Sergeant worked fine for those who knew him less well.

Still, this was a woman of courage, and it was no time to stand on ceremony. "I am the Bear," he said, nodding his large and shaggy head.

Kathleen started to laugh and cry, and the Bear sat on the edge of the bed and held her in his big arms until the ambulance came.

McGONIGAL HAD THREE of his own men with him—Jim Daid, Tim Pat Miley, and Gerry Dempsey—and Sasada.

His men were a known quantity on an operation; Sasada was not. It had been agreed that he would stay with the cars until they had completed the hit. The persuasive argument had been that a Japanese, in this backwater, would attract attention.

McGonigal was not sure how true this was. Japanese businesses seemed to be everywhere these days.

They arrived at the hospital shortly after midday. Doctors' rounds would be over. Lunch would just be starting. Visitors' hours would not start until two o'clock. The place would be just about as quiet as it could be except at night. They had considered doing a nighttime hit but had scrapped it. It was too predictable. The parking lot would be nearly empty and security, as like as not, doubled. People expected a night attack. And escaping on strange roads by night was another problem.

The hospital parking lot surrounded the hospital on three sides. To the rear was a goods-delivery area and various utility buildings, including the boiler house and mortuary. McGonigal had considered going in the back way, but there was a porter there to monitor deliveries and prevent theft. A second factor against that plan was that the route through the kitchens was longer. They were housed in a single-story extension at the rear, and the terrorists would have to pass through that before entering the main building.

The parking spaces directly in front of the hospital were reserved for the senior medical staff, and there was a clearway for ambulances. Since this facility was old and small, both visitors and emergency patients were brought in through the same entrance at the front. Emergency itself was at the front across from reception. The arrangement would not have worked in a busy city hospital.

They parked on the right side of the building, out of sight of the front of the hospital, but only a few yards away from the fire escape that led up to the ward facing the private wing. McGonigal and his men were all dressed in maintenance workers' blue overalls. They got out of the cars and opened the trunks. The weapons inside were concealed under painter's tarpaulins.

McGonigal's nerves had been at fever pitch as he drove in. Every sense was honed for the slightest hint of danger, but he could see nothing amiss.

The hospital, an ugly, raw, concrete construction at the best of times and even worse when wet, and its bumpy, black asphalt parking area looked depressingly normal. The rain had stopped, but water lay in pools everywhere. The sky overhead was still heavily overcast and obscured the slightest hint of direct sunlight. The chill air complemented the gloom. The dreadful weather and the drab environment reminded McGonigal of Belfast.

He nodded at Jim Daid.

The terrorist walked around to the front of the hospital and asked to use the rest room. The receptionist paid him little attention. Daid looked around and noticed that no policeman was present. However, a *garda* raincoat hung from a hook in the reception area.

"Excuse me," he said politely to the receptionist. There was no reaction. He cleared his throat. "Excuse me, I'm looking for my brother."

The receptionist, a middle-aged barrel-shaped woman to whom life had not been kind, looked up from the book she was reading. This was outside visiting hours and one of the quieter times in the day, and she resented the interruption. The heroine in the book with whom she identified was young, attractive, and currently being made love to by an equally attractive hero.

She was not pleased to be reminded of real life when fantasy was so much more pleasant. "Who?" she said unpleasantly.

"He's a policeman," said Daid. "I thought he might be on duty here." He nodded toward the coat.

The receptionist shrugged. "Lunch, the rest room, who knows?"

Daid looked at her and decided further conversation was pointless. He had just come from the rest room, and that had been empty. Lunch meant the cop could return at any time, which could be inconvenient.

He then remembered that the uniforms in the Republic were not armed. It would have been neater to take him out in advance, but if he showed up later, what the fuck. Daid turned and went back to McGonigal.

McGonigal thought about what Daid told him. The policeman's absence disturbed him, but it was too late to turn back now.

"Go," he said to Tim Pat and Gerry Dempsey. Immediately, they removed heavy canvas tool bags from the cars and commenced climbing up the fire escape.

The metal staircase, designed to allow the ill and elderly to escape, had originally been an attractive construction. Now it was pitted and rusty, a victim of tight budgets, sloppy management, and the unrelenting Irish weather. But it was more than adequate for fast access. The two terrorists were outside the third-floor fire door in seconds.

Beyond the fire door lay the corridor of a public wing inhabited mainly by geriatric patients who would now be having their lunch. Such patients frequently required help when eating, so it was a fair assumption that the nursing staff would be preoccupied. At the end of the corridor was another fire door, and beyond that a landing and another staircase. Across the landing was an armed Ranger, the two doors of the security zone, and the private wing.

One of the terrorists outside the third-floor fire door removed a battery-operated hand drill, made a small hole in the door, and inserted a probe.

Seconds later he had engaged the crash bar and opened the door. Just before the second terrorist entered the corridor, he turned and looked down at McGonigal and gave a thumbs-up signal. Immediately, he turned and vanished.

"Sixty seconds, Jim," said McGonigal, pressing the button on his stopwatch.

The two headed toward the entrance, muttered "We're expected" at the indifferent receptionist, and headed up the stairs. On the half-landing just above the first floor, they opened their tool bags but did not yet remove their weapons.

McGonigal checked his stopwatch again. The counterterrorist special forces were not the only people who understood timing. The Ranger outside the third-floor security zone would hear them coming, but would not be suspicious of a couple of workmen. While he was distracted, he would be shot by the boys who had come up the fire escape.

It would then be just a matter of blowing a way in with the rocket launchers. And they had Semtex, too, if something heavier was needed.

The Libyans had provided some serious firepower.

MOST PEOPLE'S mental image of a security television camera is of a highly visible, though compact, wall-mounted metal rectangular box fronted with a lens.

A security camera looks menacing. It whirs as it rotates to follow you. Its telephoto lens can watch you in intimate close-up while its operator remains concealed. It is not a friendly piece of equipment. However, its visibility and offputting presence is part of its purpose. It is there not just to observe but to deter.

Kilmara was making some use of conventional security cameras, but the bulk of his information was coming from devices which owed more to microsurgery than to the television industry.

They were small enough to fit inside a human artery. For all practical purposes they were invisible, and the information they transmitted traveled at the speed of light along optical fibers which looked to the

uninitiated—in the rare cases where they were not concealed—like ordinary house wiring.

What he saw, as he looked at his monitors, did not please him.

Of the six Rangers normally either on duty or on call, he now had
five, since one was away on emergency personal leave. Now another,
whom he had placed in a sniper role some three hundred meters away
on top of a grain silo to cover the entrance to the hospital, would be of
limited use. He had expected the terrorists to park in the front to ensure themselves the fastest possible getaway. Their parking at the side
was quite unexpected and put them out of the line of fire. By the time
the sniper could be brought into play, the main event would be over.

The second thing that caused him concern was the firepower displayed by the two terrorists on the third-floor fire escape. The image
from the miniature lens was wide angle and not as clear as he would
have liked, but there seemed little doubt that both men had rocket-
propelled grenades in addition to automatic rifles. The specially installed doors of the security zone were going to be of little use.

He was comforted that he had taken the unarmed policeman at reception off his post and had redeployed the armed Ranger who was
normally positioned outside the security zone. The terrorists might
well suspect something when they found the second man absent too,
but by then they would be committed.

Kilmara spoke briefly into his headpiece microphone and received
three one-word acknowledgments. The fourth and fifth Rangers, Ser-
geants Grady and Molloy, were concealed in a linen cupboard on the
half-landing above the third floor. From this position, using the electronic equivalent of a periscope, they could observe the landing area
between the geriatric ward and the control zone, and also most of the
last flight of stairs as it arrived at the third floor.

It was a good position, the best available, but it was not ideal. To fire,
they had to open the door, and then their field of fire would be slightly
restricted by the banisters. A secondary problem was that anyone advancing through the fire doors of the geriatric ward could jump back
immediately if not hit in the first burst and then be immediately under
cover. As a killing ground, the landing was not really large enough and
cover was too close to hand.

But then, circumstances were rarely ideal. That was why elite counterterrorist forces trained daily in the Killing House under constantly
varying circumstances.

Relentless training of Rangers who entered the unit as the best of the best could make all the difference when life or death was decided in fractions of a second. The ability to select targets in order of threat, change a magazine or unblock a weapon faster than the eye could follow, read terrain for maximum cover without conscious thought, anticipate the actions of the enemy—these and numerous other skills were basic to their particular calling.

The best CRW—counterrevolutionary warfare—troops tended to be in their early thirties to mid-forties. It was a calling where training alone and youthful reflexes were never enough. Above all, you needed experience and judgment, and these strengths only developed over time.

In the ideal world, every Ranger waiting for the assault would have had access to the monitoring equipment. In practice, only Kilmara had access to all the incoming information, and there were areas that the cameras did not cover. He lost the two terrorists who had broken in through the fire-escape entrance. Fortunately, the external camera on the fire escape showed no more attackers coming from that quarter.

The last thing he wanted was shooting in a normal ward. With automatic weapons in a confined space there would be civilian dead—not to mention the potential for hostages. It was imperative that the action not commence until both terrorists were out of the geriatric area. On the third-floor landing or in the private ward, it was another matter. In these locations he had his firepower deployed and the discretion to do what was necessary.

There was a camera halfway along the corridor of the geriatric ward pointing toward the internal fire doors and the landing. He picked up the two terrorists as they passed it.

There was a lunch trolley in the way, being pushed by a ward attendant. Without breaking stride, the first terrorist hurled the trolley to one side and his companion smashed the attendant in the face, sending her sprawling. Both men were armed with AK-47s and RPGs. The man in front had his rifle at the ready. The man behind him had his rifle slung and the rocket-propelled grenade launcher ready to fire.

"Position One," said Kilmara to Grady and Molloy. "There are two coming from the geriatric ward on your left—rifle in front, RPG follows."

Kilmara was faced with two unpalatable alternatives. He could either order fire into the corridor and the geriatric ward, which could well incur civilian casualties, or else wait until the rocket launchers were fired across the landing and into the security doors—the direction in which he and three of his Rangers and the man he was supposed to protect were located. Thankfully, the security zone and the corridor behind had been evacuated.

Tim Pat gripped his rifle and looked at his stopwatch. A glass safety panel was set into the heavy wooden fire door, but he did not want to alarm the Ranger opposite by sneaking a look. This was where surprise was all. The door was hung on a two-way hinge. He would push through it and fire. No matter how well-trained the Ranger opposite was, he would not have time to react.

The camera on the landing picked up two men in boilersuits and Halloween masks coming up the last flight of stairs before the third floor.

As Kilmara watched, they removed automatic rifles from heavy bags and slung heavy satchels over their shoulders. Shit! They could have grenades.

Tim Pat burst through the door, firing. Rounds stitched across the security door.

There was no Ranger there.

McGonigal and Jim Daid rushed up the last few stairs, slightly surprised that they had not seen the guard yet, but not concerned, as the outer security door was a good ten yards back along the corridor and did not come into view until you reached the top of the stairs and turned the corner.

Nothing! No guard sprawled on the ground in a pool of his own blood. Instantly, McGonigal knew something was wrong.

Matters started to develop very fast indeed.

Dempsey stepped through the fire door with the RPG-7 on his shoulder and fired, blowing aside the first security door and impacting on the frame of the metal and explosive detector inside and blowing it to pieces.

At the landing at the top of the stairs, McGonigal had flung himself to the ground, twisting around and searching desperately for an ambush position.

"One, GO!" said Kilmara a split second after he saw that both terrorists had moved beyond the fire door into the killing zone.

Tim Pat had unslung his RPG-7 and fired at the second security door. It exploded with a roar and blew the steel structure aside. The air was thick with fumes.

McGonigal spotted the linen cupboard at the precise moment that Molloy emerged, and fired a long desperate burst, hitting the Ranger in his torso and face, killing him instantly and knocking him back into Grady.

McGonigal then picked himself up and rushed forward down the corridor into the private ward, firing. The lust of battle was on him and he was determined that whatever happened, he was going to do what he came for and kill a few of these pigs into the bargain.

Sick at Molloy's death and cursing himself for not having moved faster, Sergeant Grady pushed his comrade's body aside and brought his weapon into action.

He was using an automatic shotgun with a twenty-round rotary magazine that fired flechette ammunition. Known as a force multiplier, it allowed one man to put out the firepower of several in the crucial first few seconds that normally determine the outcome of a firefight. Each Magnum cartridge held twelve long steel darts. It was of little use at ranges of over a hundred and fifty meters, but at close quarters it was highly effective.

The corridor was lit by recessed fluorescent tubes and, normally, such daylight as filtered in through the fanlights over each of the six doors. In addition, there was backup lighting in the event of power failure.

Some of the fluorescents had been smashed in the blast of the exploding rockets, but enough still functioned to illuminate the corridor adequately.

McGonigal crouched behind the smashed metal detector. Jim Daid came up beside him and dropped into firing position. McGonigal glanced over his shoulder. Tim Pat was in position behind the twisted door frame of the first security door, and Dempsey was just coming up on the other side. All his force was unharmed and the fellow in the ambush position had been taken out.

McGonigal began to feel confident.

Up ahead, there were three rooms on his left and three on his right. Normal procedure would be to secure each room as he advanced with grenades and a few quick bursts of automatic fire.

But in this case, he wouldn't bother. He had a target and knew exactly where it was. He and Dempsey would head straight for Room Number 4. A quick kick at the door or burst at the door lock, and in with the firepower.

It would be over in seconds. There had to be other Rangers waiting in the rooms, expecting them to clear them out as normal before heading for Fitzduane. Well, they could bloody well wait. If they opened the doors, he was confident the covering fire of Tim Pat and Dempsey could deal with them.

He made a quick hand signal to Jim Daid and readied himself to run forward. First, they both threw grenades forward. The corridor looked empty, but they could not see everything from behind cover.

The grenades exploded in two shattering blasts, blowing open the doors at either side of the end of the corridor.

Rooms 3 and 4 were now open to attack. This was an extra bonus as far as McGonigal was concerned. Both doorways seemed to stare at him blankly. Something was wrong. And then it came to him.

It was the middle of the bloody day and there was no light.

Sergeant Grady moved out of the linen cupboard and started down the stairs. One of the terrorists spotted the movement and turned, and as he did so, Grady fired a three-round burst.

Thirty-six steel darts sliced through the air and turned the wall behind the terrorist into a stipple of blood, bone, and flesh.

Tim Pat turned to see horror as the skin and tissue of Dempsey's body was flayed off him by the hail of metal.

The sight was terrible, and he was momentarily frozen as his friend's body disintegrated as if sliced by unseen blades.

He turned toward the angle of threat and started to fire. He could see a figure in black combat clothes and some sort of high-tech helmet with a microphone and strange goggles.

Grady fired a second, longer burst.

The man in front of him seemed to come to pieces, as if his clothes and flesh were being blown off him by some terrible wind. For a split second he could see the man's bone structure, and then the half-man, half-skeleton was a heap on the floor.

Kilmara cut the lights and activated a switch.

There was a metallic roar as a specially installed folding partition fell from a box on the ceiling. It was similar in design to that used to protect shop windows while still keeping the display visible, but it was painted a matte black. The principle was practically as old as warfare itself: In case you lose your outer defenses, always have a strong point to which to retreat.

The end of the corridor housing the last four of the six rooms was now sealed off.

It was now near total darkness as far as McGonigal and Jim Daid were concerned. About to rush forward, they hesitated at this unexpected development.

McGonigal fired a burst.

The muzzle flashes were blinding in the darkness, but he was just able to orient himself. He tried to fire again, but his magazine was empty. He changed in the darkness. It was an effortless maneuver practiced hundreds of times before.

He turned around, expecting to see some minimal light from the stairwell of the corridor behind him. There was almost nothing. Just a faint illumination from the safety panel of the fire door of the geriatric ward.

As he watched, that too vanished. It was now utterly dark. Too late, he remembered that the heavy curtains covering the windows of the stairwell had been drawn as they had ascended. It had been a gloomy day and the lights had been on, so he had thought nothing of it.

Rage gripped him. This was such a simple, foolish way to be defeated. It was the middle of the day. How could he have been expected to foresee darkness?

He reached out for Jim Daid, who gave a start as McGonigal gripped his arm.

"Relax, man," said McGonigal. "We'll follow the wall up. Fuck their tricks. We'll get the job done and be out of here in a moment."

He moved across to the corridor wall on the right, and with Jim Daid beside him began moving up slowly. Ahead were Rooms 6, 5, and 4.

He felt the door frame of Room 6 and briefly considered blasting his way in and opening the windows to get some light. Instead, he decided the darkness could work to his advantage also.

Grady and two other Rangers watched the two terrorists through their night-vision equipment. All had activated their laser sights. The thin beams were invisible except to those wearing the appropriate goggles. As it was, the Rangers could see each of the two terrorists fixed with pinpoints of imminent death. No one fired.

Kilmara studied the situation. Both men had removed their masks to see better in the darkness, and he could now identify them. He wanted a prisoner who knew something. This was a contract job, so probably neither of them would know much, but it was worth a try.

"Filters on," said Kilmara. He flicked a switch again and an immensely powerful light blazed from the end of the corridor, then went out again immediately.

McGonigal and Daid blinked in the light and mentally marked its source. They would shoot it out when it came on again.

Suddenly it flashed on and off again at bewildering speed, like some disco strobe light gone berserk.

Both terrorists fired, but the strobe effect was disorienting. They concentrated and fired short aimed bursts straight at the light. They could hear rounds whining and ricocheting, and it occurred to McGonigal that the light must be covered with bulletproof glass or transparent ballistic plastic. He began to feel sick and disoriented; then he started to shake. His weapon slid from his hands and he collapsed to the floor in what looked like a seizure.

He was the victim of a device which had initially been developed for crowd control and which exploited the discovery that certain people were disoriented by strobe lights. The developers had increased the intensity and flashing frequency of the beam and the results had exceeded their expectations. Prolonged exposure, even for a few minutes, could turn the recipient into a permanent epileptic. The technology was cheap and effective and belonged in a category known as "nonlethal weapons." Having seen the results of some of these toys—sonic beams designed to deafen, laser beams designed to blind—Kilmara found the category something of a misnomer. Still, he had to admit the Megabeam was a more compassionate alternative to being shot very permanently dead.

Unfortunately, shielded behind McGonigal, Jim Daid was not equally affected. Disoriented though he was, he still managed a desperate rush at the door of Fitzduane's room, his automatic rifle blazing.

Bullets splintered the door already blasted half open by the grenade. Sick and nauseated, Daid stumbled in, firing.

His last glimpse of life was of a near-solid line of light emanating from the far side of the room and terminating in his upper body. Flesh was ripped, bones were smashed, blood spewed from a dozen holes. Lifeless, he was thrown backwards into the corridor beside the gibbering McGonigal.

An electric motor whirred and the partition rose. The Rangers moved forward. The entire action, from the time the terrorists had started climbing the fire escape to enter the hospital, had taken two minutes and twenty-three seconds.

Fitzduane had slept through everything until the grenades had gone off. Then he had woken and reached for the Calico automatic rifle. The weapon was exceptionally easy to operate. The safety catch could be operated by either hand, and by touch alone. The cartridges ejected downward into a nylon bag as he fired. The weapon was environmentally friendly—no litter. The balance was perfect. It was loaded with red tracer. He just had to point and hose.

That is exactly what he did.

"Shit! Shit! Shit!" said Kilmara, turning the room lights back on. "May the Lord fuck you from a height, Hugo! Why did you have to shoot him? Why couldn't you just wound the fucker? We need someone to question. We need to know who is doing this. We need a prisoner. We need some answers."

Fitzduane was sitting up in his bed, smoke trickling from his automatic weapon. He looked as dangerous as anyone in pajamas can.

"A modest priority," he snarled, "I need to stay alive. Besides," he added, "I've been wounded—and believe me, it isn't fun."

SASADA HEARD MUFFLED explosions and his heart leaped. It's done, he thought, it's done.

He looked at his watch, imagining bursts of automatic-rifle fire as McGonigal and his people tidied up behind them and ran down the stairs. He started the engine of the Cavalier and kept his eye on the corner. Any moment now, they would appear around it.

Seconds passed, and then suddenly a figure clad in a blue boilersuit appeared and ran toward him. He flung open the door on the passenger side. The figure still wore his Halloween mask.

The fangs of a vampire told Sasada it was McGonigal. The figure beckoned to the others behind him, though Sasada could not see them. He felt relieved. He had thought for a moment that something had gone wrong and only McGonigal had made it out.

The vampire halted at the open door and pointed his AK-47 at Sasada. The Japanese stared at him.

"New rules," said Grady. "I don't get in; you get out."

Sasada reached for the door handle and suddenly flung himself out of the car. To his surprise, Grady did not fire. Sasada, now crouched behind the front of the car, drew his automatic.

"Oh dear, oh dear," said Grady patiently. "I guess I'd better count up to ten."

Sasada suddenly stood up to fire at the spot from which the voice had come, and felt the gun plucked from his hand from behind. Seconds later, he was spread-eagled over the car's hood and being handcuffed behind his back. The handcuffs were secured to an unbreakable belt made out of the same material as body armor. Looser restraints were placed around his ankles so that he could hobble but not walk and he was hauled to his feet.

He was surrounded by men in black combat uniforms wearing body armor with built-in pouches, microphone-equipped helmets, and carrying a range of futuristic-looking weaponry, none of which he was familiar with.

A distinguished-looking bearded man in the same black combat clothing and helmet walked over to him. He had an automatic weapon slung over one shoulder and a holstered handgun at his waist. He wore no badges of rank, but it was clear he did not need to.

He said nothing until two of the black-clad men completed an extremely thorough body search. Then he spoke.

"You and I are going to get to know each other very well," he said. "Normally the police and prison service handle people like you, but in this case, you will be our guest." The voice was gentle, almost friendly. "And you *will* talk."

Sasada felt weak and very much afraid. As he was being handcuffed, he had clung to the belief that he would be handed over to the police and the civil authorities. In such custody, he would say nothing, reveal nothing, as his oath dictated. Now the certainty in this man's voice cut through his resolution.

The man-in-black's eyes were merciless, though his voice remained relaxed. "Under the Irish legal system, you have the right to remain silent, and I'm sure your little group demands no less." He paused. Sasada felt as if his mind was being read. "But," the man continued, "you are an exceptional case and you are playing in a very special game."

Sasada wanted to defy this man in some way, but his mouth was too dry to spit and he did not want to give him the satisfaction of hearing him speak.

"And you know what my friends in the U.K.—you've heard of the SAS, I'm sure—say about our rather particular activities?"

Sasada could feel the sweat break out on his forehead, and he felt a quick pain in his upper arm. He turned his head sharply and saw a hypodermic syringe being emptied into him. He tried to struggle, but he was thoroughly immobilized by the Rangers on either side of him. He could no longer focus, and he could feel his limbs getting weaker.

His mind seemed to float away from his body. He could understand what was being said, but he could not reply. He was in despair and he knew, without being told, that his mission had failed. He also knew that this terrible man was right. He would talk. These people would do what was necessary to break him and there was nothing he could do to resist.

"Big boys' games, big boys' rules," said the voice relentlessly.

Sasada's eyeballs rolled upward in their sockets, and he stiffened in a last attempt to fight the drug, then collapsed.

Kilmara felt nauseated at what he was about to do to this man and the other he had captured, but events had gone far enough to demand special measures, and Molloy's death had tipped the balance.

These men would talk and their individual determination to resist would have no effect on the outcome, though their brains could well be permanently damaged. It was an unpleasant business, tinkering with somebody's mind, but the alternatives were worse.

Ranger Molloy's body was removed from the hospital in a body bag, and Kilmara accompanied it as it was carried to the mortuary at the rear of the hospital. He was married with three children, Kilmara recalled. The youngest had been born a few months ago, and Kilmara had attended the christening.

Big boys' games, big boys' rules.

I have no answers, he thought to himself, but a great deal to do.

TOKYO, JAPAN

February 1

The helicopter beat its way across the skies of central Tokyo, heading south.

Night had fallen, and the gray concrete drabness of much of the architecture was no longer evident. Instead, the city was a blaze of light, glowing with vitality. To the right, the recently erected skyscrapers of Nishi Shinjuku soared into the clouds.

Getting permission to fly across the metropolitan area was a rare privilege, but Hodama-*sensei* had made the necessary arrangements some five years previously, when private helicopters for Japan's business elite had started coming into vogue, and now the chairman of Namaka Industries could make the trip from the Namaka Tower at Sunshine City to Namaka Steel in forty minutes, instead of the normal two to three hours, and include a detour over the sea—a relaxing contrast to the urban sprawl.

There was no getting around it. Tokyo traffic was a bitch, and to use the faster subway-and-suburban-train combination was unacceptable from both a security and prestige point of view. A helicopter was the only way to go. It was also a measure of the scale of the Namaka brothers' achievement. As he looked down, Kei could still remember the desperation of the postwar years, the hunger, the fear, and above all the humiliation, of having and being nothing.

They crossed the docks, still a mass of activity, then went over the dark polluted waters of Tokyo Bay, the traditional resting ground of *yakuza* victims and still popular, though now rivaled by more scientific disposal methods. The memory of so many faces frozen in fear flashed through Kei's mind as he looked down. The climb had been hard and bloody. Staying at the top was no easier. Standards had to be kept high. Examples had to be made.

The lights of Kawasaki showed up ahead, and soon the cooling towers and industrial labyrinth that was the might of Namaka Steel. The plant was vast and operated around the clock. All kinds of steel were produced there. Pride of place was given to the well-guarded inner compound which housed the long, beige, ultramodern building of Namaka Special Steels. Special Steels forged the high-specification alloys required for the aerospace industry and it also made a range of items for the Japanese Self-Defense Forces. Accordingly, the facility was classified top secret and its security guards were legally authorized to be armed. Only the most carefully selected Namaka employees worked within it.

It was an ideal location for Kei Namaka's purposes. He found the naked power of so many of the production processes an inspiration, and certain of the facilities a convenience. His favorite items of equipment were the giant forging press—which could mold white-hot forty-ton ingots as if they were plasticine—and the tempering ovens. The ovens, some bigger than a railway carriage, were used to change the molecular structure of steel by the application of heat, and could reach 1,400 degrees centigrade. When open, radiating the incredible destructive power of pure heat, they looked like the gates of Hell.

Kei Namaka had had a private *dojo*, a training room for martial arts, constructed high up in the Special Steels facility. One wall was of *shoji* screens. When they were pulled back, it was possible to see through one-way glass the giant forging press and the ovens below. A bank of television monitors and one giant screen offered close-up observation of the factory floor and the various manufacturing processes.

Kei's interest in the martial arts stemmed from the fundamental need to survive in the confused and desperate environment that was the Tokyo underworld of the 1940s and '50s. Most of his opponents had been unskilled thugs whom he had easily been able to overcome, given his natural speed, height, and strength; but an encounter with a seasoned *yakuza* of the old school, who had actually taken the time to master his weapons, taught him the lesson that youth and brute force alone were not enough.

The grizzled gangster had disarmed Kei and was just about to kill him, when Fumio shot the man in the thigh. Guns were rare then and seldom used, but Fumio always used one in those days to compensate for his physical weakness. He was a terrible shot.

Kei had completed the termination of the *yakuza* with a thrust to the stomach, and he swore, as he watched the man writhe, that he would never again be outclassed. After a suitable interval, he had then decapitated his victim and gone to find the best *sensei* he could. The cleaning-up had been left to Fumio, who was good at that sort of thing and rarely failed to turn adversity into a benefit. The *yakuza*'s body was encased in concrete and dumped in Tokyo Bay. His head was embalmed in *sake* and sent back to his boss in a lacquer box.

Those were the days, thought Kei, good days in their way. That lacquer-box business was typical of how the brothers had prospered in the earlier years. His strong right arm and Fumio's brain had been a complementary combination, and then Hodama-*sensei* had taken them under his wing and their rise had accelerated, but their world had also become more complex.

Fumio was in his element. Kei was confused by the endless complexities. He let the *kuromaku* and his brother get on with it and devoted as much of his time as he could to *bujutsu,* the martial arts, and above all to *iai-do,* the art of swordsmanship. For much of the time, Kei Namaka wore a business suit and availed himself of all modern conveniences as required, but in his heart and dreams he was a *samurai,* a warrior and soldier like his father and his ancestors before him.

The helicopter set down on the landing pad on the roof of the Namaka Special Steels building and Kei jumped out into the brightly lit area. Armed company guards saluted, their uniforms whipping in the downdraft of the rotors as he strode impatiently toward the private elevator that linked with his office and the *dojo* below.

Kei took a quick shower and changed into *kendo* costume. *Kendo* was a poor imitation of sword fighting, in Kei's opinion, but it was an excellent sport in its own right, and vigorous exercise, and his security chief, Kitano-*sensei,* was an effective teacher and opponent.

They fought wearing full *kendo* armor: the *keikogi,* the loose-fitting quilted cotton jacket that both protected against bruising blows and also absorbed perspiration; the *hakama,* the divided skirt made of cotton; *tare,* the multilayered stiff cotton waist and hip protector; the *do,* the chest armor made of strips of heavy bamboo lashed in place vertically and covered with heavy hide and lacquered leather; the *hachimaki,* the towel-like cotton cloth wrapped around the head to keep sweat from the eyes and also act as a cushioning for the helmet; the *men,* the helmetlike combination face mask and head protector made of steel bars and heavy, layered cotton; and finally the *kote,* long leather padded gloves which also protected the lower arms. Their feet were bare.

They fought for over ninety minutes.

The *dojo* echoed to the sound of rapidly moving bare feet on the polished hardwood floor, the creak of armor, the controlled rasping of breath, and the clashing of *shinai,* the split bamboo fencing foils.

Halfway through the practice session, four men came into the room. Two were Namaka employees and reported directly to Kitano. The two visitors they were escorting were *interi yakuza,* the new so-called intellectual gangsters who specialized in financial racketeering. Their specialty was property fraud and their area was Hawaii. Recently, with the decline in value of the dollar, returns from that area had been disappointing.

Iced tea was served, and the visitors, wearing the slippers provided, watched the training session with interest, shouting applause and clapping as points were scored. The two Namaka men stood in the background, their hands folded in front of them.

The senior of the visitors thought that Kei Namaka looked quite magnificent. His *kendo* armor was crimson and his *do* was embossed in gold with the Namaka crest. He looked every inch the traditional *samurai* he aspired to be. In contrast, Kitano, in dull-black armor, seemed insignificant, despite his unquestioned technical proficiency.

The practice session ended with a spectacular blow to the throat by Kei and a laugh from Kitano. "Namaka-*san,* you will soon be *sensei,*" he said.

Kei bowed toward the master. "The skill of the pupil is but a tribute to the quality of the teaching."

Kei and Kitano greeted their visitors, then went to bathe and change. Meanwhile, the screens were pulled back and the two *yakuza* were entertained by watching the activity on the floor below. Both men were a little awed and impressed by what they saw. Iron and steel they associated with solidity and strength. Here it was being shaped and formed as if the effort were nothing. It was a stunning impression of power. There was a dynamism about such heavy industrial processes that made them compelling to watch.

Kei and Kitano returned after twenty minutes. Both were wearing the customary house clothes of a *samurai* and each had the traditional two swords that went with the rank, placed as normal in the sash of his kimono. The right of wearing two swords had been abolished by imperial decree over a hundred years earlier, but in their private homes, some traditionalists continued the custom.

The two men and their visitors sat down cross-legged on *tatami* mats, facing across a low table. *Sake* and *sushi* were brought. Kei and Kitano made a point of filling their guests' cups. The atmosphere was one of relaxation. Nonetheless, there were a few matters of business to be discussed before they could devote themselves completely to enjoying themselves. The senior gangster was relieved. His conscience was not entirely clear. On the other hand, he had rarely seen the chairman in better spirits.

"I confess I am a little puzzled," Kei said to him with a smile. "We have invested several billion yen in those beautiful islands and the return has not quite been what we expected. Perhaps you could explain. I am not a financial expert like my brother, but I suppose I should try and understand. Frankly, I find most of these schemes above me. I prefer the simplicity of the *dojo*."

He laughed, and his two visitors laughed dutifully with him. The senior gangster was grateful for the extra time to think, and he composed his answer with care. Kitano did not laugh, but smiled slightly. The man did not notice. His attention was focused on the chairman. Kei refilled all the glasses and smiled encouragingly.

"The dollar has sunk dramatically and unexpectedly," said the man. "That means when we make our returns to Japan in yen—as we have been requested to do—our return appears to have shrunk. Actually, in dollar terms, it is as planned. It is merely when denominated in yen that it appears to be below our target."

The chairman nodded and was silent, as if pondering this. Then he spoke again. "But surely, since we are continuing to invest in yen with fresh funds, the stronger yen should be buying us more. We should be getting more assets for our money."

The man nodded in agreement. "That is so," he said, "or would be so if no other money were coming in from Japan. Unfortunately, many other organizations have the same idea as we do, and they are bidding up the price of property in Hawaii. Accordingly, our investments are costing us more than we originally planned."

He was sweating a little. The *dojo* was air-conditioned, but the heat from the steel works below seemed to make itself felt. Or perhaps it was his imagination. The man tried to keep his mind clear of the numbered bank account in the Cayman Islands. The transactions had all been in cash. There was no paper trail. It had been very discreet skimming.

The chairman spoke again. "Kitano-*san*," he said, gesturing with his left hand at the security chief, who sat beside him, "has interviewed some six of the vendors of property that we purchased. They all confirmed that what you say is true. Demand has bid up supply."

The gangster's heart had been pounding, but at Kei's reassuring words he felt a flood of relief. Then Kitano spoke. "The chairman is talking about the initial interviews," he said, with a thin smile, "but it is in the nature of my responsibility to be thorough. Further interviews—conducted with some vigor by my staff—revealed an interesting reason for the high prices."

He removed a folded sheet of paper from his sleeve, unfolded it, and placed it carefully in front of the man. The paper listed the Cayman

Islands account number and each of the hidden payments. The amounts were accurate to the nearest yen. The gangster had insisted on payment in yen. He had little faith in the long-term strength of the dollar. How could you have faith in a country that would sell anything and everything for a profit? The Americans had already sold half of Hawaii and a goodly portion of California. The Statue of Liberty would be next. They were unprincipled.

His focus had been on the paper. It was, he knew, his death warrant, unless he could act quickly. Dread filled his heart. He glanced at his companion. The other *yakuza* was shaking with fear. There would not be much help from there. He looked across at the chairman. Namaka-*san* seemed almost to be in a trance. There might just be a chance to grab one of the swords from his waist and make a run for it.

There was a blur of movement, and the gangster felt a terrible agony and a sudden overwhelming weakness. In front of him, the chairman still sat, but now he held a bloody sword in his *left* hand. But Namaka-*san* was right-handed! He had been carefully watching for any sudden move, but the chairman had deceived him. He had executed a perfect left-handed draw and horizontal slashing cut from the sitting position, which had sliced open the lower torsos of the two men. The man looked down at his stomach, which now gaped open. He could see the edges of his *izumi,* the dragon tattoo covering much of his body which had been the symbol of acceptance into his group. It was now cut in two, the careful workmanship desecrated. Beside him, his companion had slumped forward.

Waves of pain engulfed him, but still, although swaying slightly, he sat upright, blood draining from his body as he waited for the killing blow. His chin was held high. He expected the customary decapitation. "Namaka-*san*," he said, pleading. He could just manage the words. Blood flowed from his mouth.

Namaka did not move. His *katana* was at rest. The blow did not come. "You have stolen from the clan," he said. "I take no pleasure in your death, nor in the manner of it, but examples must be made. You will die in the ovens."

It was at that moment that the man's composure broke. He tried to scream, but blood filled his throat. He attempted to struggle as he was strapped to a wooden stretcher and carried down to the production floor.

The end of the two *interi yakuza* was watched in close-up on the big television monitor by the chairman and his security chief. The heat of the oven was so great that in minutes nothing remained.

Kei's greatest sword-fighting expertise was in *iai-do*—the art of drawing a sword. The blow he had executed in one continuous movement following his blade clearing the scabbard was a classic cut. Kitano had rarely seen it executed better.

Kei had completed *chiburi*—shaking the blood off the blade by making an arclike movement over his head and then snapping the blade down by his side—and now commenced polishing the surface with a soft cloth and powdered limestone. He worked with care, both for his own well-being—the weapon was razor-sharp and lethal if mishandled—and for that of the sword.

Too much polishing could damage the surface. Forty-five strokes had been determined over the centuries as the recommended optimum.

He erred on the conservative side and gave the blade forty-two. Finally, he rubbed the gleaming surface with a very light coating of clove oil and replaced it in its sheath.

11

CONNEMARA REGIONAL HOSPITAL

February 8

There was the sound of heavy breathing on the phone and then a giggle.

The custom was that Fitzduane would put the phone down last, and Boots played this to the hilt at bedtime. When Boots was not sleeping over in the hospital, Fitzduane and he talked every night before Boots was tucked in. Boots still had some way to go with his telephone technique, but he made up for it with sheer zest.

His gaiety made Fitzduane's heart sing. And there was the added reassurance of knowing his son was safe. Oona was looking after him, Christian de Guevain had flown over for a few weeks to lend a helping hand, and there was now a regular Ranger presence on the island.

" 'Night and big hug for the fifth time, you little monster," said Fitzduane, laughing. "Now! GO TO BED!"

Boots burst into fits of giggles and then Fitzduane could hear Oona in the background and Boots's fading " 'Night, 'night! Daddeee . . ." as he was carried to his bed. Whatever they were feeding him, Boots was in demon form.

"Hugo?" It was de Guevain's voice.

"Still here," said Fitzduane.

"All is well here, *mon ami*," said de Guevain, amused. "The only threat here is from Boots."

Fitzduane laughed. "I can hear that." His tone became more serious. "Christian, your keeping the home fires burning is much appreciated."

de Guevain made a dismissive noise, and Fitzduane smiled to himself. His friend had film-star good looks, a debonair manner, and a way with gestures and body language that put most other Parisians of Fitzduane's acquaintance to shame. An ex-paratrooper and now a Paris-based merchant banker, the Frenchman had originally met Fitzduane as a result of a shared social interest in medieval weaponry and fencing. The two were expert swordsmen. It was a rather impractical skill in the late twentieth century, but for both, something of a family tradition.

Their friendship had nearly come to an abrupt end during the Hangman's attack on the castle. It had been a grim business which had affected all the survivors, but also created a special bond between them. When de Guevain had heard from Kilmara about the attack on Fitzduane, he had come immediately. He was confident that his bank, wife, and mistress would prosper in his absence. They were all mature elements in his well-ordered social structure. He was equally confident, with good reason, that they would welcome him back with open arms. Christian de Guevain had that kind of charisma.

"And how goes it for you, Hugo?" continued de Guevain. "I'm on red." The slight drop in voice quality and change to a more impersonal, manufactured sound confirmed the switch to encryption.

"These people are not going to go away," said Fitzduane grimly, "and I'm not to going to sit around waiting for their next play."

"Japan?" said de Guevain. "You've decided."

"Japan," confirmed Fitzduane. "The interrogation of Sasada has confirmed that the Namakas are directly involved. Sasada was briefed by the Namaka security chief, who is a member of the Namaka inner sanctum, and the word is that Kitano does nothing that does not come from the Namakas themselves."

"Is there any chance of getting the Namakas through the courts?" asked de Guevain, without any real hope of getting an affirmative response. "Using Sasada as a witness?"

"Not a snowball's chance in hell," said Fitzduane. "Kitano is the cutout, and there is the slight problem that Sasada did not come out of interrogation too well. Kilmara broke him, but there was a price."

"*Merde,*" said de Guevain, but with understanding. As a young man, he had served his time as a parachute lieutenant in Algeria, fighting in a very dirty war, and there were some situations where the Geneva conventions did not apply. Few people liked it, but in counterterrorism it was sometimes a matter of weighing unpalatable alternatives.

"Hugo," he went on, "if you go to Japan you are going to need friends. A foreigner alone won't get very far. The Japanese . . ."

". . . are very Japanese, and different from us Western types," completed Fitzduane dryly. "Yeah, I've heard that. It's even rumored they have their own language and eat with wooden skewers."

de Guevain laughed. "It is clear that you are recovering, Hugo. But you know what I mean, and in Japan, friends in high places are particularly important. If you are going to go up against people as powerful as the Namakas, you need—must have—a player of equal or greater influence. Believe me, I know. We bank there."

"Point accepted," said Fitzduane. "Kilmara has said much the same thing. He can make connections on the security side—the man has pipelines everywhere—but he says that's not enough. I'm going to need some extra weight over there." He paused before continuing. "Someone we are certain is not allied in any way to the Namakas."

de Guevain could see the problem. Japan was a pyramid. Its base was broad, but at the top of an extremely hierarchical society a small number of people and organizations constituted the main movers and shakers. And many of this ruling group were cross-connected. Some of the alliances were known, but many were not. Japan could not be considered an open society.

"Yoshokawa," said de Guevain. "He's the obvious choice."

"He's my only choice," said Fitzduane grimly. "I have a few other connections in Japan, but they are all expatriates. Yoshokawa-*san* is my only option, but whether he is connected to the Namakas or not, I don't know."

"I see the problem, Hugo," said de Guevain. "I'm going back to Paris in a couple of days, so I'll put out a few feelers. But my guess is that Yoshokawa is your man. He owes you. You saved his son's life."

"Yoshokawa would not betray me," said Fitzduane, with some force, "but there is the matter of conflicting loyalties. If he's already in bed with the Namakas, he's going to sit on the sidelines, which may be all very honorable but will be no use to me."

de Guevain laughed. "I'll check out a few sets of entrails," he said, "and talk to a few friends, but my guess is that Yoshokawa is your man."

The conversation came to an end, and Fitzduane replaced the telephone handset and watched the red encryption light wink out.

He lay back against the pillows of his raised bed, closed his eyes, and thought of his baby son and his home and of the comfort of good friends like Kilmara and de Guevain and the Bear. Life, one way and another, was a hard and random business, but all in all he considered he was a lucky man. Being shot, of course, was not so lucky, but overall he liked to believe things balanced out.

de Guevain had telephoned from the Great Hall of Fitzduane's castle, and as he thought about his home and felt more than a few pangs of homesickness mixed with impatience to get out of the damned hospital, he recalled how he had met Yoshokawa-*san*.

The Japanese industrialist had made quite an entrance.

The core of Fitzduane's castle was a rectangular stone tower known as the Keep, built by the first Sir Hugo Fitzduane in the thirteenth century. Subsequently, among other improvements, the Keep had been extended by building out to one side where the site overlooked the sea.

Unfortunately, the entire extension, known as the Great House, had been gutted by fire during the Hangman's siege. At first Fitzduane had thought of restoring it very much as it had been originally. He had grown up in Duncleeve, and its physical fabric and traditions were important to him.

He was attached to age-blackened wooden beams, oak paneling, tapestries, family portraits, crossed weapons, and mounted animal trophies with glass eyes and mange, but he was blessed with an open mind. As his ideas developed, he decided to preserve the traditional look of the exterior of the Great House so that it harmonized with the Keep, the curtain wall and its outhouses, and the gatehouse, but inside to make the rooms light and airy and uncluttered.

The general tendency of his social class to live in dusty, wood-wormed cocoons of architectural tradition and dry rot was not necessarily to their advantage, he thought. His peers tended to ossify in harmony with their museumlike surroundings.

Above all, he wanted to open the Great Hall—the magnificent open space on the top floor and the center of social activity over the centuries—to overlook the sea. It was a vista Fitzduane found endlessly fascinating, given the unusual light in the West of Ireland, but it lost quite a lot of appeal when your main visual access was confined to arrow slits designed for five-foot-high Norman crossbowmen—and you were six foot two. But he was far from sure how to implement this vision.

He was sitting on the chilly bronze of a cannon in the courtyard pondering this dilemma, when Yoshokawa arrived. Yoshokawa-*san* was the chairman of Yoshokawa Electrical, the Japanese electronics and consumer-goods conglomerate founded by his grandfather.

Hideo Yoshokawa's son, Aki, had been one of those saved by Fitzduane in the Hangman episode, and though the father had already expressed his thanks, he now had arrived in person to pay his respects and to tour the battlefield.

Four weeks later, Yoshokawa-*san's* personal architect and a supporting team arrived to make a site assessment. Two months after that, Yoshokawa-*san* himself arrived with a scale model.

Ten months later, the specially-flown-in team of Japanese craftsmen had completed the work, gotten seriously drunk on Guinness and Irish whiskey at a special dinner in the new Great Hall, and had vanished— and Fitzduane was left to gaze with considerable pleasure and not a little awe at the result.

He would wait until Christian de Guevain reported back, but his instincts said that his friend was right.

Yoshokawa-*san* could be trusted.

TOKYO, JAPAN

February 8

Sitting in his office in the Namaka Tower, Fumio studied the discussion document prepared by Goto-*san*, the group's controller.

It was a masterly piece of work. The Namaka holdings were structured in the form of a *keiretsu,* the complex corporate structure favored by major Japanese groups. Goto had reduced the financial figures of scores of interlocking Namaka companies so that the bottom line reflected cash flow—and nothing else.

The figures reflected a simple truth. While showing paper profits, the Namaka *keiretsu* was hemorrhaging cash. A graph clearly demonstrated the moment of truth. The group would crash like a row of dominoes in less than a year unless there was a major cash injection.

Goto had been the first professionally qualified man that the Namaka brothers had hired. He had worked as controller of one of the major car manufacturers until a most ingenious fraud had come to light. To save face all around, he had resigned gracefully to live on his recently acquired riches, but then Fumio had tempted him out of his decidedly premature retirement. Goto had been recommended by Hodama. The *kuromaku* had a nose for talent.

The seriousness of the situation had been known for some time, but with Hodama alive Fumio had not been unduly worried. The *kuromaku* could always come up with a friendly bank. His influence with the Ministry of Finance was legendary. A word or two in the right ear, a little administrative guidance with a few remarks about the national interest . . .

It had been done before. It was how the system worked. It was why you paid money to politicians and master fixers like Hodama in the first place.

Hodama's death had changed the game. Within days of his funeral, the climate of support that the Namaka *keiretsu* had enjoyed for so long seemed to have evaporated.

Nothing was said. Nothing specific that they were aware of was done—and yet suddenly there was a chill everywhere. It was as if someone or some group of great power and influence was actively working against them. And yet every effort to determine who was responsible had come up with nothing.

In the past, they would automatically have turned to Hodama-*sensei*. Efforts to find a replacement had so far failed. A long and intimate relationship was the basis of working with a *kuromaku*. Difficult and complex things needed to be done. The law had to be treated "flexibly." Trust was essential if prosecution was to be avoided. It was not the sort of thing you could set up overnight. All the politicians were locked into their own particular factions by obligations generated over the years. And there were very few, if any, other people of Hodama-*sensei*'s caliber.

Goto spoke with the freedom that came from a long and trusted association. Also, he and Fumio were close personal friends. Nonetheless, they still addressed each other with some formality.

"There is a certain irony to our situation, Namaka-*san*," said Goto. "Our illegal activities have remained consistently profitable. It is our entirely legal expansion that is creating these difficulties. First we invested in the dollar and that went through the floor; then we had a flyer on gold, and that, which had always gone up, now seems to be going nowhere; and finally, we bought and expanded Namaka Steel. It is the steel plant that really lies at the root of our problems. There is now overcapacity worldwide. And as to our investment in the Special Steels facility—that has been the last straw."

Fumio sighed. He adored his big brother, and Namaka Steel was Kei's passion. It made him feel like a proper industrialist. And as for the investment in the new Special Steels facility, that had been made as a result of a strategic decision by MITI, the supposedly infallible Ministry of International Trade and Industry. MITI had devised a plan to take over the international aerospace industry in the 1970s, and Namaka Special Steels had been a key element in that plan. The project had enjoyed massive prestige. Encouraging speeches had been made by a series of ministers and other politicians.

The plan had gone precisely nowhere. There had been some modest progress, but for all practical purposes, the Americans still owned the skies—with the Europeans, supposedly in decadent decline, in a healthy second place. It was frustrating for MITI, but it was disastrous for Namaka. A few defense contracts helped in the short term, but nothing would substitute for a major breakthrough.

That breakthrough was no longer possible in the time available through normal legal commercial trading. The only chance that either Fumio or Goto could see lay with the sale of some of the more esoteric products of Namaka Special Steels. Project Tsunami, the production of nuclear-weapons-plant equipment for the North Koreans, was illegal— absolutely against the laws of Japan—but it represented a vast amount of cash money.

With Hodama dead, the North Korean weapons project was now fundamental to the Namaka *keiretsu*'s survival. It was that simple.

"I don't think we will trouble the chairman with these figures," said Fumio. "He has other things on his mind."

Goto nodded in agreement. An untroubled Kei Namaka was important. As chairman, his confident dynamism was of enormous help with the major institutions. It would not do to trouble him with unpleasant details. Anyway, Kei had enough trouble just reading martial arts *manga,* the adult comics. Balance sheets and cash flow forecasts were beyond him.

Goto had never been a traditional *yakuza,* so the issue of the fullbody tattoo had not arisen. However, early on in his life he had discovered a simple truth which he had tattooed in Japanese characters—*kanji*—across his torso. The modest design was attractive, but it was designed for Goto's use principally; it could be read only in a mirror.

The elegant tattooed characters read: CASH IS KING.

THE WEST OF IRELAND

February 17

Kilmara drove the Land-Rover slowly down the unpaved track toward the beach.

They reached a grassy area at the bottom and parked. Ahead of them, a short steep path wound its way through rocks to the sand and sea below. Against a backdrop of mountains, the beach seemed to curve endlessly.

They left the car. The day before, winds of up to eighty miles an hour had been blowing. Now the breeze off the Atlantic was down to a tenth of that and the waves were almost gentle.

The sand was firm nearer the waterline and made for easy walking. From time to time they stopped to look at driftwood thrown up by the storm or at unusual stones or shells. Clouds scudded overhead and the sun darted in and out. The air, though chill, was invigorating.

Kilmara stopped and looked back. They had walked for perhaps half a mile in companionable silence, and their footsteps could be seen stretching back to the rocks below where the car was parked. Theirs were the only footsteps to be seen. He turned around, and ahead of them the beach was unmarked and empty.

"I've been to half the countries in the world," he said with feeling, "and I have seen amazing sights and the most beautiful scenery, but, somehow, nowhere compares to Ireland. This country gets into your soul and it touches you and that's it—you're hooked, you're marked for life. If you leave, there is always a bit of you that yearns to be back in Ireland. There is something in the fabric of this land that is unique. And the most beautiful part of this land is the West."

Kathleen looked at him, a little surprised. She had not expected Kilmara to have the soul of a romantic. In most of her dealings with him he had been an authority figure, dominating—a little frightening, even—in his uniform and so often in the company of his armed Rangers.

Now, alone with her and in civilian clothes, he seemed more accessible, easier to talk to, and more like a normal person. There was less of the General and more of the man. He was someone, perhaps, who could be a friend.

"The romantic General," she said with a smile. "Another romantic we both know said something rather similar."

Kilmara laughed. "I'm a part-time romantic," he said. "Very part-time. My nature is to be practical, to see the world the way it is without the expectation that I can change it. Hugo is the real thing. Even worse, he is a romantic and an idealist. He believes things can and will get better, and in such notions as honor and duty and fidelity. That's what gets him into so much trouble. Yet I envy him his nature. He can be a lethal son of a bitch, but in essence, he is a good man."

"And you're not?" said Kathleen.

Kilmara took his time answering. He was thinking of Sasada, of drugs and sensory deprivation, of other terrible techniques; of what they had done to the man to make him talk.

The man now slobbered and grunted and could no longer control his bowels. He was permanently insane.

"No," he said heavily. "My world demands other qualities, and it appears that I may have them. But goodness is not high on the list."

Kathleen had the sense that he was referring to something specific, and she shuddered. His was a fearful world and he had spent a lifetime in it. Violence was a perversion of all civilized values. How could one be exposed to such a culture of destruction and remain unaffected? And yet she was being unfair. Violence was a reality, and the relative peace that most people enjoyed depended on such men as her companion. Without people such as the Bear and Kilmara, she reminded herself, she would now be dead.

She took his arm companionably. "You're a kind man," she said thoughtfully, "and a good friend to Hugo."

Kathleen had not seen Fitzduane since the carnage at the hospital. In view of the investigations after the incident, she had been sent to a hospital elsewhere and released after a week. Her physical injuries were not serious and were now almost healed. Then there had been her father's funeral and her mother to look after. And there was a sense of shock and violation that was taking a longer time to overcome; it might take years.

In truth, her feelings about Fitzduane were hard to clarify. Indirectly he was the cause of these terrible happenings. He was not responsible but he was directly associated. If she had never met the man, her father might yet be alive and her mother would not have had a nervous breakdown.

"How is he?" she said. She missed him as she spoke and had an overwhelming desire to be with him. She felt confused. Here was a man with a son by another woman, whose life was associated with a level of threat that any sane person, given a choice, would avoid like the plague.

He was also the most attractive and stimulating man she had ever met, and she could not stay away from him. Yet she was scared of being with him and the emotional pain that might ensue. And she was appalled by the latent physical danger. The memory of McGonigal and Sasada was fresh in her mind. She had trouble sleeping and found it difficult to concentrate. Sometimes, for no specific reason, she felt herself shaking with terror and sweating.

"Grumpy," said Kilmara, in an amused voice, and then he became more serious. "For the last couple of years, Hugo has been focused on Boots and rebuilding Duncleeve and some work for the Rangers—but otherwise skating. He did not seem to be fully engaged. It was as if he needed to rest up for a little time before embarking on something new. He had hung up his wars and his cameras but hadn't found a replacement activity. He seemed to me to lack a purpose in life."

"Looking after a child and building a home is not a purpose?" said Kathleen, a little annoyed.

Kilmara laughed. "Touché!" he said.

Kathleen stopped and stared at some seaweed, kelp, the deep-brown rubbery kind with long stalks and little bubbles on the fronds that you could burst. She was reminded of summers at the seaside with her family and the reassuring feeling of her father's hand in hers, and she was gripped with a sense of loss and desolation. Tears welled from her eyes.

Kilmara looked across at her and saw the tears and put his arm around her, and they walked like that for some distance before either spoke again. The beach seemed endless and the headland in the distance was shrouded in mist. Kathleen imagined that they were walking on clouds. When she spoke again, she picked up the conversation where they had left off. "And his being shot," she said. "Are you implying that this has changed him?"

"Being shot, seriously injured, tends to concentrate the mind," said Kilmara grimly. "You'll have seen it for yourself. Some people fold and die and others draw on all their reserves and seem to get a renewed grip on life, as if they realize just how little time there is and the importance of making the most of what we've got."

"Well, Hugo is a fighter," said Kathleen forcibly.

"And there is the irony," said Kilmara. "He claws his way back into the land of the living and, insofar as it is humanly possible in such a condition, operates flat out . . ." He paused and laughed.

"And?" said Kathleen impatiently.

"And when something happens that he cannot remotely blame himself for—the attack on the hospital—he gets an acute attack of depression and just does nothing for five days," said Kilmara. He looked at Kathleen. "I think he misses you."

Kathleen did not reply at first. Her cheeks were tingling from the breeze off the sea and the salt spray. She felt defensive about Fitzduane and thought Kilmara was being a little cruel. "He feels responsible," she said slowly. "He was the target and others died. That would hurt him."

"Well, he is back on track now," Kilmara said, "and furious with himself for losing so much time. That is why he's grumpy."

Kathleen started to laugh, and it was infectious. Soon both of them were laughing as they walked arm in arm along the endless curve of the sand.

THE MOST UNPLEASANT initial aftereffect of his injuries, in Fitzduane's opinion—a judgment he felt most qualified to make, since it was his body, after all—was the external fixation the orthopedic team had used to repair his smashed thighbone. Fortunately, it had been a temporary expedient.

They had screwed four pins into the bone, two above and two below the fracture, which protruded through the skin. They had then joined the pins together externally with crossbars. When Fitzduane looked at his leg, the fixation reminded him of a scaffolding construction. He was part bionic. Frankly, he had preferred being all human.

The orthopedic surgeon had been proud of his handiwork. "The advantage of external over internal fixation is that it does not contaminate," he had said, looking at an X ray of Fitzduane's thigh with much the same enthusiasm that a normal male might reserve for a *Playboy* centerfold.

"Very nice," said Fitzduane, "but it makes me look like part of the Eiffel Tower. What's the downside?"

The surgeon had smiled reassuringly. "Just a little discomfort," he had said. "Nothing to be concerned about."

"Just a little discomfort," Fitzduane had soon learned, was a relative term. External fixation was extremely uncomfortable. There were four sites of entry in Fitzduane's leg for the pins, and despite regular dressing they were a constant source of pain and irritation. If he accidentally bashed the fixator, the skin tore. To help him sleep, a frame was put over his leg at night.

"You are able to walk almost immediately with external fixation," said the surgeon. "Exercise is very important."

Fitzduane, cursed with an imagination and his mind painting a graphic picture of shattered bone, could not at first even mentally consider walking, but he was given little choice in the matter.

On the fourth day after he had been shot, he had begun dynamic exercises.

On the fifth day, he had been eased out of bed, propped up with a zimmer frame—a walking support—and, to his amazement, made twenty yards. He had felt terrified at first and then ridiculous. He'd still had his chest drains in. He was told that what he was doing was called "shadow walking." Shadow or not, it was a start.

At the end of the first week, his chest drains had been removed. During the second week, he had been moved from the frame onto crutches. By the third week, he could do fifty yards at a stretch. Day by day after that, his stamina improved.

Not long after the attack on the hospital, he was assessed yet again by the surgeon. The sight of X rays seemed to bring out a certain manic cheeriness in the medic. "You are fortunate, Hugo," he had said, "that your assailant used a subsonic round. The damage to your femur was serious enough, but it could have been a lot worse. Your leg is really in quite reasonable shape, all things being considered. Boy, did we do a good job!"

"How the fuck do I know?" said Fitzduane in a reasonably good-humored voice. "I don't get shot regularly. I have no basis of comparison."

The surgeon was used to being addressed as some kind of supreme being by nursing staff and patients as he made his rounds, but he enjoyed Fitzduane.

"Ireland is an island behind an island," he had said, "and you were wounded on yet another, even more remote, island. Think yourself lucky you were not just painted with iodine and left to get on with it. Anyway, it's back to surgery for you. The blood flow in your leg is good and there is encouraging new bone in the area of the wound. I'm going to take off your scaffolding."

Three days later, Fitzduane returned to Duncleeve. His leg was now internally fixated. All the external protruding metal had been removed. In its place he wore a brace, both for support and to remind him to take it easy at first. He could now walk with the aid of only one crutch. Soon that would be discarded, and then the brace.

He grew fitter and stronger.

Kathleen came with him. She was not a physiotherapist, but she was a trained nurse and well-briefed by her colleagues. Further, she had a highly motivated patient who already had learned most of what he had to do in his own right. He would push himself slightly harder every day, training for an hour at a time twice, three times, and then four times a day.

His stamina increased and his slight limp faded.

Kathleen and he became very close, intimate friends. They ate together, talked together late into the night, exchanged confidences, walked arm in arm outside the castle. Yet their physical relationship did not evolve. Kathleen was still deeply affected by the assault on her home and the death of her father. Fitzduane was still recovering his health and was adjusting to his loss of Etan.

Meanwhile there was much to be done. Fitzduane's castle and his island were being transformed.

Relentlessly, Fitzduane, displaying the thoroughness and tactical professionalism of so many of his ancestors, was preparing to strike back.

—————

THE TELEPHONE RANG. Fitzduane picked up the handset gingerly; Boots liked playing with phones, and it was covered with his porridge and honey. Still, it was a reminder that he was home again in Duncleeve.

"You sound distant," said de Guevain. He was back in Paris. Since he largely owned his private bank he was something of his own master, and he had an excellent Director-General, but even so he felt inclined to show the flag now and then.

Fitzduane was holding the instrument far enough away to avoid contact. There was raspberry jam on the damn thing as well. Boots had been hungry that morning. There were toast crumbs everywhere. He hunted around for tissues while he spoke.

"I am distant," he said. "You're in France, I'm in Ireland."

He found the tissues, wiped the phone as best he could, and moved the receiver closer to him. "How are things your end?"

"The family are fine," said de Guevain, "and the bank is making money. Situation normal. I lead a predictable life. And I have heard from our foreign friends."

"This is an open line," reminded Fitzduane gently.

"I know, *mon ami*," said de Guevain. "All I want to say is that now I have every reason to believe you can rely on the builder we talked about. He is not associated with the competition. My friends are sure of it, and I am sure of them."

de Guevain's "friends" could be traced back to his college, his regiment, and his banking connections. The foreign and intelligence services would feature. Apart from his aristocratic background, Christian was an *enarques,* which meant that he had gone to one of the small group of colleges from which the key rulers of France were selected. It was an influential club with excellent sources. It was the final check. Yoshokawa-*san* could be trusted.

"Take care of yourself, my friend," said Fitzduane. He felt suddenly concerned. It was a feeling, no more. "You were with me when the Hangman was killed. Get some security. Take some precautions."

de Guevain laughed. "I'm only in danger when I visit you, Hugo," he said. "But do you know anything?"

"No," said Fitzduane. "Nothing. But I just have a sense of unease."

"Two attempts on your life. You're entitled to some paranoia," said de Guevain. He hung up the phone and thought for a while.

Everything was fine except for the break-in at his apartment two nights earlier. Fortunately, nothing had been stolen. The security system was being upgraded, and he resolved to have a word with the bank's security people.

Tokyo, Japan

March 2

Two months into the Hodama murder investigation, it was clear to Adachi that he was in for an endurance test.

Results were not coming either easily or quickly. Murder investigations typically developed strong leads in the first day or so, resulting in a quick arrest, or else turned into a matter of stamina.

After the first couple of weeks, he realized he faced the prospect of months or even years on the affair. He might be transferred off the case to let some new blood have a go, but, pending that, he was in for the duration. Hodama had been too big a fish for the case to be put quietly on the back burner. This was the killing of an insider, one of the most powerful members of the political establishment. If someone of Hodama's status could be killed and the assassins left undetected, then no one was safe.

A steady stream of government members, senior civil servants, and politicians expressed their decidedly personal concern about the progress of the investigation. There were regular calls from the Prime Minister's office. The Minister of Justice had asked for special briefings on two occasions. The brunt of the pressure was fielded by the senior prosecutor and the Deputy Superintendent-General, so Adachi was left relatively free to operate, but the extent of the concern was made well-known to him, together with regular statements of confidence in his abilities.

Adachi was not naive. He was uncomfortable being supported in this way. It put him neatly in the firing line as the fall guy, if such was required. Secondly, it was his experience that public praise normally came before private termination. The best eulogies, now he thought about it, were delivered at weddings, retirements, firings, and funerals. It was a depressing observation about the human condition. And did weddings really belong in this group of essentially negative transitional occasions? He thought they probably did—although undoubtedly most participants regarded themselves as exceptions.

Inspector Fujiwara came into the squad room looking pleased with himself. Immediately behind him, two sweating detectives appeared, struggling with a very large, heavy object neatly wrapped in the material used by the Forensics Department. The parcel was labeled and sealed with an eye for presentation. Whoever had wrapped the damn thing had obviously aspired to the high aesthetic packaging standards of the Mitsukoshi Department Store. Adachi did not know whether to be proud of this Japanese obsession with doing everything correctly—even when it really was not necessary—or to regard his fellow countrymen as being slightly nuts. It was heresy, but it was a thought worth taking further, he considered.

He glanced at the wall clock. It was nearly eight o'clock in the evening and most of the desks were still manned or their occupants supposedly doing something policelike in the field. We are nuts, he decided. We Japanese are a completely nutty nation. We should be out enjoying ourselves instead of working ourselves even nuttier. I should be in bed with Chifune enjoying long slow sex—perhaps something slightly kinky—instead of being impaled on a swivel chair in my office with my eyes gritty and my clothing sweaty and rumpled, waiting for my Inspector-*san* to pull a huge rabbit—or maybe something more interesting—out of his parcel.

The parcel was rectangular and vaguely coffinlike in shape, though taller. "I assume, Inspector-*san*," said Adachi, "that there is a woman inside that container and that you will shortly cut her in half. You have that showman's look. Well, proceed: given the pace of progress around here, we are all in sore need of entertainment."

Inspector Fujiwara took the cue. He stretched his arms out like a magician winding up a crowd, then turned and tipped the wrapping material off the object. A nineteenth-century *kurama nagamochi* stood revealed. The heavy wooden chest, reinforced with iron corner pieces, was customarily used for storing bedding and kimono.

"Nice piece," said Adachi. "It has wheels, by the way—little round things at the bottom." He looked at the sweating detectives. "Why didn't you—Tokyo MPD's finest—push the bloody chest?"

"Forensics wrapped the wheels too, boss," said Fujiwara. "They do that kind of thing. They thought it would look neater. Anyway, we wanted to make it a surprise. You've been looking gloomy recently."

"Oh," said Adachi. He did not quite know whether to feel flattered or deflated. He did feel curious.

"Miwako Chiba," said Inspector Fujiwara. "A damned attractive woman in her early fifties. Slim figure, distinguished face, great eyes, lots of sex appeal. Looks great—could be twenty years younger."

"Is she in the box?" said Adachi. "Not that I want to pry."

"She lives out in Takanawa," said Fujiwara. "Nice house, two *tatami* rooms and the rest modern. Plenty of money there—not really big money, but comfortable. A settled look to the situation."

"Is there a Mr. Chiba?" said Adachi. He was beginning to understand.

"No," said Fujiwara.

"Little Chibas?" said Adachi.

"No," said Fujiwara. "None recorded and none that I noticed."

"Ah!" said Adachi. "What does she do?"

"Has a bar in Rippongi," said Fujiwara, "but someone else manages it. Chiba-*san* is a lady of leisure."

"Whose mistress or ex-mistress?" said Adachi. The pattern was predictable. A great deal of police work was about patterns.

"She is out of a job these days," said Fujiwara, "whatever their relationship."

"Hodama, the old goat," said Adachi. "Whatever he took, I'd like to have some. By all accounts, he was fucking someone or something steadily until he was broiled. Eighty-four years of age and still at it. He was a credit to our culture."

"Hodama," agreed Fujiwara.

Adachi had remembered how tired he was. He leaned forward. "Inspector-*san*," he said politely. "Would you be so kind as to tell me what is in that fucking box?"

"The kind of thing you would leave with someone you trusted," said Fujiwara, "if you were a prick like Hodama. Mementos of negotiations, secret conversations, and the like."

"Grrr . . ." said Adachi. "It's too late. I'm too tired. What the hell are you talking about?"

"Tapes," said Fujiwara hastily. "Just like President Nixon. Tapes."

"Banzai!" said Adachi. A thought struck him. Magnetic evidence was prone to vanish into the ether. It was not nice and physical, like paper or bloodstains. One quick pass with a powerful magnet and tape recordings were history. "Have you checked them? Is there anything on them?"

"Relax, boss," said Fujiwara. "This is really something."

THE CHIEF PROSECUTOR always dressed well but conservatively.

He favored the unostentatious gray look, reflected Adachi; the guise of the silver fox. The focus tended to be on his face and, in particular, on his eyes. Day in, day out, for decades, those eyes read the souls of men. When the prosecutor stared intently at you, you just knew that it was pointless to lie. You were aware you could not hide. You understood immediately that he did not really need to ask. It was not merely that he could read your mind: *He knew.*

Smoke and mirrors, thought Adachi. Did a trick of nature slant you in one particular direction because you looked the part, or did the look follow the occupation? Either way, the success of so much that you did was so often slanted toward how you looked when you did it.

That evening the prosecutor was dressed for a function. He looked different, less like a dedicated public servant and more like a public figure; perhaps a minister or a leading businessman. The dark-blue silk suit was of Italian cut. The white shirt gleamed like a soap-powder ad. The tie was a discreet hand-painted design. The tassled black shoes had a sheen reflecting dedication bordering on obsession.

Did Mrs. Prosecutor graft away with the polishing attachment on her Makita drill, or did Mr. Prosecutor burnish his own shoes? Somehow, Adachi regarded the latter scenario as unlikely. People's personal habits were interesting in what they revealed.

He found the way the prosecutor was dressed that evening unsettling. It did not seem to reflect the man he thought he knew. Well, he was tired. Notions tended to introduce themselves when blood sugar was low.

The tape came to an end. "There were over two hundred tapes in a fireproof safe inside Chiba-*san*'s blanket chest," said Adachi, "all neatly labeled and cross-indexed. There are some prominent names mentioned on the tapes. The most interesting tape is the one you just played. The quality is not good, but the content is compelling."

"The two speakers are Hodama himself," said the prosecutor, "and Fumio Namaka."

Adachi nodded in agreement. "Both names are mentioned in the course of the conversation, and we have already obtained separate confirmation. Hodama's reedy voice is quite distinctive. Namaka's is also clear enough. No one else seemed to be present."

"So here we have Hodama saying he is withdrawing support for the Namakas," said the prosecutor, "and giving as his reasons the financial weakness of the Namaka *keiretsu* and their links with Yaibo. Hodama, despite their long association, cannot afford scandal and to go down with a sinking ship."

"That's how it sounds," said Adachi. "It is a thirty-five-minute discussion. They go over the points several times, the way one does in that kind of conversation. The message is very clear. The Namakas are going to be ditched by their *kuromaku*—with deep regret and despite their long association."

"Are these tapes genuine?" asked the prosecutor.

"Our technical boys say they are," said Adachi slowly. "But that's a judgment, not certainty. Tape is tricky, but they have put twenty of the two hundred tapes through state-of-the-art equipment and the results indicate the genuine article. Also, they pointed out there is too much here to fake. It would be a massive job. So, best assessment is: the tapes are genuine."

Despite his words, Adachi was uneasy about the tapes. Tape was a reliable enough medium if you used it yourself and kept the evidence chain intact, but where a third party was involved he was cautious. There were all kinds of electronic tricks you could play these days. Also, the fact that some tapes were genuine did not mean all were. The sheer number of tapes would tend to suggest authenticity, but what better place, when you thought about it, to hide a couple of fakes. He resolved to check the tapes further with a speech analyst. But that would take time. Meanwhile, they would have to go with what they had.

The prosecutor closed his eyes, lost in thought. He was wearing a lapel pin, Adachi noticed: miniature crossed silver brooms; the sweeping out of corruption. It had become associated with some of those who were working to clean up Japanese politics. So far, wearers were in something of a select and extremely small minority. The average voter knew the system was deeply flawed but also knew the economic gains made by Japan and the steady progress of individual well-being. The system was imperfect, but it worked. So why change it? Power would always be a money game. That was human nature.

"Means, opportunity, and motive," said the prosecutor. "I find it hard to believe that the Namakas would turn on their *kuromaku....*"

"But," said Adachi, "there is the matter of the evidence."

"Quite so," said the prosecutor. "And the evidence is quite convincing."

"Bring them in?" said Adachi.

The prosecutor shook his head. "I think we should talk to the Namaka brothers fairly soon," he said, "but not quite yet. Let us see what we can turn up in the next couple of weeks. The indicators are clear, but a successful outcome will require more in the way of proof."

"We are working on it," said Adachi. Despite some unease, which he did his best to suppress, he could feel the case beginning to crack. The feeling was that of exhilaration, the lust of the hunter. It would give him the greatest pleasure to put the Namaka brothers behind bars.

"This is encouraging progress," said the prosecutor in dismissal. Adachi bowed respectfully. He felt tired but good.

THREE DAYS LATER, the Tokyo MPD forensic laboratory cracked the encryption code which had prevented Hodama's security video from being viewed.

The encryption technology was similar to that used to prevent unauthorized viewers from watching satellite or cable TV without a decoder. The principle was easy to understand. Finding the key to the particular code used by Hodama was another matter. The permutations seemed to be endless. It was a problem for a supercomputer, it seemed, the kind of thing that the U.S.'s worldwide eavesdropping agency, the NSA, excelled at.

In the end, thinking laterally, old-fashioned police work rather than technology was brought into play. A detailed examination of Hodama's business connections revealed a shareholding in a company that manufactured decoders. From then on, it was just a matter of talking persuasively to the company president. At first he was unwilling to cooperate.

A trip to police headquarters and a tour of some of the facilities for overnight guests worked wonders.

The lab sent over several unlocked copies of the tape which could be played on an ordinary video machine. Adachi had an initial viewing in the squad room, then took a copy back to his apartment to study at his leisure. Besides, he wanted Chifune's input; and he wanted Chifune.

Surprisingly, she was available. She tended to be elusive. She said that unpredictability stimulated ardor. Privately, Adachi thought his ardor for Chifune did not need any help. He only had to think of Tanabu-*san* for his desire to become well-nigh intolerable. Other women no longer interested him. He had tried a few times since he had started sleeping with Chifune, but the alternatives paled in comparison. It was a damn nuisance.

He was accustomed to a robust and uncomplicated sex life enjoyed in much the same physical way as a bout of *kendo*—and now his whole being was involved. It was a marvelous, awful, terrifying feeling; and a bloody nuisance. Running any murder investigation required absolute focus and concentration. And the Hodama business was not just any old slice of mayhem.

Hodama's security videos were linked to the cameras directly in front of the house and inside the main reception area. There were cameras elsewhere, but these were merely connected to monitors. The lab had intercut the tapes from the two cameras linked to recorders to give some chronological sense, but had edited out nothing.

The video had a grim documentary quality about it. There was no sound and the pictures were in black and white, but nonetheless they were compelling.

Unfortunately, they appeared to be of little help.

"Dark business suits and ski masks," said Adachi cheerfully, "and surgical gloves. These are not particularly helpful people. And note the license plates are covered with black cloth or something similar. Very professional and unfriendly."

His voice was relaxed. Chifune had no sooner entered his apartment than he had taken her on the *tatami* floor, or maybe she had taken him. It was hard to know with Chifune. She now sat naked beside him, the video controls in her hand. They were drinking chilled white wine and leaning back against beanbags.

It was a rather pleasant way, thought Adachi, to carry on an investigation. He was not naked. Almost everything had come off in the encounter, but he was still just wearing his tie—his Tokyo MPD tie at that. He lifted the mangled thing off his head and threw it like a ring at the door handle. It hung perfectly on the first shot.

"We've got the make of car, the number and build of the assailants, and the makes of several of the weapons for starters," said Chifune. "Don't be lazy. You can't expect them to wear name tags."

"Whiz it back," said Adachi. He was pleased with his VCR. Matsushita, he considered, had done him proud. It featured all the latest gadgetry, not the least of which was resolution enhancement, freeze frame, and variable-speed slow motion. If there was something to be seen, they would see it.

Chifune reran the video, and again, and again, and again. And then she noticed Adachi's revived tumescent condition and decided they both could do with some attention.

Afterward, they ran the video twice more. By now they were concentrating on the figure who seemed to be giving the orders. His face and neck were completely concealed; his suit gave off no clues, except to show that the wearer was a tall, powerful man.

The camera had caught his outstretched arms as he waved his people to surround the building. Here there was an interesting detail. Through the thin surgical glove on the left hand, the outline of a heavy ring could clearly be seen.

"Kei Namaka?" said Adachi. "The build is right, the body language is right, and he wears a ring something like that—I'll get the lab to do some photo enhancement. But hell, would he do a hit himself? He would be insane to. These people never do their own dirty work. They're insulated."

"Hodama didn't die any old way," said Chifune. "This was personal. And I think it may well be political—which is interesting."

"What do you mean?" said Adachi.

"A conventional killing gets harder to solve as time goes on," said Chifune. "A hit like Hodama brings the beneficiary out of the woodwork. I don't think we're looking closely enough at who benefits. Think about it. Power abhors a vacuum. Kill a *kuromaku* and who is likely to surface?"

"Another *kuromaku*," said Adachi slowly. "A puppetmaster—and his puppets."

"Killing Hodama may be about revenge," said Chifune, "but I think it was mostly about power. Look for a power shift."

Adachi stared at her. "What do you know?" he said.

"More than you," said Chifune, "but neither of us knows enough. I'm working on it."

"Politics!" said Adachi disgustedly.

"Not just politics," said Chifune. "There are linkages here." She stroked Adachi's cheek and then kissed him. "Powerful interests, corruption, a lot of history, and terrorism. This is a dangerous, bloody business, my love. So keep wearing your hardware."

" 'My love'?" said Adachi, looking very pleased and rather like a schoolboy.

Chifune ruffled his hair. "Figure of speech," she said. "Don't go getting ideas."

The rest of what Chifune had said slowly surfaced. "Terrorism?" he said. "What the hell is going on? What ever happened to old-fashioned murder?" He was quiet for a while. "You know," he added, "our killer may just have a sense of humor, and have made the most of the moment when he found Hodama about to have his bath, but I don't think so. I don't see this as a nice, clean political assassination. I think Hodama was meant to die in agony. The thing may be political—given who Hodama was, *must* be political—but I think the primary motive was revenge."

"Nonetheless," said Chifune, "look at the politics. Look at the realignments, the new alliances in the toy box. Look at where the strings lead."

Adachi whistled a few bars of an old Beatles song. The Beatles had been big in Japan and, when still only a kid, he had once gone to see them in the Nippon Budokan. A memorable evening. He was not sure that the present generation of much-hyped midadolescent pop stars could be defined as progress. Most Japanese singers had a short shelf life and seemed to be considered geriatric by the time they were twenty. He had a feeling they were assembled by robots somewhere and were simply replaced when they wore out. Flexible production: cars one day; pop singers the next; computer-controlled, using fuzzy logic. Your every need provided by half a dozen vast corporations and the state—or were business and the state one and the same? It was a frightening thought and not entirely fanciful. Japanese homogeneity was all very well, but like food needed salt, there was a lot to be said for a useful dash of individuality.

Speaking of which: He rolled over onto Chifune and, the weight of his upper body taken by his arms so he could look down at her, entered her. She drew up her knees to bring him deeper and returned his gaze steadily, scarcely moving. Then she reached up and stroked his face before pulling him down to her.

THE MEETING TOOK PLACE in the twenty-story Tokyo building of the electronics *keiretsu*. The head office of the group was officially in Osaka, but the chairman and direct descendant of the founder worked out of Tokyo, so the facilities there were lavish.

The first floor was a showroom displaying the latest electronic products. They ranged from voice-activated rice cookers to HDTV—high definition television. A constant stream of visitors came to gaze at this Aladdin's cave of desirable technology. In its way, the whole of the building was a showpiece for the scale and scope of the group.

The twentieth floor housed the chairman's office and other facilities for the board of directors. It was also used to demonstrate the group's expertise in state-of-the-art security products and was, therefore, totally electronically secure.

Twenty-one men sat at a V-shaped conference table. At the open end of the V, a multimedia wall brought data onto the giant screens on demand. A three-person secretariat from the confidential office of the chairman manipulated the computer controls as instructed and performed such other functions as were necessary. Minutes were kept in encrypted form then and there. No other record of the meeting was kept and no member could take notes or remove any records from the room.

The twenty-one men were the ruling council of the secret Gamma Society, which, scattered throughout Japan though heavily concentrated in the capital, was over five thousand strong in all. Members were drawn only from those in senior positions in the Japanese government, business, and academic establishment—and then only after personal recommendations and lengthy vetting.

Each of the twenty-one men in the guarded and sealed conference room wore two lapel pins, that of his work affiliation and that of the Gamma Society itself. The gamma pin was in the form of the Greek letter, and, in the few cases where it had been inadvertently worn outside a meeting, had been associated with Gaia—the environmental movement. The Gamma pin was actually an indirect way of referring to *giri,* "obligation." In this case their *giri* related to their obligations toward the well-being and health of Japanese society and in particular toward the body politic.

The Gamma Society had been set up by a small but influential group who had been concerned with the increasing power of the alliance of organized crime and corrupt politics, in what was otherwise a most successful society in many ways. The founders had initially considered combating the opposition publicly—for instance, by forming a new, clean political party and lobbying for change in some of the structures. They'd soon realized that the forces they were up against were too strongly entrenched. Head-on attacks would be fruitless and could indeed be counterproductive. Instead, they'd decided to work completely behind the scenes and, in the main, through others. It had proved to be a fruitful strategy.

Some of their more notable successes to date had come by applying the principles of the martial arts—in particular, the principle of using the strength and momentum of an opponent to defeat himself. The technique's secret lay in applying a small amount of leverage at the right place and the right time.

The photograph of just such a lever was flashed up on the giant central screen. It was of a foreigner, a *gaijin,* a tall, good-looking man with steel-gray hair worn *en brosse,* and gentle eyes in a strong, well-proportioned face. He looked to be in his early forties, perhaps younger.

The photo was captioned "Hugo Fitzduane."

One of the gathering, using a laser pointer, commenced the briefing. The dossier was extensive.

12

A fter a couple of months at Duncleeve, eating well, resting, exercising, and enjoying the beauty of his island, Fitzduane was starting to feel human again and ready for the next phase. He was looking forward to the arrival of his friend.

Kilmara flew in and landed on the new airstrip that Fitzduane had arranged to have constructed down the center of the island.

The strip was short, but hard-surfaced and well-drained and entirely adequate for both the aircraft the Ranger general was using and the new machine that Fitzduane had purchased. Both were Pilatus Norman Britten Islanders, sturdy aerial workhorses capable of carrying up to nine passengers or over a ton of cargo.

Fitzduane ushered Kilmara into a black-painted Hughes helicopter and they took off immediately, as if leaving a hot landing zone.

"Sometimes it's useful having money," said Fitzduane over the intercom. "I got started on this on my second week in the hospital. Let me give you the rationale and the grand tour. As you'll see, I have made a few changes."

They flew over Fitzduane's castle. Fitzduane pointed. Kilmara could clearly see the saucer shape on top of the gatehouse.

"I like the isolation here," Fitzduane continued, "but this business has made me face up to the fact that being cut off from the world has its downside. You can do nothing today without communications, so I put in a satellite telephone dish and a slew of extra lines. We can now talk to anyone anywhere in the world without fucking with the local exchange. And we can transfer computer data the same way, using high-speed modems.

"Next on the list was the requirement to get people and goods in and out fast. This machine and the Islander now mean we can link up with Dublin in less than two hours. In addition, both aircraft are fitted with FLIR modules and other observation equipment and can retransmit that information in real time to the ground."

The helicopter looped around Duncleeve. Kilmara looked at the FLIR screen as instructed. He could just make out a series of metal posts well spaced apart.

"Microwave fencing, TV cameras, and other similar goodies," said Fitzduane. "Surprisingly affordable technology these days. No system is foolproof, but the castle itself is now almost impossible to approach undetected, and we have radar to keep an eye on the sky."

The pilot banked and flew out to sea and followed the coastline to the sprawling Victorian Gothic castle that had been the school known as Draker College. When Kilmara had last seen it, it had been boarded up. Now the windows glistened with fresh paint, the grounds had been tidied up, and there were cars parked in the courtyard. It, too, was surrounded with microwave fencing and other detection equipment.

"You've had your beady eye on the island for training the Rangers for some time," said Fitzduane. "Fair enough. You've got a deal. I need security and you need space. You can hang your hat in a wing of Draker and train to the seaward end of the island."

"What about rent?" asked Kilmara, ever conscious of budgets.

"Peppercorn—as long as you are running the Rangers. The whole deal is cancellable at a month's notice. I get to keep any improvements. You guys have to make good any damage. Oh, yes—and the whole island gets classified as a restricted military area. I want to do some building and I don't want to get delayed by filing planning applications."

He spoke into his intercom, and the helicopter banked and headed low and fast for Duncleeve. "We'll talk later. Our visitors are due soon."

They landed in the courtyard of the castle. Shortly afterward, a Range Rover rolled up from the airstrip and out stepped three Japanese.

The first was Yoshokawa. The second, a short, distinguished-looking man, was a stranger to Fitzduane. The third visitor was an extremely attractive woman.

The second man was introduced as Saburo Enoke, the Deputy Superintendent-General of the Tokyo Metropolitan Police, better known to his men as the Spider.

The woman was a Miss Chifune Tanabu. She was just presenting her card when the heavens opened and sheeted rain poured down on the exposed group. They fled inside.

THE GREAT HALL had been equipped for the briefing. Various audio-visual aids were in place. Pinboards on wheeled stands lined one wall.

Outside, the skies had darkened and rain lashed against the long glass wall. Fitzduane suggested sliding shut the *shoji* screens to keep out the beautiful but depressing picture, but his visitors smiled and shook their heads.

"We're used to the restricted landscape of an urban environment," said Yoshokawa. "The sight of the open sea is a rare pleasure—whatever the weather."

The assembled group took their seats, and Yoshokawa addressed the meeting.

"This is an exceptional gathering," he said, "because matters will be discussed here today which normally would never be communicated between parties of such differing backgrounds. National interests are involved, and no nation wishes to air its flaws and deficiencies in public. However, we are confident that we are dealing with people we can trust and that we have a mutual interest. I now defer to Enoke-*san,* the Deputy Superintendent-General."

The Spider stood up. He spoke excellent English with a strong American accent. He spoke slowly, and in such a manner that it was clear what he said was carefully considered.

"We have much to be proud of in Japan, but like every country, we have situations and elements which are an embarrassment. Naturally, we do not like to publicize those negative elements. Nonetheless, in this case it is clear that there are advantages in cooperation. It has taken us some time to reach this conclusion. I regret that it has taken so long, and I can assure you all here that there will be no delays in the future. We are committed to see this matter through to a successful conclusion.

"I will now give you back to General Kilmara. He has been conducting the investigation here and is best qualified to present our mutual findings. But before I do"—he bowed deeply to Fitzduane—"I would like to apologize on behalf of our countrymen for the injuries you have suffered, Fitzduane-*san*. Activities of this dissident minority are a source of great embarrassment to us. We are deeply sorry."

Fitzduane, sitting at the head of the table, acknowledged the bow and smiled. Privately, he was getting impatient. He already knew some of the pieces, but he wanted to know more. Above all he wanted content, not platitudes. He hoped his guests had flown twelve hours or more for more than a few elegantly delivered words of apology.

Kilmara stood up. "What I am about to say is a distillation of five months' work by my unit, with contributions from many different intelligence sources. And I should add that the most beneficial help has come from my friends in Japan. For reasons that will be obvious, this is a particularly sensitive investigation from their point of view. Not just security issues are involved, but also political matters at the highest level. It is therefore vital that confidentiality be maintained."

Kilmara turned toward Fitzduane.

"You know that the attack on you and Boots was by Yaibo, and that the second attack was also mounted by Yaibo, even though the actual assault team were members of IRAP. We have now ascertained a definite link between the Hangman and Yaibo going back over nearly a decade. In-depth interrogation of Sasada confirmed that your killing was to be a straightforward matter of revenge for the Hangman, and was expected to be achieved without difficulty.

"Sasada," continued Kilmara, "was not supposed to be directly involved with the hospital hit, but he exceeded his instructions. He was an overzealous company man. His conscientiousness may have been ill-advised, but it has proved fortunate for us. He has provided the first actual direct link between Yaibo and the Namaka *keiretsu*. The Namaka organization is headed by two brothers, Kei and Fumio. They have a security chief called Kitano. According to our friend Sasada, Kitano issued the actual order to have you killed, Hugo—but Kitano does nothing without the Namaka brothers' approval."

The Spider indicated that he wanted to contribute, so Kilmara gestured that he should proceed. The Japanese were fiercely proud, and he knew how difficult it was for them to discuss any of the internal workings of their system. Nevertheless, he could sense a growing climate of mutual trust in the room and he was delighted that the DSG was abandoning his formal posture.

The Spider explained the background of the Namakas and something about the Japanese political system and their influence within it.
"For some time," he said, "we have suspected a link between the
Namakas and Yaibo based upon an examination of who has benefited
from Yaibo killings. Nonetheless, all Yaibo activities did not directly
benefit the Namakas and we never had any hard proof. Further, the
Namakas had considerable political influence up to—and including—
ministerial level. It was not, and still is not, possible to just pick them
up and sweat the truth out of them. Though we have been tempted."

The DSG made no mention of the manner in which the Rangers'
prisoner had been interrogated, which now made him unusable as a
witness. He had been extremely angry when he had first heard, but he
was a pragmatist. The interrogation had taken place within the context
of an extreme situation. Sasada would undoubtedly have kept silent
otherwise. As it was, though they had no evidence against the Namakas
they could use in court, the Namaka link with Yaibo had moved beyond
speculation.

Fitzduane was picking up a nuance. "The situation with the Namakas has changed?" he said.

The DSG nodded. "Has changed and is changing," he said with a
slight smile. "Specifically, Hodama, a *kuromaku*—and for decades the
core of their political backing—has been murdered. Secondly, a
change in public opinion is beginning. We have a sophisticated economy and we would like a political system to match. More and more
ordinary Japanese are getting fed up with money politics and corruption. Groups are organizing and lobbying for change. It is becoming
less easy for corrupt politicians and their allies to suppress investigations and operate with impunity."

"Who killed Hodama?" asked Fitzduane.

The DSG pursed his lips. "This is a confusing matter," he said. "The
position of the Namakas has been weakened as a result of his death, but
the evidence points to the Namakas themselves as having ordered his
death. The theory is that Hodama was going to publicly abandon the
Namakas because they may be in financial trouble—and he was killed
as the lesser of two evils."

"You have conclusive evidence against the Namakas?" said Fitzduane.

"Unfortunately, we do not," said the DSG. "For some months, the
case against them increased steadily, and then the investigation ground

to a halt. Everything points towards the Namakas, but we can prove nothing. Our inquiries continue under an excellent man, but for all practical purposes we are . . ." He searched for the word:

"Stuck," offered Fitzduane.

"Quite so," said the DSG.

There was a long silence. Kilmara was tempted to speak, but he wanted to encourage the Japanese to continue if he would. It had been the devil of a job to win him over in the first place. Now he was anxious to get the Spider off the sidelines and operationally involved.

The next action would best be suggested by the Japanese. It must appear to be the Spider's idea. He would be committed to it better if he actually spoke the words. Of course, Fitzduane was going to go to Japan anyway, but politically things would go so much better if it appeared as a Japanese initiative. This was the strategy that Kilmara had sold to Fitzduane, and he and Yoshokawa had been working on from their respective ends for some time while Fitzduane got himself fully fit.

But would the Spider bite? Kilmara thought it likely, given that they had come this far, but there was the matter of human chemistry. If the Spider did not like the look of Fitzduane, all bets were off.

"Fitzduane-*san*," said the Spider cautiously, "when do you think you will be fully fit?"

Fitzduane laughed. "Pretty soon," he said. "I appreciate the concern, but why do you ask?"

The Spider looked at Kilmara and then at Yoshokawa. Kilmara smiled and Yoshokawa nodded.

The Spider drew himself up in his chair. "Fitzduane-*san*," he said, "we would like you to come and join our investigation in Japan. We would be deeply honored."

Bull's-eye! thought Kilmara. Then he nearly strangled Fitzduane. There was such a thing as playing too hard to get.

"I am equally honored by your invitation, Deputy Superintendent-General-*san*," said Fitzduane, "but I do not speak your language and I am not a trained investigator. I'm not sure I would be that much use to you." Internally, he had felt a rush of exhilaration as the Spider had spoken, because at last he would be taking the fight to the enemy, but Yoshokawa had advised that a certain modest reluctance would be in order.

Yoshokawa spoke. "The Deputy Superintendent-General knows your reputation," he said. "He knows what you did in Bern. He is familiar with the story of the Hangman. He knows how you saved the life of my son. He does not make this request lightly."

"The simple fact is," said Kilmara, "that despite all the precautions, we can't keep you safe here indefinitely. That being so, there is a lot to be said for seizing the initiative and taking the fight to the enemy. The DSG thinks your presence in Japan would force them to take some action which could open this whole thing up."

"Fitzduane-*san*," came a voice from the end of the table that had not been heard till now. "I hesitate to put it this directly, but you have a choice. You can either remain a target or act as bait." Fitzduane looked at the speaker, Chifune Tanabu, with surprise and some amusement.

"Tanabu-*san* is, perhaps, a little blunt, but in essence she is quite correct," said the Spider. "You will be well-guarded, of course, by our best people. However, I should add that it will not be possible for you to carry a firearm. Even in the circumstances, that would be quite impermissible."

Fitzduane laughed so much, his leg started to hurt. He stood up to exercise and still could not stop laughing. Tears streamed down his cheeks. He had not felt this good in months. The Spider looked uncomfortable at first, but soon everyone was laughing.

When he had calmed down, Fitzduane produced some drinks and the meeting took a break. He thanked God—or whoever ran things—for having a decided sense of humor. It looked like he would be going manhunting with little more for protection than his ability to talk his way out of trouble. And he had the feeling that verbal diplomacy, in this context, was not going to be enough.

Still, he and Kilmara had anticipated this problem.

Fitzduane would not be permitted to carry a gun, but he would not be entirely without weapons.

· PARIS, FRANCE

May 28

Since Yaibo had not been completely successful at eliminating the organ-grinder, Reiko Oshima had decided to even the score with a monkey—a monkey which would surely draw Fitzduane out of his little fortress of an island, she thought with satisfaction.

Reiko Oshima's reputation rivaled that of Carlos the Jackal.

It was based not only on the savagery of Yaibo's actions, but also on her appearance. Her gentle beauty was a startling contrast to the mayhem she caused. She was a natural for the media. The sobriquet "Lethal Angel" had soon followed.

Oshima's file was high in the pile of every counterterrorist organization and her photo was prominent on every passport control of significance, but she still managed to crisscross the globe with apparent ease. She was not just a leader and a planner. She was an activist who thrived on risk. She liked to get blood on her hands. And she knew that the media impact of an incident in which she was seen to have participated would be much enhanced.

The secret of Oshima's ability to travel unhindered by the security services lay in her distinctive appearance.

The authorities were looking for a beautiful Japanese woman in her late thirties. They were quite uninterested in a plump, bucktoothed matron with graying hair in her early fifties who was touring Europe with a party of other schoolteachers. They were quite used to Japanese tourists. The hard currency was welcome, and they gave little trouble. The tourists had a fondness, which they could afford to indulge given the strength of the yen, for European luxury goods like those of Gucci and Cardin. Further, despite the steady publicity given to the Japanese Red Army, Yaibo, and various right-wing organizations, the Japanese were not readily associated with terrorism. The typical terrorist in Europe was profiled as being from the Middle East or possibly Irish. Japanese were generally perceived—quite reasonably, given the law-abiding nature of most—as not a threat.

Oshima, plumped out around the middle, in sensible, flat, lace-up leather shoes, gray suitably applied to her hair, bespectacled and with her cheeks padded and her dental plate in place over her real teeth, entered France with her fellow teachers in a rented minibus and headed toward Paris.

No one gave them a second glance. In her opinion mainland Europe, with a dense population in which to hide and internal borders coming down, was child's play to move around. Certain other countries, like island Britain, were not so easy. Israel, no matter what the disguise, was a problem. The Israelis did not pay lip service to counterterrorism. They were permanently at the sharp end. They took the tracking down of terrorists very seriously indeed.

The greatest difficulties Oshima and her team encountered as they entered Paris were driving and parking. They stayed on the *periphique,* the multilane ring-road that circled Paris, for one full circumference before managing to find the right exit, and emerged shaken, convinced that French drivers were a special group of maniacs. This judgment was vindicated as they sped through narrow side streets, and were hooted at by impatient Parisians every time they attempted to slow down. It was confirmed when they tried to find a place to park.

As a safe haven, Libya had its merits, thought the Lethal Angel, but with its limited traffic and vast open spaces, it was poor training for the cut and thrust of congested mainland Europe.

The group consoled themselves with the prospect of a good French meal. Unfortunately, they arrived at that hour in the evening when every Parisian simultaneously decides to eat and will brook no interference from amateurs like foreigners. All the restaurants they tried were full. After the eighth indifferent shrug of rejection, they dined on Big Macs, fries, and chocolate milk shakes at McDonald's.

The food reminded them of Tokyo.

PARIS, FRANCE

May 29

The *salle d'armes* had been established in the late sixteenth century—about the time that dueling with a thin blade had become a serious pastime in France—and had continued to be well-patronized, with only a few brief interruptions, since that time.

During the revolution, since skill with a sword was considered to be an aristocratic attribute, the building had temporarily become a brothel. During the Nazi occupation, it had been an officers' club. Those interludes apart, the *salle* had operated continuously for roughly four hundred years as a place where one human being learned to kill or defeat another human being with a long piece of pointed steel.

Christian de Guevain considered the *salle* a fine monument to the human condition.

The building was in the fashionable 16th Arrondissement, conveniently situated near the Bois de Vincennes military barracks, and was no more than a few minutes from his bank, his mistress, his home, and his favorite restaurant. de Guevain could work, fence, sport, eat well, and be back in time to put the kids to bed and watch TV with his wife, if he was so inclined, without straining himself excessively. He had, he considered, a most civilized existence.

He had taken Fitzduane's cautionary words to heart, though without enthusiasm. His black Citroën was armored and was driven by an armed bodyguard. A second bodyguard sat in the front passenger seat. The windows were tinted to hinder recognition. He switched cars and routes regularly. He no longer fenced at a time when the *salle* was relatively open. Now he fenced outside normal hours with only one or two chosen opponents, and arrangements were made in advance under conditions of some secrecy.

Nonetheless, there were patterns to his life. Three or four times a week—although there was some variation as to day and time—de Guevain could be found in the *salle*. He was determined to hone his skill so that he could defeat Fitzduane. de Guevain had mastered the longbow and was already way superior to the Irishman. Now he was determined to do the same with the sword. He was fiercely competitive by nature. And besides, he enjoyed the sheer speed and elegance of the sport, and the exhilaration of the exercise.

The black Citroën entered the Rue Jarnac and stopped outside the gray cut-stone facade of the *salle*. The passenger bodyguard got out and punched a code into the digital lock. The double doors opened and the Citroën entered the courtyard inside. Behind them, the heavy doors locked shut. de Guevain felt a sense of reassurance. He was secure in familiar territory. Followed by his bodyguards, he bounded up the worn stone stairs to the *salle* at the top. The long room had a woodblock floor and arched ceiling. The walls were lined with historic weapons and old engravings. The names of the masters were inscribed in a frieze that ran around the top of the paneling. To de Guevain, the room was the essence of his France: a sense of purpose, élan, glory, the strength of tradition, the reassurance of history, the continuity of privilege, a manifestation of power.

The huge room was empty. "Make yourself at home, boys," said de Guevain. "I'm going to change." He headed for the locker room where Chappuy would be suiting up. Pierre, one of the bodyguards, moved to check the locker room, but de Guevain waved him aside impatiently. Vincent, his partner, smiled and took a seat. He was less intrusive.

Sometimes this security business could get out of hand, thought de Guevain. He was of two minds whether to continue it at all. He did not particularly enjoy conducting all his affairs under close scrutiny. God alone knew what would turn up in some glossy magazine in the years ahead. "The Private Life of a Paris Banker—by his bodyguard." He shuddered. France had privacy laws, but the rest of the continent was full of media that loved that kind of thing.

The locker room, a bright white-painted space divided into three aisles by rows of tall wooden lockers dating from an earlier century, had a tiled floor and a high beamed ceiling. He could hear the sound of dripping as he entered. Someone had obviously not turned a shower off. And yet the sound seemed closer.

He could smell something. His skin prickled. He would never forget that odor. He had first encountered it as a young man a quarter of a century earlier. It brought him back to Algeria, to the paratroops, to the broken bodies of the freshly dead. It reminded him of the slaughter on Fitzduane's island.

Blood. Death. Recent death.

Help was at hand, but his mouth was suddenly completely dry. Something caught his eye. He looked up. A thin braided climber's rope hung down from one of the beams. It was taut, as if something was suspended from it. He could not see what it was, because the rope terminated in the next aisle.

de Guevain licked his lips as best he could. As if compelled, he walked slowly down his aisle of lockers and turned into the aisle where the rope hung. He could hear a coughing sound from the *salle,* but his mind was focused on what he was about to see.

A huge irregular pool of blood stained the tiles and leached under the lockers. A bloody pile of human matter was at its center and snaked upward. de Guevain's eye followed it. The naked corpse of his fencing partner, Chappuy, was suspended upside down from the rope. The flesh was completely white, virtually drained of blood. The body had been cut open with one blow from the groin to the throat. Entrails hung to the ground.

de Guevain was momentarily numb with shock and fear. He gave a cry of desperation and horror, more animal than human, and ran from the locker room into the *salle.*

The action was futile. His bodyguards, Pierre and Vincent, the marks of bullet perforations from automatic-weapons fire clearly visible, lay sprawled in bloody heaps.

He was facing a semicircle of five people. Four held silenced submachine guns. At the apex was a woman, a very beautiful Japanese woman.

She held a sword.

FITZDUANE'S ISLAND, IRELAND

May 29

Kathleen was in Boots's room in the Keep when she heard the faint cry, but at first did not know what to make of it and then dismissed it.

It was not repeated, and the mind sometimes played tricks in an old house when you were tired. A storm was raging outside and the wind off the sea whistled around the old stonework, and with such a backdrop, sometimes the cry of an owl or some other night creature sounded eerily human.

It was after midnight and all the guests had retired, so now she was going about the final business of the house, checking Boots. She enjoyed Boots and they had become very close. Asleep, he looked adorable. His bed was dry. He was well-covered. All was in order.

There was an unusual draft on the stairs, and the hangings over the double-glazed arrow slits blew in the breeze and the air was cold and chill. Methodically, she checked each of the slim windows, but all were closed. She had already checked the external doors, but she verified it again by looking at the security alarm repeater.

That left only the door to the fighting platform on the roof.

As she passed Fitzduane's room, she noticed his door was open and his room empty. A coil of fax papers lay on the floor by the doorway. She picked it up to put it somewhere where it would not be trodden on, and glanced at it as she did so. And her blood ran cold.

She read on. There was a handwritten note from Kilmara and it had clearly been sent immediately following a telephone conversation between the two men. It was a translation of a French police report, and photographs had been faxed with the text. The photographs had been transmitted at high resolution, and though they were in black and white and the quality was far from perfect, the essential details were all too apparent. Nausea swept over her and she felt bile rise in her throat. The papers fell from her hand, and she collapsed against the ancient oak doorway and retched.

Suddenly, the significance of that earlier cry hit home, and, near panic, she turned and ran up the worn stone stairs.

Thick heavy ice-cold rain driven by wind gusting over sixty miles an hour hit her as she emerged onto the fighting platform. Instantly, she was soaked and chilled to the bone, and temporarily blinded as her hair was driven across her eyes.

She had a sense of complete disorientation as the horror of what she had read combined with her fatigue and the violence of the storm.

She reeled backwards, confused and in shock, and then felt a violent blow against her lower back as she smashed into the battlements. A gust of rain-sodden wind hit her again and she scrabbled desperately for a handhold, suddenly conscious of where she was and the danger of being swept through the battlement crenellations to fall onto the rocks and heaving sea below.

The granite fortifications were ice cold and slippery to her hands, but she gained enough purchase to pull herself upright and regain her balance.

She swept her hair out of her eyes. She tried to shout for Fitzduane, but her cry was lost in the fury of the storm. Wind, sea, thunder, and rain combined in a terrifying cacophony.

The darkness was near absolute. Only a dim shaft of light from the stairway provided any illumination, and that was obscured by the rain and lost in the blackness of the night.

Fitzduane was there. He must be. This was where he liked to come to think, she knew, even in weather as vile as this. This is where he came to watch the sunrise and the sunsets and just to feel the force of the elements. Duncleeve and this wild land were deep in his blood.

She had asked him about it and he had tried to explain, but it was clear that words alone only hinted at what he felt.

"It's impossible to describe," he had said, with a slight smile. "I like the sheer aggression of the wind, violent and exhilarating at the same time, and the sting of the spray and smell of iodine from the sea, and the sense of being as one with all this incredible beautiful energy. And it's part of my childhood and part of what I am. And that is really all I can say."

He was an impossible man, with the spirit of an adventurer and the soul of a poet. And that was a terrifying combination in a world that was reckless with life.

But she loved him. Foolish and impossible though it was, she loved him. And that carried a burden. It was almost certainly futile, but she was responsible for this man. For the time she had, she would do what she could. Everything she could.

This is where he would come if he was deeply troubled, hurt, grieving, desperate . . . as he would be, because Christian de Guevain was dead and he was a friend and his death was horrible. Truly, a thing of horror.

And yet there was nothing.

The wind gusted again, this time from a different direction, and there was a crash as the door was blown shut.

Now the blackness of the night was absolute.

Kathleen went down on one knee, her head bowed, her fists clenched, as she fought panic and tried consciously to assess the situation.

It was ridiculous. She had no reason to be afraid, she told herself. Darkness in itself posed no danger, and she had been here literally dozens of times. It was not some strange cellar reeking of menace. This was no more than the flat roof, the fighting platform, of Fitzduane's Castle, and should be safe and familiar.

But she could not see. She was blind. And the storm was of an intensity that could blow her over the edge of the platform if she did not take care.

Sheer terror coursed through her as a hard, wet, snakelike body lashed at her and wrapped itself around her neck. She rose to her feet and her hands scrabbled at her throat as she fought to free herself.

A gust of wind found her and blew her backwards, and the grip on her throat tightened and she was choking.

Suddenly, her fingertips told her what her attacker was, and relief coursed through her as she unwound the familiar rope. One end of the flagpole line had worked loose and, whipped by the wind, had caught her as she stood. Every morning, the Fitzduane standard was hoist over the castle, and every evening, at sunset, it was lowered. Boots loved the practice, and many times she had helped him with the rope. The texture was familiar, and now that she realized what it was, it was reassuring.

She could not see, but she could feel and she could think.

She used the rope to guide herself to the flagpole mounted in one corner of the platform. She could feel the painted wood of the pole and the metal of the lightning conductor that ran up one side. Now she could orient herself. Better yet, her fingers touched the casing of the external floodlight switches.

She pulled the handles down one after another, neither remembering nor caring which was the right switch for the roof alone, and the mind-numbing blackness was erased as if a curtain had been whipped aside, and within seconds the whole castle was lit up. The battlements were silhouetted. The courtyard below was a pool of light.

It was a sight from the ancient myths. The sheets of gusting rain twisting and turning made the glowing castle seem to float and shimmer. It was unreal, something from a dream.

Fitzduane stood on the other side of platform, blinking in the sudden light as if woken from a daze. He was wearing only indoor clothing and was completely soaked.

Kathleen ran across to him and took him in her arms. His body was trembling and icy cold, and on his face was a look of utter despair.

She felt strong and certain. She had seen this man come from the edge of death through weeks of pain, and he had always endured with courage. Never before had there been even a hint of despair. But now he had been pushed beyond endurance and he needed help as never before. And she was there.

She led him off the platform and closed the heavy door behind her, and the violence of the storm was immediately muted.

She took him to his bedroom below and stripped off their clothes and stood with him in a hot shower, holding him as some warmth came back into their bodies. Then she put him into bed and lit a log fire in the old stone fireplace and soon the room was warm. But still he trembled, despite the heat of the room and the comforting weight of the bedclothes. And naked she took him into her arms and held his face to her breasts as if he were a young child. And he cried. And Kathleen cried with him until they slept.

———

KATHLEEN WOKE near dawn. The blazing log fire had died down but still glowed. Fitzduane slept in her arms, but he was restless.

She stroked him, massaging his back gently and then caressing down to his thighs. Soon she felt him hardening and she reached down and took him in her hand, parted her thighs, and bent her knees and slid him into her. She was warm and wet, and her need was total.

Fitzduane awoke with a feeling of extraordinary sensuality suffusing him. Long legs gripped him. Soft, firm breasts cushioned him. Her hands touched him in the most intimate places. He could feel her breath, and it was sweet.

His lips found Kathleen's and their tongues met and he could feel her nipples hard against him. At first his thrusts were slow and regular, but then her intensity beneath him increased and her tongue was in his ear and her breath grew rasping with passion.

He had no independent thoughts and no control. All he could focus on was this all-encompassing healing sexuality, a force made of physical sensation and waves of love.

Kathleen climaxed first, her body shuddering with release and a long cry of passion on her lips, and then she gripped him very tight and he came with enormous power and it seemed his orgasm would never stop. And then it was over.

THEY SLEPT AGAIN in each other's arms, then Fitzduane got the fire going again and went and made tea and fresh orange juice and they talked in bed.

Unspoken was the thought that they had broken the rules, that this was something they had agreed not to do, that they were friends and not lovers and that now things were more complicated and that, perhaps, this was not the way it should be. All of this was true, but there was also the shared belief that what had happened was nothing but good.

Eventually and reluctantly, the talk moved to de Guevain. Fitzduane sat upright in the bed, staring into the fire as he talked, and Kathleen lay beside him, her arms around his waist, sometimes stroking him. He talked about how they had met, and fencing together, and his friend's family and the good times they had had together; and eventually, he spoke of the manner of Christian de Guevain's death. It was so horrible that Kathleen wanted to stop him, but he seemed to need to talk it through, to hear the words again so that he could accept them.

"Really, the reports and photographs said most of it," said Fitzduane grimly, "but they did not explain the significance of the method used. Ironically, Christian would have understood. We both studied edged weapons and the customs surrounding them. And one of the great debates was the efficacy of Western weapons contrasted with the Japanese. Japanese *katana* are considered by many to be the supreme examples of the swordmaker's art. They went to extraordinary lengths to achieve this.

"In medieval times in Japan, a sword had to be capable of cutting through the heavy metal and leather armor worn by warriors and still inflict a mortal wound with a single blow. This demanded blades with outstanding attributes, and since swords were handmade one at a time without the consistency of mass-production standards, the testing of swords was an important business. A sword that passed its tests was signed in gold by the examiner on the sword's *nakago,* or tang. Swords that failed were melted down to make spears—weapons for the lower orders.

"Thick rolls of straw were sometimes used for testing. Human-body testing was preferred and was common. Often, the *samurai* who tested swords was licensed by the *shogun* to execute condemned criminals. This supplied live bodies for testing, and the process was conducted as a formal ceremony. There were witnesses, special clothing was worn, particular strokes were made, and a certificate of the results was issued. The sword used was equipped with a special testing handle made from two pieces of hard wood with adjustable holes secured by metal bands, which allowed maximum force to be exerted while carrying out the testing cuts.

"It was not unusual, after the initial cuts had dismembered the body, for the pieces to be stacked up again and again until there was no piece of flesh left much larger than a hand or foot.

"And that was how Christian de Guevain was found. And to rub home the callous horror of it, a certificate was left by the bastards: Yaibo—the Cutting Edge."

Fitzduane bent his head. He felt rage, disgust, nausea, sadness. Action and reaction; this bloody business called terrorism never ended.

But it could be contained. Individual groups could be destroyed. Another would doubtless spring up, but that would be tomorrow's battle.

He focused on what needed to be done now. Then he looked down at Kathleen. "And about us . . ."

Kathleen looked at him steadily. Her face was glowing, her eyes loving. "Don't talk about the future, Hugo," she said, with calm emphasis. And then she smiled and ran her lips across his loins before looking up at him. "This is about us and now. Make love to me."

B

FITZDUANE'S ISLAND, IRELAND

June 5

Yoshokawa and the Spider had departed the following morning, their mood somber after they heard the news of de Guevain.

After they had left, Chifune stayed, and for a further week took Fitzduane through the files she had brought with her and prepared him in detail.

Fitzduane was strained and drawn for the first couple of days, but then he snapped out of his depression and reverted to his normal equable nature.

The manner of Christian de Guevain's terrible death was far from forgotten, but publicly Fitzduane preferred to focus on the happier memories of his friend. That would be the way Christian would want it, he thought. Grief returned in waves despite his best efforts, but mostly he was successful in hiding it. He also planned, with quiet intensity, an appropriate retribution.

Their groundwork complete, Fitzduane and Chifune flew to Dublin in the Islander and then on to Heathrow, London, by Aer Lingus. At Heathrow they switched to the international terminal and boarded a Virgin flight for Tokyo. The flight, via Helsinki and St. Petersburg, was to take over twelve hours.

AT 35,000 FEET somewhere over Siberia, most of the passengers were asleep, Chifune among them, her breathing deep and regular. The flight attendant had brought blankets and Fitzduane had tucked one around his sleeping companion. He looked at her for a long moment. She was small, slight, elegant, and very beautiful, but in a markedly un-Western way. Compared to Etan's leggy attractiveness or Kathleen's voluptuousness, Chifune was almost insubstantial. Yet, viewed without preconceptions, she was quite lovely.

He reclined his seat and closed his eyes. His chest wound had healed completely and his leg was now virtually fully recovered. The endless exercises and training had paid off. He was now actually fitter than he had been in some years. God knows, he was going to need every edge. Third-party protection could be relied upon just so far. He would have felt much happier if carrying a firearm. On this point, the Spider had been obdurate.

The Japanese had a history of antipathy toward firearms. During their closed period, the Shogun had structured society in a strictly hierarchical fashion and guns had been seen as its antithesis.

Anyone could use a gun regardless of rank.

This would not do. Accordingly, although guns had been used widely in Japan in the fifteenth century, from the sixteenth century on they had been virtually banned. The peasants were forbidden to be armed. Only the various ranks of *samurai* were permitted to be armed, and even then only with swords, bows, and spears. So who said you could never turn back technological developments? The Japanese rejection of the gun had worked for nearly three hundred years.

Fitzduane had been well-briefed on the Hodama-Namaka-Yaibo triangle. He had been given an extensive dossier on the whole business, including a detailed summary of the police investigation to date. The file included photos of the principals, and he had been shown covert police videos. He felt he was beginning to know the opposition. He was even beginning to develop some theories as to what was going on.

Fitzduane's mind wandered onto the concept of "degrees of separation," the thesis that everybody, even in a world of five billion people, was only a handful of contacts away from everyone else. You always knew someone who knew someone who knew someone.

For instance, a perusal of the file revealed a shared interest with Kei Namaka in medieval weaponry. Namaka had even written several articles on Japanese arms for the Medieval Warrior's Society. Fitzduane was also a member.

In addition, Yoshokawa and the Namakas, as first-rank businessmen,

were connected through the Keidanren, the powerful Japanese employers' association. The Keidanren was a major provider of finance for
the LPD, the party whose strings Hodama had helped to pull before
coming to a rather unpleasant end.

In Japan, it was not considered polite to approach an established figure directly. An introduction by a mutual friend or business contact of
the appropriate status was essential. In Japan, everything and everybody was ranked. Yoshokawa-*san* would make the appropriate introduction. He scarcely knew the Namakas, but as the chairman of
Yoshokawa Electronics and a fellow member of the Keidanren, he was
entirely appropriate.

All in all, the whole damn thing was connected in one way or another. More and more it seemed to Fitzduane that the world was
becoming a very small place. Very small and very dangerous.

He thought of Kathleen and Boots and what he was leaving behind,
and then focused on what must be done.

Much later, he slept.

TOKYO, JAPAN

June 6

His uniformed driver, in the front row of the crowd at the arrivals gate,
was holding up in his white-gloved hands a sign labeled "Namaka Industries" and bearing the group logo.

The security chief himself, Toshiro Kitano, was standing well back.
As a senior executive, he would normally have sent an underling to
greet someone at the airport, but this visitor was important. He was the
chairman of a Japanese financial institution based in London who, according to the late Hodama, possessed a creative approach toward arbi-
trage and stock manipulation. The Namakas wanted to tap into his
expertise and had been courting him for many months. The formalities
would have to be observed punctiliously if negotiations were to be con-
cluded successfully.

Kitano regarded waiting at airports as an activity he could do without. His driver could be counted on to spot the new arrival, so he was
daydreaming absentmindedly. He nearly had a seizure when a tall,

broad-shouldered *gaijin* metamorphosed in the middle distance into someone he thought had been left for near-dead in Ireland. His heart pounded so loudly, he felt that the people around him must be able to hear. His mouth went absolutely dry. A vein in his throat started to twitch.

This Fitzduane business had initially seemed an easy matter, and yet here was this *gaijin* of no consequence, not only fitter-looking than a man of his age had any right to be, but here in Tokyo! This was appalling. It was unforgivable. It would make for the most terrible loss of face.

The chairman that Kitano had been expecting approached through the crowd, guided by the driver. As he approached the Namaka director, he expected that Kitano would recognize him, show pleasure at his arrival after such a long and arduous trip, and bow deeply. These were the minimum courtesies he could expect.

Instead, Kitano, even after being respectfully reminded by his driver, stared like some idiot peasant.

The chairman's face froze.

I must kill this barbarian before anyone knows he is here, thought Kitano. Here and now amid all these people, it is impossible. I must find out where he is going, where he is staying. He ran toward the exit, just in time to see the *gaijin* stepping into a car. Frantically, he searched his pockets for a pen to write down the license-plate number.

THE ONE THING Fitzduane knew about Tokyo Airport was that only someone who wanted to take out a second mortgage took a cab from there into the city center. The experienced traveler took the limousine, which cost a fraction of the amount and was actually a small bus.

The bus was unnecessary. Yoshokawa-*san*, a broad welcoming smile on his face, met Fitzduane and Tanabu-*san* in the terminal and guided them into a waiting car. The skies were low, gray, and unfriendly-looking, and it was raining. He had been expecting cherry blossoms and sun. He thought to himself that to travel halfway around the world to get the same appalling weather as Ireland was ridiculous. Worse, it was hot and humid.

Yoshokawa caught his skyward look and laughed: "I'm sorry," he said, "it's the rainy season. We call it 'plum rain.' "

"We call it 'having a nice soft day' in Ireland," said Fitzduane, "but the stuff is still wet. When does it end?"

"It has just begun," said Yoshokawa.

"Fitzduane-*san*," said Chifune, "I fear you have spent too much time with our files and not enough reading guidebooks. Did we explain about earthquakes?"

"No," said Fitzduane.

"Tokyo is in an earthquake zone," said Chifune, smiling faintly, "and small tremors are very common. In 1923, there was an earthquake here in which a hundred and forty thousand people lost their lives."

"When is the next big one due?" said Fitzduane.

"Soon enough," said Chifune, "but I would not worry. I think more-immediate risks will come from other sources."

"Tanabu-*san*," said Fitzduane. "You are an unending source of consolation."

DETECTIVE SUPERINTENDENT ADACHI was feeling somewhat ground down by the many months of the Hodama investigation, so he was treating himself to a morning away from the squad room and a little serious thinking.

He was having a late breakfast, cleaning his gun, and generally mooching around his apartment in his nice, scruffy house kimono.

Police headquarters was all about action and work and, even more important, the appearance of work. He was not too sure how good it was for perspective. And right now he needed perspective. He needed a sense of detachment. His nose had been to the grindstone so long that *it* was being ground down. That was not quite the idea. He was after a bunch of murderers. The object was not to die of overwork, even though that was a common enough occurrence in Japan. The object was to unravel this mess and put the villains behind bars. He was doing all the right things, operating by the book, and he seemed to be getting nowhere.

He was sitting comfortably on his knees on the *tatami* mat floor with his breakfast, his gun, and various files spread out in some disarray in front of him. Rain beat down on the skylight.

He popped a pickle into his mouth and finished cleaning his gun as he munched. He was getting used to carrying the damn thing and he was getting quite good at shooting it. Recently, he had taken to practicing with it at least twice a week.

He was feeling a little paranoid, and had the sense that he was under surveillance from time to time. He was sure his apartment had been searched. His instincts told him that he was part of a wider agenda. He had a nasty feeling that there was a leak somewhere in police headquarters or maybe even in the prosecutor's office. He really had not a clue as to where, but things were just a little too pat.

The Namakas were an unsavory pair, but they were the last people who should have wanted to see Hodama dead; yet every time the investigation against the Namakas slowed, another morsel of proof against them turned up.

But nothing was conclusive. It was as if there really was no hard evidence, but someone was manufacturing tidbits to put the pressure on the Namakas. And they were succeeding. The Namakas were the only suspects. They were now under around-the-clock police surveillance and had been brought in for questioning by the prosecutor on half a dozen occasions. The noose around the Namakas was steadily tightening, based on purely circumstantial evidence—and the absence of any alternative—but Adachi was uncomfortable. He was a policeman. He was a judge of people. He trusted his instincts. The Namakas were guilty of most things, including murder in his opinion, but not necessarily of the killing of Hodama. Adachi's gut feeling told him that the Namakas were being framed. Of course, it really could not be happening to nicer people.

A few weeks back, he had started making a few inquiries of his own, independent of his team, and without telling anyone. He had used a couple of old classmates from the police academy who were now posted away from headquarters in prefecture stations—and had sworn them to secrecy. Information had begun to trickle in; and at the same time, he had begun to feel he was under surveillance.

There was one consistent element in the replies. Practically all the people who were contributing to the growing case against the Namakas had been found, upon detailed investigation, to have a Korean connection.

Adachi sipped his iced tea. Maybe it was just a coincidence. He cleaned up the room's clutter, showered, and got dressed. He slid his holstered revolver onto his belt and took the subway to Kabutcho, the district where the stock market was located, to meet the Eel.

THE EEL WAS in a quiet corner of his favorite restaurant, a dish of his favorite food—which had given rise to his name—in front of him. Conveniently, he also owned the restaurant.

He was a round, merry-faced man in his early fifties. He had been a financial journalist for many years, but had been expelled from his press club for refusing to report a story according to the docile official line. This was a serious development, because news in Japan was disseminated only through press clubs. Members were expected to report favorably in exchange for being given information. *Gaijin* were not allowed to join. Press clubs were a less-than-subtle way of managing information.

The Eel had lost his job when he had been evicted from the financial press club. This could have been a disastrous situation, but he was shrewd and street smart and financially adroit. The stock market was booming. He set up a financial newsletter. He was extremely well-informed, and the venture thrived.

The rumor was that he made most of his money, not from what he published, but from businesses paying to keep stories out. Adachi did not doubt it. The Eel operated under the benevolent patronage of one of the major *yakuza* gangs. He owed Adachi from the time a rival organization had decided that the Eel might please them better as a publisher if he lost some weight. They had in mind the removal of his two arms and maybe a few other appendages. Adachi had stumbled on the transaction when he had dropped into the Eel's restaurant for a snack, and he had dissuaded the attackers. He had borrowed one of the assailants' swords and used it to good effect. It did not occur to him to draw his revolver.

The Eel stood up as Adachi approached, and tried to bow while greeting the policeman effusively. This was difficult given the Eel's bulk, the space between the bench he was sitting on and the table, and the fact that the light fixture over the table hung rather low. He was also eating. It was nearly total mayhem.

Adachi sat down and got comfortable with a beer with some relief. He liked the Eel. The man was intelligent and good company, and frankly Adachi preferred villains with something to say. Dumb thugs were all too common and made for a long working day.

"Adachi-*san*," said the Eel. His real name was Origa. It was not good protocol to call him "the Eel" to his face, though he was quite proud of the name. Eels were associated with force and power and energy, and there were aphrodisiac and indeed financial implications. When business was brisk in the stock market, dealers rushed out to fortify themselves with eels. "Adachi-*san*, is it fair to say that you are not a financial sophisticate?"

Adachi smiled. "Probably," he said. "Origa-*san*, you've tried to interest me in your financial scams for years. I have not yet bitten. That should tell you something. I have little interest in the market."

The Eel sucked his teeth. "The Namakas, Superintendent-*san*?" he said. "I had better give you some background." His tone was rhetorical.

Adachi nodded encouragingly.

"Adachi-*san*," said the Eel, "the Tokyo stock market is not as others. On the face of it there are nearly twenty-three million shareholders, shareholder democracy personified. Closer examination reveals that corporations own seventy-three percent of the shares and that a mere six large *keiretsu*—corporate holding groups—own a quarter of the market. Individuals hold about twenty-two percent."

"I'm not sure I understand the significance of this," said Adachi.

"The Tokyo stock market is purported to be a free and open market," said the Eel. "It is not. Most shares—over three-quarters—are never traded. They are held by corporations and banks on a mutually supporting basis. The equity that is traded is widely manipulated. The trade is dominated by only a handful of dealers. Prices are fixed. The insider gets the nod, then come the corporates. Finally comes the individual, the shareholder who will pay the eventual price. Privileged insiders cannot lose. They are guaranteed against loss by the dealer. Certain politicians, in exchange for favors, are privileged insiders. Hodama-*san* was certainly such a man."

"The Namakas?" said Adachi.

The Eel, his face shiny, shoveled a portion of *umaki*—grilled eel wrapped in cooked egg—into his mouth and masticated. He positively glowed as the food descended into his stomach. "Well, there is the thing," he said. "The market is going up. Virtually all shares are being hyped up, and there is Namaka Industries languishing."

"Falling?" said Adachi.

The Eel shook his head. "Going up more slowly," he said. "Way out of step with the market."

"Maybe they've shown bad results," said Adachi.

"On paper—which means nothing—they look fine," said the Eel. "Anyway, profits are not that important. Dividends are lousy. The action is in the share price. That is how the Japanese shareholder makes his money. Shares here sell for sixty to eighty times earning, sometimes more. In America, it is more like ten to twenty."

"So what is going on with the Namakas?" said Adachi.

"They are being eased ever so gently outside the club," said the Eel.

"Who's behind it?" said Adachi.

The Eel smiled. "This was not easy to find out."

Adachi picked up one chopstick and held it in both hands in a simulation of a sword, then brought it down in a fast, cutting motion.

The Eel gulped. "Uzaemon," he said. "A holding company. Now are we even?"

Adachi grinned. "Is the life that I saved worth so little?"

The Eel gave a weak smile.

"Tell me about Uzaemon," Adachi said. "And who is behind them."

The Eel went a little pale. He leaned across the table. *"Yakuza,"* he whispered. "Korean *yakuza."*

"Who exactly?" insisted Adachi.

"Katsuda-*san,*" whispered the Eel. "The man no one ever sees. He of the hideous face."

Suddenly, Adachi realized the significance of the Korean connection among the witnesses, and that the primary motive for Hodama's death could well lie, not in current events, but in something that had happened decades ago in the chaos and confusion of postwar Japan.

He had heard something secondhand about the gang wars of the American occupation from one of the old-timers who had been his mentor. The details were hazy, but at least he knew whom to ask.

But one important question was left. If Hodama's killing was, as he now suspected, a crime of vengeance for something that had happened during the occupation, why had the attackers waited until now? Why had Hodama, with all his power and influence, lost his protection?

Indeed, who had been the true source of that protection? Japan, Korea, and the postwar period. There was only one serious contender, but many factions within it.

It was beginning to make sense.

FITZDUANE HAD GIVEN much thought to the best tactic to employ with the Namaka brothers and had discussed the matter at length with Yoshokawa, the Spider, and Chifune. He also had his own, more lethal, agenda, which he did not discuss, except with Kilmara.

The objective, as agreed upon with his Japanese colleagues, was to force a reaction from the Namakas that would break the impasse of the investigation, link them to Yaibo, and lead to their arrest. The best method was not so obvious. The tactic was the tried-and-true police technique of "rattling the suspect's cage," but it was in how to do it that the problems lay. In the end it was decided that the first move should be a meeting with the Namakas, and that Yoshokawa would make the introductions.

The overt reason would be social. Fitzduane was in Japan and just wanted to pay his respects. Research had shown that companies in which Fitzduane had investments had done some business with the Namaka group—scarcely surprising given the pervasiveness of Japanese goods—so it could be considered that they had common business interests. Arguably of greater significance, he and Kei Namaka had a shared hobby: the Medieval Warrior's Society. To further arouse Kei Namaka's interest, he had brought him a gift, a handmade reproduction of a traditional Irish weapon.

Along with the approach to the Namakas, it was agreed that Fitzduane would work with Detective Superintendent Adachi's unit, with Chifune acting as his interpreter. To give him official status with the police, Fitzduane, who had held a reserve commission with the Rangers—unpaid—for some years, would use his rank, and carry a special identity card in English and Japanese to go with it. In Japan, where appropriate, he would be Colonel Hugo Fitzduane.

FITZDUANE HAD ARRIVED in Tokyo on a Friday, so it had been arranged that he would stay with Yoshokawa for the weekend.

Mrs. Yoshokawa had been dying to meet this Irishman who had saved her son from a terrorist kidnapping, and Yoshokawa himself was anxious to pay Fitzduane for his hospitality in Ireland. Also, the two men had come to like each other. Long discussions in Ireland had dented Yoshokawa's formal facade. In the privacy of his home, he relaxed completely and revealed a warm nature. Fitzduane, who had approached the visit with some concern that he might drown in protocol, was enjoying himself immensely. The only drawback was that the delightful Chifune had disappeared. Two plainclothes detectives outside the house provided security.

Given Yoshokawa's wealth, Fitzduane had expected a large house. Instead it was a relatively new modern dwelling of about two and a half thousand square feet; comfortable but not ostentatious. Two of the rooms were *tatami* rooms, decorated in Japanese style. The rest were Western. The family dinner, held in Fitzduane's honor, was served at a full-height table and featured smoked salmon, coq au vin, and an excellent sorbet, all accompanied with French wine. Japanese elements were the serving of rice as an option with the main course and plentiful supplies of *sake*. Fitzduane stuck to the wine. *Sake* had a habit, he had discovered, of creeping up on him.

Mrs. Yoshokawa was an attractive woman in her early fifties, with beautiful eyes and a face full of character. During dinner, she wore a white silk blouse and a long black velvet skirt. After the meal, both she and Yoshokawa excused themselves for a few minutes and then reappeared in traditional kimonos to demonstrate the tea ceremony.

Fitzduane had not been overly enthusiastic about watching someone spend half an hour to make tea, but he had never seen the full formal tea ceremony. When it was over, he was both impressed and deeply touched.

He slept well that night on a futon in the same *tatami* room where the tea ceremony had taken place. The ceremony was an exercise in doing one thing just about as well as it could be done. It had scant practical purpose, but every movement was carried out with an elegance and precision that made it compelling to watch. It was a tribute to the pursuit of excellence. And it was a welcome by the Yoshokawa family of Fitzduane to Japan. He felt very much at peace.

Yoshokawa's home was in Kamakura, an hour by train south of Tokyo. In Tokyo itself, agents of the Namaka security chief scoured the city, trying to find where Fitzduane might be staying. At about the time that Fitzduane was being ushered into the *tatami* room to watch the ceremony, Kitano received his answer. The Irishman was due to check in to the Fairmont Hotel on Sunday afternoon.

Sunday, thought Kitano, is a good day for a killing. Police manpower is lighter. Traffic is less. The streets are less crowded. Escape is easier. On the day Fitzduane checked in, he would be permanently checked out. The security chief smiled at his little joke and made some calls and called in some favors. Unfortunately, the active members of Yaibo were all out of the country. However, a minor *yakuza* gang, the *Insuji-gumi*, were deeply in his debt. An *oyaban*—boss—and five *kobuns* would attend to the matter. They would use swords. There would be no question of their victim's being wounded. He would be chopped to pieces.

K A M A K U R A A N D T O K Y O , J A P A N

June 7

Fitzduane spent Saturday sight-seeing in Kamakura with Yoshokawa—trailed at all times by two armed policemen.

He found the attention restricting, but was modestly cheered that the Tokyo Metropolitan Police Department wanted their bait—as Chifune had so charmingly put it—alive.

Kamakura was a seaside town—a city in Irish terms, since it boasted a population approaching two hundred thousand—bordered on three sides by mountains and on the fourth by the sea. Land access was only through a series of passes. Its defensibility had made it the capital of Japan some seven centuries earlier. The *bakufu*—military government headed by the *shogun*—had been based there before moving to Edo, now Tokyo, at the beginning of the seventeenth century.

Fitzduane found Kamakura a delightful place. It was heavily wooded, and boasted no fewer than sixty-five Buddhist temples and nineteen Shinto shrines. Strolling through the pine trees, looking at artifacts and architecture that had been there for many centuries, he felt he was getting some small flavor of old Japan. The sense of the pursuit of excellence and the integration of the physical with the spiritual was everywhere evident in the temples and shrines. He greatly enjoyed the Buddhas. He could not see one without being reminded of Boots as a chubby baby.

Talk of the history of Kamakura as a seat of government prompted Fitzduane to ask Yoshokawa a question that had been on his mind for some time.

"Yoshokawa-*san*," he said. "I have not asked this directly before because I have been searching for the right moment, but do you have a direct interest in this Namaka matter? I know you feel compelled to help me because I was fortunate enough to be able to assist your son, but I sense there is something else. You seem more than just a helpful friend."

They were looking at the Great Buddha, a vast hollow bronze construction that towered over the temple and dwarfed human visitors. Erected the best part of a millennium earlier, it suggested considerable engineering talent. The current Japanese success in world markets had been many centuries in preparation, Fitzduane reflected.

Yoshokawa was silent for such a long time that Fitzduane was momentarily concerned that his question had caused offense. He knew that directness was not generally appreciated in Japan. However, he had gauged his moment carefully and the issues were serious. Time was running out. He needed answers quickly. He thought of the terrible moment when the back of Boots's head had appeared to open up in a crimson gash, and he thought of Christian de Guevain slaughtered like an animal. He felt a deep sadness and a cold anger. He had an obligation to destroy these people who threatened his life and the lives of those he cared about. It was a responsibility, a *giri,* as the Japanese might say, to do what had to be done.

It was then that Yoshokawa told him about the Gamma Society, about the group who were dedicated to reforming Japanese society and driving out corruption, and some of the elements in the puzzle began to slip into place.

"Is Enoke-*san,* our friend the Deputy Superintendent-General, a member?" asked Fitzduane.

Yoshokawa nodded.

"And so who suggested I come to Japan?" said Fitzduane.

Yoshokawa looked embarrassed. Fitzduane smiled. "Yoshokawa-*san,*" he said, "from where I stand now, you did the right thing. Of course, if I am killed, I'll change my mind."

Yoshokawa smiled. "I hope so," he said. "It was a decision not made lightly, but I know what you did before, and in some matters we need help. We cannot always do things the Japanese way. We must join the world."

"Internationalization," said Fitzduane.

Yoshokawa laughed. "Fitzduane-*san,*" he said. "You are learning."

14

TOKYO, JAPAN

June 8

Fitzduane was glad that his first real contact with Japan had been at Kamakura.

As Yoshokawa's car drove into the vast sprawl of Tokyo itself, he became somewhat depressed at the seemingly endless vista of unlovely concrete-and-steel boxes, overhead cables snaking everywhere, and incessant neon. Most of the buildings gave the impression of having been roughed out on the back of an envelope and built in a hurry. Functionality alone seemed to have been the guideline, and frequently not even that. Many of the buildings were just plain shoddy.

Except for occasional touches—a roof upturned at its corners, the rich blue of a tile, a roadside shrine—there was almost no trace of the aesthetically satisfying blend of form and function which had been so evident in the temples of Kamakura. The visual sense of the Japanese seemed to have atrophied over the centuries, or perhaps had been one of the casualties of the war. However, it was not entirely dead, Fitzduane mused. The slick design of so much of Japanese electronic gadgetry was proof of that. Personally, Fitzduane thought it was a poor exchange.

Yoshokawa read his expression. "Fitzduane-*san*," he said, "don't read too much into what you see. The ugliness of so much of the buildings is superficial. Tokyo's character comes from its people and their energy. As to buildings, remember that the city was practically destroyed in the 1923 earthquake and no sooner rebuilt than it was virtually flattened by American bombers in the war. And we are due another earthquake! In this context, perhaps buildings are not so important." He smiled.

Fitzduane laughed out loud. "And for this kind of security, I hear you have the highest land and property prices in the world."

"This is true," said Yoshokawa. "Land is sacred to the Japanese because we are brought up to think we have so little of it. Also, property is used as security for so many financial transactions. Accordingly, our land prices have become insane. Based upon current paper value, merely by selling off Tokyo you could theoretically buy all of America. Just by selling the grounds of the Imperial Palace in the center of Tokyo, you could buy Canada!"

"The Namakas made much of their money through property, I gather," said Fitzduane.

"What was a worthless bomb site after the war was worth many millions or even billions of yen a generation later," replied Yoshokawa. "The Namakas specialized in persuading people to sell. An unwilling owner might find his child missing for a couple of days or have a car accident or simply vanish. It was all done with great subtlety. On several major projects, their opposition was conveniently attacked by right-wing terrorists—Yaibo—and there was no direct link at all. But conveniently, the Namakas benefited."

"And Hodama?" said Fitzduane.

"Identified projects, made connections, and above all, provided political protection," said Yoshokawa, "but always secretly."

As they drove through what Yoshokawa assured him was metropolitan Tokyo, Fitzduane saw frequent patches of what looked like agricultural land. Some were in rice paddies. Others were planted with fruit or vegetables. "Given the scarcity of land for building," he said, "what are farms doing in the center of the city?"

Yoshokawa was amused. "More than five percent of Tokyo is still zoned for agriculture," said Yoshokawa. "The high price of land is not due merely to market forces. It is partially artificial. There are vested interests who want land prices driven up, even if it means the average *sarariman* can no longer afford to buy a house in the city and has to commute for three hours every day. There is a substantial political element in the land equation."

Fitzduane was silent. Most Japanese probably worked their guts out to achieve some extraordinary economic results, but much of the wealth which should accrue to the individual as a result was being siphoned off. He closed his eyes. He could almost see the web of politicians and organized crime feeding off the nation. It was a situation far from unique to Japan, but the scale of it in that country was frightening. And those who had access to such wealth and power would not give it up lightly.

He realized that the Namakas were not acting just on their own. They were part of a corrupt but extremely powerful structure—and most of it was invisible. *Tatemae* and *honne*, the public image and the private reality.

Chifune had explained it to him on the plane. "Loosely expressed," said Chifune, "*tatemae* is the public facade, the official position or party line. *Honne*, which literally means 'honest voice,' is the private reality. *Tatemae* and *honne* work together. Too much *honne* would create fiction and could destroy the harmony of the group. *Tatemae* is the polite friction which smooths the way. In Japan, if the truth is likely to be hurtful or destructive, *tatemae* will always be preferred. It is often thought by Westerners that *tatemae* is hypocrisy or dishonesty. It really is not. It is a social convention understood by all Japanese. It is a problem only for *gaijin*."

So who and what was he really up against? Whom could he really trust?

"Yoshokawa-*san*," he said, "do you really think Gamma can make a difference, or are the forces against you just too entrenched?"

Yoshokawa looked across and smiled somewhat wearily. "I have to believe we can," he said, "with a little help."

THEY APPROACHED the very center of Tokyo.

Fitzduane expected a high-rise hotel abutting on a crowded city-center street, but the Fairmont was a surprise. The architecture was unspectacular—it had a postwar utilitarian feel about it and had obviously been extended upward—but the location was superb. It was set well back from the road, with a park in front, and it was just outside the grounds of the Imperial Palace. Trees and flowers were everywhere. He caught a glimpse of water. It was the palace moat.

"The Americans did such a good job of bombing Tokyo," said Yoshokawa, "that there was a serious shortage of accommodation. The Fairmont was built and equipped not too long after the war, primarily to house American officers—so the beds are the right size for you over-sized *gaijin."* He smiled. "I think you'll like it. It has what you asked for—character. Whatever that is."

"It is something you have, Yoshokawa-*san*," said Fitzduane, taking his time with his words.

Yoshokawa smiled slightly and gave a slight bow in acknowledgment. Through his police connections, he had read the account of Fitz-duane's adventures in Switzerland and was beginning to see why the man had been successful. The man had a sensitivity, a warmth. Unlike so many *gaijin* who were overly aggressive in tone and style, he under-stood the fundamental importance of *ninjo*—human feelings. He had a quick sense of humor and he was a good listener. Though he was a big man, he did not appear to be physically dangerous in any way, though the evidence said otherwise. If anything, his manner was gentle.

Yoshokawa was recognized instantly. Though his company was not as large as Sony, it had a similar profile and Yoshokawa was widely con-sidered to be responsible for a great deal of its postwar success. He was a public figure and he regularly appeared in the media. For him to drive a guest personally to the hotel was an honor. There was much bowing and smiling. Fitzduane basked in the reflected glory. It was quite fun. He was whisked up to his room. Some packages had arrived for him by courier from the Irish Embassy and had been placed at the end of his bed.

They ran through the arrangements again in the privacy of Fitz-duane's hotel room before Yoshokawa departed. They had considered having Fitzduane permanently based in Yoshokawa's home, but had decided it would not be appropriate. It was too far out and it could well restrict the Namakas if they were going to make a move. The Fairmont was, so to speak, neutral ground. And bait should be visible.

The following day, Yoshokawa would contact the Namakas and try to arrange a meeting. Meanwhile, Fitzduane would settle in, and later that afternoon meet Superintendent Adachi. He would be discreetly guarded at all times by two detectives—he nodded at two men who had just joined them—who would be stationed in a room next to his. Chi-fune would appear on Monday to act as his interpreter. Fortunately, Adachi spoke excellent English.

"Will the detectives guarding me normally speak English?" said Fitzduane. There was a staccato burst of Japanese from Yoshokawa.

The two men looked embarrassed, and so did Yoshokawa. There was a momentary silence, which Fitzduane broke.

"Yoshokawa-*san*," he said. "Could you tell these gentlemen that they should follow me, but not restrict my movements? And could you add that I am deeply sorry that I speak no Japanese, but I feel quite confident that I am in good hands? The reputation of the Tokyo Metropolitan Police Department is legendary."

One of the detectives, a Sergeant Oga, looked visibly pleased at these comments, and Fitzduane realized that whatever the case about speaking English, the man understood it. That was progress. Meanwhile Yoshokawa translated, and as he finished speaking, Sergeant Oga spoke and both men bowed deeply. Yoshokawa looked visibly relieved. *Wa*—harmony—had been restored.

"Sergeant Oga and Detective Reido," said Yoshokawa, "much appreciate your thoughtful words and say that it is an honor to serve you, Colonel Fitzduane-*san*. Sergeant Oga-*san* says that he does speak English, but he is out of practice."

Yoshokawa left a few minutes later and Fitzduane returned to his room, poured himself a glass of *sake* from the mini-bar, and unpacked. Through his window he could see the tops of trees and the curved roof of the Nippon Budokan. It was hard to believe he was in the center of Tokyo. The gray sky looked just like Ireland, though it was not actually raining. In the distance, he could see an airship.

He turned to the parcels delivered from the Irish Embassy. They had traveled over in the diplomatic bag. One of the smaller packages held a cuff designed to be strapped around the forearm with built-in Velcro binding. Sewn into the semirigid cloth of the cuff were two sheathed throwing knives made out of a dense plastic which would not be picked up by a metal detector. The blades were weighted with inset ceramic pieces to give perfect throwing balance. Fitzduane had learned to throw a knife two decades earlier when a soldier in the Congo. The most important thing was the ability to gauge distance, though a certain knack did not hurt. Fitzduane had the knack.

He unpacked the other parcels. One of them was a surprise. It was a golf umbrella from Kilmara. Fitzduane swore. The sod must have known it was the rainy season and had said nothing. The umbrella came with instructions, which Fitzduane read. He then experimented. The thing was really quite ingenious.

The deal with the Japanese was that he should not carry a gun. That did not mean he had to be stupid.

THE OYABUN OF the *Insuji-gumi* tasked by the Namaka security chief with terminating this *gaijin*, Fitzduane, was something of an expert in the human-removal business.

Nonetheless, he had never before killed a foreigner, and he had never killed anyone at all under this time pressure. Normally, he would be given a name and an address and could determine a time and place of his own choosing. Further, he tended to be dealing with someone whose habits he was familiar with and whose behavior he could predict. In this case, he was going to have to improvise, and he would probably have to leave the body where it fell.

This was a pity. A disappearance—the *Insuji-gumi* had a meat-packing plant among their other interests, which contained all kinds of useful machinery—did not engender the same reaction from the police as a murdered corpse. Still, the *Insuji-gumi* were indebted to Kitano-*san* and obligations must be met. They were old-fashioned *yakuza,* with full-body tattoos for the initiated, and they prided themselves on their traditional values. Their code was rather like the *bushido* code of the *samurai,* and it was inconceivable that it not be followed.

The *oyabun* had been supplied with a description and photograph of Fitzduane and the approximate time he would be checking in to the Fairmont Hotel. From then on, he would have to improvise.

Fortunately, the Fairmont was well set up for observation. A coffee shop with large windows to the left of the entrance was open all day, and the hotel itself was quite small. Any new arrival could easily be seen. From an appropriate table, it was also possible to overlook much of the lobby.

The *oyabun,* armed with an automatic for emergencies and with a short sword concealed in his raincoat, settled himself in the coffee shop to wait, with one *kobun* as company. The remaining four *kobuns* waited nearby in a Mazda van with tinted windows. Their swords were in a baseball bag. The overall boss of the *Insuji-gumi* was an avid baseball fan, so a display of enthusiasm for the sport and attendance at all major matches was virtually obligatory. There was not much place for the nonconformist in Japan, and none at all in the traditional *yakuza.*

The *oyabun* boss and his *kobun* were arguing about baseball scores and working their way through the fixed-price lunch menu and a beer or two, when Fitzduane arrived. The *oyabun*'s first reaction was at the height of this foreigner. He was a good head taller than the Japanese around him and was built in proportion. It was going to be satisfying to cut him down to size. The *oyabun* was tempted to rush into the lobby and do the deed there and then, but he suddenly recognized Yoshokawa-*san* and blanched. To commit an assassination in front of one of Japan's leading industrialists, and possibly to harm him in the melee, would really be inviting an excessive police reaction. To kill the odd foreigner was one thing. To threaten Japan's industrial might would be an act of a different order of magnitude.

He looked out the window at the weather. Well, it was not actually raining and it was still early enough in the day. With a bit of luck, the *gaijin* would not hole up in his room but would do a little sight-seeing. The Yasukini Shrine was nearby. The Nippon Budokan, the concert hall where the Beatles and Bob Dylan had once played, was worth a look. The grounds of the Imperial Palace were only a stone's throw away.

He pressed the transmitter button on the radio clipped to his belt and held up his arm so that the microphone in his cuff would pick up his voice. "The *gaijin* has arrived," he said, "so stop playing with yourselves and stay alert. He has gone up to his room. When he comes down and leaves the hotel, we'll do the job."

Across the table, his companion looked relieved that he could finish his lunch, and went on slurping his bean curd soup. This kind of work made him hungry. In the van with the tinted windows, the four *yakuza* on standby opened more beer and played with their portable *pachinko* board for reasonably serious money. Pinball was a marvelously mindless way of killing time when you were on stakeout.

Yoshokawa departed and the *oyabun* looked up at the heavens and thanked whoever was up there. The skies darkened and it started to pour, and he felt betrayed. After a further twenty minutes, the rain ceased and an uncertain sun peeked through the clouds. The *oyabun* felt his spirits lifting again. The *gaijin*, he presumed, had not come all those miles to sit in his room and watch CNN on the TV. He must have some spirit of adventure if Kitano-*san* wanted to have him killed.

His heart leaped. The American—well, all *gaijins* in his experience were American—had entered the lobby from the direction of the elevators. He was checking a map and, better yet, carrying an umbrella.

This was excellent. With his heart pounding, the *oyabun* watched as the target moved out of sight as he approached the main entrance. Seconds later, he reappeared on the pavement outside and turned left and headed down toward Yasukini-dori Avenue.

The *oyabun* barked into his microphone. At his command, the driver of the van with the tinted windows abandoned his *pachinko* game, leaped out of the side door, and jumped into his seat. In the confusion, the piles of yen notes on the table in the back were dislodged. Several notes drifted out the door when it was opened. The three *yakuza* scrabbled around the floor on their hands and knees and tried to recover the others. In the turmoil, although the foreigner was quickly identified, none of the *yakuza* paid any attention to the two Japanese who were following at a respectable distance behind Fitzduane. A connection might have been made under normal circumstances, despite the excitement and chaos of going in for the kill, but it was raining. Fitzduane and both of his bodyguards had put up their umbrellas. All eyes were fixed on the large golf umbrella in green, white, and gold—the colors of the Irish flag. It was easy to follow. Apart from its color scheme, it protruded a good foot higher than the Japanese umbrellas. Obviously, it was carried either by a freak or a foreigner.

FITZDUANE, equipped with a map, had been well-briefed by the concierge at the Fairmont.

There was an obvious concern over the ability of a foreigner to find his way about Tokyo. Since he could not read a word of Japanese and most streets had no name, Fitzduane shared that concern in a mild way, but he formed the view that with Sergeant Oga and Detective Reido behind him, he should not get into serious trouble. Further, he had been advised that there were police boxes all over the place, so if he somehow lost his guardians he had a fallback. Of course, none of this should be necessary. In Tokyo, Fitzduane had been assured, he would be safe.

He actually felt safe as he strode through the rain. Tokyo was over six thousand miles from the bloodshed in Ireland. The memories of the shooting and Christian de Guevain's death faded temporarily from his mind. His injuries had healed. He was fit and greatly enjoying his new surroundings. Life is pleasant, he thought, as he quickened his pace and turned right onto Yasukini-dori. He was heading downhill to Jinbo-cho, the bookshop area, to do a little browsing.

DETECTIVE SUPERINTENDENT ADACHI had been enjoying Sunday lunch with his parents until the subject of his marriage came up.

Mostly, it came up directly, but this time his mother was talking about the royal family and looking at him in that particular way. Continuity, his mother stressed, was vital. It was essential, for example, that the Crown Prince marry sooner rather than later. The inference was clear. Adachi might not have the mystical well-being of one hundred and twenty-nine million Japanese resting on his shoulders, but he was the direct concern of his parents. If the Crown Prince could be pressured to marry—as he surely was, both by the Imperial Household Agency and the media—then the Adachi parents could certainly pressure their son.

Adachi fled rather sooner than planned and headed into headquarters to check on the team and reread the file on this Irishman. A murder investigation was distinctly more restful than his parents when they had the bit between their teeth.

He thought of Chifune and ached inside. He loved her and missed her, but even when he was with her he had the sense that he was losing her. If ever he had wanted to marry anyone, it was Chifune, but she was a New Japanese Woman and somehow marriage did not seem to be on her mind. Oh women, women! What a pleasure, what a pain, what a distraction. And these days, who knew where they belonged? Certainly, they did not, not anymore.

He returned the salutes of the smartly uniformed riot police in their jump boots and took the elevator. In the squad room, on a Sunday afternoon, no fewer than eleven of his team were present. He felt proud to be Japanese. Of course, all were watching a baseball game on television, but it was the principle that mattered. He joined the group and watched the rest of the game and drank a couple of beers.

Afterward, he wandered into his office to scan the *gaijin*'s file and found Inspector Fujiwara hard at work there. He had not even broken off to watch the game. Given Fujiwara's fondness for baseball, this was true dedication. Adachi felt quite embarrassed.

He drank some tea with Fujiwara and headed off to the Fairmont. He still had a little time since he was not due to meet Fitzduane until five, so he thought that instead of taking the subway direct to the nearest station, Kudanshita, he would get off a station early at Jinbocho, window-shop a little, and enjoy the walk up the hill. There was a police box just below Kudanshita, and he might drop in as he passed. Sergeant Akamatsu, the grizzled veteran who had trained Adachi in his first years on the street, was normally on duty there on Sundays, and Adachi visited when he could.

The sergeant's wife had died a few years earlier and his children had left home, so he found Sundays at home particularly hard. The police force was now his family. Adachi, he supposed, was a kind of surrogate son. Well, whatever he was, he was fond of the old man. Yes, he would drop in. Also, Akamatsu knew things from the old days. Perhaps the time had come to talk to him about this Hodama business. If anyone would, he would know something about the earlier years. And the old sergeant had wisdom and that elusive commodity Adachi was chasing—perspective.

He thought of the Irishman he was about to meet and wondered whether he could really bring anything to the investigation. The superintendent doubted it, but he was curious. The DSG had originated the matter. Chifune, when she had phoned after returning from Ireland, had spoken highly of him. The man must have something.

Judging by his file, he also seemed to have a talent for violence. Well, that was something he would find scant use for in Tokyo. The city was extraordinarily peaceful by any standards, let alone by those of a Western capital. His request that he be allowed to carry a gun was ridiculous; Adachi thoroughly supported the DSG's decision. Threats—if any, which he doubted—would be taken care of by the Tokyo Metropolitan Police Department.

Adachi strolled through Jinbocho, browsed at a couple of stores, then headed up to the police box—actually a miniature police station of two stories—on Yasukini-dori. A young policeman, by the look of it only just out of the academy, was at the open entrance. His main business at this time of day was giving directions. He went pink, as a couple of very pretty OLs in their Sunday gear of jeans and T-shirts approached him with an inquiry. Adachi waited politely, and when the OLs had finished, showed his ID. The young policeman became flustered when he realized he had kept such a senior officer waiting.

Adachi suppressed a smile, removed his shoes, and went through to the back and up the tiny stairs to the *tatami* room above. It was not protocol to wear shoes in a private home or traditional building, and as a relaxation area, the *tatami* room came into that category. Besides, street shoes and police boots were unkind to the straw *tatami* mats, particularly in the rainy season.

Before reaching the top, he called ahead. He had studied under Sergeant Akamatsu, so he addressed him as if he, Superintendent Adachi, were still the pupil. It was the way in Japan. The initial relationship established the mode of address thereafter. There was no rush to first names in the Western sense. A growing friendship or close professional relationship did not need to be symbolized by such a superficial change as that. If it was there, it would be felt and understood without words.

"*Sensei!*" called Adachi.

A grizzled, lined face appeared at the top of the stairs. Sergeant Akamatsu looked as if he had either seen or experienced firsthand almost everything a Tokyo policeman could have over the last half century; and he had. He had joined the police force during the occupation, and had stayed on beyond retirement because he was an institution and could still do his job better than most rookies.

The sergeant's tie was loose and there was a glass of tea in one hand and a newspaper in the other. He had removed his gun belt, the top two buttons of his trousers were undone, and he was wearing slippers. His initial expression suggested that he was not overly pleased at having his well-earned break disturbed, but his face broke into a broad grin when he recognized Adachi.

"Adachi-*kun*," he said, the *kun* appendage indicating that the superintendent had been his pupil, "this is a pleasure. Come up and have some tea."

Adachi finished climbing the stairs, sat down on the *tatami* floor, and accepted the tea gratefully. He was silent at first, thinking. He had worked in this very *koban* a decade earlier under Sergeant Akamatsu, and every time he returned he got an acute attack of nostalgia for the place. It was curious, given the cramped utilitarian nature of the miniature construction—a typical police box was little more than a booth—but he had been privileged to learn under a real master. Whatever problems he encountered on the streets, he had always known that Akamatsu would know the answer and he had never been disappointed. He had very warm feelings toward the sergeant. Coming back from patrol to the streetwise presence of Sergeant Akamatsu had been as reassuring in its way as coming home. It was a fortunate man who worked under a great teacher.

When Adachi visited Akamatsu, they tended to reminisce and talk about general gossip rather than specific cases, because the superintendent's responsibilities were now at a level much higher than the sergeant's and neither wanted to draw attention to the differences of their worlds. It was more companionable to discuss matters in common. This was not a cast-iron rule, because from time to time Adachi felt the need to pick his old mentor's brains, but he had not so far raised the Hodama investigation. It was politically sensitive and operated mostly on a need-to-know basis.

The time had now come to consult Akamatsu. He put down his cup and they talked baseball for a few minutes, as Adachi searched for the right opening approach.

There was a natural break in the conversation, and then Sergeant Akamatsu spoke. "The Hodama business, Adachi-*kun?*"

Adachi smiled. "Ever the mind reader, *sensei.*"

Akamatsu laughed. "The entire force knows you're running the investigation, and the word is that it's going nowhere. Then you come to my *koban* with that certain familiar look on your face. I don't need to be a detective to work out where to go from there. So let's talk about it."

Adachi nodded and started to speak. Akamatsu filled his pipe and listened.

"What you need is a little history," said the sergeant when Adachi had finished. "Files aren't enough and computers are dumb beasts. You need flesh and blood to get closer to what happened. Those were hard days after the war when the Namakas were building their empire."

"Can you help, *sensei?*" said Adachi.

"I think so," said Akamatsu. He was about to say more when shouts could be heard from the street below, and then almost immediately there was the sound of metal clashing and of people screaming in agony.

Both men rose to their feet, and as they did so, there was the sound of gunfire very close at hand. Then came shots from immediately below.

Adachi drew his revolver and made for the stairs, with Sergeant Akamatsu buckling on his gun belt immediately behind.

THE OYABUN OF the *Insuji-gumi* had learned from experience that too many attackers in a street hit could be counterproductive.

Armed with guns, hyped on the adrenaline rush, they had a tendency to shoot each other and a disturbing number of the passing citizenry. Equipped with swords and working close in, the only way you can with a blade less than three feet long, it became hard to tell who was hacking at who in the melee—and the victim had a fair chance of escaping amid a welter of spraying blood and wrongly targeted severed limbs.

Nonetheless, numbers definitely had an advantage if properly deployed. A would-be hero, a policeman or passerby, might go up against one assailant, but few sane people would go head-to-head with half a dozen sword-wielding assailants shouting battle cries.

The *oyabun* favored a human variation of a formation which fighter pilots, he had heard, called the "lazy deuce." Divided into pairs, the lead fighter would bore in for the kill, while the second aircraft, the wingman, stayed back and to the right and kept an eye out for any surprises—particularly from the rear.

With the "lazy deuce" in mind, the *oyabun* sent one pair in front of Fitzduane and put the second pair behind, with himself and his *kobun* bringing up the rear. All were linked by radio, using concealed microphones and hearing-aid earpieces. They were wearing sunglasses and surgical gloves and were dressed in long, light-gray disposable polyethylene raincoats—the kind you buy in a packet in a department store when you get caught short—and floppy rain hats of the same material.

These shapeless outfits not only served as effective disguises but would also shield their wearers from blood. A hit with swords almost always resulted in a kill, but tended to be extremely messy. You could not very well escape unnoticed through the subway, as the *oyabun* intended, if saturated with gore. Tokyo was so crowded there was a convention that you behaved as if no one else existed, but there was a limit. Dripping crimson on your neighbor's shoes as you strap-hung side by side in a subway car would be regarded as decidedly ostentatious.

The designated hitter, a seasoned *yakuza* in his late thirties called

Mikami, moved into position about ten paces behind the *gaijin*. When the *oyabun* gave the word, he would remove the sword concealed beneath his coat, rush forward, and strike. He would use a downward diagonal blow which would hit his victim on the right side of the neck and then penetrate deep into the torso, severing the spine and many of the major organs, and if delivered by an expert with the right-quality blade, would actually cut the body in two.

In this case, severance was unlikely. Mikami was an experienced swordsman, but the *katana* being used were not of traditional quality; they were merely mass-produced, modern utilitarian reproductions. They were razor-sharp and deadly, but they did not have quite the same cutting power as the extraordinary works of art handmade by the master craftsmen of old. Even so, they would kill.

Since the body to which he was attached had been perforated twice, thus providing some serious motivation, Fitzduane had given a great deal of thought to the appropriate response to threat. The safest solution was to stay isolated in protected surroundings. That was unpalatable. It was like being in prison. The next-best thing was to be reasonably unpredictable and to cultivate a very high level of threat awareness. That was the option he had chosen, and he had the advantage of being naturally observant and intuitive. But he had also studied—and trained, trained, trained.

The objective was never—but never—to let your guard down, and always, even if thinking about something entirely different, to have your subconscious hard at work on looking out for the unusual, the different, that small something that hinted at danger. He had become very good at anticipating the unexpected.

Since it was Sunday afternoon and raining, the pavement was not crowded and Fitzduane was able to walk as he had trained—with no one in an immediate threat area either in front or behind him. The concept of defensible space is programmed into us by centuries of having had to fight for survival. In Fitzduane's case, his awareness of that invisible but vital cordon around him was very high. If anyone came any closer, his senses were alerted. If that proximity was linked to any other unusual element, his senses screamed.

Fitzduane was walking briskly, so he became immediately aware of two men in long raincoats who overtook him as if in a hurry and then slowed down, despite the heavy rain, when they were only ten yards or so in front of him. There was something not quite right about them that he could not place at first. Without making any obvious gesture, he moved immediately to his right, near the railings, so that one flank would be secured. At the same time, using his umbrella to remain unnoticed, he glanced behind him.

He felt an immediate rush. His two police minders were a discreet twenty yards behind him, but between them and himself were two men, dressed much the same as the two in front of him. It might mean nothing, he knew, because their clothing was entirely appropriate for the heavy rain, except for their dark glasses. Still, vanity did not necessarily mean danger.

Walking well behind, the *oyabun* watched with satisfaction as his two killing teams bracketed their victim. They were walking downhill, so Mikami would have momentum on his side as he rushed in for the kill. After one terrible blow, he would then discard his sword and his rain clothing and run into the subway station.

To ensure a kill—the Namaka security chief had been adamant about that—his fellow *yakuza* would then deliver another blow to the fallen victim to completely sever his head and would then follow Mikami's example. The team ahead of the *gaijin* were there to block his escape if something went wrong. Kudanshita station was up ahead. They would have to act before reaching the station, because there was a police box a little farther down. Fortunately, the police-box entrance faced away from the location of the proposed hit.

Sergeant Oga was an experienced policeman in his forties, who'd even had special training in personal-protection work a decade earlier. However, he had forgotten much of his protection training. Because Tokyo was a safe city, when he guarded some visiting VIP, he did not regard him as being at risk. In all his years, he had never known anyone under his guard to have been seriously threatened—if one discounted the occasional politician being jostled. And giving those corrupt bastards a hard time might be a good thing.

He had heard that this *gaijin,* Fitzduane-*san,* had been attacked in Ireland, but he associated that with the IRA. Everyone knew about the IRA and that Ireland was in a permanent state of civil war. He had seen enough coverage of explosions and shootings on TV. It seemed to have been going on for the last twenty years—a crazy way to run a country. But Ireland was six thousand miles away and there were no IRA in Tokyo. Even the few Japanese terrorists were mostly in the Middle East, he had heard. The fact was that Japan was well and tightly policed, the population supportive and, except for the *yakuza*—who at least were fairly well-organized and kept in check—law-abiding. It was the way it should be. Who wanted everyone running around with guns, like in America! That was no quality of life.

The sergeant had not been too happy when Colonel Fitzduane had indicated that he was going for a walk, because it would have been easier and safer to guard the man in the Fairmont, but then he realized he was being unrealistic. There was no real risk, and no one could remain cooped up in a hotel room all day. A man needed to stretch his legs. Personally, the sergeant loved the streets and hated being confined in an office. Still, it was a pity that the weather was so terrible. The *gaijin* should have come in spring when the cherry blossoms were out and the weather warm and balmy. Whoever had advised him to come this time of year had not done him any favors. It was hot, wet, and muggy now, and it would get worse before it got better. He wondered how long the man was staying. He was agreeable for a *gaijin* and almost like a Japanese in his sensitivity. A nice man, really.

The sergeant watched in horror from under his umbrella as a figure in front of him suddenly drew a sword and in the same motion raised it high above his head and ran silently at Fitzduane. The action was so unexpected, indeed surreal, that it took him two or three seconds to react—and then it was too late. He glanced at Detective Reido, who was walking beside him, and it was clear that he, too, had been caught unawares. Both men looked at each other, shocked, and then as one drew their service revolvers. The sergeant realized that he was still holding his umbrella, and as he moved forward, he threw it behind him.

Fitzduane turned as his assailant made his rush and took the blow on his umbrella, at the same time drawing out the sword concealed in its handle. The thin blade was similar to an epee, which was his preferred weapon when fencing, though it was a little lighter and lacked a hand guard.

Mikami was taken aback by the *gaijin*'s swift turn, but expected his blade to slice right through the thin cloth of the umbrella and into his victim. He was taken aback when the blade was deflected.

Fitzduane gave fleeting thanks to Du Pont for inventing Kevlar and realized that he could now resolve a conundrum which had puzzled him for years. It was an opportunity he could have done without. He collected weapons and had had several very fine *katana* in his collection, and he had often questioned the merits of the magnificently made Japanese swords—designed primarily for cutting—as compared to the thin-bladed European weapons, which killed mainly on the thrust. He had often debated the matter with Christian de Guevain.

A cold anger gripped Fitzduane. His attacker's blade cut across in a second vicious slashing attack intended to brush aside the umbrella and cut into his victim's body.

Fitzduane stepped back down the hill, but still kept his back to the railings, as the second stroke came at him. At the same time, he dropped the umbrella.

Mikami, expecting that his blow would have to push the umbrella out of the way as well as kill Fitzduane, had slashed with all his force. At the last minute, there was no resistance and he lurched forward off-balance.

Fitzduane deflected the *katana* blade upward and away, and in the same movement slid his epee into Mikami's body. His attacker's eyes rolled and he stared in surprise as Fitzduane immediately withdrew his blade and blood spurted from his wound. A bloody froth burst from his lips, and he collapsed. Blood and rainwater cascaded down the pavement.

A second figure, holding a sword in two hands low, as if to thrust, ran at Fitzduane from the same direction as his first attacker. Fitzduane extended his sword, and this assailant came to a halt. Two other attackers, the men who had been in front of him, Fitzduane realized, also approached. All three now surrounded Fitzduane in a semicircle, as he stood on guard with his back to the railings.

Fitzduane feinted, parried, and thrust at the attacker on his right, knowing that the attacker on his left would be hindered by the man in the middle. His intended victim gave ground as the epee flickered at him, giving Fitzduane just enough time to remove a throwing knife from his wrist, but not enough time or space to throw it. He now faced his attackers with a blade in either hand. It was a style with which his ancestors in the sixteenth century would have been very familiar.

The man in the center gave a cry and ran forward in a slashing attack. Fitzduane stepped forward, seemingly into the blow, as he moved and deflected the glittering steel so that it crashed into the railings, drawing sparks. Shock, and then agonizing pain, ran through the *yakuza* and he slumped against the barrier with Fitzduane's knife protruding from his kidneys.

Fitzduane slashed at the *yakuza* on his left, and the man, appalled at the ferocity and skill of his intended victim, staggered back, his cheek laid open, slipped on the wet ground, and fell hard on his back, his sword clattering away from his hand. He turned on his side and reached for it as Fitzduane stepped forward swiftly, and without hesitation, thrust his sword into the man's throat and turned. The fallen *yakuza* made a gurgling sound as he died. Nearby, a pedestrian, too frozen with fear to move, screamed and kept on screaming.

The *oyabun* had been taken aback when he had seen what he had taken for two ordinary citizens draw weapons. He immediately made the connection and was furious with himself for not having anticipated bodyguards. Just as quickly, he had shouted at his *kobun* and the two *yakuza* had run at the policemen from behind.

The *oyabun*, mindful of the consequences of killing a policeman, had felled his victim with the blow of a gun barrel behind the ear. Unfortunately, his *kobun* had not been thinking, and Detective Reido lay on the wet pavement with his eyes glassy and his head split in two. His arm, still clutching his revolver, lay several paces away. He had turned as his attacker had run up, and his arm had taken the full force of the *kobun*'s first blow.

The *oyabun* looked at the dead policeman for perhaps fifteen seconds, as if somehow he could piece the man together again. This was a terrible development. The Tokyo MPD were implacable when one of their own was killed. Life for the *yakuza*—for all *yakuza*—would be hell until the murderer and his associates were caught and punished. And it would mean the death penalty. The *oyabun* realized that he now had nothing to lose. If he was to have any negotiation power at all with the boss of the *Insuji-gumi,* he would have to complete his current mission successfully. He drew his gun. The *gaijin* was still standing, apparently unharmed.

Fitzduane glanced up the slope and was surprised to see both his guardians lying motionless. He was now facing three attackers alone. One was nearby and the remaining two were perhaps twenty yards away. The rain had increased in intensity and was now a wall of water. Through it, he could distinguish the *oyabun*'s unmistakable movement as he drew his automatic. And this was a land where the criminals did not have guns. Fuck! He drew his remaining throwing knife and threw it hard at his nearest assailant. The blade missed, but the man skidded onto his knee as he jumped back to avoid it.

Fitzduane turned and ran for all he was worth to the police box some fifty yards downhill. There were two cracks, and splinters from the pavement jumped up in front of him. He ran on, ducking and weaving on the slippery pavement. Spray splashed in the air only to be beaten back again by the rain. The sky was black.

He skidded to a halt at the police box, and with his right hand on an upright, whirled around to face the policeman inside. The young man, immaculately uniformed, looked as if he had stepped straight out of a recruiting poster. A neatly holstered revolver was at his hip. Though he projected all the social concern of the Tokyo MPD, it was clear that there was no way he was going to react in time. The inexperience and lack of comprehension that shone from his face had an almost incandescent quality. He was going to do the right thing, and Fitzduane was going to die.

"Oh, shit!" said Fitzduane, who was imagining the consequences of what he was about to do even as he did it. He hit the policeman very hard in the stomach, then gave him a roundhouse to the jaw.

The policeman made an odd sound as he collapsed, and Fitzduane reached across and removed his revolver. He flicked open the cylinder to make sure it was loaded, then turned just in time to shoot the *oyabun* twice in the face at point-blank range. The man's nose and forehead vanished out through the back of his skull, and he shot backwards off the pavement and onto the road, to vanish five seconds later under the wheels of a tour bus.

The remaining two *yakuza* stood there frozen, with swords upraised, as Fitzduane pointed the revolver at them. He was just deciding which one to shoot first when a voice spoke behind him in American-accented English.

"Fitzduane-*san*, I presume? Please drop your weapon."

Fitzduane kept his gun on the *yakuza*. A uniformed sergeant with the look of someone who knew his way around came into his peripheral vision, his gun also pointed at the *yakuza*.

"There are two of your guys up the hill who need attention," said Fitzduane, "and I mean NOW! Get an ambulance. I'm going back up to see what I can do."

Adachi was speechless for a moment. Then he lowered his gun and picked up the telephone. Three minutes later, he found Fitzduane on his knees ministering to Sergeant Oga. The Irishman seemed to know exactly what to do.

15

TOKYO, JAPAN

June 8

The Deputy Superintendent-General of the Tokyo Metropolitan Police looked down at the open file on his desk and then up at Superintendent Adachi so many times before he spoke that Adachi, who was standing at attention in front of the DSG's desk, started to feel disoriented. He felt he was facing one of those nodding birds.

Between glances, the DSG flipped through the reports and stared at the photographs. In the time Adachi had known the Spider, nothing had caused the DSG to react to any perceptible extent, but the slaughter on Yasukini-dori had made a decided impact.

The Spider's eyebrows seemed to have been raised permanently by half an inch, and his voice was up an octave. Occasionally, it squeaked. This reaction gave Adachi a certain inner satisfaction. After all, bringing this Irishman in on the Namaka case had been the Spider's idea, and, fortunately, everyone knew it.

"This is incredible," the DSG squeaked. "This man is here only three days and he turns Tokyo into Chicago. In thirty-five years on the force, I have never seen anything like it. Five dead, including a policeman, and one policeman injured. And all of this only yards from the Imperial Palace and the War Memorial. The press are going to eat this up. If this was fifty years earlier, I'd be committing *seppuku,* and as to you, Adachi-*san,* I hate to think. You'd probably be enlisted as a kamikaze pilot, if they were feeling generous. You were there, after all, and senior police officers are supposed to stop this kind of behavior."

He shook his head. "Incredible, incredible. And not just swords, but guns too. Guns in *my* city. What is Tokyo coming to!"

The fruits of economic progress, Adachi felt like saying, but this was not a time for jokes. He also did not point out that the Emperor was not actually living in the Imperial Palace at the moment, since it was being repaired. He remained silent, as was appropriate, and waited for a signal to speak.

In truth, he was nearly as stunned as the DSG, perhaps more so. He had actually been there and seen the *gaijin* in action. He had not witnessed the sword-fighting, but he had glimpsed Fitzduane as he was checking the young policeman's revolver before turning and shooting the *oyabun* in the face.

It was his speed and the way he had acted without any hesitation that stuck in Adachi's mind. This was a truly dangerous man; but also decent. He also remembered seeing Fitzduane attend to the injured Sergeant Oga. The sergeant, lucky man, looked like he'd be coming out of the affair with nothing worse than surface lacerations on his scalp and a rather sore head.

The DSG seemed to realize for the first time that his subordinate was still standing at attention. He gestured toward a chair. "Oh, sit down, Superintendent-*san*. Thankfully, this is not half a century ago."

Adachi sat down.

"To be factual about this," said the DSG in a more normal voice, "the core issue here is that the Tokyo MPD failed to protect an invited guest. But for his own initiative, Fitzduane-*san* would have been cut down only a short distance from his hotel. And to make matters worse, he was forbidden to carry a firearm, even though I knew he was at risk." He sighed. "Frankly, I underestimated the forces we are up against."

Adachi cleared his throat. The Spider now seemed almost human. He had displayed more emotion in the last ten minutes than over the previous decade. It was almost possible to imagine the DSG as a normal person with a home life and a family.

The DSG looked directly at him. "You are not in any way to blame for this, Adachi-*san*," he said. "You behaved entirely appropriately and your report is excellent. The fault is mine, but I would appreciate your input as to what we should do now. Our immediate priority is to make a statement to the press. Then we can consider our next move with this Irishman."

Adachi removed his notebook and consulted it. "Fitzduane-*san* has made a number of suggestions," he said.

The DSG nodded.

"He has said that he is aware that this incident may be embarrassing, but that he personally does not blame the MPD in any way, and indeed regrets—very deeply regrets—the inconvenience caused."

The DSG looked extremely interested. "Fitzduane-*san* suggests," Adachi continued, "that the whole business be dismissed in the press release as a clash between rival *yakuza* gangs which was stopped thanks to the prompt actions of the police. Further, he suggests that the hero of the hour be the young policeman he was forced to knock unconscious. The *yakuza oyabun* was shot with Policeman Teramura's revolver, so it would seem appropriate. Fitzduane-*san* also respectfully recommends that Teramura-*san* be given a medal."

The DSG exhaled, and in Adachi's opinion, took an unconscionably long time about it. The Spider was a positive genius at buying time in a discussion while also managing to appear entirely in control. Those around him tended to wait with bated breath for the oracle to speak. The Spider had raised hesitation to a high art.

The seconds passed. Adachi was frankly impressed at how much air the little man contained. He must really be fit. When did he exercise? There was not even a rumor of him in the police *dojo*. Perhaps he jogged in the dead of night around Hibiya Park.

The DSG eventually took a deep breath—to Adachi's relief—and then exploded in laughter. After an appropriate interval, Adachi joined in. The DSG practically rolled off his chair, but finally got control of himself.

"Let's do it," he said. "It's a perfect solution. But weren't there witnesses?"

"Most noticed only the initial *yakuza* attack," said Adachi, "and then they fled. The involvement of a *gaijin* was seen only by a couple, and the rain was heavy. I don't think we need to worry. We'll have a quiet word about the public interest."

"Our *gaijin* friend," said the DSG, "is a very clever man. The Irish must have some Japanese blood in them somewhere. But tell me, Superintendent-*san,* what does he want?"

Adachi smiled. "He would like to continue what has been agreed upon, and he respectfully suggests that he should be allowed—"

The DSG groaned.

"—to carry a firearm."

THE VILLAGE OF ASUMAE NORTH OF TOKYO, JAPAN

June 10

The village was some sixty miles north of Tokyo, so Fitzduane's bodyguards—now increased to four—had not been overly keen on his making the trip.

Their protests had been so vigorous that Fitzduane, in his Toyota four-wheel drive with unmarked police cars front and rear, had half expected to have to fight his way through the suburbs like a stagecoach careering through hostile Indians. The reality was more prosaic. It was a long, boring trip through heavy rain and endless Tokyo suburbia, until suddenly there were paddy fields and rice growing and a line of pine-covered hills in the distance.

Fitzduane's heart lifted. The green of the forests was a different shade, but there were echoes of Ireland. He greatly missed his island and the beauty of the Irish countryside. He cursed it often for its miserable weather and its failures, but the pull of his tragic, rain-washed island was in his soul. And Japan was a land of islands. There was a bond.

The rain stopped as the little convoy drove into the village. Even as he watched, men and women came out of their houses with hoes and sickles and started cutting at the undergrowth at the perimeter. It was clear that civic pride was alive and well in the hamlet of Asumae.

A tall, heavyset figure in his early sixties leaned against a stone *ishidoro* lantern outside a modest wood-framed two-story house and grinned at Fitzduane, then bowed. It was something of a pastiche. With his height and jutting jaw and craggy features, he was a decidedly un-Asian figure.

A pipe was clenched in his teeth, and he was wearing an unpressed khaki shirt of military cut and baggy cotton trousers of similar origin.

Fitzduane had known Mike Bergin since the early days of Vietnam, and his dress sense had not improved.

"I thought you'd be working, Mike," said Fitzduane with a smile, indicating the villagers hacking and hoeing away.

Bergin removed the pipe from his mouth. His complexion—tanned, weather-beaten, and blotched with the patchwork of veins of a heavy drinker—hovered somewhere between unshaven and designer stubble. But there was a presence, a strong sense of human worth.

"Hugo, the Japanese believe that man is put on this earth to work, and that work, work, and more work is the solution to everything."

"But?" said Fitzduane.

Bergin laughed. "I ain't Japanese. Anyway, Hugo, you're a good excuse for me to revert to my decadent Western ways."

"You'd normally join in?" said Fitzduane. Mike, the old Asia hand and battle-hardened war correspondent, had once been something of a mentor to Fitzduane, and the Irishman was curious to see how Bergin had adapted to living in Japan. He had settled in Japan in the mid-seventies after Vietnam, with the comment that "the Pacific rim is where the action is going to be in the future." And he had been far from wrong, in Fitzduane's opinion.

"Sure," said Bergin. "It's important for us *gaijins* to show we aren't complete barbarians. Anyway, I rather like some of their values. Community spirit is still a big thing here. Money isn't the sum of all gods, like in the West."

"Hell, Mike, what do you know about the West?" said Fitzduane, grinning. "You spent the late forties here with MacArthur and then didn't get much further West than Singapore. The odd foray to London and New York doesn't count."

Bergin put his arm around Fitzduane's shoulders and ushered him into the house. "You've got a point, old son," he said, "but though my lips move as I do it, I can read. Anyway, it's real good to see you. And alive, at that. Given what you get up to, it's fucking amazing."

Privately, Fitzduane was beginning to think much the same, but he made no comment as they removed their shoes and padded in the slippers provided into the living room. Fitzduane's slippers fit. Either he was wearing a spare pair of Mike's, or Mike had regular *gaijin* visitors. All of which was in line with Bergin's less overt occupation.

Outside the house, the security team had safeguarded the front and rear entrances, and as Fitzduane glanced up, a liveried police car drove up. Belt and suspenders. Well, he could not blame them. He slid the *shoji* screen shut and went to sit across from Bergin at a battered pine table.

"Thanks for the trade goods," said Mike, looking up from the case of French wine Fitzduane had brought. "*Sake* is good stuff and it's cheap, but it's nice to be reminded of the fleshpots every now and then. I mean, rice is great, but sometimes I yearn for potatoes."

"Once a *gaijin*, always a *gaijin*," said Fitzduane.

"No truer word," said Bergin. He looked distracted for a moment, and Fitzduane remembered his wife had died. She had been Japanese and had provided something of a bridge to the local community. What must it be like now?

Fitzduane reached out across the table and put his hand on top of Bergin's for a moment. "It's good to see you, you old pirate," he said, with quiet emphasis. "You're a monument to the merits of hard living. You drink, you smoke, you've fucked your way through every skin shade in Asia, and you've been under fire more often than we get rained on in Ireland—and still you look terrific."

Bergin looked up, and there was real warmth in his eyes. "Goddamn liar," he growled. "I'll get a corkscrew."

The first bottle of wine was empty by the time Fitzduane had finished his story. He trusted Mike, so he related most of what had happened under strict off-the-record ground rules.

Bergin whistled quietly to himself as the narrative came to an end, then looked across at Fitzduane and grinned. "It might be a practical move to see that your life insurance is paid up."

"Thank you for your concern," said Fitzduane dryly, "but I am hoping that with the help of a few of my friends, including the odd battle-scarred veteran, I won't need it. I'm getting tired of being a target." He smiled, and added with some irony, "I'm thinking of becoming . . . proactive."

Bergin raised his eyebrows. "I would say killing four *yakuza* and knocking a policeman unconscious is an auspicious start. Now, how can this particular battle-scarred veteran help?"

"I need information," said Fitzduane, "background, context, history, perspective. So far I have been fed what other people think I need to know. Well, I need more than that. I need a sense—almost a physical sense"—he rubbed his fingers and thumb together to emphasize the tactile point he was making—"of what I'm up against."

Bergin stretched. "Where do you want me to start?" he said.

"The Namakas," said Fitzduane. "What do you know that I don't?"

"Just as well you brought a case of wine," said Bergin. "This talk is going to run to more than a couple of bottles.

"I worked for CIC—the Counter Intelligence Corps—during the occupation as a special agent before my conversion to the Fourth Estate. They used to say you had to be lily-white to get into CIC and turn coal-black to stay in. We did what had to be done and to hell with the rules. Interesting times. Long time ago. But some things linger, like our friend Hodama."

"And the Namakas?" said Fitzduane.

"The Namakas worked for Hodama in those days," said Bergin. "He picked them out of the gutter and used them for some of the rougher stuff. And, of course, all of them worked for us. All part of putting down communism and, like I said, to hell with the rules. Then time moved on and Hodama moved up the ladder and brought the Namakas with him. And they all started wearing silk suits. But inside, nothing changed. Nor did the old alliances. So there is no way the Namakas killed Hodama."

"So who did?" said Fitzduane.

"I'm not sure," said Bergin, "but I've got a few ideas. The one thing I can tell you is this game goes way back. I think there's your pointer."

Fitzduane looked at Bergin hard. "You know what happened," he said, "but you're not going to tell me. What the hell is this, Mike?"

"I guess you'd call it a conflict of interest," said Bergin. "I have added some ethics as I've gotten older. I'm not in so much of a hurry."

"If the Namakas did not kill Hodama," said Fitzduane, "and someone else did, then they've gone to a great deal of trouble to blame it on the Namakas. Which means they have it in for the Namakas—which means we have something in common. And thinking further about it, the timing of the killing has to be important. It's not just paying off an old grudge. It's more about rescheduling the pecking order."

Bergin nodded and chuckled. "That's my interpretation," he said, "but policemen have to go on the evidence. Frankly, it has been a neat operation so far and it does not look good for the Namakas. And the truth is not really very relevant. They've run their course. Now it's just a matter of time."

"You sound very sure," said Fitzduane. "I've read the Namaka file. They are redoubtable people."

"There are some forces you can't buck," said Bergin flatly.

Fitzduane thought about what Bergin had been saying. Half of what his friend was communicating was unspoken, yet the clues were there. Suddenly, Fitzduane understood.

"You said the old alliances haven't changed?" said Fitzduane.

"Different names, that's all," said Bergin, "but the same team is still pulling the strings, even if there is a problem with one of the team members. Overenthusiasm, say some. Something nastier, say others. But the trouble is, it's hard to get a rotten apple when it's at the top of this particular tree. Hard to do it without embarrassment."

"How rotten an apple?" said Fitzduane. "As a friend to a friend, Mike."

Bergin pursed his lips. "This particular apple has been rotten since Vietnam," said Bergin. "Terminal is the description I would use."

"Terminal?" said Fitzduane. "That's a rather strong word."

Bergin met his glance. "Carefully chosen," he said.

The conversation turned to reminiscing, and later they ate together. It was near midnight when Fitzduane left. As he was saying farewell, he asked a question that had been in the back of his mind for some time.

"How long have you been with the Company, Mike?"

Bergin blinked, but said nothing at first. Then he held out his hand. "Loose talk sinks ships," he said. "How did you know?"

Fitzduane pointed at the row of guest slippers. "Too many size twelves," he said.

"You always were an intuitive bastard," said Bergin, smiling. "But someone has to watch the watchers. It's been good to see you, Hugo."

Fitzduane had a lot to think about as he drove back to Tokyo, bracketed by his escorts. In particular, he was thinking about a rotten apple called Schwanberg. As the Company's head of station in Tokyo, controlling the power brokers of Japanese society, he probably felt near-invulnerable.

In his scruffy but comfortable house in the village of Asumae, Bergin finished the open bottle of Fitzduane's excellent wine, shook his head, and made a call.

16

TOKYO, JAPAN

June 19

The big man in the expensive black silk suit, handmade shirt, and club tie listened to the progress reports on the Namaka affair with interest, pleasure, and some concern, but his face displayed no emotion.

It could not.

Nearly four decades earlier, terrible burns had disfigured it. The whole of his face had been savaged by the flames, and the flesh on the left side had been almost completely seared away. His ear had been reduced to a piece of blackened gristle. The left side of his body was horribly scarred.

Plastic surgery was not possible at the time. The Korean gangs were being hunted, and a hospital could have meant his death. By the time he was able to have surgery, the medical team could do only so much. Thanks to grafts from his thigh and buttocks, he was made functional. He could eat again and make love to a woman if she could bear it. He could open and close his eyes. His nose was rebuilt, and he had what passed for an ear.

But he was still hideous, repulsive, with his scarred, seamed face, twisted features, and tight, artificial-looking skin. People looked at him and were afraid. He was a living reminder of the terrible things that can be done to the human body. And he looked exceedingly dangerous; a man who had already been embraced by death; a man with nothing to lose.

His own group had all been burned to death in the fire or cut to pieces as they tried to escape. They thought he was dead, too, that the small gang of Korean gangsters was completely destroyed. It was a deliberate object lesson in brutality. Japan was going to emerge again stronger than ever from the destruction of the war, and the power brokers did not want rivals. And they certainly did not want Koreans. The Koreans were a conquered people who had come to Japan as virtual forced labor before and during the Second World War, and then had used the U.S. occupation to try to break out of their servitude.

Japan was defeated. There was a power vacuum. The black market flourished. The *gurentai,* a new breed of more vicious gangster, emerged with little of the spirit of the traditional *yakuza.* The *gurentai* were ruthless and ran roughshod over the defeated Japanese. Many of the *gurentai* were Korean. It was an opportunity to hit back at the arrogance of the Japanese, to prey on their erstwhile masters. Their conquerors were now the defeated. The newly released Koreans were protected by the U.S. Army of occupation—at first.

For several exhilarating years in the immediate postwar period, Korean gangsters enjoyed unprecedented success in Japan. The occupation regime concentrated on demilitarization and changing Japan into a liberal democracy.

Then came a change in emphasis. The defeat of communism became the main priority. Anyone and everything that was opposed to communism, or purported to be opposed to communism, began to get active U.S. intelligence support.

Hodama was released from prison for just such a purpose. He was an organizer and a fixer, with unparalleled connections. He knew how to press the right buttons to win political support. He knew how to recruit gangs of young thugs—such as the Namakas—to enforce his will. An alliance of U.S. intelligence, right-wing politicians, and organized crime was created. This alliance set out to defeat communism and the burgeoning left-wing movement in Japan and to seize political power. This demanded cultivating popular support, and one of the quickest ways was to turn on the Korean criminal gangs. They were fiercely resented by the average Japanese and were a convenient focus of hate.

The man in the black silk suit was seventeen when the attack by Hodama's people came. The warehouse where his gang was based was surrounded by the Namakas and other members of Hodama's group and saturated with gasoline. Twenty-six Korean gang members had died in that holocaust, including the man in the black silk suit's mother, father, two brothers, and sister.

The one survivor had sworn revenge.

He lived only for retribution. But revenge would only be possible if he became strong. Hodama and the Namakas had the powerful backing of U.S. intelligence, and soon became even more powerful in their own right. The right time to exact appropriate retribution seemed never to come.

The decades passed. The man in the black silk suit worked his way up to become boss of one of the most powerful *yakuza* gangs in Japan, but still could not strike at Hodama and his supporters without excessive risk and terminal consequences. Hodama's base of support was too strong. He was needed. He could deliver the votes. He was a linchpin of the right wing, of the anti-communist alliance. He was the leading *kuromaku* behind the Liberal Democrat Party, and he was the CIA's man. He was protected.

Though some knew the story, the fire had removed most traces of the survivor's Korean background. He took the name Katsuda and initially passed himself off as Japanese, though eventually, as the Korean community in Japan prospered and searched for protection against the dominant Japanese, he reestablished his Korean links and traded upon them. Over time, as the Katsuda-*gumi* became ever stronger, he, too, established links with the right wing and the LPD and the Americans. And he waited for the right opportunity.

Sooner or later, Hodama would make a mistake. He would lose his protection and Katsuda could strike. It was a carefully planned operation refined again and again over the years, which would destroy not only Hodama but his whole base of support, starting with the Namakas. The Americans, referring to the spread of communism in Southeast Asia, called it "the Domino Theory." Katsuda thought the simile applicable to what he had in mind. Knock down the first tile and it falls on the second, which falls on the third . . .

When it was over, there would be a new *kuromaku*, Katsuda-*sensei*. Only very few people would know. Hodama had enjoyed his public reputation. He felt it increased his influence. Katsuda had no time for such vanities. He wanted power, but cloaked in secrecy. It was the way of a true *kuromaku*. Invisible but all-powerful.

While still a young man, Katsuda had been impatient for revenge.

The image of the destruction of his enemies had influenced his every action. It made him faster, more ruthless, and more urgent in everything he did.

Yet as time went on, he learned to savor his motivation. Anticipation in itself, he found, was greatly pleasurable. The fact that Hodama and his followers were blithely unaware of their nemesis gave the enterprise an added piquancy.

Katsuda wanted Hodama to die without ever knowing. He wanted to deny him even this slight and fleeting satisfaction. Katsuda would be the bringer of death, and the way of death would be terrible. The thoughts of Hodama himself were of little concern. Only his fear and pain would be important. The man must die in fear and he must suffer. Katsuda had seen his family die in agony, and he could not forget. He did not wish to forget.

Patiently, Katsuda studied his intended victims and waited. And waited. Then, at last, the conjunction of several events created the opportunity.

The cold war came to an end, and gradually it began to be perceived that the strategic importance of Japan had changed. For forty years and more, Japan had been offered unrivaled access to U.S. markets in exchange for being an unswerving U.S. ally. This was no longer so important.

Japanese economic success had made the leading Japanese power brokers cocky. They no longer felt obligated to America. Japan was now the world's second-largest economic power, and, in the opinion of Hodama and some others, the time had come for Japan's international behavior to reflect its economic power. The time for automatically playing second fiddle to the U.S. was over.

The third development was a sense by the political analysts and intelligence services of the world's last remaining superpower that the time of the postwar politicians was over. They had become associated with "money politics" and their greed had surfaced once too often. There had been too many public scandals. The old regime had run its course. It had served its purpose.

It was time for an illusion of change.

New blood would be brought in, to public acclaim. But, of course, Japan's real *kuromaku,* the U.S., would continue as normal. *Tatemae* and *honne.* The public image and the private reality. Japan might indeed be the world's second-largest economy—but the operative word was "second."

In the final analysis, a country of one hundred and twenty-nine million people on the wrong side of the globe, living on a chain of a thousand islands without almost any natural resources, could never fundamentally challenge the world's true leader. And if it thought of so doing, it would not be allowed to. What was needed to be done, would be done. Every action that might prove necessary.

The last item that made it possible, even desirable, for Katsuda to initiate his move was an act of sheer hubris by the Hodama faction. With their confidence boosted by their economic success, they started dabbling in the arms trade and then moved to supplying enemies of the West. Rumors surfaced of the North Korean deal. This was impertinent and would not be tolerated.

Nothing was said directly to Katsuda, but suddenly the signs were there that Hodama and his faction were no longer protected. It was open season, if handled discreetly and with a certain sophistication.

Katsuda made his move.

He had personally led the assault group on Hodama and had taken the greatest pleasure in linking the killing to the Namakas. Month by month, he had tightened the noose. At the same time, he had set in motion his economic initiative. The Namakas' financial power base was being weakened. The elements in the plan were working and coming together.

Yet the Namakas endured. They had taken the heaviest pressure and were still in business. And there were now signs that they were rebounding stronger than ever. Evidently, Katsuda's actions had been too subtle.

Fortunately, the Namakas' own actions had thrown up an unlikely ally. This *gaijin*, Hugo Fitzduane, could make the necessary difference if the right circumstances were created. An Irishman, another islander like the Japanese. An interesting man, by all accounts.

Katsuda picked up the phone.

FITZDUANE LOOKED UP from his *Japan Times* as Adachi made his way across the floor of the hotel restaurant.

The remains of his Western-style breakfast, except for his tea and toast, were cleared away as the policeman approached.

"Good morning, Adachi-*san*," said Fitzduane, waving the policeman to a chair. "You have a look about you that suggests developments."

A waiter rushed up and brought Adachi some green tea. The service was excellent in Japan, Fitzduane had found, though the language barrier could be a problem. His waiter, for instance, was convinced that hot milk was what the Irish *gaijin* required with tea, and he would not be persuaded otherwise. Still, that slight eccentricity notwithstanding, Fitzduane felt he was in good hands.

"Would you ever think of trying Japanese food, Fitzduane-*san?*" said Adachi. He was used to *gaijins* demonstrating their skill with chopsticks and endeavoring, unsuccessfully, to be more Japanese than the Japanese when it came to food. Fitzduane, in contrast, asked for a knife and fork and did not seem to feel he had to prove anything. Sometimes he ordered Japanese dishes, but mostly he ordered Western. It was easy to do so in Tokyo. Practically every type of national cuisine was represented there. "Fish, rice, vegetables, and seaweed," continued Adachi. "It is a very healthy diet."

"A vicar was once served a dubious egg for breakfast," said Fitzduane, "and was then asked if everything was satisfactory. He replied, 'Good in parts.' Well, that is pretty much my impression of Japanese food." He smiled. "Though it is all superbly presented—a feast for the eye. Unfortunately, my taste buds do not always agree. They have a weakness for French and Northern Italian cooking, with forays into Indian and Chinese and the occasional medium-rare steak. Doubtless, they need further education."

Adachi laughed. He had been skeptical of the DSG's initiative in bringing a foreigner into what, in his view, was a Tokyo MPD affair, but Fitzduane, for a *gaijin*—a fundamental qualification—was an agreeable surprise.

Despite their unfortunate introduction, Adachi found the Irishman easy to get along with. He had a generous, low-key personality that invited confidences and he was sensitive to nuance, to the unspoken word. Also, his style was intuitive. He could almost have been a Japanese in his respect and understanding for *giri-ninjo*, yet he was very much his own man.

Adachi was somewhat puzzled by his own reactions to the man. As a Tokyo policeman, profoundly opposed to violence, he could not forget the carnage the Irishman had wrought the day they had met, yet Adachi still found he greatly enjoyed the man's company. Here was a man whose personal code seemed to reflect the most human of values, yet who killed without hesitation and without visible remorse. Adachi had never met anyone quite like him before.

"The two *yakuza* of the *Insuji-gumi* who you captured, Fitzduane-*san*," said Adachi, "have confessed." He did not sound surprised. It had been over a week since the botched assassination attempt. Fitzduane tried to imagine what a week of Japan's famous draconian police-custody system would have been like, under these rather embarrassing circumstances for the Tokyo MPD, and decided he did not particularly want to find out, nor was he overly sympathetic. It was hard to feel much about people who tried to kill you.

Fitzduane nodded. Adachi was slightly taken aback at Fitzduane's lack of reaction. It was yet another example of the man's atypical behavior. In his experience, most *gaijin* were surprised and sometimes shocked at how consistently Japanese police were able to get criminals to confess. They would raise questions of civil rights and habeas corpus and all kinds of legal mumbo jumbo, as if the rights of the victims and ordinary citizens were not an issue also. In Adachi's view, the West were hypocrites and had their priorities backward.

"The two *yakuza*," continued Adachi, "made separate confessions and have now signed statements. The contract on you, Fitzduane-*san*, was initiated by Kitano-*san*, the security chief of the Namaka Corporation. He personally briefed the killing team."

Fitzduane raised his eyebrows. "You surprise me, Adachi-*san*. Why would he get involved personally? Isn't a cutout normal procedure? Hell, this links the assassination attempt directly to the Namakas. It sounds too good to be true."

Adachi shook his head. "Unfortunately, Fitzduane-*san*," he said, "this development is not to our advantage. Yesterday, just prior to the *yakuza* confessions, we also received a written complaint from the Namaka brothers about their security chief, reporting their suspicions that he had been using his division for his own private advantage and also accusing him of embezzling company funds. Early this morning, we attempted to arrest Kitano. We were not successful. Instead we found him and his wife dead and a brief suicide note. In the note he stated that he had disgraced his entirely innocent employers by carrying out criminal activities and associating with terrorists. Yaibo was specifically mentioned. Effectively, the trail ends with Kitano. The evidence, regarding the attempts on your life at least, no longer points to the Namakas—whatever we may suppose."

"How did Kitano and his wife die?" said Fitzduane. "Could the suicide have been faked?"

"We have already carried out an autopsy," said Adachi, "and although the results of some tests still have to come in, the findings seem fairly conclusive. The woman was shot in the back of the neck at close range by a .45 U.S. Army Colt automatic as she knelt on the floor. Kitano then placed the barrel of the same weapon in his mouth and pulled the trigger. There are no signs of struggle, and there is evidence that Kitano fired the weapon with his right hand. And though the note was typed on a word processor, it was signed and we have verified the signature. The evidence says suicide."

"Was the weapon his?" said Fitzduane.

Adachi smiled. "Fitzduane-*san*, you already know how hard it is to own a legally registered gun in this country. No, although Kitano-*san* was head of security, he was not licensed to carry a firearm. However, there is a black market in such weapons, and all too many are in circulation as a result of the U.S. forces' presence and smuggling. Regrettably, the *yakuza* are tending to use firearms more frequently than they used to and their ownership is something of a criminal status symbol."

"Leaving evidence aside, Adachi-*san*," said Fitzduane, "what do you think about the Namakas themselves? Were they behind the various assaults on me? Are they really responsible for the Hodama killing? Perhaps they are really the high-minded captains of industry they purport to be, and all of this is a smear caused by a renegade employee."

"I'm a policeman, Fitzduane-*san*," said Adachi, "and I have to go by the evidence. The fact is that there is now no evidence at all linking the attacks on you with the Namakas. Instead we have a culprit, the late Kitano-*san*, with the means, motive, and opportunity—and a signed confession. As to Hodama, the evidence against the Namakas did appear strong, but on closer examination, I'm not so sure."

"You're still not saying what you think, Adachi-*san*," persevered Fitzduane, but gently. "*Go-enryo-naku*—please do not hold back."

Adachi smiled at Fitzduane's Japanese, but not at the thoughts he was expressing. The Irishman was touching on the *amae* element of a relationship—roughly translated as "childlike dependence"—so important in Japan, which results in *shinyo*—absolute confidence in another person, confidence not only in his or her integrity but also that such a person will do whatever is expected, whatever the cost. Such a trust normally took years to develop in Japan, but curiously Adachi felt that he could have *shinyo* in Fitzduane.

"I think the Namakas are an evil pair who should be put out of business," said Adachi, "and were certainly behind the attempts on your life and are involved with terrorism as a means to commercial gain. As to the Hodama business, here I do not feel they are guilty. Instead I believe that the Hodama killings are part of a power play, and that part of that scenario is the destruction of the Namakas. It's ironic. My investigation of the Hodama affair puts me, in a way, on the wrong side."

Fitzduane thought about what Adachi was saying. "The thought strikes me, Adachi-*san*," said Fitzduane, "that unless we are both careful, we could end up as the filling in this particular political sandwich. Perhaps a little pooling of resources might be an idea."

Adachi thought of the suspected leak in Keishicho—or was it the prosecutor's office?—and the blunt fact that he no longer knew whom to trust except, irony of ironies, for the Irishman. He nodded.

"Let's go for a stroll," he said. "There is a place we can talk in private and someone I would like you to meet again, a Sergeant Akamatsu."

"The veteran in the police box," said Fitzduane. "The man with the all-knowing eyes. He wasn't too happy I messed up his pavement, but lead on."

As Fitzduane was about to leave the hotel, he took a call from Yoshokawa. The Namakas regretted the delay, but one of the brothers had been away and both would like to meet Fitzduane-*san*. An appointment had been arranged for that afternoon. A car would arrive after lunch to take Fitzduane-*san* to the Namaka Tower.

"So they are sniffing the bait, Yoshokawa-*san*," said Fitzduane.

"Be careful all they do is sniff," said Yoshokawa. "These are very dangerous people."

"I'll hang garlic around my neck," said Fitzduane, "and maybe take a few other precautions. But, what the hell, it should be interesting."

FITZDUANE RETURNED from his lengthy discussion with Adachi and Sergeant Akamatsu just before lunch and opted to eat in his room.

It made his Tokyo MPD minders happier when he was not sitting exposed in a public place, and he wanted to do some thinking. In a couple of hours' time, he was going to meet and exchange pleasantries with two people, the Namaka brothers, who he had every reason to believe had tried repeatedly to kill him.

The anticipation gave him a strange feeling. Fear and anger were components, but there were also elements of uncertainty. The initiative was still in his enemies' hands, and although he had many reasons to believe that the Namakas were behind the assassination attempts, he still had no legal proof. They would have to make the first move or he could do nothing; or he could cross a line he preferred not to cross.

He could not kill on mere suspicion. There had to be some core values to live by, even in this confusing and dangerous world. Kilmara had chastised him for a lack of ruthlessness on occasions in the past, but the simple fact was that he could not change. He had been brought up to believe in some standards, and there it was. Even to protect his own life and that of his child, he could not exercise lethal force unprovoked.

He ordered a sandwich and a glass of white wine and ran a bath. The food arrived within minutes, but was actually delivered by a smiling Sergeant Oga. He was becoming quite good friends with the sergeant, and the minders were not overly keen on an assassin disguised as room service. As they learned Fitzduane's ways, they were getting very good at their job. Surveillance was comprehensive but unobtrusive. Nonetheless, it was a bloody nuisance. Fitzduane liked wandering around strange cities on his own, and being part of an armed convoy definitely took some of the spontaneity out of the whole business.

You could not really act the relaxed tourist when surrounded by a bunch of submachine-gun-toting cops, even if they did keep their weapons in shoulder bags. The submachine guns had been added after the Yasukini-dori business. If the *yakuza* wanted to play hardball, the Tokyo cops were not going to fuck around, and they were quick students.

Insofar as any *gaijin* ever could, Fitzduane reflected, he was now beginning to get a handle on how the various players such as Hodama, the Namakas, Yoshokawa, and the others fitted in. A fresh element in the Namaka equations was their possible involvement in supplying embargoed equipment to North Korea. Kilmara had explained briefly in an encrypted phone call to Fitzduane in the relatively secure environs of the Irish Embassy, but he had been rushed and the communication had been short on detail.

All Fitzduane had understood was that intelligence reports indicated

VICTOR O'REILLY

that the Namakas and some of their personnel from Namaka Special Steels were having secret negotiations with the North Korean nuclear people, and it might well behoove Fitzduane to watch his ass, because the stakes could be even higher than originally thought. On the other hand, it could prove helpful if he kept his eyes open. No one knew exactly what was going on. The intelligence reports were a mixture of scant fact and liberal extrapolation. Disturbingly, the final conclusion of the analysis was that all of this could involve the production by the North Koreans of nuclear weapons.

Kilmara had finished the conversation by pointing out that Fitzduane's Japanese hosts might not be too enthusiastic about the Namakas' possible arms-trading coming to light.

"My guess," Kilmara had said, "is that the local fuzz—"

"Adachi—the Tokyo MPD," Fitzduane had interrupted.

"—won't know about the nuclear thing, but that their security people will want to keep it very quiet. The Japanese depend on international trade and the U.S. is their largest single customer, so the last thing they will want is for them to be found peddling nuclear-weapons manufacturing plants to Uncle Sam's enemies. We're talking serious vested interests here, so watch it."

"While watching my ass, what am I supposed to be looking for?" said Fitzduane. "They could show me a complete hydrogen-bomb plant and tell me it made chocolate bars and I would be none the wiser. A nuclear expert I am not."

"Look, I'm just passing on the ruminations of the spooks," said Kilmara. "Just keep your eyes open and remember Japan is not that big a place—and happy hunting."

The land mass of Japan, Fitzduane recalled, was actually just under a hundred and forty-six thousand square miles, or just over half the size of Texas. Sometimes Kilmara's comments could be unhelpful.

He ate his sandwich, then soaked in his bath and sipped his wine. The thought occurred to him that although Adachi, and indeed the DSG, might not be in the need-to-know loop, Koancho, the security service, almost certainly was. Which explained Chifune's presence and raised strong questions about her own personal agenda. The *gaijin* had been brought over to help break the impasse in the Hodama investigation, but supposing Fitzduane-*san* found out something which could embarrass Japanese interests?

He hopped out of the bath and toweled vigorously while singing an old Irish Army marching song, then dressed for the occasion. Light-weight dark-blue suit, pale-blue shirt, regimental tie, silk socks, highly polished loafers. He examined himself in the mirror and decided he looked the very model of a *sarariman.* All he was missing was the corporate pin.

He checked his throwing knives and the compact Calico automatic, and was just holstering the latter when his phone rang.

The limousine of the Namaka Corporation had arrived. He picked up the gift he had brought for the Namaka brothers and left. His interpreter, Chifune, was waiting for him in the lobby. She bowed, as any well-mannered interpreter would do, but when she rose he saw once again that enigmatic smile.

He was about to wave her through the door ahead of him, then remembered how the Japanese did such things. He grinned at Chifune, then walked out ahead and was ushered first into the waiting black limousine. The uniformed chauffeur wore white gloves and the seats had white head protectors like those in an airline. The Namaka corporate crest was discreetly painted on the limousine doors.

As they drove north toward Ikeburo and Sunshine City, Fitzduane reflected on the rise of the Namakas and tried to imagine what bombed-out postwar Tokyo must have been like for a pair of near-starving teenagers whose father had just been executed.

He almost felt sympathy for the Namakas, until he remembered the slicing of the bullet as it drew blood from his little son's head.

He was acutely conscious of Chifune's physical presence beside him on the rear seat, quiet and demure as befitted her interpreter role.

The Namaka Tower, Sunshine City, Tokyo, Japan:

June 19

Fumio Namaka leaned back in his chair and steepled his hands in thought.

The *gaijin* Fitzduane was due shortly, and he wanted to satisfy himself that he had considered and provided for all the issues involved.

The news from North Korea had been extremely encouraging. What had seemed like a wild card now looked like it was turning into a financial windfall, and just at the right time. It would tip the balance. Namaka Industries would survive. Fumio had been very much against the idea of supplying the North Koreans with nuclear plants, but Kei had argued strongly in favor and he had turned out to be right. Frankly, Kei's investment enthusiasms rarely worked out, but the North Korea nuclear project was proving to be a notable exception.

It was at last becoming clear who was behind the Hodama killings and the financial onslaught on the Namakas' empire. A vast counterintelligence exercise and the calling-in of favors at the highest government, civil service, and corporate levels had uncovered a trail that had led in the end to the Katsuda-*gumi*. It was a much-feared and respected organization, the second-largest *yakuza* gang in Japan, but as to why the Katsuda people were mounting such a vicious and deadly campaign against the Namakas was a complete mystery. Perhaps they were merely fronting for some other faction. It was hard to be certain. Attempts to make direct contact through a highly respected and neutral intermediary had been rebuffed.

Still, whether they were the principals or not, the Katsuda-*gumi* were certainly heavily involved and there was now a specific opponent to fight. This was hugely encouraging. The Namakas had been in such wars before and had always emerged triumphant. And recently, there were signs that the tide was beginning to turn in the Namakas' favor.

The Namaka share prices were starting to perform in line with the market again. Contacts who had been mysteriously unavailable were starting to return calls and pay their respects. Damage control to compensate for the loss of the Hodama patronage was working.

It had been a matter of rearranging certain key elements in the extensive Namaka network of influence, and that had taken time, but now the new arrangements were in place and the Namakas were on the offensive.

The Katsuda-*gumi* would soon learn the reality of true power. Shortly, a Yaibo killing team would commence a campaign of selective assassination against the Katsuda-*gumi,* and other initiatives would be implemented. Even their hideous leader, rarely seen by any outsider, would find himself vulnerable.

The Namaka brothers were old hands at fighting this kind of gang warfare. And they would have the tacit support of the police, once this Hodama business was put aside.

The police were rarely much concerned about the *yakuza* being cut down to size, providing ordinary citizens were not harmed. The *yakuza* were tolerated because some organization was needed—even in crime—but the police were still their enemies. In contrast, the Namakas headed a powerful industrial group and had friends in the highest places.

Kitano's abuse of authority had been unexpectedly convenient. It was outrageous that he should have mounted an assassination attempt on this *gaijin* Fitzduane without getting permission, but fortunately all avenues led to and stopped at him. He was a perfect scapegoat, not just for the Fitzduane attacks, but also for whatever else the Namakas were suspected of—even Hodama. He had been found out to be a rogue element. Well, these things happened, even in the best-run organizations. A single corrupt employee had scant significance in the scheme of things.

The Namakas were, of course, above such behavior. Their *bun*—the rights pertaining to their station in life—made this clear by implication. A rank-and-file *yakuza* or a junior employee might be made subject to special police interrogation, but those at the level of the Namakas were, for all practical purposes, immune. Even the much-feared Tokyo Prosecutor's Office treated those at the highest level with respect. This was Japan, the supreme hierarchical society. Rank was everything.

Ironically, it did not matter whether anyone believed Kitano had acted independently or not. The important thing was that it was a story which could save face all round. The *tatemae* was what was important. Fumio was reminded of the American phrase "plausible deniability."

The *gaijin* Fitzduane remained a loose end. Left to himself, Fumio was all for leaving him alone and concentrating on more important issues. Three failed assassination attempts suggested he was an unusually hard man to kill and, really, they had satisfied their obligation to their dead associate by severely wounding the *gaijin*. Enough was enough.

Unfortunately, Kei—who combined a limited intellect with mulelike stubbornness—did not see things this way. He had taken their failure personally and was being extremely bullheaded about it. His pride was hurt, and he took Fitzduane's continued survival as an ongoing affront. He argued that there was more to the Irishman than they knew and that he was certainly an agent sent to secure the Namakas' downfall. Frankly, some of Kei's comments were excessive, but the result was straightforward enough. Kei Namaka wanted the *gaijin*,

Fitzduane-*san*, dead, and if the hired help were not competent to do the job, he would carry out the task himself.

Fumio had pointed out that surveillance and informers had confirmed that the *gaijin* was under around-the-clock police protection, but his big brother had been adamant. He was going to kill Fitzduane and he would not be stopped. It was now a matter of *giri*. Reluctantly, Fumio had agreed, and had then applied his considerable brain to devising a method which would allow Kei his way without fear of discovery.

He had come up with a good plan, he thought. The *gaijin*'s own initiative—his desire to see the steel plant, as communicated by Yoshokawa-*san,* who had set up the meeting—would be turned against him. The plan had pleased Kei greatly. The *gaijin* would not just be killed, but he would literally evaporate.

Thrown inside a tempering oven set to its highest temperature, his body fluids—the bulk of a corpse—would soon boil away and the small residue would turn to gas. It was a scientific truth that matter could not be destroyed, but its substance could certainly be altered. A gaseous Fitzduane would not pose a problem, whatever it might do for global warming.

His telephone buzzed, and a respectful voice announced that the *gaijin* Fitzduane-*san*'s party had arrived at the security desk at the base of the Namaka Tower. The call reminded Fumio to clear his desk. The meeting was to be in the conference room, but one could never be too careful. All was secure. After a final glance, he limped to the meeting.

AFTER CHIFUNE HAD introduced her *gaijin* employer at the first-floor reception desk, a uniformed OL came forward and bowed deeply toward Fitzduane and more moderately at Chifune.

She then spoke, and Chifune translated near-simultaneously. In fact, Chifune was so good at translation that Fitzduane realized it must have been part of her Koancho training. He wondered how many trade delegates admiring their attractive interpreter realized that they were under observation by the security services. Well, doubtless the CIA and God knows who else were doing the same thing at the other end.

"Sunshine City, of which the Namaka Tower is the centerpiece, is a multifunction complex that is a center for business and commerce," translated Chifune, her face blank. "The Higashi Ikeburo ramp of the

Metropolitan Expressway connects directly to the basement parking area of the complex, and there is parking there for 1,800 cars. Sunshine City includes, in addition to the Namaka Tower, a hotel, a shopping mall, a branch of the Mitsukoshi department store, many offices, a convention center, and the world's highest aquarium."

Fitzduane blinked and tried hard to keep a straight face. The Japanese had built an aquarium on the site where their wartime leaders had been executed.

Sunshine City had been Sugamo Prison. This was making pragmatism into a high art. Well, maybe it was better to forget the past. The Irish never forgot the past and look what trouble the North was in. Still, an aquarium! He suppressed a desire to rush away and reread *Alice in Wonderland*.

"How high is the world's highest aquarium?" asked Fitzduane politely.

"It's on the tenth floor," translated Chifune, "forty meters above ground level. It has 20,000 fish covering 620 different species, and fresh seawater from Hachicho Island is supplied to them constantly so that their environment is entirely natural." Her mouth was beginning to twitch.

"If I was a fish," said Fitzduane, "I couldn't imagine anything less natural than being stuck in a tank ten floors up with 19,999 neighbors. It sounds more like the South Bronx, which certainly is not entirely natural. Still, to be fair, I am not a fish."

Since Sunshine City looked solidly rooted in northern Tokyo and the sea did not seem to be immediately available, he was dying to ask by what ingenious method seawater was constantly supplied from Hachicho Island, wherever that was, but then the elevator doors opened and their guide burst into action again. She had a cheerleader's energy and enthusiasm packed into her neat little body. Fitzduane half expected pom-poms to appear any second, but her body language was repressed and demure.

The doors closed and the elevator took off like a rocket. Fitzduane felt he had left his stomach somewhere about the level of the fish, and there were still fifty more floors to go.

"The Namaka Tower, at 240 meters above ground level, is the tallest occupied building in Japan," translated Chifune, "and on a clear day you can see a hundred kilometers in any direction, and even Mount Fuji. You may also care to know that you are standing in the world's fastest elevator, which will make the entire journey in only thirty-five seconds."

Fitzduane's stomach had reappeared and was starting to go in the other direction as they decelerated. If the Namakas went through this rocket trip twice a day, it was clear that he was up against some fairly tough people.

"Doesn't this country have earthquakes?" said Fitzduane. "Is it really a good idea to be this high up when holes open up in the ground?"

There was no time for an answer. The elevator came to a halt and the doors opened. Facing him were the two people who had casually arranged to have him killed, who had threatened the very core of his family.

He smiled and stepped forward, the gift he had brought in his left hand. It was a carefully packaged, handmade reproduction of a traditional Irish weapon, the Galloglass Axe, and with its blade and handle it was nearly the height of an average Western man. It towered over the smaller Japanese man, whom Fitzduane took to be the younger brother, Fumio. Set against the tall, broad-shouldered Kei Namaka, it looked to be a fair match.

17

June 19

Fumio Namaka had felt the chill fingers of fear caress his very soul the first time he saw Fitzduane, and ten minutes into the meeting in the luxuriously appointed conference room on the sixtieth floor of the Namaka Tower, the grim feeling was still with him.

The *gaijin* had first come into their lives as a matter of obligation. At that time he had had no substance, no reality. He was a name on a piece of paper, a photograph in a file.

Three failed assassination attempts later, and sitting across the table at the very heart of the Namaka empire, the *gaijin* was another matter entirely. This was a truly impressive man, confident and at ease with himself. He appeared relaxed and to be enjoying the discussion, and it was this very ease of manner, after he had been through so much, that convinced Fumio that his brother was right. Fitzduane was a fundamental threat and deserved to be taken most seriously, for if they failed to destroy him quickly, he would be their nemesis.

Looking across at Fitzduane, Fumio felt fear. Of course, there was always the chance that the *gaijin* actually knew nothing and would accept the story about Kitano being responsible for everything, but Fumio trusted his instincts. The *gaijin* was a bringer of death.

Kei Namaka, at his very best in the role of concerned, socially responsible captain of industry, was just expressing his shock at discovering the scheming of the Namaka security chief.

"It seems, Fitzduane-*san*," he said, "that we have all been victims of a cunning man who grossly abused his position. My brother and I were appalled to discover what our supposedly trusted employee was up to. Kitano-*san* has brought the respected name of Namaka Industries into disrepute, and my brother and I are extremely embarrassed by this. We apologize without reservation for what this renegade has done. You must let us make compensation, and of course we will do anything we can to make your trip here more interesting and enjoyable."

Fitzduane was struck by the contrast between the two brothers. Kei Namaka was truly a magnificent physical specimen, tall, broad-shouldered, and with the kind of confidence-inspiring good looks that would make him a natural for a business-magazine front cover. In contrast, Fumio, with his thin, disfigured body, was a decidedly puny-looking specimen unless you looked at him closely. There was a deep intelligence in those eyes. The physically unimpressive Fumio Namaka was, in Fitzduane's opinion, the one to watch.

"Namaka-*san*," said Fitzduane. "Your words are most gracious and are deeply appreciated, but you employ tens of thousands of people and cannot possibly be expected to be responsible for every one. All of us have suffered. I have had my life threatened, and you, I understand, have lost a great deal of money to this man. Well, let us think of ourselves as partners in our misfortune and hopefully partners in a future in happier affairs, and move on to more pleasant matters." He smiled.

Chifune, effectively invisible since she was a woman and her presence, strictly speaking, unnecessary—both Namakas spoke excellent English—was amused at Fitzduane's performance. Knowing what she did, she found the confrontation bizarre, but the Irishman was carrying off his role with aplomb. He was being quite charming, and she could see Kei Namaka responding.

Kei evidently saw himself as a leader and a man's man, and reacted well to having this self-image appreciated. In Chifune's opinion, he was a case of heart—or, more probably, impulse—over head. As for the sinister younger brother, he said almost nothing, but just sat there noting everything. He was a cold fish.

"You're most kind, Fitzduane-*san*," said Kei Namaka, "and you are right. Perhaps now it would be appropriate if we unwrapped our gifts. Thanks to Yoshokawa-*san*, I know we share an interest in medieval weaponry, so I hope you will enjoy the modest token we have selected for you."

Fitzduane unwrapped the long, rectangular package. Every aspect of the packaging was superb, both in quality and in execution, and yet again he could not but admire the Japanese attention to detail. With the paper removed, he found himself looking at a long, narrow, hand-made inlaid cedarwood box about four feet long and eight inches wide, itself a minor masterpiece of craftsmanship, but obviously the precursor to something more special.

He was enjoying this. Even under these dangerous circumstances, it was fun to receive a present, especially something that was obviously special. Of course, it could be lethal, but that was unlikely, he thought. The meeting had been arranged by Yoshokawa and was a public affair. No, whatever the Namakas had in mind, he was safe for the moment. He looked across at the Namakas and smiled in anticipation. Kei Namaka beamed back at him. The man was enjoying this as much as he was. Criminal though he might be, there was something rather likable about Kei. Fumio just sat there, stone-faced. It was hard to warm to Fumio.

"What superb workmanship!" he said, indicating the cedarwood box. "I cannot imagine what must be inside." He gently caressed the rich patina of the wood, taking his time. He could feel Kei's impatience. The man had childlike enthusiasm.

"You must open the box, Fitzduane-*san*," Kei said. "Press the chrysanthemum inlay in the middle and slide it to the left and it will open."

Fitzduane did as instructed. The chrysanthemum, he knew, was associated with the Japanese royal family, and he began to realize that what he had been given was very special indeed. He opened the box.

A magnificent Spanish cup-hilt rapier lay there, cushioned in padded crimson silk. The hilt was inlaid with scenes of hunting and warfare. The weapon was an antique, and extremely valuable. He removed it from the presentation box and it settled in his hand as if custom-made for him.

"Late-seventeenth-century Spanish," he said. "The long, straight quillons and curved knuckle bow are typical of the designs of that time—but what a superb specimen. What perfect weight and balance, and what workmanship!"

Kei Namaka looked genuinely delighted at Fitzduane's obvious surprise and pleasure. "Fitzduane-*san*," he said, "we heard from Yoshokawa-*san* that you are a swordsman of some renown and a knowledgeable collector, so this small token seemed appropriate. Your weapon of choice is, I believe, the epee, the sporting evolution of the rapier, and it was that fact that motivated this particular selection."

Fitzduane smiled his appreciation. "I do fence a little, that is true, but I'm not sure I am in the same league as this fine weapon. Also, the swords I use have blunted points. Killing your opponent in this day and age is frowned upon."

Kei laughed heartily at this observation and Chifune tittered politely as she was expected to, her hand in front of her mouth. She found the convention ridiculous, but it was not considered polite for a well-brought-up young Japanese woman to give a full belly laugh or to laugh with her mouth uncovered. Kei was acting, Chifune thought, as if he were some medieval *daimyo* or clan lord in a good mood, posturing in front of his *samurai.*

Just as quickly, she recalled, the mood of such a man could swing the other way to violence. Of course, the brutal reality was that he was indeed the modern version of a powerful *daimyo,* only his holdings spanned the continents. The wealth of a modern *keiretsu* would make a medieval *daimyo* pale. Kei was not merely acting his role. He was strong and influential. This was the frightening truth.

"Namaka-*san,*" said Fitzduane. "I am deeply honored by your gift. Now perhaps you would do me the honor of opening the simple token I have brought for you. It will not compare with your generosity, but you may find it interesting."

If Kei had been excited while watching Fitzduane open his present, then this time he was practically panting, although to a less well-trained eye than Chifune's, his superficial physical demeanor did not betray him. This was Japan, where control was important and excess was frowned upon. Nonetheless, his fingers worked a little too hard at the outer wrapping and his eyes gleamed just a little too brightly. The man acted as if it was Christmas. It was curious, this mixture of childlike vulnerability and brutality.

When the gleaming ax finally emerged, the blade double-headed and the handle inlaid with fine gold wire, Kei Namaka gave a gasp of admiration and then, being unable to restrain himself any longer, gave a shout and stood up, ax in hand, and whirled it about his head.

Kei, despite his handmade shirt and silk tie and Savile Row suit, did not look in any way incongruous as he whirled the weapon. On the contrary, he looked magnificent—every inch the Eternal Warrior, in Chifune's opinion, or a spoiled chilled with yet another lethal toy. It depended on your particular point of view.

"I heard, Namaka-*san*," said Fitzduane, "that you had an unsurpassed collection of edged weapons, so I wanted to find something that you would not already possess. Unfortunately, Ireland's troubled history is such that almost all our early medieval weaponry has been destroyed, but what you have there is a precise reproduction of a thirteenth-century Irish fighting ax. It was a weapon used to great effect against the Norman invader because it could cleave through armor."

Kei whirled the huge ax once again, then brought it back and laid it on its leather carrying case on the table. It was then he noticed the Namaka crest etched into the blade. He looked up at Fitzduane.

"You have gone to a great deal of trouble, Fitzduane-*san*," he said. "My brother and I deeply appreciate this gift. We must now make arrangements for you to visit the steel plant in which, through Yoshokawa-*san*, you have already expressed an interest. It is an awesome sight to see the hardest steels handled like putty. Also, I have a *dojo* there and most of my weapons collection. I think you'll find it fascinating."

Fumio found it hard to take his eyes off the ax. Kei and this *gaijin* were getting along like old friends and yet he could not shake the feeling of dread that gripped him. The weapon on the table reminded him forcibly of an executioner's ax. It was an ingenious gift, and perfect for the effect it was intended to achieve, but the sight of it made Fumio feel ill.

He tore his eyes away from the ax and looked across at Fitzduane and then at Chifune. The woman was every inch the well-mannered interpreter, but there was something about her that gave him pause.

"Fitzduane-*san*," said Fumio, with a slight smile. "We greatly look forward to your visit to Namaka Steel, but you will now realize that since we both speak English, you will not need an interpreter during your visit. Tanabu-*san*'s service will not be required."

Fitzduane played it very well, thought Chifune. He gave a dismissive gesture, as if to indicate that his interpreter was of no consequence, and the conversation moved on to other matters. The Namakas had taken the bait, but Chifune was now convinced they had every intention of keeping it. They had something in mind, she was sure of it, but what?

As Kei Namaka and Fitzduane joked and chatted in the relaxed and easy manner of old friends, united in their common interest in antique weapons, Chifune started to worry.

THAT EVENING, Fitzduane had dinner with Chifune, an enjoyable if sexually disturbing experience, and returned to the bows of the night porter near midnight feeling pleasantly mellow but sexually aroused—a quaint combination.

He endeavored to balance things out under a cold shower, a traditional remedy for such a conjunction, but his erection would not be subdued. Chifune had that kind of effect. Nothing explicit had either been said or done, but the sexual electricity had become strong enough, he felt, to make both of them glow in the dark like Russian sailors on the nuclear subs of the Northern fleet. It seemed a pity, he reflected, that for the balance of the night they would have to glow apart.

Women were damn confusing. There was Etan, whom he loved but who did not want to settle down just when he did. There was Kathleen, of whom he was becoming increasingly fond, who evidently did want to settle down, just when he was beginning to think perhaps he didn't. And there was Chifune, where the chemistry was just plain sexual and who had Adachi-*san* hidden in the wings, if he read the signs right. He liked Adachi, and anyway it really would not be a good idea to confuse business and pleasure. He needed, and was getting, Adachi's cooperation, so sleeping with the superintendent's woman would not be tactful. Still, life was rarely about being sensible.

Since the cold water did not seem to be having the desired effect, and he saw no point in giving the Namakas the satisfaction of dying of hypothermia, Fitzduane turned up the hot. He was endeavoring to have a pleasantly mindless soak when the phone rang. Evidently, his mind was not fooled. When he wrapped a towel around his waist, there remained a noticeable protrusion.

"I'm asleep," said Fitzduane, "more or less. The earth is round and Japan is a long way away from where you are and it's after midnight around here. Nobody civilized calls that late."

"Well, ain't that nice," said Kilmara. "That leaves me in the clear. Listen, my good friend, this is a global village these days, and the ether has been hyperactive since you visited with Bergin. Somebody wants to talk to you to make sure you don't step into something you shouldn't. 'There are things afoot we don't want to fuck up,' he says. 'We need our friends,' he says."

"Who is the somebody?" said Fitzduane, who already knew.

"Our friend, the unlovable Paul Schwanberg," said Kilmara. "Head off to the New Otani tomorrow after breakfast if you have nothing doing, and ask for him at reception. He's got offices there. Something called the Japan-World Research Federation. Well, it's better than Acme Import-Export, but not much. Anyway, everyone knows who they are. It's just that it's more fun operating from a cover than out of the embassy, though they do that too. They have a proprietorial feeling about Japan. There is nothing like dropping a couple of nuclear bombs on a country to start a special relationship."

As if on cue, the room started to shake, not violently but steadily. After about ten seconds, the movement stopped. Kilmara was still talking, but Fitzduane had not been listening. It had been frightening.

"Hell," he said, "they really do have earthquakes here. It's scary."

"They are due a big one soon," said Kilmara, "or so I hear. Something to take your mind off all this blood and guts you seem to attract. Just remember to stay away from reinforced concrete buildings and stuff like that. They do you no good at all if they fall on you—especially at your age."

"I feel pretty young tonight," said Fitzduane, eyeing the obstinate bulge which had come unscathed through the earth tremor, "but unfortunately there is no one around to share this insight with."

"Yeah, hotel rooms are like that sometimes," said Kilmara. "But not always. I remember when you and I were in . . . ."

Fitzduane laughed. He was asleep minutes later.

THE NEW OTANI, TOKYO, JAPAN

June 20

The New Otani complex was a fitting monument to the new superrich, self-confident Japan, and Fitzduane, having learned something about Japanese property prices, shuddered at what it might be worth.

It was part luxury hotel and part office complex, and doubtless there were expensive apartments hidden away there also. The atrium was spectacular and looked high enough to have its own microclimate. Certainly you could jump off one of the internal balconies and hang-glide inside it if you were so inclined—provided you were well-tailored and wore polished Gucci loafers. There was an implied dress code.

The soaring atrium was a truly magnificent waste of Tokyo real estate. Such impracticality cheered up Fitzduane immensely, and he was already in a good mood. His favorite waiter had brought *cold* milk for his tea that morning, and no one had taken a shot at him or tried to cut him into pieces when he had gone for a prebreakfast run with his convoy. Also, it had not been raining, which was a decided improvement.

It was soon clear that the loss the developers of the New Otani had taken with the atrium was being compensated for elsewhere. The offices of the Japan-World Research Federation were exquisitely finished, but tiny. It was the smallest suite of offices Fitzduane had ever seen, and everything—desks, cupboards, tables, chairs—seemed to be shrunk in proportion. Schwanberg was small, too, a not-quite-a-yuppie-anymore in his early fifties with thinning hair and a smooth, manufactured face. He wore a tie with a stickpin, and as he moved there was a flash of red suspenders. His jacket buttons were covered with the same material as his suit.

For a brief moment Fitzduane remembered that horrendous scene from decades earlier as, without explanation or warning, Schwanberg suddenly inserted the blade of his knife into that young Vietnamese girl's mouth. He could never forget the gush of red blood and the terrible animal noise she had made. It had been reported, but then the Tet Offensive had intervened, and when the fighting died down again the file had been lost and the affair glossed over.

Fitzduane despised the man. In his opinion, Schwanberg was vicious and cunning but absolutely without core values. He was also an extraordinarily colorless individual. Fitzduane had the feeling that Schwanberg knew clamps were needed to climb the slippy bureaucratic pole, but otherwise he had been chosen to match the furniture. Still, Kilmara had made the current introduction, and the game was not played by being overly concerned about personalities.

"Colonel Fitzduane," said Schwanberg, smiling broadly and taking Fitzduane's hand in both of his. "This is a genuine pleasure and a privilege. It's good to see an old war buddy. We've both come a long way since then."

Fitzduane extracted his hand, kept his face in neutral, and barely restrained himself from doing something painful and destructive to the little toad. The man's eyes were curiously dead, as if feelings and emotions were alien.

Schwanberg snapped his fingers. Fitzduane's umbrella was removed by a bowing office lady and he was shown into a miniature conference room.

Tea was brought in by another OL. Frankly, he could not see where they put all these people. The place was seriously small. They must rack up the staff in the filing cabinets. There did not seem enough space for a couple of real humans.

Schwanberg pressed some buttons on a console recessed into the conference table and the door slid shut and there was the sound of humming.

"We're now totally secure," said Schwanberg. "A bubble. A lot of dollars went into this place. Totally soundproof, totally bug-proof. Nada gets out, Hugo, so we can speak quite freely."

Fitzduane smiled disarmingly. "Speak away, Schwanberg," he said, and sat back into his miniature chair expectantly. Schwanberg looked at him, as if expecting him to say something. Fitzduane just nodded reassuringly, but said nothing.

"You know, Colonel," said Schwanberg, "you've got one hell of an impressive track record. Most in the counterterrorism business just shuffle paper, send each other classified E-mail, and maneuver to get the most out of the public trough, but you and I and General Kilmara get right in there and get our hands bloody."

He grinned. "Forget me. I've been a desk jockey too long. The fact is that, compared to most in this business, you two are right at the top in terms of hands-on experience. You guys are not the product of endless expensive training and computer war games. You people have actually done it. You've tracked down the bad guys and wasted them. You know what to do and how to do it and how to get others to do it. In fact, apart from maybe the Israelis, there are few people more experienced at the game."

Fitzduane drank his tea. He had absolutely no idea where Schwanberg was heading, except that he was being flattered for some, doubtless unpleasant, purpose.

"Schwanberg," he said, "what you say is probably true about General Kilmara, but if your records are accurate, they will show that apart from a stint in the Irish Army, I have spent most of my life, including my stint in Vietnam, as a war photographer. I became involved in counterterrorism by accident, by being on the receiving end, and I am here as a consequence of that accident. I am not the expert you imagine. My rank is a reserve title, nothing more."

"Colonel," said Schwanberg, the thumb and forefinger of his right hand repeatedly pinching the flesh on the back of his left in an irritating mannerism, "you're entitled to your story, but how you tracked down our friend the Hangman is a classic right up there with the Entebbe raid. You may have gotten into this business by accident, but you sure operate as a professional and you come highly recommended. And that's why we're talking. You're one of us. You're a member of the club, and, frankly, it's hard to get into, but it's even harder to leave."

It crossed Fitzduane's mind that even if he had not realized it, he *had* crossed the line between amateur and professional. What the unpleasant Schwanberg was saying was true. Circumstances had forced him into the bloody world of counterterrorism, and the reality was that he seemed to have a talent for it. But it was not a concept he enjoyed.

Violence might be necessary on occasion, but it was corrosive to the spirit. He thought of Boots. He wanted desperately to shelter his small son from that world. But the paradox was that, to shield him, he was prepared to do what had to be done. It was the endless spiral of destruction that seemed integral to the human condition.

"The club?" he said.

"The small group of us," said Schwanberg, "who do what is necessary so that Mr. and Mrs. Average Citizen have nothing more serious to worry about than the IRS. The protectors of Western values, if you want to be pompous about it."

"That is being pompous about it," said Fitzduane. "I am really not overly keen on flag-waving. And to focus this discussion a little more, where does Japan fit into your Western values?"

Schwanberg flashed his organization man's professional grin. "That's the question that preoccupies us local boys," he said, "and right now it is a little delicate. Bergin will have told you some of it, but he's an old man now and out of the game, so he doesn't know much. I'll tell you what you need to know. It's a minefield out there, and we don't want a good friend and a fellow club member treading on any of the mines. They are there for a purpose. We have specific targets in mind."

"Hodama and the Namakas," said Fitzduane. "Onetime allies who strayed a little and got too greedy and now have exceeded their shelf life. Time for a little stock rotation. It's something the CIA is pretty good at. Look at what is happening in Italy these days, to name just one other country."

Schwanberg was no longer smiling. He was looking at Fitzduane intently, as if weighing the issues, and as if one of those issues was the Irishman's continued existence. "You sound judgmental, Colonel," he said. "I would be disappointed to find that you are that naive. Japan has notions of going its own way, but that is just *tatemae*. The *honne* is that Japan has always had a *kuromaku*, and since the end of World War Two that has been Uncle Sam's job. People like Hodama were the tools of power but not truly powerful in themselves—and circumstances change and tools wear out. That's the way life really is. People are organic. They degrade."

Fitzduane spoke coldly. "Spare me the lecture, Schwanberg, and get to cases. What do you want and what have you got to offer?"

"Hodama is gone, so that's history," said Schwanberg. "Now we want the Namakas permanently out of circulation. When they go, we can move another Japanese *kuromaku* into place who will be more amenable, and then engage in a little rearranging. The government has served us well, but the public is getting unhappy. We need an illusion of change."

"Katsuda," said Fitzduane, "with some politician on a reformist platform fronting for him."

"Jesus Christ!" said Schwanberg slowly. "You've only been here a couple of weeks. How the hell did you come up with that one?"

"People talk to me," said Fitzduane, "and some have long memories. Who had reason to want to kill Hodama in that gruesome way and who was filling the power vacuum? Means, motive, and opportunity—the classic criteria—and they end up pointing clearly at Katsuda. The method of Hodama's killing was a mistake. It was so obviously personal. It should have looked like a professional hit. No signature. Just a dead body."

"All the evidence is stacked against the Namakas," said Schwanberg, "and there is no way of tying this in to Katsuda. Believe me, I know. Katsuda may be guilty, but it will never be proved. A lot of care went into clearing up the loose ends. The Namakas will take the blame."

Fitzduane shook his head. "There is a good cop on the case, and I think your frame-up has been detected."

Schwanberg looked surprised. "We'd have been told."

"As I said," said Fitzduane, "the man is a good cop—and he's also smart. I think he knows you've got a mole in there, and maybe even who."

"Fuck this," said Schwanberg. "We're supposed to be on the same side on this. We both want the Namakas. Sure, they didn't kill Hodama, but so what. They certainly were behind the hits on you. So let's work together and nail the suckers. As to your cop friend Adachi, he's been showing signs of being difficult for some time, so there are arrangements in place. He's a natural for a domestic accident."

Fitzduane, his face masking his inner feelings, wanted to reach across and strangle the man facing him. The cynicism and callousness of this little shit appalled him. Here was this bureaucrat talking about the death of a fellow human being as if it were of no more significance than ordering more photocopy paper.

He imagined the Namakas ordering his killing in the same indifferent way, and was extremely angry. His heart wanted him to rush out and somehow contact Adachi and prevent whatever was planned. His head advised caution. He must stay longer. There was more to come out of Schwanberg, and the man must not suspect the thoughts going through Fitzduane's brain.

"So what do you want me to do?" said Fitzduane.

"Help steer the whole Hodama business towards the Namakas and keep Katsuda in the clear," said Schwanberg, "and keep us informed." He was silent, but clearly he was working toward something of greater significance.

"One way or another, we'll get the Namakas," continued Schwanberg, "but they are only part of our mutual problem. There is also their tame terrorist organization—the people who shot you. Whatever you may think, these are a group we are *not* responsible for. We didn't make the connection with the Namakas for some time, and so far we haven't been able to do anything about it. But we want Yaibo taken out. The Namakas are the right place to start, but putting them out of business will still leave a very lethal residue."

Fitzduane nodded. "I see the political logic and I agree with it, but I don't have to like it."

Schwanberg shrugged.

"One extra thing," said Fitzduane, "lay off Adachi. Let me worry about him."

Schwanberg looked uncomfortable. "We influence matters," he said, "but we don't necessarily run them."

"What the fuck does that mean?" said Fitzduane.

"The word about Adachi has been passed to Katsuda," said Schwanberg. "I think an operation is already in the pipeline and that it is going to happen soon. Of course, I don't actually know any of the details. And nor do I want to."

"How soon?" said Fitzduane.

"I don't know exactly," said Schwanberg, "but maybe today. Maybe it has even already happened. Katsuda is the impatient type when let off the leash. Proactive on wet matters, you might say."

"Nothing personal, Schwanberg," said Fitzduane, "but if anything happens to Adachi, I'm going to break your scrawny little neck. Now open this bell jar and let me out of here."

TOKYO, JAPAN

June 20

Fumio Namaka limped into his brother's office.

Kei was swinging the Irish ax he had been given by Fitzduane in much the same casual manner as another executive might fool around with a golf club. Kei was not keen on paperwork and detail bored him, but his interest in the martial arts rarely flagged. In his mind, he was a medieval *samurai,* and the twentieth century an unfortunate error in timing.

"Kei," said Fumio, "I'd like you to come into the corridor and tell me what you see."

"I'm busy," said Kei, as he whirled the long-handled ax around his head and then slashed it down in a scything diagonal blow. "I'm trying to get the hang of this thing. It's trickier than it seems. It builds up enormous momentum, but that very force makes it hard to control. If your blow doesn't hit, then the ax blade carries on and you're vulnerable. Still, I'm sure there is a technique that can compensate for that, if I can just work it out."

Effortlessly, he brought up the blade again, and Fumio felt both irritation and a rush of affection for his older brother. Kei could be maddening, but his enthusiasm was infectious.

"It concerns the disposal of this *gaijin*, Fitzduane-*san*," said Fumio. "I'm running a small experiment which I think you will find interesting."

Kei snorted but put the ax down. "Where do you want me to go?" he said.

"Open the door and look left and tell me what you see in the corridor," said Fumio patiently.

"Games!" said Kei disparagingly, and marched across to the door, opened it, and peered out. He was back instantly, his face pale.

"It's the *gaijin*," he said, "the Irishman. He's here, just standing there at the end of the corridor with his back to the window. What's he doing here? How did he get past security? What's he up to?"

"I have absolutely no idea," said Fumio. "Are you sure it's the *gaijin*?"

"Of course I'm sure," said Kei instantly, and then took in Fumio's expression. "What do you mean?" he said.

"The man in the corridor is not Fitzduane-*san*," said Fumio. "Same height, same build, same clothes, same haircut and color—but he is not the *gaijin*. His back was to the window so his face was in shadow, but if you look again more closely you will see the differences. But the important thing is that he fooled you the first time and you were not expecting to see him. People see what they expect to see."

Kei opened the door again, and this time went down the corridor a dozen paces until he was much closer to the figure. Now he could tell the difference quite easily, but it was still a good likeness.

"Remarkable, Fumio," he said to his brother, as he returned to his office and closed the door, "but what is the purpose of this proxy—this doppelgänger?"

Fumio told him.

AT LEAST ONCE A WEEK Adachi had reported to Prosecutor Sekine, and this time as he stood outside his mentor's door his heart was heavy.

Loyalties that he had taken for granted all his life were now in question. Like most Japanese, he had never held politicians or the political system in high esteem, but he had always had a great deal of faith in the basic administration of the country. Now he was beginning to think he had been naive.

Political corruption *must* spill over into the civil administration. Vast sums of money were not paid over to politicians merely to perpetuate an ineffective political system. No, the money was handed over to get a very real return, and the only way that could be done was by involving senior civil servants. They comprised the very kernel of the power structure. To accomplish anything at all, politicians had to work through them. The strings of the *kuromakus* led directly to these people.

The logic was unpalatable but inescapable. The cadre of elite civil servants who mainly came from his, Adachi's, social circle, must be tainted. To what extent, he did not know, but that the rot was there he was sure. And he was equally positive that he was already a victim.

He knocked a second time on the door. There was no reply, so he turned the handle and entered. It was the accepted custom that he would wait for the prosecutor in his office.

Toshio Sekine, the much-respected and loved friend of the Adachi family, a civil servant widely renowned for his integrity, lay slumped back in his chair, his head back and tilted to the right, revealing the gaping second mouth of a slashed throat and severed jugular. Fresh blood matted his clothing from the neck down and stained the desk in front of him. Beside his right hand was the file Adachi had sent him and a blood-splashed, sealed envelope. Adachi looked at it. It was addressed to him. He slipped it into his inside pocket unread and moved to examine the body.

The carpet beneath the prosecutor's chair was also sodden with blood. The traditional folding razor he had used to cut his throat lay just below his right hand.

Adachi bent his head as a wave of grief swept over him, and stood there for several minutes in silent sorrow and tribute. Then he summoned help and did what he was trained to do. Whatever Sekine had done or thought he had done, there lay a fundamentally honorable man.

FITZDUANE FOUND HALF his convoy—two Tokyo MPD detectives, including the ever-reliable Sergeant Oga—waiting patiently in the corridor outside the miniature offices of the Japan-World Research Federation.

The other two were in the car below. It did not do much for spontaneity to be trailed around by four men all the time, but there were times when it had its advantages.

"Sergeant-*san*," he said urgently. "It is very important that I talk to Superintendent Adachi—now!"

Oga, a man of few words, blended a brief *"Hai,* Colonel-*san"* with a quick bow of acknowledgment and barked into his radio. Short bursts of conversation were interspersed with periods of waiting. Fitzduane could hear nothing as police headquarters replied, since Oga was using a miniature earpiece. The minutes passed and Fitzduane grew increasingly impatient, though he remained silent. It was clear that Oga was doing everything possible. He had read Fitzduane's body language. This was clearly a serious matter.

Fitzduane glanced at his watch. Eleven interminable minutes had passed. So much for instant communication. He looked back at Sergeant Oga. The sergeant shook his head. "We can't find him, Colonel-*san*. Normally, the superintendent-*san* carries a radio, and always he has a beeper. We have tried both, with no result."

Fitzduane tried to think under what circumstances a man might not carry either his radio or beeper, and to relate his conclusions to what he knew of Adachi. "The superintendent is a *kendo* enthusiast," he said. "Maybe he's in the *dojo* practicing, or in the shower. Send someone to check."

Oga shook his head. "I'm sorry, Colonel-*san*," he said. Everyone is logged in or out of headquarters, and he is logged out. We checked the building anyway, but with no success. He was last reported at the prosecutor's office—there has been a death there—but apparently he left alone. The dead man was someone he was close to, and he was very upset."

Bloody hell! thought Fitzduane. The man could be anywhere—drowning his sorrows in any one of Tokyo's tens of thousands of bars or just walking to clear his head. But we are all creatures of habit. What I need is someone who knows his habits. No, fuck it! There isn't time.

"Domestic accident." Schwanberg's phrase came into his mind. Almost certainly, it had not been meant literally, but it was a logical angle. You don't kill a policeman at his place of work. You hit him when he is off duty and he is relaxing and his guard is down. A bar or a girlfriend's

bedroom or the street would do fine, but who knows when a cop working the lunatic hours of the Tokyo MPD would turn up in such a place,
and a good, well-executed hit demands predictability. But almost everybody returns home sooner or later, and Adachi, he had gathered,
lived alone.

"Sergeant-*san*," said Fitzduane. "Do you know where the superintendent lives?"

"*Hai*, Colonel-*san*," said Oga in affirmation. "It is quite near your
hotel and no more than twenty minutes or so from here. A lot depends
on the traffic."

"Then I suggest we get the hell over there very bloody fast," said
Fitzduane, and started to run down the corridor. Sergeant Oga spoke
into his radio to alert the driver below to bring the car around to the
entrance, and only then headed after Fitzduane. The *gaijin* was still
waiting for an elevator. Oga restrained a smile.

"Sergeant Oga," said Fitzduane, with a snarl, "you're a good man,
but I think you should know I can read your mind. Now listen. When
this turgid technology arrives and we get down to the street, I want the
driver to break every rule in the book and get us to the superintendent's as fast as he can. Someone is trying to kill Adachi-*san*, and I think
it would be a real good idea if we stopped it. What's your opinion?"

Oga's internal smile vanished. He swallowed and nodded. The elevator arrived.

ADACHI STARED unseeing into the still water of the Imperial moat.

He had switched both his radio and beeper off. He needed time to
grieve alone and to think his situation through. A gray mood of depression gripped him. Everywhere he turned he seemed to be faced with
corruption and betrayal. Even the best of men like the prosecutor was
contaminated.

The bloody envelope had laid out the story. An indiscretion years
earlier had made Sekine vulnerable. More recently, the marker had
been called in and the prosecutor had been enrolled as part of the
move by Katsuda against Hodama and the Namakas. He did not even
have to do anything except keep Katsuda informed and push the prosecution forward in his normal, thorough way.

But then Adachi had upset the plan. Instead of taking the easy way
out and working the case based upon the evidence against the Namakas

so carefully provided by Katsuda, he had played the master detective. His foolish cleverness had destroyed the case against the Namakas, who well deserved prosecution, and had placed the prosecutor in the position of having to make a choice between his obligations toward Katsuda and his affection for Adachi. And the resolution had been his life. Mistakes or not, he was an honorable man and his death was an honorable death. But what a waste, what a terrible waste.

There was not a scrap of evidence against Katsuda. Even Sekine's suicide note had avoided the man's actual name. The context was clear enough to Adachi, but the letter would be useless for legal purposes. No, Katsuda would end up as the new *kuromaku* and there was not a thing that Adachi could do about it.

The system was corrupt at the top and, subject to some window dressing, that would remain the situation. If he had any sense, he would bend like the proverbial bamboo or else someone was likely to break him.

The final betrayal was the confirmation that the informant inside his team was his ever-reliable Inspector Fujiwara. The man had been operating under the orders of the prosecutor, so he may have thought he was doing the right thing, but his behavior hurt horribly.

Fujiwara had been implicated by name in the prosecutor's letter. Adachi had already guessed as much since the Sunday of the baseball match, but had pushed the thought to the back of his mind. Of course, it was unlike Fujiwara to be working on a Sunday when the rest of the team were glued to the TV, but that just might not have been significant.

Unfortunately, it was. Adachi's instincts had been right. The question now: Was Fujiwara merely working for the prosecutor or did the trail lead right back to Katsuda? Did the sergeant have *yakuza* connections? Adachi was not looking forward to finding out. Anyway, did it matter? He felt drained and bone-weary.

The gray sky was looking ominous. Adachi turned away from his contemplation of the moat as the first drops rippled into the water. Soon, the warm, oily drops were falling in sheets and every stitch of clothing on his body was soaked. The only dry thing left was the prosecutor's letter in his pocket, tucked bloody but safe into a plastic evidence bag.

Adachi knew he should call in or at least return to headquarters, but he could not do it. He could not face the pressure and the questions. The DSG would certainly want to talk to him about the prosecutor's death. What could Adachi say? Would the truth serve any useful purpose? Where did the DSG's loyalties lie? No, he could not face this kind of thing for the moment. Today was one day he had to be alone.

He headed away from the grounds of the Imperial Palace and back toward Jinbocho and his apartment. The rain grew heavier.

INSPECTOR FUJIWARA had had a set of keys to the superintendent's apartment since he had been sent to pick up some things for his boss shortly after the start of the Hodama investigation.

It had been a simple matter to have an additional set cut, and since that time he had made periodic use of them. There was little risk. He normally knew where Adachi was, and the man lived alone. Even if Fujiwara had been caught, he had a story about arranging a surprise party for the superintendent. It would have been awkward, but it would have worked.

It was during one of these visits that he had first learned of Adachi's parallel investigation into the Hodama affair. Paradoxically, he had been annoyed at first. The man did not even trust his own men. Then the inconsistency of his reactions had hit him. The truth was that Adachi was a smart cop and an excellent man to work for. And as a smart cop, Adachi had smelled something wrong. But he had not suspected that Fujiwara was the mole. The sergeant was sure of that.

Fujiwara let himself into the superintendent's apartment and relocked the door. As a reflex he started to remove his shoes and then realized the ridiculousness of the action. Instead, he used his jacket to dry his wet shoes so they would make no mark on the *tatami* mats and moved across the living room into the bedroom.

Inside, he unzipped the flight bag he had been given by his *yakuza* contact and removed the silenced submachine gun. It was a British-made 9mm L34A1 Sterling, curved with a thirty-four-round box magazine inserted from the left side. This gave the weapon a low profile when firing from the prone position. The *yakuza* was a gun enthusiast and had spelled out the weapon's specification in detail.

The most important element, from Fujiwara's perspective, was the effectiveness of the silencer. He had been reassured on that point. The silencer, in this case, was integrated into the barrel and was so well-designed it could use standard high-velocity ammunition and still make no more noise than the sound of a person spitting. The seventy-two radial holes drilled into the bore bled off enough of the propellant gas to make the rounds emerge subsonic. This model had been issued to the British SAS.

Fujiwara had to wonder about the gun's history and how such a weapon had ended up in Japan. Internationalization, he thought. It is not always a good thing.

He inserted the magazine, cocked and locked the weapon, and settled himself on the bed. It was now just a matter of time. Then one long burst and a second close up to make sure, and he would vanish into the night. His long coat, hat, and glasses were a sufficient disguise if he met anyone on the stairs. Once in the nearby subway, he would be anonymous.

In the most unlikely event of the subsequent investigation including him among the suspects, he had a foolproof alibi arranged. It would almost certainly be unnecessary. It was more likely that he would be a key member of the team doing the actual investigation.

How did I get myself into this situation? he thought as he waited. Very few Tokyo MPD cops are on the take. Money, money, and more money. It was a simple answer, and one he found greatly satisfying. He enjoyed the rewards of his activities.

The general lack of police corruption had created its own opportunity. The price of inside information became higher, and then it was just a matter of initiative and displaying an entrepreneurial streak and knowing whom to connect with. Working in an anti-*yakuza* unit made the last part easy. The coming gang were the Katsuda-*gumi*, no question about it. Hard men, but they paid well. For this hit, they paid superbly. A double squeeze on a trigger would bring him enough money to retire. Well, it was all a matter of being in the right place at the right time and knowing what moves to make.

He could hear keys in the lock, and then the door opened.

OVER THE YEARS, Fitzduane had developed an aversion to walking straight into places where something unpleasant might be waiting.

A planned "domestic accident" certainly put Adachi's apartment into that category. God knows what the Katsuda-*gumi* might have planned. So far—though he was still learning—the Japanese seemed to favor direct action and edged weapons. Opening the front door and walking straight into a bunch of sword-wielding *yakuza* struck him as being not a good idea.

Granted, he could send his convoy of bodyguards in first, but it really did not seem like the decent thing, and explaining a diced quartet of Tokyo MPD detectives to the Deputy Superintendent-General would be embarrassing.

No, the indirect approach was required here, combined with reconnaissance. Your parents might have done their very best to bring you up direct, honest, and forthright, but there were times when there was a definite role in life for sneakiness. Kilmara was a strong advocate of guile in a combat situation, and Fitzduane had been an apt pupil.

Adachi's apartment was on the top floor of a six-story building and was reached through a locked front door that was squeezed between a martial-arts store and a bookshop. The locked door looked solid. That was another argument in favor of sneakiness. They did not have any keys, and Fitzduane did not want to alert anyone who might be inside by playing with the bells. Apart from the radio and beeper, he had tried phoning Adachi at the apartment, but there had been no reply. A further check revealed that there was a fault on the line. This did not make Fitzduane feel good at all.

"Sergeant-*san*," he said. "Leave two men here and tell them to stop anyone entering or leaving—and in particular to stop Superintendent Adachi from entering. The rest of us will find a way up to the roof."

The block consisted of some ten adjoining buildings. From the pavement looking up it was hard to tell, but the roof looked roughly flat, and getting across to Adachi a simple matter of crossing a few parapets.

It turned out to be more complicated. Having reached roof level from an entrance three houses away, after some badge-flashing and shouting by Sergeant Oga to a remarkably stubborn little old lady, they found themselves one level below the next building.

The rain continued to emulate a lukewarm power shower as Fitzduane assessed the situation. The adjoining roof was not just one floor higher, there was a parapet involved as well. They would have to climb about fourteen or fifteen feet, and the only way he could see to do it was to scale a drainpipe on the front of the building, with the street directly below.

"Sergeant Oga," he said. "Send your colleague for some rope. God knows what we'll find when we get to the top. Meanwhile, you and I are going to do some climbing."

Oga snapped out instructions and the detective rushed away. Then the sergeant ran toward the parapet and moved to reach out to the drainpipe. Fitzduane caught up with him and interposed an arm.

"*Gaijins* first," he said, "and besides, this was my thoroughly stupid idea." He started to climb. Six feet up, he noticed that whatever was true about Japanese craftsmanship, the drainpipe fixings had not been installed on one of their better days.

He paused to get his breath.

A crack sounded beneath him, and the pipe below him slowly broke away from the wall at the brace where his feet rested.

Fitzduane looked down. Sergeant Oga was shouting something, and far below he could see faces looking up. All his weight was now being suspended by his arms, and the pipe he was hanging on to felt greasy. That was the least of his worries. If the brace above him was of the same standard as the one below, he was going to die in Japan, and in the rain at that.

Oga was pointing.

Fitzduane turned his head and looked where the sergeant was indicating. There was a metal protrusion a foot to one side and a couple of feet farther up from where his feet had been resting; it seemed to be doing something for a neon sign that flashed below.

He stretched out his left foot and found the piece of angle iron and slowly rested his weight on it and levered himself up. The iron held. He was now able to move his feet up to the next pipe brace, and soon after that got his hands over the parapet. He tensed himself for one more effort. As he pushed at the brace to gain the momentum to swing his legs over the top, the rest of the pipe gave way.

Fitzduane lay on the parapet for a few seconds to regain his strength. His head was on the edge and, looking down, he could see an excited crowd scurrying back after the impact of yet another section of pipe on the pavement.

This was one hell of a way to effect a covert entrance. He just had to hope that whoever was inside Adachi's apartment—if anybody—was not looking out through the window or, failing that, would not make an association with the chaos below. He was shaking with stress reaction, and he felt nauseous and he hoped the fallen pipe had not hit anybody. Given the population density in Tokyo, he was not sure the odds were in his favor. Still, he had more immediate concerns. He pulled himself together and carefully transferred his weight from the parapet to the roof.

Soon afterward, he was sprawled at the edge of Adachi's skylight, peering in cautiously at the scene underneath. On a bright day, he would have been silhouetted immediately against the sky. On this gloomy day, with the rain pounding down and smearing the glass, he would be less obtrusive.

It was some consolation for having to lie in a pool of dirty water. The drainage off Adachi's roof left a great deal to be desired. He was getting a whole new perspective on the Japanese economic miracle.

ADACHI HAD ARRIVED, scarcely a minute ahead of Fitzduane, wet, exhausted, shivering, and burdened with an overwhelming fatigue.

The prospect of climbing five floors was more than he could contemplate. He climbed the first flight and sat down and rested his head wearily against the wall and for a few minutes fell asleep. Rainwater from his sodden clothes dripped from him and formed a pool at his feet.

The crash of a closing door on the floor above woke him, and then there was the sound of footsteps on the stairs and a peremptory shout, as his neighbor saw him and mistook his dripping, beaten-down figure for a beggar. Stumbling apologies followed as the man realized who Adachi was. Then he offered help, but Adachi brushed his concern aside.

"A touch of flu," he said, rising to his feet and bowing politely, "but nothing serious. Thank you, Samu-*san*, for your concern."

Samu-*san* bowed in acknowledgment, but still looked at Adachi as if wanting to help. The policeman was pale and shaking, and was clearly ill.

Adachi resolved the situation by commencing to climb the stairs again. As he passed Samu-*san* he smiled, and this reassured the neighbor. He clattered off down the stairs once more and Adachi was left in peace. He rested again for some further minutes, then climbed another flight.

In all, it took him nearly twenty minutes to get to the top, and he stumbled through his door, exhausted, and closed it behind him. He removed his shoes and socks and sodden jacket, and, barefoot, trembling with fatigue and cold, walked slowly into his living room. He wanted nothing more than warmth and the escape of sleep.

It was then that he saw Fujiwara.

The sergeant walked out of the bedroom with the weapon in his hands, its thick, silenced barrel pointing straight at Adachi. The silencer made his intentions obvious. To Adachi's surprise, he felt neither surprise nor fear. Instead, there was a bittersweet blend of betrayal, sadness, and surrender. He stood there in his wet clothes, still trembling but otherwise immobile, his hands at his sides.

Fujiwara had always liked Adachi and regretted having to kill him. But his considerable regard for his superintendent was outweighed by his regard for what he was being paid. His years on the streets had taught him that life was about compromise and tough decisions. Still, faced with this pathetic figure, he was reluctant to pull the trigger.

"So, Sergeant Fujiwara-*san*," said Adachi, giving a slight bow. "A friend is going to kill me. Under the circumstances, it is, I suppose, curiously appropriate."

Fujiwara bowed in return, but though his upper body moved, the Sterling remained pointed at Adachi. "You do not seem surprised, Superintendent-*san*."

"Nothing surprises anymore," said Adachi. "I have suspected you for a little time—and then the prosecutor left a letter. So much betrayal, so much corruption."

"Please kneel down, Superintendent-*san*," said Fujiwara, "and place your hands behind your head. You will not suffer, I promise you."

Adachi sank slowly to his knees and rested his clasped hands on his head. As he had lowered his body, he had felt the firm outline of his holstered pistol press into his back. From where Fujiwara stood, it could not be seen. But thoughts of using the weapon were futile. He was shaking with cold and fever, and the submachine gun would cut him in two before he could get the weapon out of his holster. Nonetheless, the thought was implanted in his mind and, irrationally, he found the weight of the weapon comforting.

"Who sent you, Sergeant-*san*?" he said. "Who has ordered my execution? I would like to know that before I die. Was it the Spider?"

Fujiwara laughed. "The Deputy Superintendent is a model of probity as far as I know," he said.

"Katsuda?" said Adachi.

Fujiwara nodded appreciatively. "You always were a fine detective, Superintendent-*san,* unfortunately for you. A less talented investigator would not be in your present position. Yes, it is the Katsuda-*gumi* who have ordered your death. You should have kept the Namakas as suspects. That was the way it was supposed to work. It was never planned that you be killed."

"I am relieved to hear that," said Adachi with a faint smile. "So this whole business is part of a Katsuda power play—and the paying off of an old grudge. But who did the actual killing? Was it Katsuda himself?"

"Will it help you to know, Superintendent-*san?*" said Fujiwara. "Will it make any real difference?"

Adachi opened his hands in a shrug. "I'd like to know the end of the story before I die," he said. "Tell me, Fujiwara-*san,* for old times' sake. I would appreciate it."

"I was one of the assault group who killed Hodama," said Fujiwara. "The others were members of the Katsuda-*gumi.* As to who led the raid, well, he was masked. Was it Katsuda-*san* himself? Frankly, I think so, but I don't know."

"A rather uncertain note on which to die," said Adachi.

Fujiwara looked regretful. "Superintendent-*san,* I am sorry," he said, "but it's all I know." He leveled the weapon.

Glass splintered, and a concrete block crashed into the middle of the floor.

Fujiwara stepped back in surprise, and in reflex fired a burst from his weapon at the skylight, bringing down more shards of glass and ripping into the ceiling. The silenced weapon itself made so little noise that the mechanical sounds of the weapon could be heard.

Plaster dust, wood splinters, and other debris showered down, together with heavy rain from the now-open skylight.

Fujiwara moved his position and crouched down to try to see if anyone was at the skylight.

Adachi rolled, reached around to the small of his back for his revolver, and fired single-handed twice. His hand was still trembling, but the range was short and the second .38 round smashed into Fujiwara's cheekbone, cutting open the side of his face.

Fujiwara fell back from his crouched position at the shock of being hit, and the Sterling fell from his hand. Adachi looked at the wounded man, the revolver dipping in his hand. He knew he should fire again while he had the chance, but this was someone he was close to and had trusted, an intimate member of his own group, and he could not bring himself to do it.

Fujiwara, streaming blood, groped for his weapon and started to crawl back to the safety of the bedroom.

There was the sound of a body hitting the floor hard, as Fitzduane jumped down from the skylight and did an immediate parachute-roll away from Adachi but facing the bedroom. He had the 10mm Calico in his hands, loaded with tracer multipurpose ammunition.

Fujiwara turned at the noise and started to bring his weapon around. Adachi also looked across, the revolver waving in his hand, anticipating a new threat. He was now completely exhausted and in a state of shock.

Fitzduane fired a five-round burst at Fujiwara. At such a short distance, there was scarcely time for the tracer to ignite, just pinprick flashes of red before they vanished into flesh and bone.

The tight group hit the sergeant as he was turning to his left to bring his weapon to bear on Fitzduane, tore open his rib cage on the left side, and smashed him back against the bedroom door. A split second later, a second burst aimed at Fujiwara's head, in case he was wearing body armor that the multipurpose could not penetrate, blew his throat and skull apart and he fell backwards into the bedroom.

Adachi brought his left hand up to steady his aim as he had been taught, and tried to point his weapon at Fitzduane. The image in front of his eyes was a blur, and he found it desperately difficult to align his sights.

"Superintendent-*san!*" The shout came from the ceiling, and the voice was familiar. "Superintendent-*san*, don't shoot. It's Fitzduane-*san*—the *gaijin*—a friend. He has come to help. You are safe now."

Oga—Sergeant Oga—that was the owner of the voice, said Adachi's mind. He lowered the revolver and felt it removed from his hands. Finally, exhaustion and illness triumphed, and he slid gently to one side and into unconsciousness.

A rope dropped down from the skylight and Sergeant Oga, in his well-cut suit, slid down. The rain was so heavy through the aperture, it looked like the policeman was descending through a shower.

"Sergeant Oga," said Fitzduane. "It is certainly nice to see you, but how the hell did you get up on the roof after the drainpipe fell away?"

"Colonel-*san*," said Oga, "it took us some time to find, but there is a metal stairs behind the water tank at the back of the roof. The drain-pipe was not necessary."

"Terrific," said Fitzduane sourly.

Sergeant Oga smiled. "But without that drainpipe, I do not think the superintendent-*san* would be alive."

18

Fitzduane and Yoshokawa were walking along the beach in Kamakura.

"I have news of Superintendent Adachi-*san,*" said Yoshokawa. "His father called just before we left. The fever has broken and he has been released from hospital and is resting at his parents' home. He hopes to be back at his desk again in a week or so. He is deeply appreciative of what you have done."

"Adachi is a good man," said Fitzduane, "but the Hodama affair is a cesspool of an investigation. It must have been grim for him to be so betrayed. Still, better to discover what was going on than to leave it fester."

"Fitzduane-*san,*" said Yoshokawa, "you should know that Adachi-*san* feels under an obligation towards you. It is difficult for him, because you will be leaving soon and he does not know what to do, nor how to express what he feels."

Fitzduane laughed. "Between you, me, and the gatepost, Yoshokawa-*san,* it is a moot point as to who should be more obligated to whom. If he, dizzy with fever, had not put a round through Fujiwara as I was coming through the skylight, we wouldn't be enjoying this sea air together and I could advise you from direct experience of the afterlife which shrine to keep in your living room. Hell, tell him to forget it."

Yoshokawa smiled, but then turned serious. "Adachi-*san* is from an old and distinguished Japanese family," he said, "and takes his obligations very seriously. You must understand that he cannot and will not forget. It is not in his nature. It is not possible."

Fitzduane was imagining Kamakura in its medieval heyday when it was the capital of Japan. He and Yoshokawa were nobles—well, who would want to be a peasant in those days?—at the military court. They would be wearing full *samurai* regalia as they walked the beach enjoying the sea air. Guards and followers would be standing at a discreet distance, banners flying in the breeze. The two nobles would be discussing strategy and tactics, preparing for the power struggle ahead.

"Yoshokawa-*san,*" he said. "Nothing ever changes. I was thinking of us as two *daimyo* from six centuries ago; and their concerns would have been similar. There were *kuromaku* then as there are *kuromaku* now. There was intrigue and betrayal then, and there is intrigue and betrayal now." He looked across at his bodyguards in their neat gray suits. "But their clothing would have been a lot more colorful."

"And the technology marginally less refined," said Yoshokawa, "and since you are a *gaijin,* we'd have chopped your head off."

Fitzduane laughed out loud. "You're giving it a good try as it is," he said, "and there is still time—I haven't left yet. I have the Namakas to see again. They are giving me that tour of their steel plant tomorrow, though I doubt anything will come of it. They don't seem to be rising to the bait. Being able to blame Kitano has given them room to maneuver. It's a pity, but that looks like an account that will have to be settled some other time, because I have to get home. I don't like being away from Ireland too long these days. I miss Boots. He is growing up so fast. A month is a long time at that age."

Yoshokawa nodded. "My group is grateful for what you have done. The Namakas are still there, but some corruption has been exposed and we do, at least, know who was behind the Hodama killings. Modest progress, but progress all the same. That is what is important. We have always known that reforming our structures will not be easy."

"Not easy is putting it mildly," said Fitzduane. "The Namakas sail on and there is not a scrap of evidence against Katsuda. We have displaced a few pawns, but the main players remain untouched."

"We shall see," said Yoshokawa. "Personally, I am optimistic. But I fear you, Fitzduane-*san,* will return to Ireland with a jaundiced view of my country."

Fitzduane grinned. "Relax, Yoshokawa-*san.* A handful of rotten apples haven't turned me off the whole barrel. No, if someone were to ask me tomorrow about the Japanese, I'd say you are hard people to get to know, but well worth the effort. People of caliber, guardians of some special qualities we can use my side of the world. Sure, there are changes you must make, but mostly you have reason to be proud."

Yoshokawa was deeply touched by Fitzduane's words. Then Fitzduane spoke again. "One of the best things about coming here, Yoshokawa-*san,* is that I will never think of 'the Japanese' again. I'll think of individuals—you, your family, Adachi-*san,* the DSG, Sergeant Oga, the people in your plant I met yesterday, so many others with all your special individual qualities. That's the way I think it should be."

"And those like the Namakas and Yaibo who have tried to kill you?" said Yoshokawa.

"It is neither here nor there that they are Japanese," said Fitzduane. "They are just people that, in all our mutual interests, I hope we can consign on a one-way trip to hell. So far, I haven't been too successful, but the game is not over."

"And what is this game called?" said Yoshokawa. "This matter of obligation?"

"Vengeance," said Fitzduane, with a grim smile.

T O K Y O ,   J A P A N

June 27

Chifune sat at her desk at Koancho headquarters and again went through the arrangements she had made.

The Tokyo Metropolitan Police Department had the primary job of both running and protecting Fitzduane, but Koancho had its own interest and had made its own preparations. When she had first joined the security force, she had been taken aback at the service's reluctance to share information, but as time had gone on she had seen the merits of this approach.

Security issues tended to be very sensitive, and organizations such as the police, whatever their merits, were far from leakproof. Also, there were often advantages in having parallel operations, the overt and the covert. If the overt operation failed, the other was already in place, but set up in such a way that it was complementary and unlikely to have the same weaknesses. And, of course, if the secret operation ran into trouble, by definition nobody knew. Sometimes, both operations were unsuccessful. Well, she had been taught to accept a casualty rate. That was the reality of the dangerous world in which she operated.

Still, she found it hard to view the developments in the Hodama affair with equanimity. The assault on Adachi had left her deeply shocked, all the more so because it was so unexpected. Senior police in Japan were virtually never attacked.

Then there was the *gaijin* Fitzduane. Despite her strong feelings for Adachi, this was a man who, against all common sense and other loyalties, her body, and maybe her heart, wanted.

One of these days she was going to have to make some decisions. She was a modern woman, she hoped, but she had some traditional needs. She shook her head, annoyed at this undermining of her will by biological instinct. It was maddening. Men were not so encumbered in this way, or, at least, not so physically restricted. Meanwhile, there was an operation to be run. She worked her way through the file and checked that they had covered every foreseeable contingency.

Her conclusion was depressing. The *gaijin* had good basic security cover, it was true, but if anything untoward happened, he was on his own. Full cover made the operation impossible. The whole enterprise was predicated on a degree of risk.

What might the Namakas do? She dug into the files and looked at their resources. What did they like to do? What could they do?

Koancho's records were not restricted by police regulations and were buoyed by extensive covert surveillance. In addition to facts, they contained extensive analysis and speculation—some low-key and some provocative. She listened to tapes, watched surveillance videos, and read on into the night. Brawn and brains—every avenue led to the natures of the two brothers. The specifics could not be forecast, but there were patterns of behavior.

In the early hours of the morning, she began to develop a feeling about the Namakas' next move. She had also worked out how the problem of Fitzduane's police surveillance might be overcome. Unfortunately, an appropriate countermove was harder to define. The bottom line was a constant. Fitzduane-*san* was vulnerable. Whatever the pretense of security, he had to be left vulnerable if the Namakas were to be enticed to make a move.

———

FITZDUANE HAD DINNER in his room at the Fairmont and then worked late into the night on his notes.

As he closed his eyes, he thought of his father and how much he had loved him and how terribly he missed him. John Fitzduane had been killed in a skydiving accident when Fitzduane was fifteen. It still hurt Fitzduane when he remembered.

Few Fitzduanes died in their beds. Violent death was something of a Fitzduane tradition.

I don't want Boots to be alone, he thought. I'm taking enough risk as it is.

He slept.

T O K Y O , J A P A N

June 28

"Good morning, Sergeant-*san*," said Fitzduane cheerfully to Sergeant Oga.

After his late-night work, he had slept briefly but well. He was going back to Ireland in a couple of days and would see Boots and Kathleen very soon. He missed them. But he must go shopping first. Boots had been conditioned by a fond father to expect a present every time he returned, and Kathleen deserved something special.

Fitzduane was feeling very domestic that morning. The visit to Namaka Steel was not in the forefront of his mind. The sun was shining for a change and the humidity was bearable, and he felt good. And, the peculiarities of his visit aside, he was enjoying the limited amount he was seeing of Japan and, more to the point, he was interested in the Japanese. True, you needed a pickax and a miner's lamp to break through the wall they put up, but inside there were rewards. Sergeant Oga was a case in point.

Oga and the day shift bowed. "Sergeant Oga," said Fitzduane, "I'm going to miss you. I'm getting used to spending every day with four of Tokyo MPD's finest, and I just want you to know I appreciate what you're doing. But for you, I might well not be alive. Of course, I would not know if I wasn't, but I'm grateful to you that I am."

Sergeant Oga blushed. He did not understand exactly what the *gaijin* was saying—especially the last part—but the sentiments were clear. He explained briefly the gist of what Fitzduane-*san* had said to the other three detectives, and they all bowed in unison.

Fitzduane bowed back, then got on with the briefing. He had discovered that bowing could go on almost indefinitely unless you had a breakaway technique—an elevator arriving, or a cab you had to get into—anything to break the cycle.

"A Namaka limousine is coming at nine-thirty to take me to the Namaka Tower," said Fitzduane. "From there, I'm driving with the brothers to their steel plant. I'll be there most of the day."

"The Namakas do not make me feel comfortable, Fitzduane-*san*," said Oga. "They are dangerous and devious people."

"They are why I'm here," said Fitzduane.

Sergeant Oga nodded. "I don't like it, Fitzduane-*san*," he said.

"I'm trying to rattle their cage without being eaten," said Fitzduane with a smile. "Think of yourself as a keeper."

Oga was not amused. He knew perfectly well the limitations of police protection under such circumstances. "Are you armed, Fitzduane-*san*?" he said. "And wearing your bulletproof vest?"

"You're like my mother when I was small, Sergeant-*san*," said Fitzduane, "but yes to both."

"I would like to put two of my men in the Namaka limousine with you, Fitzduane-*san*," said Oga. "Following behind is not adequate, nor is one escort car. Strictly speaking, we should have at least two."

Fitzduane laughed. "Sergeant-*san*, I am neither the President of the United States nor an anti-mafia judge in Italy. One car behind me with the four of you inside as normal will be fine—unless, of course, you have fresh information?"

Oga shook his head.

"Look, Sergeant-*san*," said Fitzduane. "We're trying to strike a balance here between reasonable precautions and moving the Namakas into play. If I'm too crowded, there will be no freedom to maneuver and then we will have accomplished nothing. There has to be an element of calculated risk. It's a high-risk world out there."

"*Hai*, Colonel-*san*," said Oga, his face impassive. Orders were orders. Nonetheless, he had a bad feeling, and his concern for the *gaijin* was not purely professional. But he would be relieved when Fitzduane left Oga's jurisdiction alive and in one piece.

CHIFUNE, sitting in the back of what looked like a standard Mitsubishi delivery truck, but which was actually a Koancho high-tech surveillance vehicle, watched the Namaka limousine pull up in front of the Fairmont and a white-gloved, uniformed driver jump out and open the door.

Something about the action struck her, then she realized that the man had left the front passenger seat on the left and not the driver's seat on the right. She turned up the video camera's magnification. The limo had tinted windows, but the camera had been developed specifically to cope with this kind of problem, and using the thermal mode, she could make out the shape of a driver inside. A driver and a codriver, and there had been only one driver last time. Interesting.

The limousine pulled away, drove down the narrow access road, and paused by Yasukini-dori Avenue before pulling into the traffic. Close behind was Sergeant Oga's unmarked escort car. Farther behind was the Koancho vehicle. Chifune did not need to maintain such a close tail. There was a small transmitter concealed on Fitzduane that showed up his position at all times on an electronic map. Japanese technology was not just about Hondas and VCRs.

Sergeant Oga felt easier when they left the dense city-center traffic and moved onto the expressway. Traffic lights and intersections and two-way traffic offered too many opportunities for a hit. Cruising along the two-lane expressway on the inside lane, with traffic going the same way and no sidewalks, was considerably safer.

"There's a job for the traffic boys coming up," said the detective, who was driving, after glancing in his mirror. Sergeant Oga, sitting in the passenger seat, also had a mirror, but when he looked, the vehicle behind was so close he could not make out any details except that it was a large truck and it was tailgating them.

He began to turn for a closer look. There was a roar, and the car shook in the wash, as an unmarked high-sided Hino container truck painted a deep brown shot past, pulled in front of the police car, and then proceeded to slow down.

"Stupid bastard," said the detective, braking to match the vehicle's speed. "Why don't you take the prick's number and radio it to traffic?

That would be careless driving in a car. It's positively lethal in a truck."

"Forget the truck," said Oga. "Overtake it—we're losing the *gaijin.*"

The driver began to pull out, just as a second Hino pounded up and started to pass. There was a shriek of metal as the two vehicles touched briefly, and sparks flew, and then the driver wrenched the wheel and pulled back into his lane. The second Hino pulled ahead until it was running parallel with the first truck. The escort car was now completely blocked off from the limousine.

"Fuck!" said Sergeant Oga, who rarely swore. He hit the concealed siren. If the Hino blocking the overtaking lane did not move, it was a hit for sure. He made a precautionary radio call to central control, read out the two Hino plate numbers for a vehicle check, and kept the channel open, his thumb poised to transmit further.

As soon as the siren sounded, the blocking Hino started to accelerate to clear the lane. At this speed, the huge vehicle's acceleration was not good, but still not much more than a minute had passed before it pulled in ahead of the other truck and left the way clear for Oga's vehicle to pass.

Siren still screaming, the detective driver dropped a gear and put his foot on the floor and shot out into the passing lane.

Several hundred yards ahead was what looked like the *gaijin*'s limousine, but it was too far away to read the plate. The police car closed the distance rapidly until the plate could be identified. It was the Namaka limo.

Oga realized that his heart was pounding and his body was flushed with adrenaline. He switched the siren off and tried to calm himself down.

"I thought we were going to see some action," said the driver. "Looks like we were flapping for nothing, Sergeant-*san.* There is our target in absolutely pristine condition."

There was a searing yellow silent flash and the *gaijin*'s limousine and its contents exploded into jagged metal, splinters of glass, burning upholstery, and severed limbs.

A split second later came the thunderous roar and blast of the explosion, and the police car, already decelerating as the driver instinctively braked, was hurled against the parapet. It spun several times laterally but did not overturn, and finally the much-dented vehicle came to a halt of its own volition in the middle of the debris.

Sergeant Oga tried to get out, but the door pillar on his side had been smashed in and neither door on his side would open. The driver was unconscious, slumped in his safety belt, blood dripping from a gash in his forehead where flying glass had struck. The two detectives in the back were badly shaken but otherwise uninjured. They got out of the one backseat door that would open, and Oga squeezed between the front seats to the back and followed them.

Leaving the two detectives to look after the driver, he walked the short distance to where the still-smoking remains of the Namaka limousine lay, and looked inside.

He felt his mind separate as he looked. The interior reeked of explosive residue and cooked flesh and was plastered with the blackened bloody fragments of human remains, and he wanted to be sick. Another part of his mind, that of the trained detective, noted that the bottom pan was still intact, though bowed outward. Clearly, the device had been placed inside the car or was a projectile like a rocket which had penetrated from the outside and then exploded. There was no entry hole in the metal frame that he could see, but it could easily have come through one of the windows.

Repulsive though the task was, he tried to work out how many bodies could be made up from the pieces in the limousine, and whether he could recognize the *gaijin*.

After several minutes, he reeled away, nauseated, and with all hope destroyed. The corpse in the rear of the vehicle was the right size, weight, and build of Fitzduane-*san* and was definitely Caucasian. The clothing, insofar as he could tell, was Fitzduane's. He could just make out a watch similar to the military Rolex that Fitzduane normally wore.

There was no doubt. The *gaijin* was dead. Deeply shocked and depressed, Sergeant Oga went back to the battered unmarked police car and tried the radio. To his surprise, it was still working.

He began to make his initial report. When he finished, he found Tanabu-*san* examining the wreckage. He was not particularly surprised. Koancho made their own rules, and Chifune Tanabu certainly had her own agenda; and a special, though discreetly displayed, interest, he had noticed, in the *gaijin*.

"Sergeant-*san*," said Chifune, "did you see what happened?"

Oga noticed that she looked more puzzled than saddened, and he was surprised. Granted, Koancho agents were a hardened lot, but he had expected a more human reaction in this particular case. He explained briefly.

Tanabu-*san* stood in thought for about half a minute when he had finished. Then she turned to him. "Sergeant Oga-*san*, I think we can help each other. Come with me."

19

June 28

There was the sound of a slap, then another.

A pause followed, and then another blow, and Fitzduane felt pain and realized that he might be directly involved with what was happening. He was not sure, though. His head was muzzy and his eyes were closed, and for a short while he thought he was back in the hospital in Ireland, recovering from an anaesthetic after a surgical procedure. This business of being shot was a great deal of work. He wanted to go back to sleep.

There was yet another blow, this time even harder. "Kathleen," he murmured in protest. Why were they hitting him?

He could hear people speaking but could not understand what they were saying. That was odd. He felt suddenly cold and wet and started to splutter. There was water everywhere, cascading into his mouth and nose, and it kept on coming. It was like being under a waterfall and he was drowning. He could not breathe.

The waterfall stopped. He opened his eyes. They would not focus properly, but something wooden seemed to be suspended over him. He could see the lines where the boards joined, and he was reminded of a barrel—a rather small barrel. What was a barrel doing up there?

The image above him came reluctantly into focus. The next hard task was to link the sight with his brain. Suddenly, like a car that will not start that is being pushed and is gathering momentum, he felt a sputtering ignition. His brain cells started to do what they were designed to do, and almost immediately he wished they had not. They were coming up with the most unpleasant findings.

He was not in Ireland with a solicitous nurse bending over him. He was in Japan, and the person ministering to him, judging by the full-body tattoo that protruded from his kimono at his chest and arms, was a *yakuza*. And the barrel was not a barrel; it was a wooden bucket with a rope handle.

He was conscious and he could see, but he still felt sick and groggy. He gave himself a couple of minutes, and then when the *yakuza*'s back was turned he tried to raise himself. As he did so, the *yakuza* turned and almost absentmindedly kicked Fitzduane in the stomach and sent him flat on his back again.

The bad news, thought Fitzduane, is that I now feel even shittier. The good news, to look on the bright side, is that I can now be reasonably sure the natives are not friendly. And knowledge supposedly is power.

It really did not seem worth the effort. He closed his eyes and concentrated on trying to restore some sort of equilibrium. Clearly he had been drugged in some way, but he had no idea how.

What had happened? Where was he? Who were his captors? It did not seem as if they were going to kill him immediately, else why had he been allowed to wake up—but what sort of plans had they for his longer-term well-being? On reflection, he was not at all sure he wanted to know. The *yakuza* were fond of edged weapons and making their victims disappear. Fitzduane contemplated without enthusiasm ending up as fish food in Tokyo Bay, or being sunk in the earthquake-proof foundations of one of the examples of Japan's building boom. Alternatively, if that was going to be his fate, he could do without advance warning. Anticipating a painful death was not the most pleasant way to pass the time.

He decided he had better find something more cheerful to think about. The subject of women came to mind, but that was not exactly pain-free. Instead, he thought of Ireland and his island and Boots's ridiculous antics and his laughter.

Fitzduane started to smile at the memories, and then a voice cut in. "Fitzduane-*san,* I am glad to see you are enjoying yourself. It is part of the *samurai* code, you must know, to make the best of adverse circumstances. In your case, your position somewhat exceeds adverse. Technically, you are dead. Dismembered. Blown to pieces. A tragic loss. It was a simple matter to arrange a double."

Kei Namaka! The confident booming voice was unmistakable. Fitzduane opened his eyes. Kei stood there in full traditional *samurai* regalia, down to the two swords tucked into his sash. He looked decidedly pleased with himself.

"And I'm in heaven, Namaka-*san*," said Fitzduane dryly. "I have to tell you it's a big disappointment."

Kei laughed and then translated what the *gaijin* had said. Other laughter could be heard. Fitzduane, bearing in mind what had happened the last time he had tried to rise, did not move or look around, but he estimated there were three or four others in the large room. He was lying on a hard wooden floor. Looking straight ahead past Kei, he could see antique weapons on the walls. That information, tied in with the Namaka chairman's costume, suggested he was in a *dojo*, the Japanese equivalent of a *salle d'armes.* Christian de Guevain had died in such a place, he remembered.

"You are a brave man," Kei said, "and I like you, so I had better explain." He talked for several minutes, describing with immense satisfaction the operation to snatch Fitzduane.

"So you blew up three of your own people to snatch me," said Fitzduane.

Kei made a dismissive gesture with something he was holding in his right hand. Fitzduane looked closer, and realized with incredulity that it was a folded fan. The man was really getting into his role.

"So what is on the agenda now, Namaka-*san*?" said Fitzduane. "You certainly get an A for effort for grabbing me, and I'm flattered, of course, but I imagine you have something more in mind—a bottom line to this exercise, if I may borrow some financial terminology."

Kei beamed expansively. "Fitzduane-*san*," he said. "I am looking forward to being your host without the constraints that have limited our relationship up to now. At last we can speak freely. Complications like the police are no longer something we have to worry about, and I can tell you everything you want to know. We shall enjoy each other's company, and I can promise you that you will be fascinated. We shall start with a tour of a place you expressed particular interest in, Namaka Special Steels."

"I tour factories better when I'm vertical," said Fitzduane. "Can I get up without someone kicking me in the balls?"

Kei barked an order and two *yakuza* rushed forward and helped Fitzduane to his feet. Then Kei spoke again and another man came forward. He also wore traditional *samurai* clothing, but somewhat awkwardly, as if slightly embarrassed.

"My name is Goto," he said. "I am the new security chief of the Namaka Corporation. The chairman has asked me to explain a few points. Unfortunately, there have to be some restrictions on your freedom."

Fitzduane felt his arms being seized, and seconds later his arms were handcuffed in front of him and secured to a chain around his waist. Leg restraints were then placed around his ankles.

Goto pointed to a corner of the *dojo* and Fitzduane saw his Calico and throwing knives on a small table, together with the other contents of his pockets. They had left him his shirt and trousers, but everything else, including his shoes, had been removed.

"Shortly after you were shot with the tranquilizer dart, we found a miniature transmitter attached to your belt, Fitzduane-*san*," said Goto. "It was immediately deactivated, so please do not expect any help from that source. You are outnumbered, physically constrained, and have no weapons, and your friends think you are dead. You would be wise to accept your fate and cause us no trouble. Frankly, you can do nothing."

Fitzduane shrugged, and his chains clanked. He had been brought up to look on the brighter side of things, but was having a hard time finding any positive element in his present situation. "Goto-*san*," he said, "it is not considered polite, in my part of the world at least, to belabor the obvious."

Goto blushed. Fitzduane grinned. "Let's go and see a steel mill," he said. Inside, he was fighting hard to keep control. There had to be something he could do, but he could not imagine what. Hope had taken a serious knock with the discovery of the belt transmitter.

"You should know, Fitzduane-*san*," said Goto, indicating three unfriendly-looking thugs glowering at Fitzduane, "that your *yakuza* guards are members of the *Insuji-gumi*—the very organization that you humiliated outside the Fairmont upon your arrival. They feel they have a score to settle."

"And is that on the agenda?" said Fitzduane.

"Oh yes, Fitzduane-*san*," said Goto, smiling unpleasantly. Fitzduane stayed silent, but he made a mental note to remove Goto permanently from circulation if ever a suitable opportunity should arise. Unfortunately, it did not seem likely.

THE *DOJO*, Fitzduane judged, as he shuffled across the floor, legs hobbled between two *yakuza* guards, was about the size of a Western school gymnasium.

The decor was understated simplicity, but the room was quite magnificently finished and appointed. Japanese craftsmanship at its best was truly something to see. The floor, made of planks of some richly hued hardwood, was seamless, every plank impeccably aligned. The roof was arched and paneled with the same wood. The walls were plastered and racked with an extraordinary selection of medieval pikes, swords, and fighting knives from all over the world. Glancing across, Fitzduane noticed everything from Spanish rapiers to Malayan fighting knives.

Firearms were conspicuous by their absence. Kei Namaka's orientation was more toward fantasy than fact, though that did not make him any less dangerous.

The small procession made its way through two sets of double doors, donning shoes in the lobby in the middle. As they passed through the second set of doors, which were double-glazed and of heavy industrial quality, the noise level rose and Fitzduane could see the highly specialized equipment of a modern steel plant spread out ahead of them.

So the *dojo* was actually in the plant. Now he was beginning to understand things better. The Namaka Tower was the symbol of the brothers' joint success. The steel plant was Kei's personal baby. Costing billions, it was a grown-up box of toys.

They were standing on a railed catwalk of perforated metal. The catwalk, in turn, led to metal stairs which would bring them to the factory floor, but instead of continuing, Kei Namaka held up his hand to indicate they should halt and turned to Fitzduane.

"Steel, Fitzduane-*san*," he said, "is my passion and joy. It is at the same time so elemental and yet so extraordinarily sophisticated. It is a manifestation of man's superiority and the supreme link between man and nature. It is the very stuff of legend. It is the raw material of the sword, the very symbol of Japan. It is strong, beautiful, infinitely malle-

able, supremely versatile, and technologically elegant. It is the principal material of war and one of the major blocks of peace. Ships, aircraft,
and all wheeled communication depends on it. Nations have been built
with it. We cut our very food with it." He paused. "And the creation of
steel products on the scale we operate at here is a process of unsurpassed excitement. It is physically exciting—indeed, sexually arousing
in its power and drama and beauty."

After he had finished speaking, Kei Namaka stared at Fitzduane
with an extraordinary intensity, as if he were trying to communicate his
enthusiasm for steel telepathically.

The scene was quite bizarre. Kei, in the foreground, in full *samurai*
armor including an ornate horned helmet, looking like something out
of the Middle Ages, and over his shoulder the vast machines, ovens,
and other devices symbolic of advanced late-twentieth-century metals
technology. Yet curiously, Kei did not really look out of place. The relationship of steel and the warrior was ever valid.

Steel, for so much of history, was indeed at the cutting edge of
power.

Fitzduane held up his hands as far as the handcuffs and the restraining chain permitted. "I am bound by steel, Namaka-*san*," he said quietly. "It tempers my enthusiasm."

Kei's face flushed with rage, and for a moment it looked as if he was
going to strike Fitzduane. Then he started to laugh. " 'Tempers my enthusiasm' indeed, Fitzduane-*san*. A clever pun. You have a good sense
of humor for a *gaijin*."

He gave an order, and one of the *yakuza* placed safety glasses on
Fitzduane. The incongruity of following safety regulations while escorting their prisoner around in chains caused him to give a wry smile.

"We Japanese," said Kei, "achieved some of our earlier postwar successes with steel. While the West was working with old technology—
too greedy to invest and lacking in vision—we built new modern steel
plants and produced cheaper, higher-quality steel faster. This, in turn,
provided the raw material at the right price for car production and for
shipbuilding. It was the beginning of our economic recovery. Later, of
course, we developed into electronics and other high-added-value
products, but steel was our initial breakthrough."

Fitzduane nodded. The Japanese achievement was undeniable, but
it had not occurred in a vacuum. Without U.S. military protection,
Japan had stood a good chance of being grabbed by Soviet Russia at the

end of the Second World War. Subsequently, Japan had benefited enormously from U.S. expenditure in Japan and virtually unrestricted access to U.S. markets. Still, this was no time to get involved in a geopolitical debate.

"But Namaka Special Steels has little to do with cars and ships, I think," shouted Fitzduane.

The noise had increased as they had approached the center of operations. The primary sound was like a wave, loud and continuous. He had been around Vaybon's steel facilities in Switzerland and remembered that it came from the burning flames of gas. It was the noise of the tempering ovens generating the awesome temperatures that steelmaking required.

There was something frightening about the sound, as if it represented a ferocity beyond the ability of mere humans to resist. In fact, almost all the machinery he could see was vastly larger than human scale. It looked like a workshop for giants. Humans might have conceived it, but now their very creations had surpassed them and seemed to have a life of their own.

In the center of the floor was an immense vertical construction of tubes and black metal and cylinders that looked like a cross between some insane scientist's vision of the ultimate destructive robot and a rocket complete with strapped-on boosters on a launching pad.

It was roughly the size of a six-story building, and Fitzduane felt dwarfed by it. It emphasized the scale of the facility they were in. The huge machine was in turn comfortably accommodated by its surroundings. The roof must be well over a hundred feet up. He looked, but his gaze was lost in darkness.

"Project Tsunami," shouted Kei into Fitzduane's ear. "This is what makes it all possible."

"What is Project Tsunami, Namaka-*san*?" said Fitzduane. "I haven't the slightest idea what you are talking about."

"Hah!" said Kei. "You know exactly what I am talking about, *gaijin*, and it is why we could not let you live, even if we did not have a past obligation to kill you."

The thought occurred briefly to Fitzduane that, in the interests of self-preservation, it might be a good idea *not* to get to know any more about Tsunami. Then he thought, What the hell! For one reason or another, Kei, quite obviously, had no intention of letting him live. He had not blown up three people just to have the pleasure of Fitzduane's company for a pleasant half hour or so.

"Indulge me, Namaka-*san*," said Fitzduane. "Let me put it as simply as I can. What the fuck is Project Tsunami?"

Namaka looked at him curiously. Perhaps the *gaijin* did not know. Perhaps he was not the threat he had appeared. That would be ironic. Well, it was too late to turn back now.

"Project Tsunami," said Kei, speaking into Fitzduane's ear to counteract the noise, "is the name we have given to our North Korean project. In defiance of the U.S. and, indeed, world embargoes, we are providing North Korea with the specialized plant and equipment necessary to manufacture nuclear weapons. It is an immensely profitable project and will restore the fortunes of Namaka Steel and indeed the *keiretsu* as a whole. And this machine—we call it Godzilla—is an important element. Godzilla allows us to forge the huge pressure chambers required for an essential part of the process. Few companies have the technology, and fewer still have production plants of this scale. Look! They are just about to forge another chamber. You can see the whole process for yourself."

Fitzduane looked across to where Kei was pointing. A giant crablike machine running on tracks had scuttled up and extended two metal arms and was manipulating an enormous glowing cylinder. A darker material seemed to surround it, and as Fitzduane watched, the cylinder was beaten by what seemed to be a giant flail of chains.

"That is the ingot for one chamber," said Kei. "It weighs forty-two tons and it has just been heated to forging temperature by one of the ovens. The ingot oxidizes on the surface, so the impure surface layer—it is called scale—must be removed or it will hinder forging. Scale is peeled away partly by the chains and then by the initial forging."

For all the talk of high technology, beating a white-hot lump of metal with chains seemed to Fitzduane to be a crude process, but Kei certainly got some fun out of it. His face was glowing with enthusiasm and the ambient heat. Under his *samurai* helmet with its ornamental horns, he looked like some demonic goblin king.

"The ingot is now going through a series of preliminary deformation processes," said Kei. "The next stage is that it will be given a predetermined diameter by one of the smaller presses."

The crab moved the ingot away from the flail and placed it under a giant ram. The ram descended and deformed the ingot, making it shorter and wider. As this happened, the remaining scale fell from the shape and there remained only glowing, pulsating steel. It was as if this was new life emerging from a chrysalis, and it was a dramatic sight. Even Fitzduane, who felt he should be preoccupied with more important issues—like his imminent death—was impressed.

The crab next lifted the cylinder of pure steel and placed it under a 12,000-ton press. The cylinder, an approximate shape up to now, was placed in a mould and pressed to be dimensionally perfect. Then a further process pierced the cylinder to make it ready for the main extrusion.

"By doing the piercing process first," said Kei, "you cut down on the maximum amount of energy needed in Godzilla. It is like preparing a screw hole by drilling a small hole in advance. The total amount of energy used is the same, but it is spread and the peak is lower."

The crab now inserted the squat, pierced, forty-two-ton cylinder at the base of Godzilla while Kei explained the procedure.

"That cylinder of steel now has a temperature of over 2,000 degrees Fahrenheit—or over twenty times body temperature. It is placed upon a pedestal, and then the FE punch, or mandril, determining its internal diameter—in this case, one meter—comes down, and the vertical press forces the steel up, compressing it and reducing the wall thickness, so that what emerges at the top of the press as the process reaches its conclusion is a longer, thinner cylinder with the same diameter. To achieve this result—to extrude white-hot steel like toothpaste—it exerts a force of up to 45,000 tons."

The background noise of the gas ovens and the hammering of the pumps providing the hydraulic pressure to Godzilla was now dominated in turn by a long, appallingly loud, high-pitched screeching sound, as white-hot steel was compressed and squeezed.

The sound receded, and like some huge pink erection, a long, thin, hot shape—compared to the original ingot—was withdrawn from the top of Godzilla by a crane in the roof.

Kei looked delighted as he exhaled. "Now, *gaijin*," he said. "That— THAT—is power. It is beautiful to watch, don't you think?"

Fitzduane took a flier. He was talking to an enthusiast, and enthusiasts were notoriously indiscreet. Also, who was he going to have time to tell? He decided he had better throw in some positive sounds. Kei clearly expected an appreciative audience.

"That is singularly impressive, Namaka-*san*," he said. "And part of Project Tsunami?"

"Oh yes," said Kei. "You have just seen one pressure chamber made. There are two hundred required for one phase of the process alone. So far, we have shipped one complete chamber to our customer. That will be tested, and then Godzilla will be put seriously to work. As you have seen, a pressure-chamber section can be forged from ingot to tube in under ten minutes. Allowing for finishing, welding on flanges, polishing, and so on—the really time-consuming elements—we shall still be able to complete the shipment in one year."

Fitzduane felt very depressed at what he was hearing. So this was the world that Boots was entering. What he was seeing was illegal, but nonetheless, here was Japan, the one country that had demilitarized and dedicated itself to peace, involved in the wretched business of nuclear weapons as well. It was a grim note on which to die. An inner rage began to burn.

Kei shouted an order, and Fitzduane was roughly pulled away and propelled between two *yakuza* across the vast floor and back up the steps to the *dojo.* As he was pushed through the soundproof double doors, he could hear the screeching of Godzilla once again as another pressure-chamber length emerged.

Inside the *dojo,* the silence could almost be felt.

Fitzduane was pushed to his knees. Ahead of him, a magnificent if barbaric figure in his medieval *samurai* armor, was Kei Namaka. Behind him and slightly to one side stood Goto, similarly attired. On either side of Fitzduane were his *yakuza* guards. Two more *yakuza* stood against the wall. All six were armed with swords. The *yakuza* also had submachine guns.

"It is time, *gaijin*," said Kei Namaka, "for you to die." He spoke rapidly in Japanese, and Fitzduane felt his handcuffs and leg restraints being removed. He rose to his feet, rubbing his wrists to restore circulation.

"The only issue here, Fitzduane-*san*," said Kei, "concerns the manner of your death."

Fitzduane smiled. "I would prefer, Namaka-*san*, if you don't mind, to debate the timing."

THERE WERE FOUR passengers in the Koancho helicopter besides the pilot, and one of them was Sergeant Oga, who was not at all sure what he was getting into.

The only thing he was certain of was that anything involving the *gaijin* Fitzduane-*san,* even after he was dead, was sure to be trouble. He had much the same feeling about Tanabu-*san* as he sat across from her. Even had he not harbored a deep suspicion about the games the security service got into, the Howa Type 89 5.56mm assault rifle she held resting on her knees would have given him serious cause for concern.

The folding-stock weapon was fitted with laser sight, sound suppressor, under-barrel 40mm grenade launcher, and hundred-round C-Mag. The U.S.-made C-Mag was an extremely compact, spring-loaded, plastic double-drum that fed rounds from each drum alternatively and provided over three times the capacity of a conventional magazine.

The combination of elements added up to the most vicious personal weapon he had yet encountered, and it did not look like the kind of thing you would carry on a routine investigation.

He leaned across the tiny cabin and spoke to Tanabu-*san.* The intercom would have been an easier way of overcoming the engine noise, but the fewer people who heard their discussion the better.

"Shouldn't we do this through channels, Tanabu-*san*?" he said. "This is really a job for a large force of *kidotai.* My men are not really trained for this sort of thing."

Chifune bent forward to meet him halfway. Supremely feminine as she was, and dressed in a tan linen suit with skirt ending well above the knee-line, she should, thought Oga, have appeared slightly ridiculous with all this firepower; but that was not the case. She handled her weapons system as if nothing were more natural.

He could smell her perfume as she moved close. Her complexion was flawless, her deep-brown eyes, flecked with gold, compelling. She was going to be a hard woman to resist. In fact, she had already proved that she was a hard woman to resist, or he would not be in this helicopter.

"Oga-*san,*" Chifune said, "time is critical, and we do not have the evidence to get a large raid approved without hacking through the bureaucracy. We're following a suspicion based upon my knowledge of how the Namakas work and the one slim fact that Fitzduane-*san's* beeper continued to function for five minutes after the explosion. Further, where we are going is a defense installation. To get approval to raid that would mean going right to the top, which would take forever and blow security. The Namakas, you must know, have friends in the highest places. At a certain level in the power structure, it is hard to know where loyalties lie. That is the reality of money politics in Japan today. There are those who will be very happy to see Fitzduane-*san* dead and the status quo preserved."

Oga gulped. The woman was making it worse. If this thing went wrong, he was risking not just his life but his career. He could imagine what his wife, a thoroughly practical woman, would say. Still, she was not here, and Tanabu-*san* very much was.

"As to your competence for this kind of operation, Sergeant-*san*," said Chifune, "I know you are very highly thought of and that you were in the paratroops, just like Adachi-*san*, before you joined the police."

Oga nodded.

"And as to your men," continued Chifune, "I have the greatest confidence in the Tokyo MPD and I have no doubt they will do their duty with distinction."

Oga sighed. He had not a chance against this woman. Without being aware of the transition, he mentally switched from his police role to his previous airborne training. They were going in and they would do what had to be done, and that was that. The pieces could be picked up afterward.

He turned to his two detectives. He had had to leave his other men behind because of space limitations in the helicopter, but the men he had kept, Detectives Renako and Sakado, were rock-solid.

"Check your weapons, lads," he said. "Where we're going may be hot."

The sprawling industrial mass that was the Namaka Steel empire showed up on the skyline, and Chifune spoke an instruction to the pilot. Seconds later, the helicopter was speeding along at only a few feet above wave-top height, and Sergeant Oga was totally back into airborne mode and wondering why he had ever left. He loved this kind of shit.

"AIRBORNE!" he shouted.

"AIRBORNE!" repeated his men. Neither had seen military service, but if it was appropriate for the redoubtable Sergeant Oga, it was appropriate for them. Group solidarity was all important. And somehow it sounded just right.

Chifune smiled and made a punching gesture with her right hand. "All the way," she said.

"FITZDUANE-*SAN*," said Kei, "I must tell you that I regret you have to die.

"You are a brave man and an honorable man—but you must understand that I have no choice. We have an obligation to kill you. It is a matter of *giri*. And now it is also a matter of self-preservation. You know too much."

Fitzduane looked at each man in turn. Two *yakuza* stood against the *dojo* wall near where his personal belongings, including the Calico, lay. The other two stood on either side of Kei Namaka. Goto stood several paces behind him.

Fitzduane was about to remark on the insanity of the whole ghastly business, but then realized the futility of saying anything. Kei was following a different agenda. From his and the *yakuza*'s perspective, Fitzduane was an obstacle that must be cleared away. It was not personal; it was business. And so, if you accepted this warped logic, killing him in the most interesting and entertaining way also made sense.

"Fitzduane-*san*," said Kei. "You and I are both members of the Medieval Warrior's Society. We both share an interest in medieval weapons. We are both expert swordsmen. Accordingly, it seems appropriate to use this opportunity to resolve an old debate—the merits of the Japanese sword, the *katana*, against a Western equivalent. *Katana* versus rapier is what I have in mind, but I am open to suggestions."

Fitzduane went through the options. The obvious alternative to the rapier was the sabre, but that would be no contest. *Katana* and sabre were both designed primarily for cutting, but in this respect, in his opinion, the *katana* was incomparable. It was lighter, better balanced, could be manipulated faster, and had a vastly superior cutting edge.

No, any chance he had lay with the rapier. The rapier was designed to kill with the point. It was the type of weapon he had trained with. It was where he had the maximum advantage, and Kei must know this. The man was a murderer and a criminal, but he was not without some honor. Or perhaps honor was not the motivator but merely simple curiosity. Either way, it was academic. Motivation was no longer an issue. It was now down to the fundamentals: who would live, who would die.

"I also thought," said Kei, "that this would be an excellent opportunity to try out the ax you so kindly gave me. It is not an original medieval weapon, of course, but the workmanship is outstanding, so I am giving it honorary status."

He hefted the glittering weapon as he spoke and then swung it around in a circle. "If anyone is seriously wounded, they will be dispatched with this ax. If you kill my two champions, I shall fight you with the *katana,* but finish you with the ax. One way or another, this weapon will be blooded today. We shall field-test the quality of Irish workmanship."

In more ways than you know, if I have half a chance, thought Fitzduane. A great deal of effort by the Ranger Operations Research people had gone into preparing the presentation ax for Kei, but Fitzduane's own decapitation was not one of the results that Fitzduane had in mind. Instead, the objectives had been twofold: to intrigue Kei Namaka—and this had certainly succeeded—and to kill Kei, if an opportunity arose.

Under a thin coat of hardened steel, and lined with lead to resist X rays, in case the Namaka security people were as routinely paranoid as most of their breed, the thick center of the double-edged ax head contained a pound of plastic explosive surrounded by five hundred miniature ball bearings. The device was totally sealed in and could not be detected by a chemical sniffer or even by removing the head from the shaft. The decorative wire binding on the shaft made an excellent radio aerial. The effect when detonated would be roughly the same as two Claymore directional mines placed back-to-back.

Unfortunately, the radio detonator—Fitzduane's watch—had been removed from him and lay across the room with his other belongings, beside the two *yakuza* in the corner. Well, as a British Army friend of his liked to say, plans had a habit of turning to ratshit. Like it or not, he was going to have to fight with a sword. Close to the end of the twentieth century, it seemed like a ridiculous weapon to have to use, but at close quarters it would kill just as surely as a firearm.

"Fitzduane-*san,*" said Kei. "I do not wish to cause you unnecessary anguish by raising false hopes by not making your situation quite clear. You may be harboring thoughts of escaping from this *dojo.* Forget them. Your efforts would be futile. The door to the helicopter landing pad on the roof is locked, and outside it is guarded by a special team of a dozen men loyal only to my clan. Frankly, your situation is hopeless. Your only recourse is to die with dignity. I am sure you will not disappoint me."

He bowed as he finished speaking. "The first, and I expect the last, man you will fight is Hitai-*sensei*. He is the instructor of the *Insuji-gumi*."

Fitzduane took his time replying. Hitai was a muscular *yakuza* of medium height with intelligent eyes and a peacock's-head tattoo showing at his throat. He looked to be in his mid-forties. His sword was still in its scabbard in his sash. The suffix *sensei* was not the best of news. This was not any thug with a blade, but a master with probably a quarter of a century's experience behind him. Experience with Japanese swords, though. European techniques were very different.

Fitzduane looked across to Kei and bowed back slightly. "Thank you for the morale-raising speech, Namaka-*san*," he said dryly. "I shall endeavor to meet my obligations in the appropriate way."

Another *yakuza* came forward and laid a rapier on the polished floor several yards in front of Fitzduane, then backed away hastily. Fitzduane moved forward almost casually, keeping his eye on Hitai, and dropped to one knee and picked it up. Hitai did not move. He just gazed impassively at this *gaijin*.

Fitzduane had learned not only to sword-fight from his father, but also something of the history of swordplay. It was Fitzduane Senior's belief that skill with a blade should be instinctive rather than consciously premeditated, so he used to talk to his young pupil while fighting, trying both to teach and distract. The result, after many years, was that Fitzduane, while fencing, fought almost entirely on instinct and by reflex, and before a major bout actually found it helpful to clear his mind and think of something other than the minutiae of tactics.

"The first recorded sword, as far as I know, Hugo," his father had said, "was an Egyptian weapon made of bronze from the nineteenth century B.C. called a *khopesh*, with a long grip and a sickle-shaped blade. Actually, it was more of a knife than a sword, but it was interesting metallurgically in that it was made from one piece.

"Around fifteen hundred B.C., longer bronze swords were produced, and these were narrow thrusting weapons up to three feet long and only half an inch wide. The thinking was right, but not the technology. Bronze is a soft metal and such a narrow length would bend, so eventually a shorter, leaf-shaped blade evolved."

Fitzduane, rapier in hand, slowly backed away from Hitai. The *yakuza* looked at Kei Namaka in surprise, then advanced toward the *gaijin*. Hitai's *katana* was still in its sheath.

"Slowly, around a thousand B.C., iron replaced bronze and the leaf shape became a little narrower and the short, broad-bladed weapon carried by the Roman legionaries, the Spanish sword, emerged. This was about two feet long and two inches wide, and it was state of the art at the time. It was designed primarily for thrusting. It was long enough to allow close-in work when carrying a shield, but not so long it bent or got in the way of your neighbor. It was worn on the right side for a quick draw unencumbered by the shield, and it was light, compact, and deadly. In contrast, the Gauls had long, slashing swords. Throughout the history of sword fighting, there has been a debate about whether the sword is primarily a thrusting or a cutting weapon. Well, the Romans liked the point, and their empire lasted longer than most. They had a saying: *Duas uncias in puncta mortalis est,* which is worth remembering even today. 'Two inches in the right spot is fatal.' The thrust, in my opinion, expressed over two thousand years after the Romans came to the same conclusion, is still the most deadly technique for a sword."

The *yakuza sensei* was looking impatient. The *gaijin* had backed away slowly but continually, and he would soon be off the wooden floor and onto the *tatami* mats where visitors sat. Still, he could not retreat much longer. Two *yakuza* guards with slung Uzis and drawn *katanas* stood against the wall. They would soon prod this cowardly foreigner back into action.

There had been some mystery about what had happened during the abortive hit on Yasukini-dori outside the Fairmont and some talk about the *gaijin*'s fighting prowess. It was now clear that the *gaijin* had had nothing to do with his escape. The police must have intervened unexpectedly and it was as simple as that.

"The Romans were primarily infantry," Fitzduane's father had said. "After they lost high ground, cavalry in the form of Attila the Hun and the Goths, for example, became the dominant arm for a while, and swords became longer and more used for cutting. You needed a long sword if you were going to fight from a horse, and using the point if you are a horseman is near impossible. From a horse, you slash. The point only comes into play with a spear or lance, and even then it is largely limited to one kill. A pointed weapon sticks in its victim, and if you are on a horse, either you let go or else you get thrown."

Kei Namaka stepped forward, his face red with anger. "Fitzduane-*san,* what you are doing is not permissible. You must not retreat over the *tatami* mats. It is not proper. Fighting must be confined to the wooden floor. If you do not follow the rules, I shall order my men to cut you down. Frankly, you are a great disappointment."

Fitzduane stopped retreating, as if unsure what to do next. His shoulders were bent and he was carrying his sword low. There was a decided aura of defeat about him. He looked around, and the two *yakuza* wall guards brandished their weapons and made it clear that if he retreated any more, he would be killed. It was an imminent threat. The guards were only a couple of paces behind him. He was barely out of sword range.

He remembered his father again. "From the end of the Roman Empire for about the next thousand years, Western swords tended to be long, straight, wide-bladed, and heavy—and used primarily for slashing. This was the case whether horsemen or infantry were involved. Either way, a long heavy weapon was favored. Disciplined fighting in shielded, mutually protecting lines, Roman-style, was no longer practiced, and a long heavy weapon was deemed necessary to cut through armor and had the added advantage of keeping your enemy a reasonable distance away.

"Armor," Fitzduane's father had continued, "became somewhat redundant when guns were introduced in the fourteenth century, and evolving technology, thanks in no small part to the Arabs, found a way of making swords thinner and lighter. And so, in the sixteenth century, the rapier emerged. It was a lighter, narrow, two-edge-bladed weapon with a primary emphasis on killing with the point."

Fitzduane looked up, first at Hitai and then at Kei Namaka. "Namaka-*san,*" he said. "What we are doing is insane. All of this"—he made a gesture encompassing all in the *dojo*—"is unnecessary. The result can only be death and imprisonment. Why? Why? It's pointless. Even if you succeed in killing me, there are others who know what I know."

Kei Namaka's initial anger had turned to a black, sullen rage. The *gaijin*'s behavior was no longer merely inappropriate. It was embarrassing. It was causing him, the chairman of the Namaka Corporation, to lose face. It was an unendurable humiliation. He made a gesture of contempt. "Kill the *gaijin*," he said in Japanese, "and take your time about it."

20

Because of its involvement in defense, Namaka Special Steels was a restricted military area, so Chifune ordered the Koancho pilot to circle the rooftop landing zone twice, while announcing that this was a special police inspection through the loudspeaker.

Half a dozen armed uniformed guards could be seen on the roof and a small control tower doubtless held more, so she did not want a hot landing if it could possibly be avoided.

The helicopter was in Tokyo MPD livery, and police authority was respected in Japan, so she did not expect any serious difficulty in actually landing. Whether she would be able to get much farther than the roof was another question, but she would worry about that after they had touched down. Normally, her Koancho credentials could get her into just about anywhere. The security service was held in some awe.

The reaction from the guards was unexpected. The helicopter was energetically waved away and then a booming amplified voice from the ground announced: "Warning. This is a restricted area. Do not try and land or we will open fire. I repeat. Do not try and land or we will open fire."

Chifune and Oga looked at each other in shock. This was unprecedented. "Extraordinary," muttered Oga. What was nearly violence-free Japan coming to when guards on a steel plant could threaten an official aircraft with lethal force? Respect for authority was going to hell.

"Decidedly odd, Sergeant-*san*," said Chifune. She ordered the pilot to circle again, and perused the landing pad through a pair of pintle-mounted, high-power, gyroscopically stabilized glasses. Because of the vibration inherent in their design, helicopters were horrible things to use binoculars from, but the gyro stabilization made all the difference. The picture was rock-steady and, magnified fifteen times, the guards looked nearly close enough to touch.

She pushed the glasses on their mount over to Oga. Koancho has all the latest surveillance toys, he reflected, as he focused the instrument on a group of guards below. Suddenly, the strange reaction of the guards made sense. *"Yakuza,"* he said forcefully. "I recognize some of the faces. These cannot be proper Japanese Defense Agency–cleared guards. These people are criminals. What are they doing here?"

"I expect the Namakas know the answer to that," said Chifune grimly.

She called up Koancho control, transmitted a picture of the faces below in real time to the duty officer, and called for backup. A voice in reply told her not to try to land until reinforcements arrived. She started to argue, then noticed that a panel on the top of the control tower had opened and several guards carrying something had emerged. The video link with control was still running. There was a brief warning cry from the horrified duty officer, and then a line of red tracer stabbed into the sky toward them and the radio went dead.

A line of holes appeared in the cabin fuselage and Detective Sakado spasmed in his seat belt, as two heavy .50-caliber rounds punched through his side and blew the best part of one lung and half his rib cage out of the front of his body.

The helicopter dropped like a stone and sideslipped over the roof, as the pilot implemented immediate evasive action away from the line of tracer. It was a reflex action and effective in that it was unexpected, but it brought them closer to the control tower.

A second burst from the .50 punched through the airspace they had just left, but then a third burst caught the tail rotor. The helicopter started to spin in its own axis, but they were now so close to the roof landing area that they hit almost immediately.

There was the sound of screaming metal as the skids dragged across the metal grating of the landing area, showering sparks everywhere, and then the rotors disintegrated as the wrecked machine came to a halt against the base of the control tower.

The impact had been severe, but the short drop made it far from fatal, and the slide across the pad had dissipated much of the energy. Strapped in as they were, Chifune and the surviving detectives were bruised and shaken but otherwise unharmed. Immediately, they scrambled out of the cabin door and took shelter at the base of the tower away from where the helicopter had impacted. The pilot tried to follow them, but just as he was climbing out, the fuel tanks blew and engulfed the near side of the control tower and much of the landing pad in burning fuel and red-hot debris.

A guard staggered toward them. A long piece of rotor blade had hit him in the back as he ran away from the crashing helicopter, and as they watched he pitched forward, thick blood spewing from his mouth.

A figure peered over the roof parapet of the control tower. They were too close to the base of the tower for the .50-caliber to be brought to bear on them, but the guard had a submachine gun and was bringing it to the point of aim as Chifune fired. The guard jerked and blood sprayed from him as the burst cut him open, then he pitched over the parapet edge and crashed to the ground beside them.

Chifune crawled toward the body. They had to take out the heavy-machine-gun team on the control tower roof, and she needed grenades. Her effort was in vain. The guard had none. Her movement attracted the attention of other guards firing from a doorway about fifty meters away. Rounds cracked over her head and smashed into the base of the tower behind her.

Sergeant Oga and Detective Renako mounted a furious hail of fire in reply, and under its cover Chifune crawled back to where they were. Effectively, they were pinned down in a crossfire between the guards on the control-tower roof and the others around the door.

FITZDUANE HELD up his left hand, effectively stopping Hitai, in front of him, and the two *yakuza* guards, behind him, in their tracks.

The *gaijin* was responding at last. He was doing something other than retreating. This was good. This was what Namaka-*san* wanted, and what he wanted, his men wanted.

"Namaka-*san*," said Fitzduane, "I was thinking about the difference between Western swords and those of Japan. Is it not true that Japanese swords were perfected around the eighth century and that a sword made a thousand years later is more or less the same in appearance?"

Despite his rage, Kei was interested. The *gaijin* was a fellow weapons expert. What he had to say, particularly under these extreme circumstances, could well be worth hearing. "Wait," he said in Japanese to his men.

Hitai had been preparing to kill the *gaijin* by drawing his sword and slashing in one continuous flowing move. Kei Namaka was famous for it and Hitai wanted to show that he, too, was a master of *Iai-do*—the art of drawing a sword.

The *gaijin* did not look to be presenting much of a problem as an opponent, but his behavior was upsetting. His method of retreating meant that it was hard to keep the appropriate striking distance away. And this ridiculous conversation was just distracting. It upset the dignity of the occasion. Hitai found it irritating, and it was hard to clear his mind as he had learned to do.

His object was to make his mind like water: *A reflection in water is the symbol of a clear, calm mind in harmony with its surroundings—the highest level of training in a martial art.* The *gaijin*'s behavior was the mental equivalent of throwing pebbles into that water. Hitai could not focus.

"Yes, it is so," said Kei. "The classic Japanese sword, the *katana,* reached perfection at a time when Europeans were fighting with crude lumps of steel—and then how do you improve on perfection? Instead, the emphasis changed to perfecting the use of the sword. One hundred and twenty draws and a thousand cuts per day was normal for a warrior's training. It is only through constant practice that perfection is achieved, and that warrior and sword become as one."

"I have to admit, Namaka-*san,*" said Fitzduane, "we're a sloppy lot in the West by comparison. Instead of settling on perfection, we keep on trying out new things. It makes for a disorderly but creative society. Take the rapier, for example. At one stage, some models were all of five feet long—rather difficult to wear on social occasions. Of course, trial and error produced a more acceptable result. But then we all switched to the gun. What do you do with degenerates like that? Fickle. No staying power."

Kei Namaka was nonplussed. The *gaijin* was playing with him. Hitai glanced toward Kei in a silent plea that this nonsense be stopped.

Fitzduane stepped back three paces, and as the two *yakuza* stumbled in surprise at this totally unexpected move, he executed one ferocious thrust which pierced the neck of the man next to him and continued without pause to sink its point deep into the second *yakuza*'s eye.

Kei gave a bellow, and Hitai turned back to his opponent and drew his *katana* with incredible speed and slashed in a reflex at where Fitzduane had been. The blade caught the second *yakuza* as he fell away, mortally wounded from the sword in his eye; after cutting through his spine, it severed his right arm.

Fitzduane, who had little time for style over substance when his life was on the line, left his rapier in the first *yakuza*'s neck and grabbed the man's Uzi. The strap would not come away, so he cocked it and fired it while still attached to the *yakuza*'s body.

The weapon hammered and Hitai's weapon shattered as the first rounds hit it. It did not seem quite the occasion for restraint, so Fitzduane fired again, and Hitai sprouted red flowers as he shot backwards into the second *yakuza* master swordsman.

The Uzi jammed. Fitzduane pulled his rapier out of the dead *yakuza*'s neck with some effort and met his new opponent as he advanced. The *yakuza* delivered a series of slashing blows in a vertical cloverleaf arrangement that effectively prevented anyone from getting near him. It was an aggressive defense, because the man advanced as he deployed this flashing perimeter.

Fitzduane scooped up Hitai's damaged *katana* and used it to parry the *yakuza*'s blade, and as he did so thrust his rapier into the *yakuza*'s stomach. The man sagged forward onto his knees.

Fitzduane whirled to meet any possible attack from Kei Namaka, and was stunned to see that neither he nor Goto had moved.

Kei just stood there, the ax in his hands, enjoying the spectacle. Then Fitzduane moved forward and the ax was a blur in his hands. There was a fountain of blood, and the *yakuza*'s head flew across the room. The headless body slid to the ground, as Kei watched, mesmerized. Then he looked at the dripping weapon. "Superb," he said. "The balance, the craftsmanship, quite superb."

"Namaka-*san*," said Fitzduane, "clearly you did not eat enough fish as a child. There can be too much of a good thing. Put that weapon down."

Kei looked across. The *gaijin* had moved again. Now he was by the small table where his belongings had been placed and there was something in his hands.

"Don't disappoint me, Fitzduane-*san*," he said. "Let us fight man to man."

Fitzduane looked at the carnage around him and then at Kei. "Don't be ridiculous," he said. The familiar Calico was now in his hand. The exploding ax had been a nice idea, but he did not relish being in the same room when it went off. Metal fragments traveling at high velocity had no discrimination.

"FIGHT ME, *GAIJIN!*" Kei roared, and charged at Fitzduane, the ax held high above his head.

This is the man who arranged to have me killed and who nearly killed my son, thought Fitzduane. Still, there was deep regret, as he squeezed the trigger of the Calico and 10mm red tracer winked across the room, smashed effortlessly through the ornate *samurai* armor, and tore the magnificent body of Kei Namaka into shreds.

The remains that had been the chairman of the Namaka Corporation crumpled, and streams of crimson spread out across the seamless wooden floor.

"Namaka-*san*," said Fitzduane to himself, "we *gaijins* have our weaknesses, but we know—we truly know—about the business of killing. And there is scant glory in it."

In a far corner of the room, the new security chief of the Namaka Corporation crouched. Under the *samurai* war helmet, he was white-faced and shaking with fear.

Fitzduane walked across to him, the Calico loosely trained on the terrified man. "Goto-*san*," he said mildly, "are you sure you are on the right career path?"

Goto shook and could not speak. The *gaijin* had killed five armed men in less than a minute, and he was certain it would soon be six. He had taken the job of security chief after Kitano's abrupt demise to consolidate his power in the Namaka *keiretsu*, but had never dreamed he would be much more than an administrator. The reality of violence made him sick.

"Goto-*san*," said Fitzduane. "If you don't want me to add to your normal quota of body apertures, you're going to get up and show me how to get out of here."

The terrified man did not move.

Fitzduane straightened his aim so that the Calico was pointing directly between Goto's eyes. "Please," said Fitzduane dryly.

THE ONLY REASON they were not dead, Chifune reflected, as heavy automatic fire cracked inches overhead and drew splinters from the base of the tower, was the thin double line of sandbags about two feet high and eight feet long behind which they were sheltering.

She could not at first figure out what the bags were doing there, since the layout in no way constituted an emplacement, and then realized that they were probably used in high winds to help secure the skids of parked helicopters.

The bags had been filled with a thin, high-quality sand, unfortunately, and as the gunfire ripped open the bags, the sand was flowing out at an uncomfortably fast rate. In a matter of minutes they would be well-equipped to build sand castles but devoid of cover. They were going to have to do something very soon.

Oga was lying on his back, his Heckler and Koch MP5 pointed up at the top of the tower. From time to time, a head would appear and someone would try to shoot down, but Oga's accurate snap-shooting in semiautomatic mode to conserve ammunition kept the situation under control. He was talented at this sort of thing, observed Chifune. It was more than standard airborne training.

"How is your CQB, Sergeant-*san*?" said Chifune. She was referring to Close Quarters Battle training, the highly specialized skills acquired for hostage training or close-in counterterrorist work.

Oga fired twice rapidly at a silhouette appearing over the tower parapet and red mist stained the air. "Rusty, but coming back to me," he said. "They say it's like riding a bicycle. When you get older, you can still do it, but your joints creak."

Chifune smiled briefly. She had heard much the same comment made about another popular human pastime.

"If we stay here, we're going to get killed," she said. "If we advance to attack the guards in and around the doorway, we're not going to make it. There is at least a half-dozen of them and there are forty-odd yards to cover. Also, they will be able to hit us with the fifty on the roof from behind."

"Which leaves the tower or waiting until help comes?" said Oga.

"Help is going to take twenty minutes or more," said Chifune, "even with the quick reaction team."

"So put a 40mm into the doorway and have Renako hose them down for a few seconds while we kick in the tower doorway," said Oga. "My guess, after the helicopter blew up beside them, is that all the survivors are on the roof."

"How many do you think?" said Chifune.

"Less than there were," said Oga grimly. "Two or three, four at the most. So let's do it."

Chifune looked up at the tower again. She could take the top off with a 40mm grenade, but they were too close for the projectile to arm, and even if it did the resultant explosion could well take them out too. She made a mental note to take good, old-fashioned hand grenades with her in the future. This obsession with direct-fire weapons was ridiculous. Within seconds of any firefight starting, every sane participant was under cover, and then grenades were the best tools for the job.

Renako cried out and Chifune looked across. The detective's face was screwed up with pain. He reached down and pulled his leg under cover as if it could not move of its own volition. A round had smashed into his foot when it had strayed from behind their meager barrier into the line of fire. His face was gray with shock and there was sweat beaded on his forehead. The pain from such a wound would be intense, even if it was not immediately life-threatening.

"Renako-*san*," said Chifune. "Can you take the roof? We are going to clear it, but you must keep their heads down for a few seconds. Then we can help you."

Renako nodded weakly. Oga helped him onto his back so that he could watch the parapet, and checked that his weapon had a full magazine and a round chambered. He too had an MP5, but Oga set it to automatic.

"Nothing clever, Renako-*san*," said Oga. "Just spray the fuckers if they show."

"*Hai*, Sergeant-*san*," said Renako. He felt dizzy and the parapet was going in and out of focus, but he thought he could hang in there long enough.

Chifune had been reluctant to fire her grenade launcher into the doorway since, if Fitzduane was alive, the chances were he would be in that direction. Still, they had just about run out of the luxury of options.

"On my mark, Sergeant-*san*," she said, looking at Oga. He nodded.

"NOW!" she shouted.

Oga rose behind the barrier, weapon blazing, causing the guards in and around the doorway to duck temporarily. Almost immediately, Chifune added to the hail of fire with her C-Mag-fed automatic rifle and then sighted the grenade launcher and fired.

The bulbous projectile, looking like a massively oversized bullet, shot from the under-barrel grenade launcher and vanished through the doorway.

Flame and bodies erupted. Chifune hosed the area with the rest of her C-Mag, reloaded, and followed Oga around to the side of the tower and the door. Still-hot pieces of the wrecked helicopter lay everywhere, and as she was running, firing recommenced from across the roof. The grenade had inflicted casualties, but the defenders were far from out of action.

The tower doorway was half-broken and still burning. Oga hit it at a run, went straight in, and rolled and came up shooting. There was no one there, just metal stairs that led straight up to the small control room and the roof.

A face looked down and Oga fired again. The face vanished, but Oga thought he had missed. He was furious with himself for having fired unnecessarily and thus alerting the guards on the roof.

Chifune crouched beside him. The stairs led to an open door. She mentally worked out the distance and the angle and what the effect of the blast might be. The alternative was to climb up the stairs under fire. The advantage would be with the defenders, and she and Oga certainly did not have surprise on their side.

She did not blame Oga for firing. Had the base been occupied, they would have been dead if his precautionary fire had been delayed for even a fraction of a second. Combat, like most things in life, was about choices. You made decisions and you pushed ahead and you took the consequences if you were wrong. Regret rarely made a useful contribution.

Oga was changing magazines, so Chifune kept a hail of fire going in a series of tight-aimed bursts at where she expected the opposition to be. She could see no one.

"Do you want to be shown up or blown up, Sergeant-*san*?" she said in a brief lull, and fired again. The hundred-capacity C-Mag was a thing of joy. It fed rounds effortlessly and gave the firepower of a full machine gun.

Oga got the point immediately. "Go for it!" he said, holding up his thumb. She could not hear him, but the gesture was unmistakable. She flashed him a grin.

Chifune, crouched near the base of the stairs, fired the grenade launcher almost straight up. She imagined she could see the projectile as it entered the control room, and envisioned it continuing and impacting against the roof.

She crouched down and put her hands over her ears. The blast was awesome in the confined space, and a wave of concussion hit her. Debris and dust filled the tower.

She reloaded and fired again at a slightly different angle, in case the roof had blown open at the point of impact the first time, and again there was a violent explosion, though the concussion seemed to be less this time. The roof or some part of the structure had definitely been perforated and was dissipating the shock wave.

"Let's go," said Oga, and bounded up the stairs. Chifune followed him. They had both received similar training for CQB, and without discussion they both fell into mutually supporting roles.

They found two bodies in the wrecked control room. The center of the roof had fallen in and there was a third body under the debris. A single flight of perforated steel stairs led to the remains of the roof.

Oga advanced up it, covered by Chifune. At the top, he vanished for a few seconds and then reappeared with a smile on his face. "I'm going to look after Renako," he said. "You'd better take a look, Tanabu-*san*. Don't worry. It's safe to look over the parapet."

Oga, grinning from ear to ear but saying nothing more, rattled down the stairs past her to look after his man. Somewhat mystified, Chifune ascended. Two more dead lay there, their bodies severely mutilated from the grenade blasts and their blood leaching into the dust that was everywhere.

Despite Oga's reassurance, she was extremely cautious in looking over the parapet. First a snatched look to gain an impression, and then a longer perusal. What she saw made her rise to full height.

Several guards sat crosslegged on the ground, their hands clasped on their heads. Sitting slightly apart, very dazed, hands also on his head, was someone dressed in what looked like the remains of traditional *samurai* armor. It was an incongruous sight in this late-twentieth-century battlefield.

Standing behind the prisoners, the unusual automatic weapon she had learned was the Calico in his hands, was Fitzduane. He was wearing a torn white shirt and slacks and his feet were bare, but he looked very much alive and he was smiling.

He cupped his hands. "Chifune, you have never looked more beautiful. But what I want to know is—who is rescuing who around here?"

Chifune felt a surge of emotion. She wanted to run down and throw her arms around this unusual man, to make love to him, to hold him. She felt tears coming to her eyes and fought them back. She did not move. She struggled to regain composure. Then she started to laugh. It was not easy at first, but then she felt so good she did not want to stop. Exhilaration gripped her. She abandoned the sense of control that was so important to her, that was so much a feature of her every action. She felt liberated and joyous and infused with a sense of optimism.

"I thought you were dead, *gaijin-san*," she said, smiling.

"I nearly was when you fired that 40mm grenade, Tanabu-*san*," said Fitzduane cheerfully. "Fortunately, my friend here"—he pointed at Goto in his shattered armor—"took the blast and he was equipped for it, though it did not make him happy."

Chifune's cheeks were wet with tears. I want you, Hugo, she mouthed silently in Japanese.

Fitzduane looked up at her and then blew her a kiss.

OUTSIDE TOKYO, JAPAN

June 28

Fitzduane felt too languorous and relaxed to open his eyes.

He did not know where he was and he did not much care. All he knew was that he was warm and comfortable and safe; and tomorrow, whenever that was, could take care of itself.

Eyes closed, he daydreamed. Images and thoughts floated in and out of his mind: Chifune looking at him in a very particular way, her face smoke-blackened, her neat business suit torn and grimy, a high-tech assault rifle hanging from her shoulder; police helicopters and heavily armed riot police; bright lights and police video cameras; body bags and uniforms in surgical masks; an angry police officer and Chifune's calm insistence that they make statements later; a calm authoritative voice on the radio and the policeman backing away and saluting; a helicopter ride in the darkness; a long, low house with a verandah and overhanging roof and *shoji* screen in the traditional style; a long, hot shower and water tinged with blood as the last traces of those he had killed were washed from his body, and the nausea he had felt; the steam rising from the hot tub as he climbed in and Chifune telling him not to move and that it would be fine and it was. And then nothing except a delicious sense of peace as he slipped into sleep.

He stretched. He felt weightless in the water and greatly refreshed. It was a delicious sensation, this sense of half-floating—free of cares and responsibilities.

Hot tubs were an invention of the gods. The Romans had used them and they had done pretty well. The Japanese were fanatical about them, and that probably accounted for most of their economic miracle. Hot tubs had not made it to Ireland, which explained a great deal.

In Fitzduane's opinion at that moment, hot tubs were the solution to most of the world's problems, and you could even float a plastic duck in one. This was excellent. He was a great believer in yellow plastic ducks. Boots adored his, though he liked to sink them and then watch them bob up again. Curiously, someone had once told him, ducks seemed to be a male thing. Was this really so? Was there some deep-rooted sexual significance to bath ducks? Was there a Freudian thesis lurking somewhere which might explain the whole thing? Well, what did it matter, anyway? If ducks were sexy, good for ducks. You couldn't really do very much if you were plastic. Personally, he liked ducks, but he preferred women.

Women were soft and warm and caring and interesting and fun to talk to and they made nice babies like Boots and it had taken him a long time to really learn it but he really loved babies and children and he missed Boots greatly and he wanted to go home and give him the biggest hug in the world and then another.

But, of course, women were also dangerous sometimes, and complex always, and that did make for difficulties. Still, anything or anyone worthwhile was difficult.

That's really what life was about: babies, hot tubs, plastic bath ducks, women, and difficulties. People searched endlessly for the meaning of life, and here he had discovered it by floating in a hot tub for a couple of hours—or was it days? He really had not the faintest idea.

He opened his eyes. He could see stars in a glowing night sky and the air felt fresh and cool on his face and there was the smell of the sea. Everywhere in Ireland was near the sea, and in Duncleeve you could hear the sound of the waves on all but the calmest days and it was a sound that he greatly loved, that made him feel at peace. But here he could not quite hear the sea. It was close, but not close enough. The house and grounds were set back and, he now seemed to recall, built into the side of a hill. There would be a magnificent view of the sea and the bay below. He was sure of it, but it was impossible to check.

The hot tub was in an inner courtyard that was laid out as a traditional Japanese garden, and the house surrounded the space on all four sides. There was total privacy and silence except for the normal sounds of the night air. There was no traffic noise, so they could not be in or very near Tokyo, a city of relentless energy that never rested.

The setting was extraordinarily beautiful and a miniature world unto itself. There was something about the proportions of traditional Japanese architecture that was particularly pleasing and restful. It was a combination of line and texture and balance that in the most unostentatious way conveyed a feeling of harmony with life and with nature.

The secret of a Japanese garden, he had been told, was restraint, simplicity, and integration with what was most natural. Instead of flower beds bursting with artificially reared hybrids and the general excess of a Western garden, there appeared to be only simple features of mainly natural materials, such as sand and rocks and gravel and a few carefully selected bushes and some wildflowers. Of course, the naturalness was an illusion, but even though you knew that every natural item had been meticulously selected and arranged, it was an illusion that worked. *Tatemae* and *honne.* The way of Japan.

He felt gentle hands on his shoulders, and then his neck and shoulders were being massaged slowly and tenderly. Her touch was exquisite, and he closed his eyes and let waves of pleasure wash over him. From time to time, her hands left his back and caressed slowly down his body to his loins, stroking him in the most intimate of places.

After some minutes, he took her hands in his and kissed them one by one, running his tongue across the palm of each hand. She was wearing only a thin silk *yukata,* and through the thin material he could feel her breasts where they rested against the back of his head and her nipples hard and firm.

"Come with me," she said into his ear, her tongue licking it. Naked, he rose from the hot water into the cool night air and stepped from the tub onto the tile surround. His penis was erect and hard. The faintest lightening of the sky indicated the promise of dawn.

She draped his shoulders in a thick towel to dry him and to shield him from the night air, and took another towel and knelt down to dry his lower body. Again, she touched him without restraint, as if they had been lovers without secrets for some time.

Her beautiful hair, thick and glossy and normally worn up on a chignon or some other restrained style, now cascaded around her shoulders. He let the sensations wash over him until he could scarcely bear it, and then he bent over and lifted her up and took her in his arms.

She smelled of an exotic perfume he could not identify, but which was intensely stimulating. It was a subtle, sexual fragrance, and it blended with the clean, musky odor of her own arousal. Her arms around his neck, lips gently stroking, tongues intermingling, he carried her from the courtyard through the open *shoji* screens to where he could see the golden flickering light of a dozen candles.

The floor was of fresh *tatami,* but instead of the futon he had expected there was a low-slung, king-size bed. He lowered her feet to the floor and, still kissing her, stripped the gossamer-thin *yukata* from her body and placed her on the bed.

IT WAS DARK when Fitzduane awoke, and then he realized that he must have slept right through.

It was not surprising. The Namaka Steel business had been exhausting enough, but Chifune had been a marathon of exquisitely sensual endurance.

He fumbled for his watch and then tried opening his eyes. It made the process a whole lot easier. He noticed the candles were fresh and Chifune was leaning over him. She bent down and kissed him. Her hair was still damp from the shower, and she was wearing a toweling robe.

"Fourteen hours," she said. "More or less."

"So much for the sex," he said sleepily. "How long did we rest for?"

Chifune laughed. "There is a razor in the bathroom," she said. "I'll have some food ready in fifteen minutes. Are you hungry?"

Fitzduane undid her robe.

———

"PILLOW SPEAK," she said.

She was naked and lying with her back to him, staring unfocused at the candles, enjoying the constantly changing pattern as the flames flickered in the night breeze off the sea.

Fitzduane smiled, but did not correct her. Chifune had excellent English, but just occasionally would make a slip. He drank some more champagne. He was not quite sure whether it was breakfast, lunch, or dinner, but it tasted good anyway.

He felt recharged after the long sleep and the lovemaking and a shower and a shave and food and more lovemaking, and now that he thought of it, there were few things more pleasant in the world than lying in bed in a postcoital glow talking to a beautiful woman—unless it was doing exactly that with a bottle of decent wine to hand. Fitzduane liked the company of women. Women had good minds; a much-neglected resource in his opinion. And based on what he had seen and heard, a particularly neglected resource in Japan.

Chifune turned to look at him. "Pillow speak?" she said. "I could hear you smiling, *gaijin.*"

Fitzduane laughed. "Pillow talk," he said.

Chifune pulled back the covers and kissed his dormant penis quickly and then covered him up again. "Thank you," she said. "English is such a quirky language."

Fitzduane did not want to spoil the mood, but there were matters he was curious about and Chifune seemed to want to speak. "What about this pillow business?" he said quietly.

Chifune smiled without looking at him. "To pillow" was a euphemism for lovemaking in Japanese.

"You don't say anything explicitly, Hugo," she said, "but you're a man who invites confidences, an easy person to talk to. I think it is because you have values and you care. So many people go through the motions, but they don't really care and in their hearts there is nothing. They take up space but they do not contribute. To contribute, you have to care. And caring is about risk. You have something to lose. It exposes you. It makes you vulnerable. It is dangerous."

Fitzduane put down his wineglass and turned toward her. Her back was still to him, but he put his left arm around her and drew her to him. She snuggled up to him and pressed his hand against her breasts.

"Don't speak, Chifune," he said, "unless you must. It is not necessary."

" 'Don't say anything you'll regret afterwards,' " she quoted. "Relax, Hugo, I know the disciplines, the way it should be done in Koancho. I've been well-trained for this game, and I live it. But sometimes I need to breathe, to talk freely, as if I were not part of a world of paranoia, corruption, and deception. Security may be necessary, but it's stifling. Sometimes I wish I could live a normal life and have children and become an education mother and be married to a *sarariman*. And then complain because he is never at home—always out working or drinking with his colleagues or stuck on some commuter train."

"Who are you, Chifune?" said Fitzduane. "What's your background? How did you get into this business?"

Chifune was silent, and at first Fitzduane thought she was not going to answer, but then she spoke. "My father was a politician and the son of a politician. This makes a joke of democracy, but it is not so unusual. More and more political posts are handed down father to son, like some aristocratic birthright, and that happened in this case even though my father was estranged from my grandfather. Some alliances endure regardless. Like my grandfather, my father was a member of the Hodama faction, but something of a maverick nonetheless. He had been brought up in a world of money politics and at first regarded this as normal, but then started to think for himself. He had ideas, there were policies he wanted to pursue, but everywhere he turned he was frustrated by the system. Special interests ruled the day, and the amount of money going through the political system was such that they were not going to allow anyone to stand in their way. I'm talking about billions of yen here, millions of dollars. The bribe paid to one provincial governor, for example, to win construction contracts came to nearly twenty million dollars."

"Just one bribe?" said Fitzduane.

"Just one single backhander," said Chifune. "Politicians, certain senior civil servants, key businessmen, and the *yakuza*—the four pillars of power and corruption in Japan. Not everyone is corrupt, by any stretch of the imagination, but enough of the center of power is rotten for the tentacles of corruption to stretch far and wide."

"So what happened?" said Fitzduane.

"My father tried to change things. He and some younger faction members got together and set up a study group, and for a while they made some progress, but then the group started to fall apart. Some were simply bought, others were arrested on trumped-up corruption charges, and a few were simply scared away. It was an orchestrated campaign of intimidation conducted with ruthless brilliance, and the man behind it was my grandfather. He had power and he was not going to relinquish it to anyone—even his own blood—except on his own terms and in his own good time. And that was not yet, if ever. He was a *kuromaku* of genius and an evil corrupt old man, but no one was better at the power game than he, and no one was going to oust him."

Fitzduane gave a start as the full significance of her words hit home. "Hodama?" he said. "Your grandfather was Hodama?"

Chifune turned toward him. "There are other *kuromakus*," she said. She was leaning on one arm facing him, only inches from him. He could feel her breath as she spoke. The candles were behind her, so her face was in shadow. He could see her breasts and the dark outline of her nipples and the taut flesh of her stomach and the curve of her hip. He had to remind himself that this was a woman who was trained to kill and who could put that training into action with ease. This was a woman who had risked her life for him and whose body he had shared. This was a woman with blood on her hands. As he had. Theirs was a shared world.

"You're Hodama's granddaughter," said Fitzduane, ignoring her denial. "My God, who else knows this? What are you doing on this case? Doesn't conflict of interest mean anything around here, or is that just another difference between Japan and us *gaijins?*"

Chifune leaned across and kissed him hard on the lips. "That evil old man killed his own son," she said. "He killed my father to preserve his rotten regime. When almost all his group had been destroyed or dispersed, my father was found in his office with his throat cut and a razor in his hand. Money and other incriminating material was subsequently found in his safe. The suicide verdict was automatic. A disgraced politician kills himself. It's not so uncommon."

"How do you know it wasn't suicide?" said Fitzduane. "How do you know all this?"

Chifune smiled sadly. "Believe me, I know," she said. "My father and I were very close. I did secretarial work for his group and worked with him on the reforms they planned. I kept his records and knew what was in his safe and what was in his mind on the day he died. It was a setup and it was murder. Of that, I have no doubt. I confronted my grandfather with this and he virtually admitted it, and then he laughed at me. He despised women. We were instruments in his eyes, not people. We were there to serve and to be used."

"And so you worked the system," said Fitzduane. "You used your connections to get into Koancho and worked there under a false name. The security service was the best place to get to know the dirt on the people you hated. And sooner or later an opportunity would come up for you to strike back."

Chifune nodded. "My father had made the initial contact with Koancho. They were the people who fully understood the extent of the corruption, and the Director-General was a friend of his. If he had lived, the security service was to supply the information which would enable my father to push through his reforms."

"Your father was a clever man," said Fitzduane, "and dangerous. I can see why he had to be stopped. His plan might have worked."

"No," said Chifune. "He never had a chance and he was too trusting. The rot ran too deep."

"Hodama's death," said Fitzduane. "The strike team knew all the security precautions, the kind of things only an insider would know."

Chifune was silent. "He deserved to die," she said. "It had to be done and I'm glad it was done—but I wasn't involved. . . ."

"Directly?" said Fitzduane.

Chifune sighed. "Very well," she said. "I supplied information. I knew about Katsuda and his plans and that the Namakas had stepped out of line. We had them under surveillance because of their suspected terrorist connection, and that in turn led us to hear about this weapon they were making. At last Hodama and the Namakas became vulnerable. The Americans were not happy and Katsuda was let off the leash. I just eased the process, and I've no regrets."

"Adachi?" said Fitzduane. "He damn near got killed."

"I love that man, in my way," said Chifune, "and I got myself assigned to the case to keep an eye on things and keep him out of trouble. I never thought Katsuda would go so far, and I never suspected that the prosecutor and Sergeant Fujiwara were his men. But it just goes to show how widespread is the cancer."

"Are you working with Yoshokawa's clean-government group?" said Fitzduane.

Chifune nodded. "It was my father's death which convinced them that Gamma must be kept secret. Eventually, the money politics of the government will be exposed, but meanwhile it's safer to fight them in secret."

Fitzduane poured Chifune and himself some more champagne. "So now Hodama has gone and one Namaka has gone, so you are making progress. And doubtless you have a whole lot on Katsuda to bring him into line when he thinks he's the new *kuromaku*. What a web you people do weave. No wonder Adachi-*san* blew a fuse. Which leaves our terrorist friends, Yaibo: what about them? The Namakas may have planned it, but they are the people who tried to terminate my worries once and for all."

Chifune shrugged unhappily. "We thought they were contained," she said. "We had driven them out of Japan and believed they were safely isolated in Libya."

Fitzduane looked at her. "You have someone on the inside of Yaibo," he said. "Hell, that's why you let them play. These people are almost impossible to penetrate, and you've done it. So now you think it's better to keep them on a long leash than have them break up into a number of cells you know nothing about. But," he snarled, pointing at his scarred chest, "the one flaw is that even if they are not running around much in Japan, they've been pretty busy in my part of the world."

Chifune put her arms around him and stroked him. He could feel her breasts pressed against him and the heat of her sex as she wrapped her legs around him. "We didn't know," she said. "We didn't know. It made sense at the time."

Fitzduane felt himself become erect and slip inside her. Still inside her, and his arm around her, he lay back so that he could look at her.

"Chifune," he said, emphasizing every syllable. "You are the most beautiful and desirable woman and you have the most heartrendingly beautiful name and you touch my heart. But why do you tell me all this? I'm an outsider, a barbarian, a *gaijin*. This is not my battle."

"Don't move, Hugo," she said, and she put one arm down between her legs and took him in her fingers and wrapped the other around his lower body and did things to him and kissed him and did not speak again until they came together.

"It's because I love you," she said, "and I want to give to you and I want to help you in every way I can."

Fitzduane put his arms around her and caressed her and held her close. "Chifune," he said, and soon they slept.

TOKYO, JAPAN

June 30

Looking down from the Koancho helicopter at the seemingly unending urban sprawl that surrounded and then became Tokyo, Fitzduane tried, at first, to put his feelings about the women in his life into some sort of order.

After Anne-Marie had been killed in the Congo only a few short weeks after their marriage, he had been involved with, and had enjoyed, many women, but had been reluctant or unable to commit. The pain of Anne-Marie's death had taken a long time to fade, and the nature of his job, traveling from one war to another, did little to encourage lasting involvements. Then came Etan and a strong desire to settle down and build a life with this woman whom he loved and the sheer continuing joy of his first child.

But life did not work merely because you wanted it to. Fate, in Fitzduane's opinion, was heavily laced with black humor. And in this vein, Etan departed because she wanted her own freedom, just when he wanted to give up his. The next stage should have been simple enough, but it was not because he continued to love her, and she was the mother of his child, so she could never just fade into the past. Still, they had never married and they had parted and they lived separately, so their relationship was the most clearcut.

When he thought of Kathleen, Fitzduane felt a surge of emotion and love, together with feathers of uncertainty. Kathleen was a marvellous, tender, beautiful woman, physically desirable and a natural homemaker, yet she had come into his life almost too conveniently when he had been at his most vulnerable, and he was far from sure about his own feelings. Also, he was concerned about her ability to live under the permanent state of threat in which he now found himself. Kathleen was a gentle and caring soul, and she deserved a normal way of life. Yet clearly she loved him and Boots adored her, and she had settled into Duncleeve as if born for the role.

Unfortunately, Fitzduane thought, for no reason that made logical sense to him, he seemed to like a hint of danger in his women. It was an immature trait and troublesome, but its reality could not be denied. Etan had it and Chifune had it in spades, but it was the one element missing in Kathleen. Still, that was more his weakness than Kathleen's.

Chifune was an impossible situation in just about every way and should just be put down to a magnificent sexual conflagration, and yet the thirty-six hours they had spent together had affected Fitzduane deeply. Although he had been as promiscuous as any highly sexed young male in the past, as he grew older Fitzduane found it hard to sleep with a woman without his emotions being engaged, and Chifune, giving herself physically without any restraint and confiding in him both the confidences of her trade and her feelings, had won a place in his heart.

It was also true that there was an affinity between them that was not merely sexual. Both he and Chifune needed the stimulus of danger and were at their absolute best when living at the edge. But this was a recipe for eventual destruction, and if Fitzduane wanted nothing else, he wanted a stable and happy home for Boots, and hopefully some other children, too. He did not really want Boots to be an only child. Children should have other children to play with.

Fitzduane found no solutions as the helicopter flew on. He reflected that life was more about choices than answers—and then living with the consequences.

THE STAFF at the Fairmont—who had heard he was dead, and were not entirely surprised; and then had heard he was alive, and were not entirely sure they were relieved—still greeted him as if nothing untoward had happened.

Their bows were deep and friendly. How exactly you could tell a bow was friendly, Fitzduane was not quite sure, but there was a difference.

Fitzduane liked the staff at the Fairmont and found their behaviour reassuring. He reflected that when the world is going to hell, it is nice to find that some standards are maintained. It was not an academic thought. The hotel was going to be his home for a little longer.

His killing of Kei Namaka had accomplished part of his objective, but it had upped the stakes. He, Fitzduane, and, almost certainly, Boots and Kathleen, were now in even greater danger. Faced with the loss of his beloved elder brother, Fumio Namaka would be like a man possessed. Something serious was going to have to be done about him and Yaibo before Fitzduane could return to Ireland with any degree of equanimity.

It had come down to an elemental reality: Destroy or be destroyed.

21

TOKYO, JAPAN

July 1

L et's kick this thing around," said Schwanberg.

He was sitting in the secure bubble in the offices of the Japan-World Research Federation at the New Otani, together with the two other members of what he thought of as his "private team." The private team were paid, as was Schwanberg, by the CIA, but their motivation was profit and their loyalty was only to their boss.

That loyalty had nothing to do with Schwanberg's personality. It was based upon mutual self-interest. Their charmless superior had used the CIA as his personal profit center since Vietnam, and had made all three men extremely rich.

The best pickings of all had come in Japan. The scale of corruption in the second-most-powerful economy in the world was, for the three men, beautiful to behold. And what better cover for their operations than the CIA, with its obsession with secrecy.

As station chief, Schwanberg had brought "need to know" and compartmentalization to such a high art that not only did few people know what the others in the station were doing, but Langley counterintelligence had even praised him for his operational security. They were right. Schwanberg attached great importance to operational security, even if it had little to do with the well-being of the United States. And operational security meant leaving no loose ends.

"We've lost the North Korean thing," said Palmer, a thickset, hard-faced man in his mid-forties who was the muscle of the private team.

"Your pal Fitzduane and that Koancho chick have fucked us. Namaka Special Steels is now crawling with cops."

Schwanberg shrugged. Hodama's refusal to pay more was what had precipitated the move against him and his supporters, and their involvement in supplying North Korea had always been difficult to handle. The private team could not be seen to be overtly involved in the enterprise. That would have given Hodama and the Namakas too much leverage. Skimming was one thing. Direct involvement in supplying a hostile foreign power was something else.

Instead, Schwanberg had tried to squeeze some of the nuclear profits from Hodama and the Namakas without letting on that they knew about the North Korean deal, and the effort had backfired. They had not realized that the Namakas were in such a financial mess and could not pay more even if they had wanted to. But once they discovered that, there was only one logical move. Destroy Hodama and the Namakas and bring in a new, financially stronger *kuromaku*. Enter Katsuda, who had his own reasons to do the actual work. It was perfect.

"The Namakas were a lost cause anyway," said Schwanberg, "and now Kei is dead and that's one less person who knows about us. Also, look on the bright side. The North Koreans are now going to be screaming for product, which is going to raise the price. And there are other plants around. Relax, we'll work something out. We'll channel it through Katsuda."

"I've got two concerns," said Spencer Green, the third member of the private team, "the cop, Adachi, and Bergin." Green was tall, thin, balding, and looked like the bookkeeper that he was. He handled the paperwork for the group's operations. He was something of an administrative genius, but he was a worrier. "Adachi is now back on duty and he is pursuing the Hodama investigation with a vengeance. And Hodama was our main connection. Just suppose Adachi turns up something. A link with us. Hell, we know he kept audio- and videotapes. Suppose we missed something."

"Why do you think I went along on the Hodama hit," said Schwanberg, irritated, "except to sanitize the place? I missed fucking nothing. Unless, of course, one of the hit team displayed some private initiative." He thought for a moment. "Like that bent cop, Fujiwara. Anyway, if Adachi turns up something, we should be the first to know. The guy is bugged to his eyeballs, and we've still got friends on the inside."

"So what's this about Bergin, Spence?" said Palmer. "The guy's retired. He's practically senile."

Green shook his head. "I dunno," he said, "he's been talking to people. I think he's up to something. In my opinion, if he doesn't know, he at least suspects. The guy may be old, but he's no fool, and my gut tells me he's still a player."

Schwanberg was silent, thinking about what had been said. There was some merit in being concerned about Adachi, he thought, but he really could not see Bergin posing any threat. Of course the guy had lunch with his old friends every now and then. He must go nuts rotting out in that little Jap village.

He looked across at Green. "So, Spence, what does your gut tell you about Fitzduane?"

Green smiled. "Namaka Special Steels apart," he said, "Fitzduane's no problem. On the contrary, we're on the same side. There is still one Namaka brother to go, and it looks like he's going to do the job for us. Now, what could be neater?"

"It's nice to see you smile, Spence," said Schwanberg thinly. "You should smile more and worry less." He nodded at Palmer. "Chuck, let's talk some more about Adachi-*san*. We were unlucky last time. Let's have no mistakes the second time around. And after Adachi, let's put something terminal in the pipeline for Fitzduane. He is going to be useful in the short term, but I don't trust the fucker."

FITZDUANE'S ISLAND, IRELAND

July 1

General Kilmara donned earmuffs and peered through the thirty-power spotting telescope. It was matched to the telescopic sight the sniper was using.

A target eighteen hundred meters away looked as if it was within sixty meters, easy hailing distance. Alternatively, every body tremor or movement was magnified thirty times. The latter was the downside of long-range shooting. The very business of staying alive, of your heart pumping, of your nervous system reacting to its surroundings, of doing something as utterly normal as breathing, worked against you. The issue was leverage. The more accurate your rifle, the more the slightest movement—if your point of aim was initially correct—would send the round off target. And that was just the beginning.

Other factors entered the equation. Wind and weather were the major ones, but there were many others.

Was the propellant blended correctly? Were the grooves in the barrel perfectly machined? Was there wear? Had a shade too much oil been applied with the pull-through?

Kilmara had watched the finest of shooters at their art and afterward had spoken to many of them. He was not a religious man, but eventually he had come to the conclusion that with those at the pinnacle of perfection, it was more than a matter of science. It was almost something mystical.

The figure lying prone twenty meters away was oblivious to him. He lay there as if in a trance until the three random targets popped up.

There was a pause of about half a second as the shooter absorbed the visual information and mentally programmed ahead the three-shot firing sequence, and then the huge .50-caliber semiautomatic Barrett gave its distinctive, deep, repetitive crack. The muzzle brake absorbed most of the shock, and dust rose in the air from the deflected blast.

Three hits. All were within the kill zone, though one was near the edge. Given the lethality of the multipurpose armor-piercing explosive ammunition, all hits would have been instantly fatal, but the sniper shook his head disgustedly. Since the shooting of Fitzduane, he had become obsessive and practiced at every conceivable opportunity.

That day, he should have been faster. The image of the consequences of being slower than his aspirational optimum stayed with him. A little boy, whose back of the head had been laid open in a crimson line. Fitzduane lying there, soaked in blood as if he had been bathed in it, the light fading from his eyes.

It was not good enough. Deep inside, he knew it. He could—he really could—do better.

Kilmara left the spotting telescope and walked over to the shooter. The man had risen to his feet and was engaged in the routine rituals of range safety management. There was the final check that his weapon was safe and his magazine clear, and only then did Kilmara speak.

"Remember Colonel Fitzduane, Al?"

Lonsdale did not salute. In the Rangers, saluting was reserved for the parade ground. But he smiled, a little ruefully. "I'm scarcely likely to forget him, General," he said. "I saw him shot and I visited him afterwards in the hospital a few times. I wish I could have been quicker."

Kilmara had little patience for what might have been. "Colonel Fitzduane has asked for you, Al," he said. "How do you feel about shooting accurately from a slow, moving platform a thousand feet up?"

"How slow?" said Lonsdale.

"Thirty to fifty klicks an hour," said Kilmara. "Maybe slower. And one extra detail . . ."

He paused.

"It will be at night."

TOKYO, JAPAN

July 10

Adachi had recovered from the virus that had laid him low, but the sense of alienation and betrayal which had gripped him after the prosecutor's suicide and Fujiwara's attempt on his life was harder to shake off.

His ordered world was shattered, and since his return from leave he had found it next to impossible to integrate back into his role as leader of the team. If Fujiwara, his most trusted subordinate, could have been suborned, then so could anyone else in his operational group. All were suspect. None could be trusted absolutely. And if none could be relied upon absolutely, then he must work virtually alone.

Ironically, he knew he could trust Chifune and the *gaijin*, Fitzduane, but then he saw them together, and though nothing was said he knew instantly what had happened. He did not blame either of them, because that was not his nature and such things were natural, but inwardly he wept.

He focused on the Hodama investigation. That whole miserable business had turned his life upside down, and he had now adopted the view that only with its resolution would sanity be restored in his life. He craved some peace of mind, and he had become convinced that only wrapping up the Hodama affair would bring it to him.

He was listening to tapes in his office when the summons from the Spider came. That was another twist in this affair. If he had suspected anyone of corruption it would have been the enigmatic and ambitious

Deputy Superintendent-General, but it turned out that the Spider was one of the reformers. His father had told him so. Both were involved in some organization called Gamma.

More intrigue, albeit in a worthy and decidedly uphill cause. Adachi, the policeman, craved duty and simplicity. It was why Adachi Senior, who was immensely proud of his son, had not asked him to join Gamma. Whatever the rationale, Superintendent Adachi was not made of the stuff of conspirators. He had simple direct values, and Gamma had to deal with complex issues, where sometimes difficult decisions had to be made for the greater good. The reform of Japan was a life-or-death struggle, and the stakes were immense.

The Spider waved Adachi to a chair and tea was brought. Adachi was taken aback by the wave. The slightest gesture of the right hand was more the Deputy Superintendent-General's style. Further, there was a definite nuance of friendliness in the Spider's demeanor. True, it was no more than a nuance, but that, for the Spider, was downright extroverted behavior.

"Superintendent-*san*," said the Spider. "It is good to have you back. How long has it been?"

"I have been back on duty one week, *sensei*," said Adachi.

Adachi had lost weight and was looking pale and gaunt. In the Spider's opinion, another few weeks' rest and relaxation would have been in order, but he made no comment. The aftereffects of the virus were not the problem. This man's very foundations had been shaken to the core. First, learning that the prosecutor was betraying him, and then the near-fatal assault by Sergeant Fujiwara. The man must be feeling quite paranoid. Perhaps the best solution lay in work, after all. He must learn that the failings of a couple of people were not representative of the majority.

"I am sorry that we have not had an opportunity to talk earlier," said the Spider. "Tidying up this regrettable business at Namaka Steel has been distracting and there have been many ramifications. However, you must know, Superintendent-*san*, that you have my full support. The full resources of this department and other friends of goodwill are right behind you. You must remember that."

Adachi inclined his head respectfully. "Other friends of goodwill": it was an interesting euphemism for Gamma. He felt sudden warmth for the Spider. That apparently distant, elusive, cold-blooded manipulator was reaching out, was genuinely trying to help. And, of course, he was right. One venal policeman did not mean the whole department was dirty. He should still be able to trust his team, he thought.

But then doubt clouded his mind. Of course corrupt cops in the Tokyo MPD were the exception, but that did not mean that Fujiwara was an isolated case. Who else might be playing a double game? He could talk freely to the Spider, he now knew, but who would back him up in the field? Who could he trust with his life at the sharp end? Who could he be *absolutely* sure of?

The Spider, his face impassive, his eyes hooded, contemplated his subordinate with concern. He could sense the raging conflict in the younger man's mind, and he realized that a satisfactory resolution was going to be a more difficult task than he had thought. The man was suffering. The first move would be to stop his brooding.

"I hear there has been progress on the Hodama matter," he said. "Perhaps, Superintendent-*san,* you would be good enough to brief me."

Adachi's eyes lit up with enthusiasm. His world had been badly shaken, but his faith in his ability as a policeman was undiminished. This was one case he would resolve no matter what—or die in the trying.

Nearly ninety minutes later, the Spider's opinion of his subordinate's ability and sheer perseverance, already high, had notched up further.

"I have one suggestion, Superintendent-*san,*" he said. "It concerns the tapes."

Adachi was immensely encouraged as he left the Spider's office. The bloodline of his *samurai* ancestors was clear to see. His back was straight and there was a confident spring in his step, and a sense of purpose suffused his whole demeanor.

This man, the Spider reflected, would slay dragons with his bare hands, if that was what his duty dictated.

If only dragons were the problem.

KAMAKURA, JAPAN
July 10

They were sitting on either side of a low table in the tea room in Yo-shokawa's house in Kamakura. They had dined earlier with Yo-shokawa's family, but now the two were alone.

Both were cross-legged and seated directly on the *tatami* mats of the floor. Yoshokawa had offered Fitzduane a low chair with a supporting back to ease his untrained *gaijin* posture, but the Irishman had remarked that since he felt comfortable enough with Yoshokawa to rub his limbs or move about when pins and needles set in without upsetting protocol, he would try sitting the Japanese way. Yoshokawa had been pleased at the implied compliment. Subsequently, the intensity of the discussion caused Fitzduane to forget, temporarily, his physical discomfort. He was to be reminded when he tried to stand up.

"Your plan is brilliant and daring, Fitzduane-*san*," said Yoshokawa, after Fitzduane had run through it the first time, "but quite outrageous."

The Japanese industrialist looked a little shaken. As one of the leaders of Gamma, he was aware of the very real dangers inherent in the struggle to reform the Japanese system, but Fitzduane's easy familiarity with the world of violence was unsettling. Yoshokawa's wars stopped at trade and politics. Fitzduane's wars had no such limitations. The Irishman might not like the necessity of killing, but he did not shirk it. Faced with no alternatives, he thought pragmatically in terms of what had to be done. His cause might be just, but such an approach was chilling to encounter for the uninitiated.

"We are dealing with multiple forces here," said Fitzduane. "And each element is strong enough and well enough entrenched to reconstitute itself when damaged. Yaibo lose a handful of terrorists. No problem, they can always recruit more. The Namakas lose a few contract *yakuza* and then their head of security and, for all practical purposes, they are absolutely unaffected and even turn Kitano's death to advantage. Then Kei Namaka is killed and Namaka Special Steels is exposed as making illegal nuclear plants for the North Koreans—and not only does Fumio claim innocence, but he gets the plant back within a couple of weeks, because he has massive political support and all the blame can be shoved on the dead brother. And in the shadows we have Katsuda, *kuromaku* in waiting, who bumps off Hodama and gets way with it, and behind him, Schwanberg, doubtless with some other candidate lined up in case Katsuda comes down with a cold.

"Hell, this is like Vietnam. Slogging through the boonies won't work. We need a little *chutzpah* here, Yoshokawa-*san*. Think in terms of fencing, if you will. The clash of blades is all very exciting, but there comes a time when you have got to end it with a single aimed thrust."

Yoshokawa made a gesture of helplessness and then filled Fitzduane's wineglass. "But what you are proposing, Fitzduane-*san,* can only be done with the cooperation of the police, and they will not accept it. It involves setting up a situation where the loss of life is certain, and that will not be tolerated."

"The Tokyo Metropolitan Police won't officially back this, I'll grant you," said Fitzduane, "but Gamma has enough political muscle to set it up and do damage limitation afterwards. For all practical purposes, the Spider runs the department. If he backs it, it can happen. And Koancho will cooperate. That I already know."

"What about the Americans?" said Yoshokawa. "Schwanberg is senior CIA."

"Leave the CIA to me," said Fitzduane.

Yoshokawa sipped some wine and was lost in silence. Then he looked at Fitzduane and shook his head regretfully. "The ruling council of Gamma are moderates," he said. "They want reform, but they will not support something as drastic as what you have proposed. Things are not that desperate."

"They are," said Fitzduane grimly, "and if we do nothing, they are going to get worse. Believe me."

Yoshokawa felt dread as he heard and agreed with his friend's words, but he knew his colleagues on Gamma. The key man to persuade in this situation was the Spider, and Yoshokawa just knew he would not support Fitzduane's scheme unless pushed to the edge.

TOKYO, JAPAN

July 10

Adachi let himself into his apartment. It had been cleaned up and redecorated while he was ill and staying at his parents', and now there was no trace of the gunfight and of Sergeant Fujiwara's violent death.

He had thought of moving, but he liked the place, and the unpleasant memories of that particular incident were more than compensated for by other happier recollections. Most of all, he was reminded of Chifune. When he closed his eyes, he could see her and smell her and touch her, and when he slept at night she slept beside him.

He opened his eyes. Reality was an empty apartment and he was hungry and he had work to do.

He had bought some take-out food at the restaurant on the corner and now he laid it out on the low table and went to the fridge and got a beer.

The cold liquid and the food gave him a lift. He smiled to himself as he thought about finding the tapes. Now, that was an example of good police work and stamina if ever anything was. He, Adachi-*san*, might be a flawed human being and incapable of pinning down a beautiful butterfly like Chifune, but, whatever his limitations, he was a good policeman and that made him very proud. And he knew now that his achievements made his family proud also, and that was very satisfying. They had not been so keen on his choice of career in the early days.

When Adachi had been at home convalescing he had thought about the late Inspector Fujiwara. The man had been an excellent administrator, well-organized and thorough. Indeed, it was his organizational skills which had made it possible for him to lead his double life without detection for so long.

The investigation that had followed Fujiwara's death had been extraordinarily thorough and controlled directly by the Spider. Secret bank accounts had been found, together with other evidence of the policeman's duplicity, yet, in Adachi's opinion, as he read the reports, there was still something missing. Fujiwara, the investigation showed, was a greedy man, yet cautious and prepared for the downside. He was the kind of man who kept a flashlight by the bed in case of power failure and had spare batteries for the flashlight and candles in reserve. The spare tire in his car was nearly new and correctly inflated. He had regular health checks more often than was absolutely necessary. His substantial life insurance was paid up.

Something told Adachi that such a man would take some precautions against his criminal employers. Supplementing his police salary by taking bribes from the Katsuda-*gumi* was a hazardous business. He was not a full-fledged member of the gang. That meant he was deniable and disposable, and he would have known this. So he would have made sure to have something on his extracurricular employers, a little blackmail to create a balance of power.

And yet the Spider's team, despite their success in further confirming that Fujiwara was dirty and in turning up considerable sums of money he had hidden away, still did not find the blackmail material

that Adachi was convinced was there. Better yet, Fujiwara had personally participated in the Hodama hit. He had been in Hodama's house.
And Hodama was a man who kept records.

Possibly, Fujiwara had even participated in the sanitizing process.
Surely, he would not have missed such an opportunity. Surely, he
would have pocketed something to help secure his position if matters
turned against him. If he could deceive the Tokyo MPD day after day,
he could certainly pull a fast one on the Katsuda-*gumi*.

When Adachi returned to duty, he went to his office off the squad
room and tried again to imagine where Fujiwara might have concealed
something. The reports were meticulous in documenting every detail
of the searches. Checklists had been compiled and each item methodically ticked off. Rooms had been photographed and each search area
marked. The houses of friends and associates had been searched.
Fujiwara's desk and locker had been searched and the squad room as a
whole turned over.

Nothing.

Adachi had lain back on the too-small sofa and closed his eyes. It had
taken him several days, but he had read every document in the now-
vast Fujiwara case file and he could not think of a single thing the
search team had missed. The Spider's close supervision was apparent.
Where a report was not clear enough or some shortcut had taken place
the first time around, there was a margin note by the Spider in his distinctive hand, and a page or two later in the file, a memo would turn up
ordering a fresh search or a further check.

Adachi realized that he and his colleagues had approached, and
were continuing to look at the problem, in a Western way. They were
being logical and methodical and punctilious to a point where a Prus-
sian bureaucrat would have been proud of them, but they were not
using their famed Japanese empathy. They were not feeling their way
through the dead policeman's thought processes, sensing the answer
intuitively.

Of course, not many of the investigating team would have known
Inspector Fujiwara personally. It was the nature of such an investiga-
tion that fresh, unsullied faces would be brought in from outside.
Those who were close to the dead man were potentially contaminated.
Only Adachi had escaped being a suspect and, who knows, perhaps he,
too, was under surveillance.

Adachi brushed aside such negative thoughts and focused on

Fujiwara. There was something about his personality that the numerous reports and interviews had missed and which, indeed, had been demonstrated more by his actions than by his demeanor.

The missing elements were arrogance and nerve. In Adachi's opinion, Inspector Fujiwara had been an arrogant man, and in leading his double life he had been brave to the point of foolishness. Sooner or later, given the company he was keeping, it was inevitable that he would have come to a bad end. And yet, in his arrogance, he did not seem to have realized this.

Arrogance to the point of stupidity. Adachi thought not. He had worked with Fujiwara long enough. No, Fujiwara was very far from stupid, but he had certainly not thought too highly of the powers of observation of his fellow men.

Adachi's eyes had snapped open. A horrible thought had occurred to him. Fujiwara was a baseball fanatic. Adachi swung his legs off the sofa and looked above his desk. One year after the formation of the squad, there had been a wild squad party, and the high point of the evening had been the presentation by Inspector Fujiwara, on behalf of the team, of an inscribed baseball bat symbolic of the striking down of wrongdoing. All the squad had signed it, and it was mounted proudly beside a group photo directly behind Adachi's own desk.

Not in the squad room; not on the wall behind where Inspector Fujiwara sat; but in the private office of his very own squad commander, the very man he was deceiving.

The memory had come back: Fujiwara working in Adachi's office on that Sunday and the rest of the squad watching that baseball game. Could it be?

Adachi had tried to remove the bat, but a screwed-in brace held it in place and the signatures to the front. This was a symbolic presentation. It was not meant to be used. He remembered the ever-efficient Inspector Fujiwara himself screwing it to the wall. Very thoughtful.

Adachi had looked closely. The bat looked solid, but it was made of some composition material. He put his hand on the base and turned it. Nothing happened at first. Perhaps it was solid after all. He tried once again, and suddenly the base turned and a line of screw thread appeared. The join was virtually invisible inside a red and black decorative ring. He went on unscrewing. Seconds later, he inserted two fingers and extracted a long, taped package. He opened it up and slid eight microcassettes onto the table.

He felt a warm glow of satisfaction at the discovery itself and then a sense of mounting excitement at what it might signify. "Inspector-*san*," he said to himself. "You have been true to your spirit."

Adachi's discovery of the tapes had occurred only a couple of hours before his meeting with the Spider, and he still had to listen to most of them. He roused himself from his reverie, pushed the remains of his food aside, and drained his beer. A certain amount of private gloating was in order, but now there was work to be done.

He debated getting another beer, but decided that a clear head was the priority. The quality of the recordings was variable, and he had found he had to concentrate to understand some of what was said. The tapes were labeled clearly enough with names and dates and sometimes the subject matter, but the names were in code. Still, that was only paying lip service to security. Most of the speakers were identified by name on the tapes as they were shown in to Hodama by one of the servants. Untangling the identities of the others was something the Tokyo MPD could do with ease.

Adachi loaded the third microcassette into the tape recorder. He was just about to press the play button when the phone rang. He picked it up with irritation. This was no time to be interrupted. His salutation was abrupt.

It was the Eel, and he sounded very frightened.

"Superintendent-*san*," he said. "Many apologies, many apologies, but I must see you immediately."

Adachi modified his tone. The Eel had to be kept in line, but he was a good informant and a little friendliness toward him did not go amiss.

"Origa-*san*," said Adachi, "I am busy this evening, but I can drop in to see you tomorrow. An early lunch would be pleasant."

"Superintendent-*san*," said the Eel, in a voice of desperation, "I must see you now. It is vital, absolutely vital. But you must not come to the restaurant. It is being watched."

Adachi looked at the tapes. It was annoying, but they could wait another couple of hours.

"What do you want to see me about?" said Adachi. "What's wrong with the phone?"

"Please, please, Adachi-*san*," beseeched the Eel, "this is not something we can discuss on the phone. It concerns the man we were talking about."

Adachi's mind went back to their conversation. The Eel meant Katsuda, the real murderer of Hodama. First the tapes and now a breakthrough on the mysterious Korean. Matters were looking up. "The Korean connection?" he said.

"Yes, yes," said the Eel frantically, "but, please, no names."

Adachi debated having the Eel come around to his department, but he had never had an informant there before and did not feel like starting now. "Origa-*san*, where are you?"

"Sunshine City, Superintendent-*san*," said the Eel, "hiding in the aquarium."

Adachi was amused. "Very appropriate," he said, laughing. He then looked at his watch. "But it must be closed by now."

"Superintendent-*san*," said the Eel desperately, "this is no laughing matter. Members of the Korean's gang are hunting for me, but no one would suspect the aquarium and I have a cousin who works here who is helping me. I am safe here until I can work out what to do. But I need help, Superintendent-*san*, and I can help you. I have documents and other evidence. But you must come to me. It is too risky for me to move."

Adachi thought for a moment. The Eel had been a good source in the past. It was worth the effort. "Very well," he said. "Tell me how I can get in."

The Eel, sounding immensely relieved, gave Adachi instructions and hung up.

Adachi contemplated his next move. Up to the Fujiwara business, he would have telephoned for someone in the squad to drive him over and provide backup if need be. Now he hesitated. Suppose there was another leak. The investigation was still ongoing. There was no one he could trust absolutely.

He settled for calling a uniformed patrol. They could drive him up and wait outside while he spoke to the Eel. That would keep the contact secure while providing some backup on call if needed.

He checked his weapon and then looked at the tapes. He did not feel safe leaving them anywhere. Then his eye caught the hideous parrot alarm clock given to him by Chifune. He opened up the back and slid out the battery pack. There was room. He inserted the eight microcassettes and replaced the batteries. Now, who would think of searching a parrot?

His door buzzer sounded and he looked out the window. The reassuring sight of a Tokyo MPD patrol car was below. "I'll be right down," he said into the door intercom.

This is turning out to be an extraordinary day, he thought to himself, as he descended the stairs. He thought again of the Eel hiding in the darkened aquarium with nothing but twenty thousand fish for company and laughed out loud.

He was still laughing when the policeman showed him into the back of the patrol car with a sharp salute, then leaped into the driver's seat to await instruction.

"Sunshine City," said Adachi, trying to control his mirth, and then the thought of the Eel and his fishy companions hit him again and he roared with laughter.

He was still smiling when he reached his destination. He had not felt so good in years.

22

TOKYO, JAPAN

July 10–11

The telephone seemed to explode in Fitzduane's ear. Muzzy from being arbitrarily awoken from a deep and satisfying sleep, he looked at the bedside clock. It was 2:20 A.M.

The telephone erupted again. As he picked it up, there was a banging on the door. He ignored the door while his caller spoke. Thirty seconds later, he replaced the receiver slowly in a state of deep shock.

The banging on the door continued. It was forceful but polite and very much in the style of Sergeant Oga. Fitzduane opened the door. "I'll be down in five minutes, Sergeant-*san*," he said to Oga, then closed the door and headed for the shower. He allowed himself two minutes of icy water under full pressure and then dressed.

The roads were quiet as, lights flashing, the convoy containing Fitzduane headed toward Sunshine City and its centerpiece, the Namaka Tower. No one in the car said anything. Fitzduane felt sick inside.

Access to the complex had been cordoned off. There were dozens of uniformed police there, and some wore the distinctive paramilitary uniform of the antiterrorist riot police, the Kidotai, and carried automatic weapons.

Chifune arrived as they were about to ascend in the elevator. Fitzduane touched her briefly on the arm in a gesture of support, and their eyes met. For a moment, Chifune's guard was down, and then the elevator doors opened and some police he did not know entered with them, and her formality and mask returned.

Much of the aquarium had been taped off, and inside the cordon a white-overalled scene-of-crime team was at work.

They were guided outside the tape to a small group, and as the new arrivals approached, Fitzduane saw the Spider and Yoshokawa-*san* and a tall, distinguished-looking man in his sixties who looked familiar but whom he did not know. All three men were in evening dress, and then Fitzduane remembered Yoshokawa's saying something about a formal dinner of Gamma's ruling council. As he made the connection, he realized who the third man must be: Adachi's father.

The Spider made the introductions. He looked devastated. There was little trace of the imperturbable Deputy Superintendent-General here. His normally slicked-back hair was tousled, and shock and grief were etched into his face.

The Spider acted as their guide. He took them past the cashier's office to where the fish tanks started.

The floor was slick with fresh blood. There was so much of it, the atmosphere reeked.

First there was an immense irregular pool of thick crimson, with a pile of what looked like blood-soaked clothing to one side. Then a long, broad streak indicated where something had been dragged toward some tanks in the farther distance.

Floodlights had been brought in to supplement the aquarium's normal lighting, and shoals of multicolored fish of every shape and size swirled and pirouetted and flashed and glinted in the unaccustomed glare.

Bloody footprints marked other parts of the floor.

"We can reconstruct what happened, I think," said the Spider. "Adachi-*san* was going to meet an informant, a man with criminal connections known as the Eel. Adachi-*san* entered the aquarium, and as he turned the corner here"—he pointed at the pool of blood—"he was struck by an assailant with a sword. The blow split his skull and cut deep into his body, killing him instantly. He was then struck a second time. This second blow was not necessary, but it was made, I surmise, as a gesture of contempt for the victim. It opened up his torso down to the groin. Effectively, it eviscerated him.

"Next, Adachi-*san's* clothing was removed and his body dragged to the fish tank across there." He pointed again.

Fitzduane, fighting hard to suppress nausea, walked to the tank and looked through the glass.

The water inside was pink and streaked with long strands of crimson. In it, Adachi's naked body was suspended like some giant medical specimen in a container. Entrails drifted from it. As Fitzduane watched, the body moved slightly in the current of the oxygenating system.

It was without question one of the most horrific sights he had seen in his life. It was the stuff of the worst of nightmares, and it was real.

This man had been his friend. He wanted to cry out loud.

Chifune stood beside him, her face immobile, and then she swayed. Fitzduane caught her as she crumpled. He held her, and she seemed to regain strength. Her face was a mask.

Fitzduane, with Chifune at his side, walked back to where the Spider and Adachi's father stood. "How do you know about the Eel?" he said.

The Spider made a gesture toward the farther recesses of the aquarium. "We found the Eel back there," he said, in a voice of barely controlled rage. "One of my officers knew he was an informant. He had been shot once in the back of the head. No evisceration, no removal of clothes, no fish tank. That charade was reserved for the superintendent. The informant, having lured Adachi-*san* to his death, was merely executed. He had outlived his usefulness."

"Why was Adachi-*san* stripped?" said Fitzduane, and then answered his own question. "They were looking for something. The question is— did they find it?"

"I have already ordered the superintendent-*san*'s apartment sealed," said the Spider. He looked at Chifune. "Tanabu-*san,* I would appreciate it if you would search it first. You knew him well."

Chifune nodded in acknowledgment, and then the Spider indicated that Fitzduane should go too. Help her, help us, the Spider's eyes pleaded.

Aware that time was critical, they made it to Adachi's apartment in less than twenty minutes. There was a police guard on the door when they arrived, but as soon as they ascended the stairs and entered Adachi's living room, they knew they were too late.

The apartment had been methodically ripped apart. The systematic nature of the destruction made it seem, for some reason, even more distressing. This was not the casual vandalism of a burglar. This was the cold-blooded clinical dissection of their victim's home.

Walls and ceilings had been opened up and the wood and plaster swept into tidy piles. All the furniture had been taken apart and the pieces stacked. The floor had been raised. Electronic equipment had been taken apart. All bedding and clothing had been slashed open and cut up and then stacked.

Chifune surveyed the damage as if mesmerized, then suddenly darted into the bedroom. "I know where," she said. "I know what he would have done."

Fitzduane followed her slowly into the bedroom, respectful of the fact that he was an intruder, but also wanting to give support. In truth, he could have done with a friendly shoulder himself.

The implacability of these people was terrifying. Always they seemed to be one step ahead. Steadily, their pursuers, despite all their resources, were being whittled down. One of the most powerful men in Japan had been murdered and the bloody trail of death never seemed to stop. Their opponents were people who considered themselves above the rule of law. Adachi, a senior officer of the Tokyo Metropolitan Police Department, had been slain with contempt. No one was safe.

Chifune gave a cry of anguish and then fell to her knees, her hands scrabbling for something. Pieces of multicolored plastic were thrown up on the bed and then she started to arrange them, crying softly all the while. The shape of a parrot emerged, and then Fitzduane could see that it was a clock. A rather ugly clock.

Chifune looked up at him and gestured wordlessly at the pieces of the clock, and Fitzduane understood. The attackers had got everything. Whatever was hidden in the parrot was long gone. Every facet of Adachi's life seemed to have been ravaged. He had been killed, stripped, eviscerated as if in an abattoir, and then his home and his personal possessions had been destroyed. He had not just been killed. He was being erased. His killers were without pity, arrogant beyond belief.

Fitzduane took Chifune into his arms and held her. With her defenses down, she felt slight and vulnerable. At first she just pressed against him, seeking reassurance from the warmth of his body, and then she started to shake and sob, and then terrible anguished cries came out of her.

Fitzduane held her and stroked her, and long minutes passed and then it was over. She pulled away and then kissed him on the forehead and went into the bathroom to wipe her eyes.

The Spider and Yoshokawa stood in the living room when Fitzduane came out. Clearly they had been there for a little time. Both wore expressions of concern and grief.

"Tanabu-*san?*" said the Spider.

"She'll be . . ." Fitzduane started to say, and then realized that he did not know what to add except platitudes. This was a wound that ran very deep. Chifune was as resilient as anyone he had ever met, but this was something, he felt, against which she had no defenses. This was the death of someone she had loved. She would not recover from this loss easily. Nor was it something she would ever forget.

Chifune emerged from the bathroom, her face washed and her composure restored, and only spots of water on her blouse betraying her recent outburst.

The four stood there in the wrecked room and there was an awkward silence, and then the Spider started to speak. Fitzduane held up his hand for silence. In it was a plaster-covered, miniature black rectangle with a hair-thin wire protruding from it.

The Spider, puzzled for a moment, put on his reading glasses and took the small object and examined it more closely. Almost immediately, he gave a nod of comprehension.

They left the bugged apartment and by mutual agreement headed immediately to police headquarters. It was now after four in the morning, and the streets of Tokyo were as quiet as they ever get. It started to rain, and that added to the somber mood.

Chifune stared straight ahead as Fitzduane drove, but her hand rested on his thigh, not in a sexual gesture, but merely as if to seek reassurance. From time to time, she shivered. Fitzduane glanced at her with concern, debating whether he should stop the car and put his jacket around her, but the journey was short and soon she would be in warmth again.

They assembled in the Spider's office around the huge conference table, and tea and other refreshments were brought. The Spider also poured four large brandies. Chifune demurred at first but then drank, and some color came back into her cheeks.

It was strange, Fitzduane thought, that although there had been no discussion of why they had assembled, all knew why they were there. Adachi's death had marked a turning point. There was now a common imperative for immediate and drastic action. Adachi's death was not going to go unavenged. It was not merely a police matter. It was personal.

The Spider began the discussion. "Adachi-*san* and I met yesterday," he said heavily, "and I think you should know what transpired.

"The superintendent was determined to solve the Hodama murders. He clung to this objective, despite all else.

"Immediately following the Hodama killings, the evidence pointed towards the Namaka brothers. First of all, a Namaka identity pin was found in the cauldron itself, and then a series of other clues were discovered, all of which pointed towards the Namakas. The puzzle was the motive. Hodama was the Namakas' political mentor and had been such for many decades, so why would they turn on him after all this time? And then some tapes were found and they purported to show that there had been a falling-out between Hodama and the brothers and that he was going to abandon them politically.

"On the face of it, the steady buildup of evidence against the Namakas was damning, but Adachi-*san* was not convinced. Instinct is an important part of a good detective's skills, and Adachi-*san's* instincts told him that something was wrong. He would have been delighted to bring down the Namakas, but he felt that, paradoxically, the one crime they were innocent of was the Hodama affair.

"The aspect of the case that caused Adachi-*san* most concern was the manner of Hodama-*san's* death. Of course, the method could have been an attempt to confuse the investigators, but overall, murder by boiling someone while still alive was such a horrible technique that the superintendent felt it must be personal and that the true motive for the killing was revenge.

"A great many people had reason to be revenged on Hodama-*san,* of course, but Adachi-*san* focused on the flaws, in the chain of evidence involving the Namakas, as he saw them. Investigation here showed a common denominator. In virtually every case, there was a Korean connection. Eventually, it looked to the superintendent as if a Korean or someone with strong Korean connections was behind the hit. Accordingly, he narrowed his search to looking for such a person or organization who might harbor a grudge against Hodama, even from many years ago. He further qualified that by looking for some particularly vicious incident. Some action that would result in a response as excessive as that meted out to Hodama-*san.*

"Adachi-*san's* search was not easy. The postwar period was a confused time, and initial record-keeping left much to be desired. Additionally, Hodama was rarely involved directly in violence. Almost always, it was his practice to have such acts carried out by intermediaries, and, of course, in the early postwar years his favorite enforcers were the Namakas. Later on, the Namakas also became too respectable for much direct involvement and they, too, started to use someone else for their dirty work.

"The superintendent was eventually pointed towards Katsuda and his organization, when an elderly sergeant he had worked under told him the story of a rival Korean gang being burned to death by the Namakas at Hodama's instigation. This was the kind of crime Adachi-*san* was looking for. Here was the motive, and it came clearer when it transpired that a survivor of that Korean gang, Katsuda-*san* himself, was now running the second-largest *yakuza* gang in Japan. In other words, Katsuda not only had the motive but he also had the means. The Hodama attack smacked of a well-drilled *yakuza* operation, the kind that only one of the larger organized-crime groups could mount. Naturally, the Namakas could have carried out such an exercise, too, but at least Adachi-*san* now had another suspect and one that, in his judgment, made more sense.

"The superintendent's suspicion of Katsuda was further reinforced when an informant, generally known as the Eel and an expert in some of the murkier depths of the financial world, told Adachi-*san* that a major move against the Namakas was being made by various institutions backed by Katsuda. Of course, it could have been coincidence or Katsuda merely seizing the opportunity to avail himself of the power vacuum caused by Hodama's death, but all in all it seemed to Adachi-*san* on the balance of probability that Katsuda was the man. Apart from anything else, further investigation revealed that the scale of the financial assault on the Namakas could not have been mounted without considerable preparation, arguably a matter of months, and yet these moves by Katsuda were initiated within hours of Hodama's death.

"Suspecting Katsuda and proving it were two different things. Of course, Katsuda could theoretically have been arrested and subjected to interrogation, but, frankly, with his political backing—and I include here the Minister of Justice, who receives handsome campaign contributions from him—such interrogation was not possible.

"As any good policeman does, Adachi-*san* went over the case file and other evidence again and again. Previously, he had had some success in enlarging the Hodama security videos. There he was convinced that the evidence he had uncovered was planted, but in subsequent viewings he concentrated on the other figures."

Here the Spider smiled. "Adachi-*san* made the perceptive observation that it is a natural human tendency to focus on movement, on the action, if you will. This time he studied every figure individually, regardless of whether that figure was doing anything significant or not. He came to an interesting conclusion. One of the figures was a *gaijin*"—the Spider looked apologetically at Fitzduane—"a foreigner."

"I saw the video," said Fitzduane. "The attackers all wore suits and were masked. How could he possibly tell?"

The Spider felt very proud of Adachi. The Spider was a self-made man and the organization that had given him his opportunity was the Tokyo MPD, so he took a strong personal interest in the achievements of its personnel. Superintendent Adachi, he felt, was in the tradition of its very finest.

"It has to do with body language," said the Spider. "The superintendent examined the video enlarged and in the minutest detail. From it, he could see clearly that there was a leader and a group of subordinates. The leader was easy to pick out, and in contrast his men stood and moved in a particular way. Let me summarize it. Their demeanor, through how they stood and held their hands and numerous other small signs, conveyed respect. It demonstrated the natural ranking that underpins this society. Except for this man."

The Spider pushed a rather grainy print across the table. It was a printout from a video recording and had been enlarged so the image was slightly blurred. Nevertheless, Fitzduane saw instantly what the Spider meant. This man stood as an impatient equal, and, examined closely, his build was decidedly not Japanese. This man carried more body weight than would be normal for a Japanese of that height, and his neck was thicker. Further, the camera had caught him as he was carrying out a gesture that was somehow familiar.

The Spider tossed a second print on the table. This was a close-up of the man's hands. It showed the right hand pulling at a fold of the skin on the back of the left in a nervous or impatient gesture.

"Holy shit!" said Fitzduane. He looked back at the first print and studied the suit. All three buttons were done up. He looked closely. The buttons were covered with the same fabric as the suit. Suddenly, the masked figure was clearly recognizable. Once you made the connection, it was not hard to identify the characteristic strutting stance. "Schwanberg!" he breathed. "The decidedly unlovable Schwanberg. I guess he could not resist seeing someone boiled alive."

The Spider nodded. "It took Adachi-*san* longer to identify Mr. Schwanberg. A great deal of work, in fact. But eventually he came to the same conclusion. And then, at last, the significance of the timing of the Hodama killings became clear. Katsuda had been let off the leash by his CIA masters. The killing was Katsuda's revenge, but really that was secondary. The prime motive was a bigger game. And that game was political. Adachi-*san* did not know the precise reasons, but he suspected that it was merely that Hodama-*san* and the Namakas had out-lived their usefulness. They were well-contaminated by their money-politics reputations. It was time to reshuffle the deck and put some more-acceptable faces on the top."

The Spider looked at Fitzduane, almost as if accusing him. "Superintendent Adachi now knew who had killed Hodama and his people and why, but this very discovery made the whole business vastly more dangerous. It now appeared that he was no longer just up against one of the most powerful *yakuza* leaders in Japan, but also against a covert arm of an agency of the United States. This was very difficult. The relationship of this country with America is"—he paused, searching for the appropriate words—"friendly but not entirely harmonious at all times. There are certain areas of friction."

Fitzduane sipped at his brandy. Dawn was breaking outside. It was still raining. "Deputy Superintendent-General-*san*," he said. "A couple of points. Firstly, I am the wrong man to blame for the policies of the United States regarding Japan. Frankly, I think the U.S. has a few good reasons to be sore, but that is neither here nor there. The bottom line is—I'm Irish.

"The second point is that Schwanberg is not advancing the policies of the U.S. these days. He has his hand in the cookie jar, and Uncle Sam has found out and is moving to do something about it. Which means he is vulnerable."

There was an intake of breath from Yoshokawa, and then a burst of Japanese directed at the Spider. The conversation hurtled back and forth.

Fitzduane felt very weary. He stood up and beckoned to Chifune, and side by side they looked out through the picture window at the end of the conference room at the emerging Tokyo day.

The sky was gray and the street below was black with rain. Across the street was Hibiya Park, and that was green and verdant from the rainy season. He was reminded for a moment of Dublin and Stephen's Green. And then he thought of his island and the unspoiled land in which he lived, and he felt homesick. He missed his castle and he missed Boots and he was mixed up about women. He missed Kathleen, and Etan was God knows where, and right now Chifune needed him. But soon she would not. She was very strong.

And then he thought about Adachi.

"It's a commodity in short supply," he said.

Chifune turned to him, and at that moment, though there was no physical contact, they were as close as they had ever been. As close as either had ever been to any other person.

"Adachi-*san?*" she said.

Fitzduane nodded. "Decency," he said. "Basic human decency. That's what Adachi had more of than many of us. He was a decent human being. He tried to do the right thing, he cared about people, he reached out and he cared."

"And I deceived him," said Chifune.

"No," said Fitzduane, "I don't think we deceived him. That is useless guilt he would not want you to feel. But I think we made him unhappy. And that is a sad thing."

"I feel he's still here," said Chifune. "I feel I could reach out and touch him." She started to cry, and Fitzduane put his arm around her, and they stood silent together as Tokyo woke up below them and the rain never ceased. Chifune, his arm around her, gripped his hand.

"Adachi-*san* had a strong spirit," said Fitzduane. "That's not going to go away." Then he thought of Christian de Guevain and other friends he had lost and he grew very angry with people who played with human life.

He thought about what had to be done.

The conversation ceased behind them. The Spider cleared his throat. "Fitzduane-*san,* Tanabu-*san,* I think you should know that the people who killed the superintendent did not find what they were looking for."

Fitzduane thought of Adachi's wrecked apartment. It was, without doubt, the most thorough search he had seen. He doubted very much that the intruders had missed anything. And he said as much.

"Adachi-*san* found eight tapes that Sergeant Fujiwara had con-

cealed," said the Spider. "He believed that they might prove to be conclusive evidence against Hodama-*san*'s murderers, but he had not listened to most of them when he left me. They were certainly found by
the attackers."

Fitzduane looked at the Spider. "That's what I feared," he said.

"No, Fitzduane-*san*, you don't understand," said the Spider. "The
superintendent was a professional. He followed procedure. He made
copies and left them with me."

"Have you listened to them?" said Fitzduane.

"Not yet," said the Spider. "There has been no time."

Fitzduane smiled grimly. "Well, let's get to it, Deputy Superintend-
ent-General-*san*. If there is one place that should not be short of tape
recorders, it is Japan."

There were eight tapes. The fifth tape they played recorded
Schwanberg's abortive attempt to extract more money from Hodama
and the Namakas. Matters were now very clear.

Yoshokawa caught the Spider's eye, and the Spider nodded. "Fitz-
duane-*san*," said the Spider. "You outlined a plan of action to resolve
this matter to Yoshokawa-*san* and requested Gamma's backing to implement it."

Fitzduane nodded. "There are quite a few players in this game," he
said. "We use each one's strength against the other and then cheat a
little as well. We want a predictable outcome. Following the rules really doesn't come into it."

"This is an exceptional situation," said the Spider. "We have discussed it. Fitzduane-*san*, you now have the backing of Gamma."

"It's going to be bloody," said Fitzduane bluntly. He wanted no hesitation once the plan was under way. "Are you sure you can handle
that?"

Both the Spider and Yoshokawa nodded.

Fitzduane looked over at Chifune. "Let's go to work," he said. "We'll
start with the airship."

23

W HO?" shouted Fumio Namaka into the phone.

He was completely taken aback and then felt sudden anger at this incompetent private-switchboard operator who had undoubtedly misunderstood her caller. "You must be mistaken, woman. That *gaijin* would never call direct. It's impossible. Quite impossible."

There was silence at the end of the line, as the operator tried to figure out what to do. She knew she had not misunderstood, yet Namaka-*san,* normally a quiet-spoken man, sounded ready to strangle her.

She was tempted to cut the connection to the incoming caller, but then decided to have one more try. "I am very, very sorry, Namaka-*san,*" she said quietly, the respect evident in her voice, "but the *gaijin* insists that he is Fitzduane-*san* and that he must speak to you as a matter of urgency."

Fumio saw his hands were shaking from shock and a rush of near-uncontrollable hate. This was the man who had killed his brother, the only person in the world that he had ever really loved. This was the man that, at the very moment the call had come in, he was plotting to destroy. And he had the nerve to call Fumio directly.

It was outrageous. What did this assassin want? Yet again, could this call be turned to advantage? The *gaijin* had proved to be a hard man to kill, but perhaps he could be maneuvered into a situation where he could be taken.

Since the death of Kei, nothing was more important to Fumio than seeing his brother revenged. Nothing.

Fumio regained his self-control. "Put the *gaijin* through," he said abruptly.

The conversation lasted less than three minutes. After he replaced the receiver, Fumio could feel his heart pounding. He could see Fitz-duane's face as he was being killed, smell his fear, hear his cries. He could taste vengeance, and the *gaijin* was going to deliver himself to his executioners.

This time there would be no mistakes. He would use the most lethal killers he had under his control. This was definitely a task tailor-made for Oshima-*san* and Yaibo. Reiko Oshima was definitely one of the deadlier of her species.

Fumio thought of the job she had done on the Frenchman, Christian de Guevain, and for the first time since Kei's death, he smiled.

THE ROOM WAS in near-darkness.

Schwanberg was used to Katsuda's eccentricities, and, frankly, the *yakuza* chief was not a pretty sight in normal lighting, but on this occasion the CIA man required some illumination.

He had brought with him a plan of the building and, more important, its surrounding garden. He wanted to talk it through, but that was impossible if no one could see the fucking thing.

Katsuda took the point and gave a clipped instruction, and a directional light shone on a table. Katsuda himself, as always, remained in the darkness.

Schwanberg had known Katsuda too long to spend any time on the social niceties. In his opinion, the *yakuza* leader, however powerful in his own milieu, was bought and paid for way back and could be treated accordingly. There was always another hotshot in a hurry. If push came to shove, Katsuda was replaceable.

For his part, Katsuda despised his backer for his crudeness and lack of manners and hated him for his arrogance. But he endured him because it had been, in the past, a mutually beneficial relationship.

Recently, he was beginning to have doubts. The Hodama killings were supposed to have had a domino effect which would have swept away the Namakas and instituted Katsuda as the new *kuromaku*. But it had not happened, and despite losing their chairman, Kei Namaka, the

Namaka empire, though perhaps somewhat bloodied, looked set to endure. Which was profoundly disturbing and did not reflect well on Schwanberg's judgment and influence. Schwanberg had initiated the Hodama business with the promise that he had enough political muscle to carry it through, but manifestly he had not delivered.

Katsuda wondered if this was just this thoroughly unpleasant man himself or symptomatic of an overall decline in U.S. influence in the Pacific rim. On balance, he rather thought the former. He had substantial investments in the U.S., and over the last few quarters they had been showing healthy signs of life. But a reviving U.S. economy did not solve the Schwanberg problem.

Schwanberg spread the plan on the table and weighed it down with several jade ornaments and a small bronze Buddha. Katsuda shuddered. The value of the ornaments came to several times more than Schwanberg's official salary for a year. The man was an uncouth barbarian.

Schwanberg tapped the plan. "Just as I figured," he said, "that fucking Irishman has played right into our hands."

The plan looked disconcertingly familiar to Katsuda. Typically, given Schwanberg's consistent thoughtlessness, it was upside down when viewed from the *yakuza*'s direction, but it still looked very much like the drawing of the Hodama house they had used to plan the hit.

Katsuda was normally courteous, but years of dealing with Schwanberg had taught him that here was a man on whom politeness was wasted. The man had the sensitivity of a bucket of night soil.

"Schwanberg-*san*," said Katsuda with some asperity, "I have not the faintest idea what you are talking about."

The CIA man was practically chortling. "Fitzduane, the naive prick, has set up Fumio Namaka for us. And with that gimpy fuck out of the way, we're home and dry as planned."

"A little detail would not go amiss, Schwanberg-*san*," said Katsuda dryly.

"Fitzduane came to see me," said Schwanberg. "He doesn't like me, but he thinks we're allies on this one. He wants Fumio out of the way and he knows we do, too, so he has set it up that we—or, to be more precise, you—can finish the job. And the punchline is that the Irishman thinks Fumio was responsible for Adachi's death. Putting the bodies in the aquarium was a neat move. It was near enough to the Namaka

Tower to be too much of a coincidence, in Fitzduane's opinion. It's beautiful."

Katsuda was feeling profoundly irritated with this uncouth idiot. He was beginning to have a glimmering of understanding, but he really could not see where the plan of Hodama's house came into the equation.

"Schwanberg-*san*," he said. "Since we moved on Hodama-*san,* I have had a team of people trying to get near the Namakas with absolutely no success. Fortunately, Kei Namaka is now dead, but since that happened, the security surrounding Fumio has tripled. He cannot be got at, and I fail to see how Fitzduane-*san*'s involvement changes the situation."

Schwanberg leaned over the table toward the *yakuza* leader to emphasize his words. Katsuda stood in the shadows perhaps four feet away, but he still imagined he could feel Schwanberg's breath, and certainly the man's spittle as he spoke excitedly was no illusion. Katsuda stepped back in disgust.

"Let me make it simple, Katsuda," said Schwanberg. "What do you think Fumio wants most in the world right now? What does he have wet dreams about?"

Katsuda thought for a moment. It was not a difficult question to answer. He had studied Hodama and the Namakas in detail before making his move. "The Irishman killed his brother," he said. "He wants Fitzduane-*san*'s head on a plate." Katsuda smiled slightly. "After that, he probably wants mine."

Schwanberg beamed. "You're business, Katsuda. Fitzduane is personal. You're not even close."

"So Fitzduane is the bait," said Katsuda slowly. "He is the one reason Fumio will show himself."

Schwanberg nodded. "Very smart," he said. "What has actually happened is that Fitzduane approached Fumio directly and suggested a meet. His spiel is that there must be an end to the feud between them, now that Fitzduane has nearly been killed and lost his best friend and Fumio has lost his brother. And Fumio has agreed to the meet, not with any peaceful intent but because he wants Fitzduane carved up so badly he can taste it."

"And where is this meeting?" said Katsuda.

"That's the elegant part of it," said Schwanberg. "Fitzduane came up with the bright idea of using Hodama's place. He wanted some location that was private, convenient, and secure, and Hodama's walled garden was his suggestion. The premises are sealed off right now, but Fitzduane has been working with the cops and can gain access. It is just locked up these days. It's no longer guarded."

Katsuda pondered this for a few seconds. The idea of using Hodama's place was a clever idea. It met all the criteria for a meeting and it also was where the whole business had started. It would be fitting to end it there.

"I would assume that Fumio will take precautions," said Katsuda, "so how do you propose we do this, Schwanberg-*san*? He will probably involve Yaibo, and they are no idle threat."

Schwanberg's hand came down flat on the table with a resounding crack, and two sixth-century jade ornaments fell to the ground and shattered.

Katsuda felt ill. He valued his jade ornaments considerably more than he did most people. He wondered if Schwanberg had any idea how near death he was. If he was not so dependent on the man's backing, he would have Schwanberg killed painfully here and now. Well, even if Katsuda could not implement the thought for the time being, it was a soothing prospect to anticipate.

Schwanberg was so pleased with his cleverness that he had forgotten he had not followed up his triumphant table-pounding with words. He was just staring at Katsuda with a self-satisfied grin on his face.

"Well, Schwanberg-*san*?" said Katsuda.

"You'll have the edge, Katsuda-*san*," said Schwanberg. "It will be arranged that you and your people will be at the meet instead of Fitzduane, and we will run interference over the whole operation from on high. We'll have the whole thing covered. Night-vision equipment, sniper rifles, heavy firepower. That fuck Fumio won't have a chance."

Katsuda tried to imagine having a discreet meeting with Namaka while a swarm of armed helicopters clattered overhead, and came to the conclusion that Schwanberg must have been out in the sun in Vietnam too long.

"Helicopters are not entirely discreet," he said politely.

This time Schwanberg actually jumped up and down with excitement. "Not helicopters, Katsuda-*san*, we're going to use the airship. That giant, motherfucking inflated condom is part of the scenery in this city. It floats around and no one pays it the slightest bit of attention. We'll fuck Fumio from a height. It's brilliant."

Katsuda contemplated Schwanberg with surprise. Clearly there was more to this unpleasant man than he had thought. It really was a clever idea. Inspired, even. Then it dawned on him where the idea had probably come from.

"And the *gaijin* Fitzduane? Where will he be while I am disposing of Fumio Namaka?"

"Oh, he'll be in the airship," said Schwanberg. "As I'll explain, we need him to bait the trap. But when Fumio is terminated, Fitzduane-*san* will have an accident. Frankly, it will be a pleasure."

"So no witnesses?" said Katsuda.

Schwanberg had every intention of getting the killing of Fumio by Katsuda on video in close-up. The more strings he had to control his new *kuromaku,* the better. "No witnesses," he replied.

Katsuda smiled to himself in the darkness. Schwanberg's devious mind was not hard to read. He was already thinking of appropriate action. Perhaps the time had come for the renegade to have an accident. Have a crash, indeed, or fall from a height. The man's plan had interesting implications.

"Your proposal has great merit, Schwanberg-*san,*" he said. "Let us now talk about the details."

"Fucking A," said Schwanberg, and as he leaned forward over the blueprint of Hodama's premises, his feet crunched on the shattered pieces of the ornaments.

Katsuda hissed.

Schwanberg, as was normal for him where human sensitivities were involved, noticed nothing.

BERGIN HAD GONE to some lengths to arrive at Fitzduane's room in the Fairmont undetected.

The blond wig and moustache made him look ten years younger, and he was wearing an expensive double-breasted business suit and Guccis, but his principal *coup de théâtre* was the platinum-and-gold Rolex inset with diamonds and the matching identity bracelet on the other wrist.

The combination was so ostentatious you scarcely noticed the wearer. Bergin's shirt cuffs were tailored short to optimize the impact.

Fitzduane eyed his visitor.

"Mike," he said dryly, "clothes really do make the man. You are un-recognizable. You look like you run a small Southern bank and wash drug money for the Medellín cartel. You're probably on your third wife and she's thirty years younger than you. Alternatively, you produce pornographic movies."

Bergin spread his hands in a mock gesture of modesty and his wrists glinted in the light. Fitzduane poured him a drink and the two men sat in armchairs on either side of a low table. The blinds were drawn and the room had been electronically swept.

"Everything ready, Hugo?" said Bergin.

"Pretty much," said Fitzduane. "The hunt is going to take place as scheduled, with a full attendance as planned. It's now a matter of finalizing the rules. I don't want the CIA unhappy. Kilmara and I work with you people too often for that to be neighbourly."

Bergin took off his blond wig and scratched his head. "Horrible things," he said.

"Lice love them," said Fitzduane helpfully.

"Which brings us back to Schwanberg," said Bergin. He drank some wine and then looked directly at Fitzduane. "We've been finalizing his case. It's a rough estimate, but it looks like he and his cronies have lifted, one way or another, the best part of a hundred and twenty million dollars."

"And who says the U.S. can't succeed in the Japanese market?" said Fitzduane. "So now you're going to arrest him and bring him to trial."

Bergin looked pained. "Really, Hugo," he said. "You can't be serious."

Fitzduane smiled grimly. "Schwanberg had Adachi killed," he said. "That is not something I am likely to forgive or forget. But how it's done is the issue. He's your operative."

"The director feels it would be more appropriate if it's handled in-house," said Bergin. "Caught in the crossfire, killed in the line of duty, something of that nature. So I'd like to hitch a ride and take care of matters personally. I'm rather fond of balloons, you know."

Fitzduane looked at his friend thoughtfully. "You know, Mike, I never saw you as a practitioner of extreme prejudice."

"That was the general idea, Hugo," said Bergin with a regretful smile, "and mostly I'm not. But every so often there is a requirement and, really, Schwanberg has been running around long enough."

"Too long," said Fitzduane quietly. "Not a personal criticism, Mike. More a truth we share. Isn't that so?"

Bergin nodded his agreement. He felt uncomfortable, perhaps even ashamed. The simple truth was that Schwanberg had been under suspicion for some time and only the reflex bureaucratic desire to prevent scandal had prevented action. And meanwhile people had died.

Cover-ups were not confined to Watergate. In the real world of big government and big business, they were the norm. Exposure was the exception. The price was just a cost of doing business.

Fitzduane emptied the bottle into their glasses. "Drink up and listen, Mike. If you're going to be flying with us, there are a few extra angles you should know. Preparation for the unexpected. What the training manuals call 'making an appreciation of the situation.' "

He ran through what was necessary, and as he spoke Bergin's eyes widened. Bergin wasn't altogether displeased. At his age he had not been sure they could do that anymore.

24

T he entire perimeter was sealed off as they approached a side
entrance of the military base at Atsugi.

Security floodlights pierced the darkness.

Located just outside Tokyo, Atsugi was the headquarters of the elite
Airborne Brigade of the Japanese Defense Forces, and it was there
they were to board the airship.

With a pang, Fitzduane thought of Adachi, who had trained and operated from there. It was appropriate, he mused, that retribution
against the policeman's killer should originate from that location as
well. He felt a great sadness when he thought of Adachi, and there was
that familiar twinge of guilt which so often seemed to accompany the
death of a comrade: why him and not me? He pushed such thoughts to
the back of his mind. Right now, there were more urgent issues to consider. What they were about to do was intricate and dangerous and
would require all his concentration.

The black Tokyo MPD limousine containing the police driver, the
Spider, Yoshokawa, and Fitzduane was stopped at a striped pole barrier and they were asked to leave the car while each man's credentials
were checked thoroughly.

Beyond the token barrier of the striped pole, Fitzduane saw retract-
able spiked metal anti-ram barricades and two well-camouflaged inter-
laced machine-gun posts.

The airborne troopers were taking security seriously. Other troops with blackened faces and in full battle order patrolled the perimeter and all key installations. Apart from being a military installation, Atsugi was also the training area for the *kidotai,* the antiterrorist riot police, and, as such, was a prime terrorist target.

The white-helmeted gate guards waved them through and held salutes as they drove past. Five minutes later, they could see the black silhouette of the airship in the distance. It looked impossibly large in the darkness and brought to Fitzduane's mind the image of some vast, menacing space monster.

"It's awesome," breathed Yoshokawa, as they emerged from the limousine. "And beautiful in a rather sinister way. But what a creation!"

"It's quite small by traditional airship standards," said the Spider modestly. Actually, he was proud of the Tokyo MPD airship. "It's about seventy feet high, fifty feet in diameter, and two hundred feet long. That is big enough to hold just under a quarter of a million feet of gas."

It's going to be like flying in a mobile city block, contemplated Fitzduane. He was used to smaller things buzzing around in the skies. On the other hand, he tried to have a reasonably open mind.

Yoshokawa was lost in thought. The engineer and inventor in him was fascinated. "When I think of airships," he mused, "I always think of zeppelins and then the horrible crash of the *Hindenburg.* I saw it on an old newsreel when I was a boy. A truly dread-inspiring sight to see that huge balloon burst into flames and incinerate all those people."

"It did not do a lot for airship sales," said Fitzduane dryly. "And I would add, with respect, Yoshokawa-*san,* that such stories don't do a lot for me. In case you had forgotten, I'm going up in this particular one tonight."

"Oh," said Yoshokawa. "Oh, dear!" He was quite disconcerted. Then he recovered somewhat and went into damage limitation. "But I was talking about the past, Fitzduane-*san.* Airships are much safer now."

"Well, I should hope so, Yoshokawa-*san,*" said Fitzduane with a straight face. "I have no desire to descend lightly toasted or maybe even resembling a well-done steak. I think you should know that."

There was a strange noise from the Spider. Yoshokawa looked at Fitzduane, then at the Spider. Finally, the Spider could not contain himself any longer and a belly laugh emerged.

It was only the second time Fitzduane had heard the Spider laugh. The first time had been back in Ireland in his castle. It had been merely a matter of weeks, but it seemed a different age.

"STOP THE CAR," said Schwanberg suddenly.

They were through the Atsugi base perimeter, but there was still half a mile to go before the airship. "We're not there yet, Paul," said Palmer, who was driving.

"STOP THE FUCKING CAR NOW, YOU ASSHOLE!" shouted Schwanberg.

Startled, Palmer jammed his foot on the brakes and the medium-sized embassy Ford fishtailed to a halt. He waited in silence. Schwanberg had no manners at the best of times, but when he was in one of these moods all you could do was keep your head down.

"Cut the fucking lights, Chuck," said Schwanberg deliberately. "All of them."

Palmer switched off the lights.

The two men sat in the darkness and stared out through the windshield of the car. The airship was ahead of them, silhouetted against the night sky. The airfield lights showed the ground crew moving about their business. They were dwarfed by the immense mass of the gas-filled envelope.

Schwanberg removed his Browning, checked the clip by touch and feel, and slapped it home again with the palm of his hand. Humans were devious shitheads, but there were some things in life you could rely on. Put a couple of 9mm hollow-points in a target's kill-zone, and he, or she, ceased to present a problem. God knows, he'd proved it often enough. The back of the neck was best. The victim dropped as if poleaxed.

"It's a hell of a plan, Paul," said Palmer quietly.

Schwanberg turned toward him, his face suffused with rage. "That's the problem, you stupid fuck," he snarled. "It's a terrific plan, and that goddamned Irishman thought it up. So what else did he think up?"

Palmer had seen Schwanberg have these feelings before. It was as if the man had an additional sense dedicated solely to his survival. They would embark on an operation and then for no reason that Palmer could ever figure out, Schwanberg would suddenly pause and think. Sometimes he would then proceed as if nothing had happened. Other times, he would arbitrarily cancel the project. Again and again, he had been proved right. It was no small reason why he had been able to succeed as a player in this dangerous game for so long.

"I don't think he has thought up the ending on this one," said Palmer reassuringly. The words just came to him. He was not particularly articulate, but he felt good about this mission and he had complete faith in Schwanberg's ability to pull something out of the hat if anything went wrong. And he wanted to fly in the airship. He had never been in one before.

Schwanberg's mood suddenly switched. He had been worried, but now he felt confident again. Chuck was right. They were in control.

"Let's go," he said. Palmer restarted the engine. Schwanberg was now laughing. " 'Hasn't thought up the ending on this one,' " he repeated. "Too goddamn right."

Palmer joined in the laughter as he drove the short remaining distance to the airship.

TWO HOURS LATER, after a host of checklists—most relating to the mission—the airship was released from its tethering mast and the mission team were airborne.

Below, the Spider and Yoshokawa waved and then were quickly lost in the darkness as the airship climbed to 1,500 feet.

Fitzduane stared out of one of the windows at the panorama below and ran through the operation plan one more time, trying to consolidate his overall mental model of what had to be done. Checklists were necessary and all very well, but the endless items covered tended to buzz around distractingly in your mind and then weigh you down with detail. Fitzduane now sought a clear overview. He was keenly aware that, prepare as he might, the operation was highly unlikely to go according to plan. His opponents were clever and devious people who would have their own agendas. He had to try to prepare for the unexpected.

He smiled to himself. Another way of looking at it was to anticipate the unknown, and that was a decided contradiction in terms. Well, all you could do was to give it your best shot and then make sure that you acted with reasonable grace under pressure. And the last element was luck.

Summarized—and there were a few interesting moves to add to the scenario—the basic plan was simple. Fumio Namaka had been enticed out of his normal heavy security to meet Fitzduane in the seclusion of the walled gardens surrounding Hodama's villa. The villa would be searched by two representatives of both parties to ensure there were no hidden surprises, and then the two principals and one driver each would be allowed in. Then the conference would commence. It would be held in the open garden under floodlights, so that everyone could see everyone else and to minimize the chance of eavesdropping. If it rained, there was the adequate protection of the open-sided summer house.

Fitzduane had been far from sure that Fumio would agree to an open-air meeting, but logic was on his side. It did make sense to have all involved in plain sight, and Fumio Namaka was known to be paranoid about being bugged. As an additional concession, Fitzduane had agreed that Fumio could enter the villa grounds first, immediately after the initial search, so that there would be no opportunity for any ambush to be set up.

The first twist in the plan was that it would not be Fitzduane in the second limo. But from then on, it was up to the players on the ground, with just a little help from on high.

The requirement of having a tactical edge, if at all possible, had been drummed into Fitzduane when serving under Kilmara in the Congo. There he had found he had a natural talent for thinking this way, and its application had been accelerated by being repeatedly shot at. In modern high-technology combat, so much of death was random, but it still made a difference to have an edge.

Fitzduane had been taken aback by the Tokyo MPD airship when he had first seen it floating past his bedroom window at the Fairmont, but he had very quickly taken it for granted. And it was the fact that all Tokyo residents seemed to regard the craft in the same way that had given him the idea of using it.

Vast though it was, it was such a regular of the Tokyo skyline, it was, for all practical purposes, invisible.

A further curious but helpful fact about the airship was that it was very hard to judge its proximity. Most people knew the approximate size of a helicopter or aircraft and could make a rough guess at range, but the airship was seldom seen by people on the ground, so range estimation in its case was problematic in the extreme. If you do not know the size of something, it is virtually impossible to estimate distance unless there is a familiar object at the same distance.

What this boiled down to was that you could use the airship as a monitoring platform for activities on the ground below without attracting any undue attention. An extension of that premise was that you could shoot from it, too. Of course, the other side could shoot back, but at least there was the consoling thought that a modern airship could not do a *Hindenburg*. Early aircraft got their lift from ultravolatile hydrogen, which was a fair definition of an accident waiting to happen. Today's birds had switched to the much more expensive but more stable helium. You could fire an incendiary round into helium and no reaction would occur.

The stability of helium was the good news. The bad news, if hostiles started shooting at you, was that an airship the size of the Tokyo model was an easy target to acquire and a hard target to miss. Then, having found the overall target, a hostile would not have to be a rocket scientist to work out that the vulnerable humans were likely to be in the gondola below. And better yet, flying slowly.

Maximum speed was only just over seventy miles an hour. In reality, if shooting did start, their initial protection through speed would be considerably less. They would be optimized for monitoring, which would mean hovering or traveling at a purely nominal rate, and the airship's acceleration left a great deal to be desired. The thing was supposed to float serenely. It was not designed to hot-rod.

Fitzduane played out various scenes in his mind.

Some of the possibilities were distinctly unpalatable.

The thought of an air-to-ground running gunfight over densely populated central Tokyo made him shudder. It was for that reason that he had agreed with the Spider that only aimed rifle fire would be used within the urban confines and even then be confined to targets within the grounds of Hodama's house. It had been a reasonable request, but it would have been nice to know that the opposition was going to follow the same restrictive rules. Frankly, he did not think they would, so invisibility and surprise were his best weapons. Of course, if the action switched to over the sea, then the Spider's rules would not apply. Then they could play hardball.

Al Lonsdale had been gazing out of one of the large observation windows that lined both sides of the gondola and now turned and came over and sat by Fitzduane. When they had converted the airship for the operation, they had left a walkway around the periphery of the gondola and a row of seats in the center.

They would be airborne for four hours before the 2:00 A.M. time of the meeting. The airship could not suddenly appear. It was unlikely that anyone would look up past the glare of the floodlights when reconnoitering the meeting, but on the off chance they did, the ship had to be established as part of the scenery. The delay was a nuisance, because waiting was the hardest part of any action, but it was unavoidable. The endurance of the airship itself was not a problem. At slow speeds it used minimal fuel and could stay up for up to forty hours if necessary.

"Hell of a craft, isn't she, Colonel?" said Lonsdale, looking around the gondola with a proprietorial air. "Frankly, I'm surprised they're not more popular. I mean, what a way to see to the country. Smooth as silk."

Fitzduane was amused. Since Al had trained in the borrowed Airship Industries Skyship 600—a model similar to the one they were flying in now—the Delta marksman had become something of an instant airship expert and advocate.

"Smooth as silk if the weather holds," said Fitzduane. "Now, some serious wind could make you reach for a brown paper bag—or so I hear."

Lonsdale grinned. The Achilles' heel of an airship was its behavior in high wind. With all that surface area, an airship's gas-holding envelope acted like a giant sail, and could pitch and roll just like a boat. On his first training flight, Lonsdale had been airsick.

"Someone's been talking," said Lonsdale cheerfully. "Anyway, that was a particularly shitty day and my pilot wasn't as expert as these boys. I don't think we're going to have any trouble tonight." He saw Fitzduane's eyebrows rise, and hastily added, "Well, not from the weather, anyway."

Fitzduane laughed. Lonsdale was right. Fortunately, weather conditions were ideal, and flying at night, unless you were flying directly over a factory or similar heat source, eliminated interference from thermals. The airship was powered by two Porsche air-cooled gasoline engines driving twin-ducted variable-pitch propellers located on either side of the rear of the gondola. It seemed to float across the sky.

It was a remarkably pleasant way to travel.

Schwanberg's good humor as he had boarded had faded and had been replaced with a sour feeling in the pit of his stomach as the airship took off.

At first, he had put it down to a touch of airsickness. Now, standing up in the front of the gondola looking out of one of the port observation windows, Schwanberg felt distinctly uneasy again, and it was not physical. He did not know what it was, but something just did not feel right. And, over the years, if there was one thing that he had learned to rely on, it was his instinct for self-preservation. There was no question about it, something was not kosher; but what?

He fingered the grip of his 9mm Browning automatic as it sat reassuringly in his shoulder holster. What the hell had set him off? Everything seemed normal.

He had initially been thrown when he had arrived at Atsugi. He and Chuck Palmer had expected to board with everyone else after a final briefing session. That would be normal procedure. Instead, Fitzduane and his people were already installed on the airship and there had been little discussion before the airship cast off and they rose near-vertically into the sky. Fuck, it was almost as if this was entirely Fitzduane's operation, which was not the way it was supposed to be.

The second disconcerting element was the presence of Al Lonsdale and that Japanese bitch on board.

He had expected only Fitzduane and the pilots, and under those circumstances an accident for the Irishman would have been easy to arrange. The pilots were shielded from the main cabin and would see nothing. Fitzduane would just have disappeared. An accidental fall out of the door. Something simple like that.

But instead, there were two unexpected and unwanted witnesses, and both were loaded for bear. The Delta man had a .50-caliber Barrett with some high-tech telescopic sight, and the bitch had some custom self-loading piece chambered, it looked like, for the .300 Winchester Magnum.

For no reason that he could identify, Fitzduane was thinking about Schwanberg. He looked across at the man. He seemed as relaxed and unperturbed as anyone could be under the very special pressures of an operation which was going to result in the imminent death of a number of fellow human beings, but Fitzduane could just feel the tension. There was nothing to see, but to Fitzduane the signs were as evident as if Schwanberg were radiating blue sparks.

Fitzduane's mind went back to the CIA chief's boarding of the airship. Had there been any sign of suspicion then? He thought not. On the contrary, both Schwanberg and his henchman, Palmer, had seemed in exceptionally good form. They had been laughing at some private joke. There had not been the slightest hint of suspicion. Or had there?

He replayed the scene in his mind. There was something—an excess of joviality?—something. He was missing some element.

He thought of Bergin. Could Schwanberg and Palmer possibly know? Surely not. There was not even a hint that they suspected their nemesis was at hand.

And yet . . .

WHAT THE FUCK is going on? thought Schwanberg.

He turned toward Chuck Palmer. Palmer was looking contentedly out a window at the Tokyo lights below and seemed quite unaware that anything was amiss. Of course, Chuck would be content, since he was flying in a real airship for the first time and knew pretty much for certain that he was going to be able to kill a few people in the near future. Chuck was easy to please.

Schwanberg tried to work out a few possibilities as to what might be going down, and then, as the options clicked into place, started to sweat. It suddenly dawned on him that what he had planned to do to Fitzduane, that fucking Irishman was intending to do to *him*. Suspicion became certainty.

He leaned across and spoke into Chuck Palmer's ear. Palmer's back stiffened as Schwanberg spoke. If the boss had a funny feeling, there was no point in debating it. The man had a nose for trouble.

Schwanberg felt easier now that Chuck was alerted. The next question was what to do about it. Frankly, backing up Katsuda was all very well, but the prime directive was personal survival.

He looked at his watch. Shit! It was 01:38 A.M., only twenty-two minutes before the meet. They were going to have to act soon if they wanted to resolve this thing before the main action went down. After it, he had a feeling it would be too late. He had a disconcerting feeling he was being set up to die in the line of duty. He and Chuck would probably get Distinguished Intelligence Medals—posthumously—and maybe get bronze stars and their names on the memorial wall in Langley.

Some motherfucking consolation when you were a heap of ashes sitting in someone's filing cabinet because they had forgotten to sprinkle you in the Garden of Remembrance. Well, it would be how Schwanberg would arrange things if roles were reversed. Death in the line of duty was a nice touch. No trial. No scandal. The Agency really did not like scandal.

The more Schwanberg thought about it, the more he was convinced he was on the button. Fuck logic! It felt right. Which raised two questions: why had they not acted already? and who was going to do the hit?

The delay in making their move was easy to work out. They did not know what was going to go down at the meet and wanted all the firepower they could get. A reasonable decision, but a fatal one for them.

FITZDUANE TENSED for a preemptive move against Schwanberg—and then relaxed. His instincts screamed danger, but his head argued with cold logic that the scenario should be played out. The first priority was what was taking place below.

Schwanberg would have to wait—and he was covered by an ace in the hole. A very experienced ace who knew exactly what he was doing.

An ace who was not as young as he had been, whose reflexes were perhaps a little slow?

Fitzduane suppressed his doubts. The situation was complex enough already without his taking any precipitative action.

He would wait. He glanced across at Schwanberg and Palmer again. Nothing untoward.

AS TO WHO was going to make the hit, Schwanberg started to give some serious thought to Bergin. He had dismissed the threat from that source before, but now it looked as if he had been wrong. This was the kind of thing the Agency liked to handle internally. Allowing outsiders to liquidate your personnel was not a good precedent. So maybe someone here worked for the Agency or . . . maybe he was anticipating a threat from the wrong quarter.

Schwanberg took a fresh look at his surroundings. He had read a briefing document on the airship before deciding it was worth using, and now he tried to recall what he could from it. What he saw was now illuminated only by dim red light. They were on night-vision status. Shortly, the light would be extinguished altogether, as the focus of attention switched to the meeting below. If they were going to make a move, it would have to be very soon or they would not be able to see what they were doing.

The gondola was, in effect, a long thin room that was suspended under the main balloon. At the front end were the two pilots, separated from the main cabin by only a three-quarter-height partition. Strictly speaking, he recalled, the airship did not need two pilots, but there was some safety regulation which made belt and suspenders mandatory.

In the middle was the main cabin. In passenger mode, it could seat up to twenty-four, but now there was only a short double row of seats down the middle. Fitzduane was speaking into a microphone, and sitting beside him was the Delta sniper, busy checking his weapon. Farther back on the left, the Japanese bitch stood half leaning against the rear bulkhead. She appeared to be dozing. At any rate, her eyes seemed closed. Most probably she was into some meditation shit.

Beyond the bulkhead, at the rear of the gondola, was a major thickness of soundproofing and the engines. Schwanberg again tried to recall the layout of the airship. Wait! He had forgotten the head on the left and a small galley space on the right.

He had used the head, so there was nothing untoward there. He looked toward the galley space and it was not there—there was just a door—and suddenly their whole fucking game plan became clear.

"CHUCK!" he screamed, and drew his Browning and pumped seven rounds through the galley door.

The door crashed open and Bergin stumbled out, blood spewing from a wound in his neck.

There was a silenced automatic held high in his right hand, and Schwanberg watched as the barrel swung toward him and the black circle jumped twice, as two rounds were fired. They missed him, as he knew they would.

Schwanberg felt a rush. Once more he had beaten them to it. The

VC could not get him, nor could anyone else. He was whip-sharp and fucking well invulnerable.

He shot again three times and watched Bergin's skull come apart and his body slam back toward the galley door.

Chifune dropped to the ground just as Chuck Palmer fired his pistol, and the round smashed through the gondola wall just above her. She was now hidden behind the center row of seats, and Palmer fired a burst of shots trying to guess her position.

She had moved forward as he was shooting, and now raised herself on one knee and put two shots into Palmer's stomach.

He folded in two, and she shot him again in the crown of his head. The bullets exited at the back of his neck.

Schwanberg could not understand the sudden terrible pain.

He knew he had not been shot, but his vision was dimming and there was no strength in his limbs.

He looked down, and the haft of a throwing knife was protruding from his chest.

He saw Fitzduane's face, and then the pain was overwhelming as the blade was removed from his torso and plunged in once again under his rib cage and up into his heart.

Fitzduane removed his knife from Schwanberg's body and saw with horror a double hole in the low screen immediately behind the pilot's chair.

He leaped forward and ripped the screen aside.

The copilot's face, frozen with shock and fear, looked up at him in desperation. The side of the screen in front of the pilot was black with blood.

The digital chronometer on the instrument panel read 01:47 A.M.

There were thirteen minutes to go before the meet.

Fitzduane looked down at the police copilot. "We will proceed as planned, Inspector-*san*," he said grimly.

He began to wipe the blood and brain matter from the windshield while the copilot went into a slow circuit around the Hodama residence far below.

The parameters of the residence were defined by infrared strobe lights that were invisible at ground level and even from the air, unless seen through the appropriate goggles.

The object was to keep the Hodama garden below at a constant diagonal from the airship. A predictable range made for more accurate shooting.

Behind Fitzduane in the main cabin, Lonsdale and Chifune clipped up observation windows and readied their weapons.

As he went through the necessary actions, every fiber of Fitzduane's being screamed in pain and sadness at his friend's death and then focused totally on what had to be done. Grieving would wait. Mike Bergin, if anyone could, would understand.

You shut out the sadness and you did what had to be done, and only afterwards did you weep. That was the way of it. There was no other.

THE SPIDER WAITED in his command vehicle as the deadline approached, and although he had no official status, Yoshokawa waited with him.

The meeting at the Hodama residence was the focal point for a vast police operation involving concentric rings of the top-secret Airborne special antiterrorist unit and armed riot police. In all, over eleven hundred men and a host of specialized equipment were deployed, and the hardest part of planning the operation had been devising ways of concealing the buildup. Fumio Namaka and his terrorists and Katsuda and his *yakuza* must be allowed into the trap before it was sprung, or the whole exercise was pointless.

The downside of that vital qualification was that response time to Hodama's villa would not be as fast as the Spider would have preferred. However, he was reassured that whoever got into the residence would not get out, and he had the advantage of Fitzduane and his team visually monitoring the operation from on high.

He had broached the question of downloading a video picture of the scene from the airship's observation cameras, but Fitzduane had looked straight at him and shaken his head. Silently, with only the slightest movement, the Spider had nodded his agreement.

There were some things he, the Deputy Superintendent-General of the Tokyo Metropolitan Police, should not be officially aware of.

FUMIO NAMAKA sat in the back of his long, black armored limousine and rechecked his arrangements. What he had planned would, perhaps, not have been so unusual in a country such as the U.S., but in tightly controlled Tokyo, it was unorthodox in the extreme.

He thought it possible that he would not need his full reinforcements. The irony was that the *gaijin* Fitzduane would quite likely be there as arranged, seriously thinking he could arrange a truce after all that had happened. Actually, a truce would make sense. This kind of endless war was a gross distraction from the more productive business of ever expanding the Namaka organization. Further, given that the feud with Katsuda was unresolved, it was not very wise to be fighting on two fronts.

Still, Kei's death had to be avenged. It was the overarching imperative and had to be accomplished whatever the price. And in a fundamental way, the ultimate price had already been paid.

From the moment Fumio had seen his brother's bullet-riven corpse in the chill surroundings of the mortuary, and the last vestige of hope that somehow he had been misinformed had vanished, Fumio had died inside.

He no longer had a life. He only had obligations.

"*Sensei,* it is time," said his driver.

"Very well," said Fumio. The limousine slid forward out of the private parking space and turned into the street. Since timing was critical, they had waited in a safe house only three minutes from the Hodama residence. Within five minutes, ten at the most, this accursed *gaijin* Fitzduane, this murderer of his beloved Kei, would be dead.

Deep inside, Fumio knew that even this vengeance would make no real difference, and inside he despaired. Whatever he did or tried to do, his splendid big brother was no more.

His mind went back to the ruins of postwar Tokyo and those earlier poverty-stricken joyful days when all they had was each other and every day was a new adventure. He was smiling to himself when they arrived at Hodama's gates.

ALL INSIDE THE AIRSHIP were now linked with head-mounted headsets equipped with miniature boom microphones. The airship was, in fact, quiet enough for normal voice communication, but the use of an intercom meant that you did not have to move your head and look at your audience to be heard with perfect clarity.

Such a detail was important. The watchers were focused with total intensity on the scene below. They knew that whatever was going to happen was likely to be unexpected, sudden, and lethal, and they would have to react immediately. A tenth of a second could make the difference between living and dying. They were dealing with some very dangerous people.

Fitzduane was acting as spotter and fire commander. He was observing the scene below through gyroscopically stabilized, twenty-power, range-finding field glasses.

The diagonal to the garden below as they circled was almost exactly five hundred yards, and this range appeared in the bottom left-hand corner of his vision, together with other targeting details. The picture quality was outstanding. In visual terms, he was a mere twenty-five yards away. There were night-vision options, but he did not need them. Within its fifteen-foot-high walls, as agreed, the Hodama gardens were brightly illuminated. The benefit of this level of brightness was not just that everything in the garden could be clearly seen, but also that looking up meant looking into glare. The airship could not be detected.

The gondola was now in darkness. This was something of a relief to Fitzduane, since the slaughter surrounding him could no longer be seen. His own hands and clothing were covered in blood, and though the observation windows were open he could still detect the acrid smell. A split-second picture of Mike Bergin's body flashed before him, and he thrust it from his mind.

That was then and this was now. Focus, focus, focus on the scene below.

Fortunately, the copilot was turning out to be damn good. After the initial shock of seeing his superior's face half blown away and deposited on the Plexiglas, Inspector-*san* had rallied and now was flying superbly. There was the occasional very slight variation in height and distance due to variations in the night breeze, but mostly the airship held its circular course as if tied to the Hodama garden by some invisible line. Thrust vectoring of its two duct-mounted propellers, the ability to swivel the complete drive units in flight, was supposed to give an unusual degree of control—and it showed.

Fitzduane was also linked to the Spider on ground control. Now he watched Fumio drive into the Hodama grounds, leave his limousine, and take up position as arranged.

Fitzduane took care making his identification. Bearing in mind what he had planned, he was acutely conscious that Fumio could attempt a switch. His instinct told him it was unlikely. Fumio would want to be there personally to see his brother's killer destroyed.

Still, it was best to be certain. Fitzduane examined Fumio's distinctive crippled walk, his build, and his features with great care and quickly switched to infrared mode to detect any mask or similar anomaly. There was little doubt.

"Fumio has entered and is in position," said Fitzduane on the open net. "No surprises so far."

The Spider's people were watching all approaches, leaving Fitzduane and his team to concentrate on the garden. "Katsuda's limousine should arrive in about thirty seconds," said the Spider.

"Any sign of backup for either of them?" said Fitzduane.

Surely there would be car- or vanloads of reinforcements ready to rush in. Both men were always heavily guarded and were devious in the extreme. He found it hard to believe that neither of them would be planning anything. It would be downright unnatural. And yet the Spider's men, who had the area saturated, had reported nothing so far.

Very weird.

Where were Yaibo? What was Katsuda really up to? Probably Schwanberg had known, but he was not going to tell anyone anything now.

"Still nothing," said the Spider. He, too, was unsettled.

KATSUDA'S TRULY REPULSIVE appearance severely limited his public appearances.

He lived in the seclusion of his own world, in the darkness and shadows of his own creations. This behavior limited neither his work nor his ambition, but regularly he felt a need for release. Apart from his women and the ambivalence he felt toward them because of his burn-distorted features, his relaxation and his window to the outside world were the movies.

He watched them to the point of obsession. The movies were not inwardly disgusted by how he looked. They were pleasure, pure and simple.

Film fulfilled his need for escape, stimulated his imagination, and appealed to his sense of the dramatic. Privately, Katsuda considered that if events had not taken the direction they had, he would have made an outstanding actor. He had a fine voice and projected it well, and his movements were well-coordinated. All that was missing were looks.

From the movies, Katsuda had followed the extraordinary developments of special effects and, of even more interest, specialized makeup. Sometimes, the results on the screen were so good that it seemed to him he could apply them to his own situation and appear, albeit for a limited time, normal.

He had cultivated one of the leading makeup artists in Japan and had even sent him to Hollywood to advance his craft to state of the art. The results were encouraging, brilliant even, if he was seen from a short distance away, but in close-up the artificiality was always detectable. It was a bitter disappointment, but he persevered. One day, he thought, they would get it right, and it was undeniable that makeup skills were steadily improving.

For the meeting with Fumio Namaka, such an artifice was arguably not necessary, but it appealed to his sense of theater.

It would be an entirely appropriate way to lead into the final act of his destruction of the Namaka clan; and the actual execution method he planned to employ deserved such a buildup. Decades ago, Hodama and the Namaka brothers had eliminated Katsuda's family in a locked, burning house. Now the last of the Namakas would also die in flames.

Katsuda was very aware that Fumio might have a few tricks up his sleeve, so had devoted a great deal of time to taking precautions. He had studied the plan of Hodama's residence for several days and finally had come up with something that he was sure beyond any doubt at all would guarantee surprise. And, of course, his own preparations were in addition to the fire support he would be getting from Schwanberg in the airship.

Nothing was certain, but as his limousine approached the gates of Hodama's house, Katsuda was as sure as any reasonable man could be when making a major move that his preparations would ensure success.

"SEE ANYTHING?" said Fitzduane.

"Negative," said Chifune, who was all business when operational.

"A lot of pebbles," said Lonsdale, who felt the mood could do with some lightening.

Both Chifune and Lonsdale were professional and would report instantly anything untoward, but Fitzduane was getting increasingly concerned and a little strain was showing. He could still see nothing but Fumio standing beside the open-sided summer house where they were to have the meeting and Katsuda being checked in and searched at the gate. Surely, he should have detected something else by now. He could not see the pair of them meeting and just sticking out their tongues at each other.

He had two snipers, Lonsdale and Chifune, eyeballing the confrontation, but their vision was severely restricted because their eyes were glued to their telescopic sights. That had been the original plan and had made sense with Fitzduane and Mike Bergin and the pilot monitoring the bigger picture, but it was somewhat problematical now they were short two pairs of eyes.

It was time to make a change in the arrangements.

Lonsdale was targeted, but Chifune was not yet allocated, and right now it was not much good having an extra sniper if she had nothing to shoot at. Also, in training he had noticed that Chifune was about as fast as anyone at acquiring a target, so if she had to return to her scope in a hurry, it should not cause any serious grief. Chifune was not as good with the Barrett as Al, but she was one hell of a combat shot up to about a kilometer.

For both of them, five hundred yards, with precision equipment, made for virtually guaranteed single-shot kills. The best of special-operations people were somewhat frightening.

"Chifune," said Fitzduane. "Try binoculars. We need a second kibbitzer. I think I'm missing something here."

"Affirmative," said Chifune, and put down her rifle. Her binoculars gave her a much wider field to examine, and the brilliantly lit rectangle seen from above was easy to search.

She followed the driveway in and searched the open garden area to the right. There was a bench, some stone pots containing dwarf plants, and a couple of stone lanterns strategically placed on a bed of pebbles. It was very simple and beautiful, and the thought came to her that whatever villainy Hodama had been up to, he had good taste. The entire garden was an exercise in simplicity. Which meant there were very few places to hide in, and the house had already been searched by representatives of both sides and sealed. No, Fitzduane was right to worry. Something they had not anticipated was going to happen.

She swung her binoculars to the left of the driveway and began searching the much larger area of garden there. Her glasses rested on an ornate well with a small pagoda top, but she was looking diagonally and could not see down it.

"The well," she said. "It's a possibility. It's big enough."

"Maybe," said Fitzduane, "but it doesn't lead anywhere and it was searched and sealed when they did the house."

"They're going to zap each other with telepathy," said Lonsdale.

"Shut the fuck up, Al," said Fitzduane politely. "Please," he added.

Chifune scanned to the open-sided summer house. Still nothing, except Fumio Namaka standing there and Katsuda, still about thirty yards away, walking toward him on the irregular stone path that circumscribed the house. By agreement, their respective drivers had both stayed with the limousines.

She was running out of time. She searched a bank of ornamental plants. No room to hide even a midget here. She swept on past another *ishi-doro* to a decorative pond which was positioned to the side of the house fairly close to the surrounding wall. A stone bridge led to a miniature island which actually touched the perimeter wall.

"A way-out thought," she said. "Could they have tunneled under the wall?"

"Supposedly not," said Fitzduane. "There are sensors against that possibility and the police have the outside walls under observation."

Chifune did a quick sweep along the back of the house past an inscribed Garden Tablet and then moved on to a boulder garden. Still no sign of anything except what was supposed to be there.

Something niggled at her.

The circling airship had now moved on so that she could see not only Hodama's residence, but also the adjoining house and gardens. This was an area of luxury residences. The neighboring house also had a pond and it was on the other side of the wall from Hodama's. Neither actually touched the wall, but the congruence looked more than a coincidence.

Suppose they both shared the same water? A culvert between them or maybe just a grating. Sensors in the water with goldfish and turtles paddling about the irises? Unlikely!

"The pond," she said urgently, her binoculars now focused on the black surface of the water. "Hugo, LOOK AT THE POND!"

Fitzduane had been concentrating on Fumio Namaka and the approaching figure of Katsuda, but at Chifune's shout he looked quickly at the black water. Something was decidedly odd about it.

As he watched, it began to undulate, as if it was coming to a boil or was haven to a mass of writhing snakes.

Suddenly, he understood at least part of what was happening. And he had an uneasy feeling that this was only the beginning.

"Hold your fire, people," he said. "But stand by on my mark."

This was a scene that would have to be played out. Chifune returned to her .300 Winchester Magnum.

Fitzduane focused on Namaka and Katsuda and the summer house with its broad-eaved thatched roof. Katsuda, aware of the airship on high and assuming support from Schwanberg, knew better than to go inside. His guardians had to be able to see him.

It was going to start happening any second now.

"Fitzduane-*san*," the Spider's voice sounded in Fitzduane's headphones urgently. "Something we did not expect in central Tokyo. I have received reports of two Huey helicopters without lights approaching low and at speed. No flight plan has been filed and they are headed precisely in your direction. ETA within two minutes, perhaps sooner."

Civilian helicopter overflight was supposed to be banned in central Tokyo, particularly in Akasaka, where not only did Hodama have his exclusive residence but so did the Emperor of Japan. Clearly, the imminent arrivals were no respecters of the rules.

A neat operation looked like it was turning very messy; or maybe a great deal worse.

Their invisible airship suddenly felt like the very large target it was.

25

TOKYO, JAPAN

July 12

Fumio Namaka watched the *gaijin* walk toward him.

In the glare of the perimeter floodlights and from a distance, he looked somehow smaller and slighter than when they had met in the Namaka Tower, but doubtless that was an illusion. The Irishman was wearing a dark suit, and that tended to reduce the impression of size. Or perhaps it was natural to imagine a much-hated enemy as larger than he really was.

The steel-gray hair and features were unmistakable. As he looked at Fitzduane, Fumio almost regretted the imminent arrival of the Yaibo helicopters. His anticipation of this man's death was fulfillment in itself. The actual execution would be almost an anticlimax.

"Namaka-*san*," said the *gaijin*. He had stopped about ten yards away. "It is good to see you," he said. "It is a long-deferred pleasure."

Fumio started. The voice was different, and the *gaijin* was speaking in Japanese! He did not know what, but something was definitely amiss.

He looked around uncertainly. Where before the garden had been empty, now heavily armed masked figures in black rubber suits and hoods were emerging from the pond like some nightmare of hell.

Within seconds, he was surrounded, his arms and legs pinioned, and he was rammed against one of the summer-house uprights. He felt cold steel against his wrists, and he realized that he had been handcuffed in place.

He could hear the distant *whump-whump-whump* of helicopters. It was not too late. There was still time.

The *gaijin* approached, put his face close to Fumio's, and as Fumio watched helplessly, the *gaijin* put his hand up and tore his own flesh from his skull.

Fumio gagged as gobbets of flesh and tissue and hair were torn away. And then came sudden realization as the deformed face underneath appeared. His bowels turned to liquid and he could smell his own reeking fear.

"Katsuda," he whispered.

The hideous head nodded.

Pieces of artificial flesh still adhered to it, and the effect was to give a leprous, rotting look to Katsuda's features.

It looked as if the real flesh was also peeling away. The man seemed to be decaying in front of him.

"Your executioner," said Katsuda.

Fumio smelled the liquid before it was poured on him, and instantly he knew how he was going to die.

The noise of the helicopters was now overwhelming, and a split second later two black shapes appeared overhead and black ropes snaked down from one.

Katsuda stood well back and a frogman handed him a short cylinder. A moment later, it burst into brilliant pink light.

The burning flare arced through the air toward the screaming, struggling Fumio.

A DISTINCTIVE BLACK SHAPE blocked out Fitzduane's vision and then settled in the front garden, and once again he could see Fumio Namaka and Katsuda.

Fitzduane had lost a few seconds and was not quite sure what was going on. He had seen the eruption of the frogmen and Fumio being seized, but then had lost continuity.

As Fumio and Katsuda reemerged, he saw the flash of a pink flare and then Fumio erupted into flame. He, the summer house, and the ground around him must have been saturated in something like high-octane gas or charcoal lighter fuel, because the explosion of flame was startlingly violent. A searing white flame shot into the sky, and within split seconds the thatch had caught and was burning with extraordinary ferocity.

"Al, take Katsuda now," said Fitzduane deliberately. "Chifune, focus on the frogmen. Fire at will."

Katsuda spread his arms and, fists clenched, shouted up into the sky to celebrate his triumph.

Now he was THE *kuromaku.*

Lonsdale took first pressure on the Barrett trigger. Katsuda already filled the reticle of his telescopic sight.

"Banzai! Banzai! Banzai!" Katsuda shouted, oblivious to the gun battle that had erupted between his frogmen and Fumio's terrorists, who had arrived too late to save their master.

Lonsdale gently squeezed the trigger. The .50 round, developed originally in World War I to destroy tanks, caught Katsuda in the upper torso and exploded, blowing his heart, rib cage, lungs, and spine into bloody fragments and the rest of his body into the flames where Fumio Namaka's body spat and flared in the vicious heat.

The two enemies burned together.

The first Huey had landed in the largest clear space available, the front garden between the well and the blazing summer house.

The Huey had a nearly fifty-foot rotor diameter and the second helicopter made no attempt to touch down. Instead, it hovered about twenty feet up.

Four figures rappelled down ropes, and other terrorists remained in the cabin, shooting at targets of opportunity.

Chifune was firing rapidly.

Three frogmen had dropped in as many seconds, but then the survivors headed for cover and her rate of fire slowed as she sought out targets.

One frogman hunkered behind a man-height stone lantern carved from volcanic rock, but the .300 Magnum round cut effortlessly through it and through the man hiding on the other side.

A second man had made it to the pool and was under six inches of water when the round seared through the back of his skull.

In Chifune's opinion, the effectiveness of the airship operation was severely hindered by the agreed-upon restrictions on firepower, but the rules of the hunt were quite specific. They were over a densely populated city. Automatic-weapons fire, whether machine gun or grenade launcher, was out. The Spider had been adamant. It was a minor miracle the Barrett had not been prohibited, too. The .50 round could penetrate brick, stone, or plate steel and had been known to cut through six wooden houses. A loose round could take out a complete *sushi* bar counter and give a whole new meaning to the term "friendly fire."

Fitzduane assessed the situation below. It was getting time to hand over to the Spider and his people. The airship had limited objectives. It was a superb observation platform and had given them the crucial element of surprise, but now it was only a matter of time before someone looked up. That would not have mattered before the helicopters arrived on the scene, but now the situation could get unhealthy.

The airship could do just over seventy miles an hour if wind conditions were favorable. The Huey was rated at around a hundred and thirty. True, the rates of climb under power were around the same, with the airship, ironically, having a slight edge, but when it came to maneuverability, there was no comparison. The Huey won hands down. The issue of which aircraft presented the better target scarcely bore contemplation. It was nearly time to bug out.

"Spider-*san*," said Fitzduane. His mind was not on protocol.

The Deputy Superintendent-General and his attendant staff looked at the loudspeaker in his mobile command vehicle in a state of shock.

"*Gaijin*," he muttered under his breath. "What do foreign barbarians know about good manners!" His staff looked at each other with smiles of relief. The Spider had just defused a potentially serious case of loss of face. Honor was restored.

The Spider keyed the microphone. "Fitzduane-*san*," he said in acknowledgment.

"We're going to try and take out the helicopter on the ground," said Fitzduane, "and then we're getting the hell out of here. Engaging the second Huey is too dangerous unless you want central Tokyo shot up. I just hope the other side feels the same way."

"Affirmative," said the Spider. "We'll move in in thirty seconds." He gave the orders, and the inner ring of armed riot police spearheaded by armored cars roared toward the Hodama residence.

"Al, go for the engine and fuel tanks of the grounded Huey," said Fitzduane. "Chifune, try for the pilot. I don't want that bird flying."

Lonsdale knew that the .50 could pierce the Huey with ease, but it was another matter hitting a vital spot. He focused on the turbine engine under the rotor and methodically fired five rounds. He was certain he had hit, but the explosive armor-piercing ammunition seemed to have no effect. With horror, he saw the helicopter begin to lift off, and fired until his magazine was empty.

Beside him, Chifune rapid-fired an entire magazine of .300 Magnum at the pilot.

The Huey rose about fifteen feet, then half-rolled and smashed into the still-burning summer house. Seconds later, there was a series of explosions as the fuel tanks, ignited by the exploding .50 and the surrounding flames, blew up.

The leading police armored car smashed through the locked double gates and rolled forward, its machine gun chattering.

More armored cars moved in and gave covering fire, while an entry team of *kidotai* in helmets and body armor moved in on foot.

The terrorists on the ground fought till they died.

Katsuda's surviving *yakuza* in their frogmen's suits raised their hands.

REIKO OSHIMA, the leader of Yaibo, was in the copilot's seat of the airborne Huey when Lonsdale fired, and she saw the holes of the .50 as they punched through the engine compartment of the landed helicopter.

The significance of the direction of fire was immediately apparent.

"UP AND EVADE!" she screamed into her microphone. "UNLESS YOU WANT US ALL TO GET BARBECUED LIKE THAT OTHER IDIOT. GET THE FUCK UP. WE'RE TAKING FIRE FROM ABOVE."

Startled both by Oshima's screaming and by the explosions in front of him from the other helicopter, the pilot was overheavy on the foot pedals and the Huey's tail wagged from side to side in what was known as the "Huey Shuffle."

He recovered and then banked the machine away from the combat and climbed at maximum revs for his life.

Beside him, Oshima scanned the sky for the source of fire. She was looking for a police or army helicopter, so she initially disregarded the airship. She could see nothing, and that was not believable, because an official helicopter would not leave the scene while all hell was breaking loose below.

She knew how official minds worked when airborne. They liked to buzz around and report things and follow procedure. If there was a police unit up there, any moment some uniformed idiot with a microphone was going to fly alongside and ask her to surrender and she was going to blow his interfering brains out and send his machine in flames down on top of the Ginza. That was the way these people thought and acted. She had been outmaneuvering them for years.

Could it be the airship? She had never remotely considered the airship in the past—it was just part of the sky over Tokyo, like clouds in the rainy season, and it had never entered her thinking one way or another—but now she focused on the huge floating structure as it receded into the distance.

It was inconceivable that the Tokyo cops would actually think of firing down into an area of the city which housed some of the most exclusive residences in Tokyo, but she had temporarily forgotten to factor in the *gaijin* Fitzduane. He had already demonstrated a flair for the daring and unorthodox. An aerial ambush from the airship would be exactly the kind of tactic he would employ.

A shiver of anticipation ran through her as she thought of the significance of the mayhem in Hodama's gardens.

The *gaijin* was still alive.

She had caught a brief glimpse of Namaka as they had flown in, but there had been no sign of Fitzduane.

He should have been there. He was the bait. But was it not more likely that, having baited the trap, he would withdraw and watch events play out from a safer location? The *gaijin* was daring and clearly did not lack courage, but he was no fool.

Suddenly, Fitzduane's plan became clear to her. He had used the strengths of his opponents against each other and he had been not only the bait but the catalyst of their destruction. Fumio Namaka, normally so farseeing and cautious, had been blinded by his obsession with the destruction of his brother's killer. Katsuda had been impelled by his desire for revenge against the Namakas and his ambition to become the new *kuromaku*. Who knew what other elements were involved? And worst of all, her own organization had committed nearly its full strength out of obligation to the Namakas and had been caught in the trap.

The full realization of how they had all been outmaneuvered by this foreign barbarian filled her with gall. But if her analysis was correct, it also meant that Fitzduane was in the airship. He had achieved complete tactical surprise, like a hunter concealed on high in a tree hide, but his main defense had lain in remaining undetected. And clearly he had not fully considered the possibility of his prey being airborne too.

Oshima felt confidence in her judgment restored. It had been her idea to use the two stolen Japanese Defense Forces helicopters. Several Yaibo members had received helicopter training in Libya, ironically from North Vietnamese instructors using captured South Vietnamese equipment, so they were particularly familiar with Hueys. For some time, she had seen the relevance of air power in terrorist operations and saw no reason why the authorities should have a monopoly on air mobility and firepower.

The roles were now reversed. The hunter in his hide would now be the hunted. And the airship would be a hard target to miss.

This time Yaibo would have the high ground.

Oshima pointed toward the receding airship. It was already several miles away. They had lost time looking for a police helicopter, but they would soon make it up. The Huey, she knew, was much faster than that huge bag of gas.

"Pursue the airship," she said, "and maneuver so that we can attack from above. They won't be able to see us and they won't be able to shoot back. And hurry. I want that craft downed right over the city."

The propaganda significance of destroying such a large and visible symbol of authority over Japan's capital city would be immense.

The pilot increased power, and the Huey sped above the neon-lit city toward a target they could not miss.

"FITZDUANE-*san*," said the Spider. "Radar confirmed by visual observation reports that your airship is being pursued by a helicopter." There was a pause. "Two helicopters were reported stolen by the JDF five days ago. We regret—but we have every reason to suspect terrorist action."

"Roger that," said Fitzduane, who was thinking.

The Spider's voice was urgent. "You may well be attacked, Fitzduane-*san*," he said, "but I would ask you to remember the rules of engagement. There must be NO civilian casualties. Whatever the provocation, you must not return fire over Tokyo. Evade and escape, Fitzduane-*san*, but do not open fire."

"How long do we have before the Yaibo chopper gets within range?" said Fitzduane.

"Two to three minutes minimum," said the Spider. "Maybe longer. And they may never attack. But it is important you be warned."

"Out," said Fitzduane. The world now divided into his team and the rest, but there was one member he did not know too well. He went to sit beside the pilot. The inspector-*san* looked scarcely out of diapers, but most Japanese looked young for their age. In a few words, he told him the situation.

The pilot grimaced and turned to Fitzduane. "Colonel-*san*," he said, "I have been trained in all normal aspects of airship operation, but this ship is not a fighter." He paused for half a beat and then spoke again. "But I will do whatever can be done."

Fitzduane had initially thought the pilot looked about eight. He revised his opinion after sitting closer. Close up, the kid was undeniably over fifteen. To have achieved the rank of police inspector, he was clearly on the fast track.

"Inspector-*san*," he said. "Where did you go to university?"

"Todai," said the pilot proudly. All roads led to and from Tokyo University.

"Well, that's all right, then," said Fitzduane cheerfully.

The pilot turned and looked at this lunatic *gaijin* blankly.

"You move and shake when I tell you, Inspector-*san*," said Fitzduane. "It's kind of like lateral thinking, only different. No looping the loop or Immelman turns. Just a couple of sexy maneuvers at exactly the right time. Understand?"

The inspector-pilot-*san* still looked puzzled, until Fitzduane spoke for about twenty seconds. Then realization dawned and his face lit up. "Ah so!" he said with enthusiasm.

Fitzduane looked genuinely pleased. "I always wanted to hear someone say that," he said.

THE YAIBO HELICOPTER was a scant hundred yards away from the airship, but slightly above and behind.

The gondola was below and out of sight. They could see the airship and could get so close they could almost reach out and touch it, but the airship crew in the gondola below could not see them.

The enemy was blind.

"Open fire. Empty your magazines," said Oshima, and two AK-47s and five 9mm submachine guns crackled into action.

The Huey was flying with both doors open, but still the noise was deafening. Cartridge cases cascaded out of the automatic weapons, bounced off the cabin floor, and then slid into the neon-lit glow of the darkness to fall two thousand feet to the city below.

Three hundred full-metal-jacketed rounds penetrated the sausage-shaped balloon of the airship in under ten seconds.

Helium gas began to leak from the holes.

TURBINES WHINING, a flight of JDF Super-Cobra gunships on full military power climbed into the night sky over Atsugi and headed toward the airship.

"ETA ten—one zero—minutes," said the Spider. There was no acknowledgment. "Gunships will rendezvous in ten—one zero—minutes," he repeated.

Static came back at him. In midcommunication, the airship had gone suddenly silent.

"BLOODY HELL," said Fitzduane, with some understandable irritation, as the radio in front of him shattered in a cloud of sparks.

The rounds, judging by the angle of entry, were coming from above and the rear. Before striking their communications, the fire must have punched through the double polyester coating of the envelope twice on its way in and out and then through the Kevlar-reinforced plastic of the gondola itself.

He had hoped that such a combination would have stopped the light automatic fire normally used by terrorists, but he was being disabused. He was learning more and more about airships and modern firepower in a hurry. Frankly, he did not object to the acquisition of this information as such—he rather liked airships—but the manner of learning left a great deal to be desired.

The back of his hand oozed blood from an encounter with a piece of razor-sharp plastic blasted out of the casing by the bullets, and he sucked the wound. A cut about an inch and a half long was revealed.

All in all, they were being very lucky. The terrorists had been shooting at them for well over a minute, he estimated, but so far nothing too vital had been struck.

Yaibo was discovering the hard way that scoring hits on something as large as an airship was not the same as doing it damage. True, they were losing the gas that kept them up, but the bullet holes were so small in relation to the overall size of the envelope that it was going to take some time before lift was affected. Fitzduane had heard that pilots in World War I had had much the same problem with German zeppelins before the incendiary had been invented. On the other hand, zeppelins were allowed to shoot back.

Fitzduane looked down. They were just crossing the coastline. Tokyo Bay lay straight ahead. Lots of nice water in case they had to touch down in a hurry, and better yet, no Tokyo citizenry.

"Any sign of the bat out of hell?" he said into his headset microphone. There was a fighting chance the intercom was still working, and he wanted to give the pilot-*san* some moral support while he could.

"He's still up top," said Lonsdale. There were more thuds on the top of the gondola roof, and dimples appeared in the ceiling. "The way I figure it, they're using a mixture of 9mm and AK-47, and only the AK stuff is getting through."

"Well, that's very interesting, Al," said Fitzduane dryly. "How about you, Chifune?"

"They're going to figure out soon they should be firing at the gondola, Hugo," said Chifune. "Or at least at the engines."

"We're entering a free-fire zone," said Fitzduane, then added a qualification. "Well, Al, providing you point your elephant gun away from Tokyo, what is that thing's range?"

"Unaimed, about eight miles," said Lonsdale proudly.

Fitzduane winced, but said nothing. He had followed the Spider's rules, but now that they were over the sea it was going to be a matter of self-preservation. Time to play ball.

"DIVE! DIVE! DIVE!" he said to the pilot with absolute urgency. "MAX POWER! MAX ANGLE! POUR IT ON!"

The pilot thrust the control wheel forward and the airship headed toward the murky waters below. The lights of several ships could be seen. The crews were going to have some unexpected free entertainment. He just hoped they had enough sense to keep their heads down.

The terrorist helicopter suddenly appeared on their right, the side marked by Lonsdale, and started to slow down to match their speed and riddle the gondola at point-blank range. At first when the airship had dived, Oshima had thought the Yaibo fire had achieved a mortal hit, but then she had realized that either way it made sense to make sure. The airship was not going to crash into the city as she would have wished, but its destruction would still be a major victory.

There was a thundering series of explosions as Lonsdale rapid-fired a complete ten-round magazine from the Barrett at the terrorists crowding the open doors of the helicopter flying beside them. In turn, automatic fire smashed into the gondola.

The helicopter was only sixty yards away. Through his telescopic sight, Lonsdale saw the expressions on the faces of two of the terrorists as the huge 750-grain explosive bullets punched into them.

There were vivid flashes as the .50 shells ignited and holes appeared in the cabin and windows of the Huey, but still it flew on. The damn things had been shot down by the thousands in the Vietnam War, but this one and its crew were bloody tough.

A body fell from the helicopter and plummeted into the sea below.

A split second later, the Huey peeled away and vanished into the darkness. The encounter had taken just a few seconds.

Chifune had taken a 9mm round in her upper right arm just as she was turning to add her firepower to Lonsdale's, and the shock and impact made her stagger against the cabin wall, the .300 Magnum dropping from her hands.

Fitzduane turned ashen as he saw her, and for the briefest of moments he saw her and felt her naked in his arms as they had made love.

He leaped from his position beside the pilot and helped her to a seat. A brief examination revealed that the wound was not serious, and he quickly bound it, conscious that he was perhaps hurting her but there was no time. He kissed her on her forehead briefly and picked up her weapon and checked the magazine. Chifune smiled weakly at him. She was still in some shock.

The airship had now leveled off and was flying so low, they passed a huge oil tanker heading in the opposite direction toward Tokyo and found the gondola was actually lower than the bridge of the ship.

The watch crew stared openmouthed as the vast black shape appeared to head straight toward them, then flashed by their port side at a combined speed of around eighty miles an hour. As the watch commander remarked afterward, he had heard of the Flying Dutchman but this was ridiculous. For a few seconds, the scale of the airship made him think he was going to be rammed by some flying supertanker.

Fitzduane was now focusing on the left observation windows, while Lonsdale covered the right.

The helicopter had attacked them from above and the side. Both attacks had been of limited effectiveness, but he expected the next attack to be roughly level with the gondola and from the rear. That was the airship's most vulnerable remaining blind spot, in his opinion. The Huey could not get underneath them, because they were flying so low, and a head-on pass would not allow enough time to bring adequate power to bear.

There was no practical defense against an attack from the rear. The airship's visibility was all on the sides and to the front. The rear of the gondola housed the engines, and they were enclosed in a windowless compartment. In some ways, Fitzduane was surprised that the terrorists had not attacked there immediately, but then they would not be so intimate with the airship's structure, and on-the-job training tended to be mostly trial and error. But he had an uncomfortable feeling that Yaibo was learning fast.

"Colonel-*san*," shouted the pilot. Fitzduane had taken off his headset to go to Chifune's aid, and now the pilot had twisted around in his seat and was shouting at him. All the observation windows were open to facilitate firing, and the roar of the engines at full speed filled the gondola.

Fitzduane made his way to the front and leaned over to hear the pilot.

"Fitzduane-*san*," said the pilot urgently. If we are to be successful with our maneuver, WE MUST LOSE WEIGHT."

There was the crack of the Barrett as Lonsdale leaned precariously out of the window and tried to fire to their rear. "Hugo, they're maneuvering behind us," he said. "Sling a harness around me and I'll try and have another go. I can do it."

Fitzduane considered for a moment and tried to imagine Al's line of fire shooting backwards. It could work for a shot or two, but all the Huey would have to do would be to maneuver slightly and it would be out of range again.

He looked hard at Lonsdale. They'd already discussed another option, but Al's harness idea had certainly been worth considering.

He discarded it. "We stick with Plan B," he said. "Pilot-*san* wants more lift, so when I give the word, we dump everything we can. Then we should have an opportunity, and we'd better not miss."

Lonsdale grinned. "This is a very crazy tactic," he said, "but then you're a very crazy man."

Fitzduane smiled. "Let's go to it."

"Mike Bergin and the dead pilot, too?" said Lonsdale.

Fitzduane hesitated for a moment, and then there was a banging sound from the rear as the attacking Huey fired at them. He knew the time had come to finish it, and noble gestures would be of scant worth if the terrorists had their way. On the other hand . . .

"Not unless we have to," he said. He turned to the pilot. "NOW!" he shouted.

The pilot switched both engines to vertical thrust and at the same time activated the control that dumped half a ton of water from ballast tanks in the gondola.

Simultaneously, Fitzduane and Lonsdale pushed the bodies of Schwanberg and Chuck Palmer out the door. Other heavy items followed.

Modern airships flew "heavy." That meant they got around ninety percent of their lift from the helium contained in the envelope and the remaining lift from the aerodynamics of the envelope and the engines. That combination made the airship easier to control and to land without bleeding off expensive helium. The normal rate of climb was based on that heavy configuration.

The dumping of the ballast and the bodies changed the equation dramatically.

The airship, within a few seconds relieved of over 2,000 pounds of weight, was suddenly lighter than air. Further, the rotation of the two Porsche engines meant that thrust was now vertical and not forward.

The airship shot skyward and slowed. Within seconds, it was above and behind and slightly to the right of the terrorist helicopter.

Fitzduane and Lonsdale, resting their weapons on the sills of the open observation windows, had near-perfect firing positions. Magnum and Barrett cracked simultaneously. Both men fired precision shots until their magazines were empty, then took fresh magazines from Chifune and reloaded.

The Yaibo helicopter had reacted with surprising speed, and was just attempting to climb and turn when the first rounds plowed into it.

The pilot's incomplete maneuver had actually placed it in an even more vulnerable position. The full diameter was exposed as it reared up, and through the circling blades the marksmen had a perfect view of the engine and where the fuel tanks were located.

A .50 Barrett round caught one of the rotor blades near the hub and shattered it, spinning the aircraft helplessly out of control. A fraction of a second later, one of the fuel tanks blew and ignited the others.

There were high explosives aboard. They were a Yaibo trademark. The puttylike blocks were stable against rifle fire, but the exploding rounds of the Barrett acted like detonators.

There was the searing white flame of a violent explosion, and the Huey blew apart a moment before it hit the water. The blast rocked the airship.

And then there was no trace that the helicopter had ever existed, except for a thin smear of bloodstained oil and floating fragments of human flesh.

EPILOGUE

TOKYO, JAPAN

July 15

Fitzduane felt a definite lump in his throat as he prepared to say farewell to the line of Japanese facing him in the VIP departure lounge at Tokyo Airport.

It was ridiculous—he had known them only a few weeks—but there it was. The bonds were strong and the relationships, tested under the most extreme circumstances, would endure. For the rest of his life, he would be linked in some important but indefinable way to Japan and to his friends there.

He smiled to himself for a moment as he noticed that the line of well-wishers was ranked in order of seniority. Adachi's father, trim and upright, and bearing a remarkable resemblance to his dead son; Yoshokawa-*san* and his wife, bringing back memories of Kamakura; the Spider in the full uniform of the Deputy Superintendent of the Tokyo Metropolitan Police; the young airship copilot, Inspector Mikio Ueda, who had performed so magnificently under fire; the lined and seasoned face of Sergeant Akamatsu from the police *koban*; and Sergeant Oga and all of the twenty-three men and women who had served on his bodyguard at various times.

It was just as well that Tokyo was a peaceful city. The duty roster of the Tokyo MPD was at the moment depleted.

There was no sign of Chifune, and he missed her very much. But typically, Tanabu-*san* was elusive and independent to the last.

The boarding announcement was made, and as if that was the

agreed-upon signal, the entire line suddenly broke into three cheers—
"*Banzai! Banzai! Banzai!*"—and then, faces frozen in formal expressions, bowed deeply.

Fitzduane, draped in farewell gifts, bowed in return. And the line
bowed and he bowed, and the process might have gone on indefinitely
if a Virgin Airlines hostess had not tactfully intervened.

His mind in something of a jumble of emotions, Fitzduane made his
way to his first-class seat in the front of the aircraft. There was a beautifully wrapped package on the seat, but he ignored it until he had put his
belongings away, assuming it belonged to another passenger. Then he
saw that the package was addressed to him.

He smelled her perfume and the scent of her body before she spoke,
and a sharp feeling of both longing and loss went through him. He
turned around. And there she was: luscious black hair, perfect skin,
huge eyes, breasts he could feel against his lips, the body of a lover. A
beautiful and extraordinary woman. And an enigma.

"It's for Boots," she said. "A soft toy, a cuddly sumo wrestler. I think
he will like him." Chifune hesitated. "Or is he too big for such things?"

Fitzduane thought of Boots and what he felt like in his arms and
suddenly was impatient to be home again. "No," he said, with a smile,
"he's not too big for cuddly toys. He's only three. He's still a very
cuddly boy."

Chifune was silent at first, and Fitzduane was acutely conscious of all
that was unsaid that was passing between them. There were tears in her
eyes, and as he watched, one trickled down her cheek.

"That's what I remembered," she said.

A newly boarded passenger pushed by with an apology, and Chifune
winced.

"How is the arm?" he said. It had not been a serious wound, but
being shot was never much fun.

"Healing," she said with a slight smile, "but still a little tender."

Fitzduane was forcibly reminded that the aircraft was leaving
shortly. He asked the obvious question, already knowing the answer.

"Chifune," he said. "Are you traveling, too?"

Chifune shook her head. "I wanted to see you alone, Hugo," she
said. She smiled again amid the tears. "With Koancho, such things as
boarding a departing aircraft can be arranged. But I have to go now."

"Or they'll make you work your passage," said Fitzduane, with a smile he had to force. He felt a terrible sense of loss, but also knew somehow that this was not the time to say anything.

He moved forward and held out his arms to embrace her, but Chifune stepped back. "No, Fitzduane-*san*," she sobbed. And then she bowed deeply and was gone.

And then Fitzduane saw Adachi, which was impossible for he was dead, and he smiled and felt tears come to his cheeks. Then Adachi reached out his hand and Fitzduane took it and his grip was firm and warm. "My friends call me Aki," he said, and then Adachi too vanished.

Fitzduane was deeply moved. He put Boots's present on the seat beside him and fought to get a grip on his emotions. He thought of Christian de Guevain and Mike Bergin and Aki Adachi and other comrades-in-arms and how honored he had been to fight beside them and how irreplaceable they were. He thought of Etan and Chifune and the other women he had known and loved. And he thought of those who were still living and of Kilmara's words:

"I have no answers, but much to do."

He slept and dreamed extraordinary dreams, and when he woke the hostess was leaning over him to remind him about his seat belt and they were approaching London. One more plane flight and he would be in Dublin. And then he would board the Islander and fly to the West and he would be home.

DUBLIN AIRPORT, IRELAND
July 16

As he flew the London–Dublin leg of the journey Fitzduane reflected on the chain of events that had culminated in Japan.

The origins went back about seventy years, arguably even longer. World politics, seemingly so remote, had impacted directly in this case. And individual actions had had terrible and unforeseen consequences.

Who would have thought that fate would eventually catch up with Hodama the *kuromaku*. He had survived so much only to be struck down at the height of his power as a consequence of a routine bit of thuggery decades earlier.

If the Namakas had not had their father executed and been left alone and starving in postwar Tokyo, would they ever have become criminals? Today, they would probably have graduated with distinction from Todai and be model citizens.

As for Katsuda, his criminal imperative could be traced directly back to the Japanese occupation of Korea and the appalling treatment in the past of so many Koreans in Japan, including the killing of his own family. He was a man motivated by hate. Given his background, it was easy to understand.

Fitzduane did not know what distortions in his upbringing had caused Schwanberg to go bad. Frankly, he did not care. Certainly Vietnam had not helped. Many brave men and women had fought in it, but it had not been the best of wars.

In the final analysis, the origins did not matter. You dealt with the situation as it existed now and you did what was necessary as well as you could and accepted the consequences. And that was the end of it.

When the aircraft landed in Dublin, Fitzduane thought at first he must have taken the wrong flight. The weather was near perfect, the sky a rich blue, and the temperature downright balmy. It was like landing in the South of France. For a moment he expected to see the vivid scarlet of bougainvillea and to smell the perfume of oleander and hibiscus and to be surrounded by tanned bodies. He was soon disabused. The patrons of Dublin Airport looked as pale and sun-starved and as cheerful as ever. The Irish, he conceded, were an odd lot, in truth. They loved their rain and windswept land.

He smiled to himself. The day was a false promise, a temporary illusion, but Kathleen and Boots running toward him were very real.

He swept Boots into his arms and kissed and hugged him, and soon Kathleen was in his arms, too, and as he felt her body against him and her lips against his, he had a feeling of returning to normality, to values that were important and worth building on.

Boots, jumping up and down with happiness and impatience, immediately opened Chifune's gift to him, and his face shone as he beheld the cuddly sumo doll inside. It was love at first sight.

"It's a sumo, Boots," said Fitzduane. "A Japanese wrestler."

"Zoomie! Zoomie! Zoomie!" shrieked Boots, and shot around in circles, alternately hugging his new friend and then throwing him in the air.

Kathleen, alone with Fitzduane for a few seconds, put her arms around his neck and looked up at him. She had forgotten what a big man he was. He looked pale and tired and pleased to be back, and, she thought, rather magnificent. Her lover looked what he truly was, every inch the warrior.

"So, my love," she said quizzically, "how was Japan? Cherry blossoms and geisha girls?"

A thousand images flashed through Fitzduane's mind too fast to comprehend, and then they were gone and only Kathleen in his arms was real.

He laughed. "It rained a lot," he said. "It was surprisingly bloody wet. I felt quite at home."

Author's Note and Acknowledgments

Quite a number of people helped to assemble the information that underpins the story *Rules Of The Hunt*. One question tends to lead to another if you have a curious mind and only afterwards does the true scale of the research journey involved become clear. Just as well.

Games of the Hangman—the first Hugo Fitzduane book—was inspired by real events, specifically an actual hanging that this author discovered. In turn, this sequel, *Rules Of The Hunt,* is based upon real events, real experiences, and real institutions. Counterterrorism is not something that most of us experience up close in our day-to-day lives, but it is a reality nonetheless. And without counter-terrorist professionals our world would be a much more dangerous place. Of that, have no doubt.

Much of this book is set in Japan and in that context I have one thought to communicate: Japan, like any nation, has its problems, but it has a great deal to contribute to our flawed world. Certainly, its political system is far from perfect, but, in this writer's personal experience, there are many talented and thoughtful people over there and we should be talking to them more than we do—and they to us. I value my Japanese friends and I appreciate them. As to what I think about leaving rain-sodden Ireland to arrive at the start of the Japanese rainy season, well, Fitzduane has conveyed but the faintest flavor of my true feelings . . .

The inspiration of reality apart, this book is a work of fiction with all its associated conventions and should be treated as such.

Some people who have contributed to this book cannot be mentioned for security reasons. Well, that is a reflection of the state of the world and I thank you nonetheless. As to the others who have been kind enough to help in some way, thank you also.

The errors, such as they are, are mine. My gratitude is yours.

A concluding note: Visitors to Tokyo should note that despite Hugo's experiences, Tokyo, by international standards, is a remarkably safe city. The Tokyo Metropolitan Police Department do an excellent job. Visit and enjoy. I did.

Ireland

The Irish Army: Lt. Col. Des Travers; Captain Tom Aherne; Captain Cathal O'Neill; Commandant Charles O'Malley; Commandant Jim Carvey; Cpl. Paddy McGarrigle.

The Irish Police, the Gardai Siochana: Superintendent Liam Nolan; Marie Egan; Mary O'Connor.

The U.S. Embassy: Col. Michael Ryan, Military Attaché; Kay Mulligan.

From the Medical World: Patrick Plunkett; Louise Irwin; Jackie Murphy; Denis Mehigan; Vincent P. Lynch; Mr. Sugars; Agnes Hayes; Alice McGarvey; Carol Cotter; Miriam O'Callaghan; Gillian Darling; Oscar Traynor; Robert Campbell; Rodney Peyton; Dr. David Taylor.

And also: Jill Kennedy; Julia Kennedy; Pat Kenny; Yoshii Ishi; Ivan O'Brien; Virginia Colter; Peter Byrne; Bill Gallagher; Gerry Hanlon; Michael Kilduff; John Kinahan; Jim Comerford; Enda Rohan; Pierce Butler; The Meteorological Office, Dublin.

Very many thanks to Brendan O'Sullivan of Apple Macintosh Ireland for introducing me to computers that really work.

Japan

Metropolitan Police Department, Tokyo: Deputy Superintendent General Masaharu Saitoh; Katsuomi Fukushima; Masataka Ishizuka.